SHOCK WAVE

JASON TRAPP
BOOK 11

JACK SLATER

Copyright © 2025 by Jack Slater

All rights reserved.

No part of this book may be reproduced in any form or by any electronic or mechanical means, including information storage and retrieval systems, without written permission from the author, except for the use of brief quotations in a book review.

❋ Formatted with Vellum

ONE

The flash of cameras momentarily blinded Qiao Yuhan on the tiny stage. He stood there, unsure if his voice would still work, with his right hand raised as the weight of the moment surged like a tide.

"I hereby declare," Qiao recited in his accented English, practiced daily at every opportunity, "on oath... that I absolutely and entirely renounce... and abjure... all allegiance and fidelity to any foreign prince, potentate, state, or sovereignty... of whom or which I have heretofore been a subject or citizen... that I will support and defend the Constitution and laws of the United States of America against all enemies... foreign... and domestic."

As the words departed his lips, he sensed a fragment of himself slipping away. A swell of sadness mingled with the hope that had sustained him throughout these harsh months, propelling him headlong to this moment.

If his homeland had not made it impossible for him to return, would he still have made this choice?

He thought of the friends he'd left behind in Hong Kong, of

the dire warning in the night that had sent him fleeing with only his bug-out case. The journey out of China still haunted him.

His citizenship oath concluded, and applause rippled from the small crowd in the community hall. Qiao lowered his hand, his heart and throat swelling with a maelstrom of sorrow, pride, and bittersweet relief.

"Congratulations," the official said. "You are now an American."

Qiao nodded, not trusting his voice. He stepped off the little stage at the head of the community center, where amateur plays, local political meetings, and children's dance recitals were the norm. As he and his companions gathered backstage, their oath completed, they all embraced as if they were reuniting after years apart.

"We did it," Li Wei said. "We're free."

Qiao's smile brought a mild sting to his eye, moistening it with what he would pass off as joyful tears. "Yes, but our work is not finished."

Now that they were citizens, safeguarded by the full weight of American law, they could campaign more openly for democracy in Hong Kong and urge America to maintain its protective embrace of Taiwan.

"Mr. Yuhan!" a man's voice called.

He turned to see a local reporter approaching, notebook in hand. He'd been warned that news outlets would send people to cover the session, that he should respond concisely because there was no telling if it was an outlet friendly or hostile toward immigrants.

The journalist sounded friendly as he asked, "How does it feel to be an American citizen?"

Qiao straightened his posture, lifting his chin. "It is an honor and a responsibility," he said, giving a deliberately mundane but truthful response. "We came here seeking protection and freedom, and now we have a duty to use that freedom to aid others."

The reporter nodded, scribbling fervently. "What are your plans moving forward?"

"We will continue to speak out against oppression," Qiao said, anxious that he was revealing too much, but the last-minute jitters he'd suppressed had transformed into a different kind of mental energy. "To advocate for democracy and human rights in Hong Kong and every other place that China suppresses its citizens."

As the reporter moved away, Li Wei appeared at Qiao's side. "Bold words. Are you sure it's prudent to be so outspoken in public?"

Qiao didn't know, but there was no taking it back. He chose to project assurance instead. "We are American citizens now. What can they do to us?"

Before Li Wei could respond, the master of ceremonies called for attention. "If I could have all our new citizens gather for a group photo, please!"

They assembled on the steps before the small stage, arranging themselves in neat rows. Qiao found himself in the front, next to the master of ceremonies. But as the photographer prepared to take the shot, a wave of dizziness washed over him.

Qiao blinked, trying to clear his suddenly foggy vision.

"Is everyone ready?" the photographer called.

A glance at his friends showed similar expressions of confusion and discomfort. The other new citizens around them did too, frowning in bewilderment, hands resting on stomachs and necks, eyes wide and terrified.

Qiao opened his mouth, but no words emerged. His throat closed, then began to burn, as if reflux were shooting up from his stomach. The world tilted, swaying like a ship in a tempest, and Qiao staggered, almost losing his footing.

What's happening? Am I sick? Are we all...?

As darkness encroached on the periphery of his vision, Qiao's thoughts returned to the oath he'd just sworn—to defend his new country against all enemies, foreign and domestic.

What the hell *was* this?

The world erupted from nausea into agony. Qiao's stomach twisted. His skin felt as though it were on fire, his insides turning to acid. His brain sent desperate signals to the rest of his body, to run, to scream, but he could not move, and his throat constricted further, choking off the sound.

Around him, friends and new citizens collapsed, their bodies contorting as if possessed by demons.

The master of ceremonies stumbled backward, horror etched on his face as he was clearly afflicted too. He paled and swayed slightly, as did the photographer, but neither was writhing in pain.

Qiao's vision blurred, red-tinged and pulsing. His heart raced, each beat sending waves of searing pain through his body. He could smell flesh roasting, a nauseating scent that made bile rise in his throat as he realized it was his own.

Li Wei, lying face down, crawling God only knew where, reached for Qiao, his fingers reddening, eyes bloodshot. "Help..." he gasped before crumpling to the ground.

As consciousness slipped away, Qiao's final thought was of the irony. They'd escaped China for freedom, only to perish on the steps of American democracy.

FANG CHEN WATCHED the Chinese assassin stride into a warehouse which, on paper, was owned by an online retailer that utilized it to store goods subject to tariffs. In reality, the company traded no physical goods except for a bare minimum of the cheapest items, procured from Chinese-run Internet-only retailers and used to launder digital funds into projects like the proof-of-concept demonstration that had just completed. If successful, that demonstration represented a significant step forward in their mission here in the US.

Isabella Knight emerged from the threadbare office, her blond hair pulled back tightly, her stance alert and—it seemed to Fang—predatory. Knight joined Fang and the two men she'd brought with her.

"Well?" she asked, her clipped British accent echoing in the cavernous space.

The assassin hefted an item that did not look like a weapon. It was boxy, about the size of a leaf-blower and similarly shaped, only the long blower tube had been replaced with an outlet at the front that served as a barrel of sorts, and power cables hung loose from the body of the device.

He nodded and replied to Fang in Chinese. "It worked as she declared it would. But it is too bulky and highly inefficient. A bomb would accomplish the mission with the same result, but cheaper, and I would not have to conceal the kit in a janitorial cart. There is also a higher risk of personal exposure."

One of the misgivings about the device was its need for an additional battery pack which the user strapped to their back. It was, supposedly, the most advanced weapon of its type and certainly the most compact and lightweight. The assassin had predicted that its size was a tick in the "con" column, but Isabella Knight promised that this aspect had already been addressed in its next iteration. Today was about function, not form.

"Show us," one of the suited Chinese men demanded.

The assassin set the weapon aside and pulled out a tablet,

bringing up the footage from the ceremony. Fang knew what was coming, had even helped choose the target. But the reality was... unsettling. She forced herself to watch impassively as the new American citizens writhed and perished. *Traitors*, she reminded herself.

"Impressive," said the Chinese investor. "But General Gao will need more than this before he approves deployment of the mesh."

The mesh. Big promises. Light on technological detail.

Fang stepped forward, her voice steadier than she felt. "Was it necessary to be so messy? We discussed a more discreet approach."

The assassin shrugged. "I acted as instructed. Collateral damage was minimal."

Minimal? Fang thought, recalling the screaming bystanders in the footage. *Is this truly what it takes?*

"The next demonstration will be more... precise," Isabella was saying, her tone businesslike. "We'll need additional resources, of course."

Fang cleared her throat. "The timeline?"

The assassin turned to her. Fang knew he would be dead within minutes of leaving this place—a disposable asset who could, if necessary, be held up as the culprit so that no one would be looking for an attaché based in Washington, D.C.

"Six weeks," Knight replied. "As long as we receive the shipment on time, we'll fulfill our side and supply the final project."

Fang nodded, again striving to project confidence she didn't feel. She was committed now. Committed to a path she still wasn't sure she could—or should—follow. But the alternative was unthinkable. If it was a choice between returning to her past self and evolving with the inevitable changes in the world, evolution was the only choice.

"Can you guarantee delivery on time?" Fang asked. "We understand Mr. Ashenhurst is under some logistical stress. And we have a specific deadline in mind."

Knight's smile wasn't friendly at all. "He has already invested heavily in personnel and infrastructure. It will guarantee our ability to fulfill this and future orders. Mr. Ashenhurst takes the long view."

"Very well," Fang said, reading approval on the two experts General Gao had sent as his proxies. "Proceed."

Isabella Knight stepped forward. She scanned the group before settling on Fang. "Let's be clear. This isn't a free trial. We need capital. Funnel it through the Taiwan facility. They'll make sure it isn't traceable to you or to us."

Fang fought to maintain a neutral expression. Lian Zhelan was placing a tremendous amount of trust in her. She could not afford to miscalculate. "How much?"

Knight's lips curved into a humorless smile. "Enough to make your backers sweat. But I assure you, the results will be... spectacular."

The assassin shifted, his hand brushing against the concealed weapon Fang knew to be at his side.

"And six weeks is definitely sufficient?" Fang asked.

"Six weeks," Knight confirmed. "Pay what we require upfront, hold up your end, and I guarantee a demonstration that will make Pittsburgh look like a warm-up act."

Fang swallowed, her mouth dry. "And the target?"

Knight's eyes glinted dangerously. "Oh, we'll address that soon enough. But it will be impossible to ignore."

TWO

Five Weeks Later

AN UNMARKED BLACK SUV rolled to a halt on the fringe of a private airfield nestled deep in the Virginia countryside. Its headlights cut a lonely swath across the rain-slicked tarmac, illuminating the waiting jet. It was a Gulfstream G700, shark-gray and silent save for the low hum of its auxiliary power unit. There were no logos on its fuselage, no call signs on its tail.

Jason Trapp stepped out into the humid night air, the scent of jet fuel and damp asphalt sharp in his nostrils. A lone figure in a dark suit, whose face was a carefully constructed mask of anonymity, waited at the base of the aircraft's stairs. He gave a single, curt nod as Trapp approached. The hiss of the jet's hydraulics was the only sound as Trapp ascended into the cabin.

The interior was a sterile, efficient tube of cream leather and polished chrome, smelling of nothing at all. No crew on this flight. No champagne, no canapes. Black budget or not, this was still a government charter. So Trapp had twelve hours of solitude ahead of him to catch up on sleep.

Except the jet wasn't empty.

At a small workstation bolted to the fuselage, Madison Grubbs was already at work, her back to the door. Her fingers flew across the keyboard of a ruggedized laptop, her focus absolute. A half-empty coffee cup sat beside a stack of folders and notepads, her only companions.

Trapp paused on the top step, the surprise registering as a tightening in his gut. "I wasn't aware this was a two-person job."

Madison finished typing a sentence before swiveling in her chair. Her eyes, framed by the exhaustion of too many late nights staring at screens, held the same sharp intelligence he'd come to rely on.

The tension between them, a low-frequency hum from their last mission in New York—when Trapp had betrayed both her personal and professional trust in him—was still there, barely buried under a thin topsoil of courtesy. Madison was still pissed at him. And he knew he'd earned every bit of it.

"Someone has to do the actual analysis, Jason," she said, her voice even. "You just get to break things."

"Right. The 'fun part,'" Trapp countered, settling into his seat. "Remind me of that next time someone's shooting at us."

A taut smile touched Grubbs' lips, but instead of a comeback, she turned back to her console. "Speaking of which, the director is waiting." Her fingers moved with practiced speed. "Establishing secure uplink now."

On the forward bulkhead, the large screen flickered, displaying a cascade of security protocols and authentication handshakes scrolling by. After a final *ping*, the code resolved into the live, craggy face of Deputy Director Mike Mitchell. He looked as tired as Trapp felt, the lines around his eyes etched deeper than usual.

"Glad you're both aboard," Mitchell's voice crackled through the speakers, devoid of pleasantries. The jet's engines began to whine, the pitch rising as they prepared for takeoff. "We have a break in the Pittsburgh attack."

An image flashed on the screen: a grainy photo from a naturalization ceremony. A red arrow pointed to the smiling face of a man Trapp only recognized from the news broadcasts he usually tried his hardest to ignore.

"One of the victims was Qiao Yuhan," Mitchell stated. "A high-profile Hong Kong dissident the Bureau had under light observation. His death, and the bizarre nature of the scene—the complete cellular breakdown of the victims—is what triggered a multi-agency alert."

The jet surged forward, pressing Trapp back into his plush leather seat. The airfield lights blurred into streaks, then fell away as they ascended steeply into the dark sky. Below, the lights of Washington, D.C. began to shrink into a glittering web.

Mitchell swiped, and a satellite map of West Africa replaced the photo. A red dot sat on a desolate, sun-bleached patch of northern Nigeria.

"Hours after the attack, the Nigerian NIA—take a wild guess what the acronym stands for—intercepted a coded phone call. It was short, but it contained the keywords 'delivery' and 'Pittsburgh package.' It took a couple of weeks, but eventually it got handed to us, and our friends at the NSA managed to geolocate the call to this specific location." He zoomed in, revealing the sprawling layout of an industrial site. "A lithium mine deep in territory controlled by Boko Haram."

Trapp leaned forward, his focus sharpening. The city lights were gone now, replaced by the black, featureless expanse of the Atlantic Ocean. "What the hell is Boko Haram doing mounting a killing spree in Pittsburgh? Doesn't fit their profile."

"No, it doesn't," Mitchell agreed. "That's not their signature. But we know they use that area as a major hub for their human trafficking and smuggling networks. They move fighters, refugees, political dissidents... anyone they can profit from. Our working hypothesis is that the Pittsburgh attackers were foreign nationals, likely Chinese state assets, who were smuggled into the US via this route. Same MO as the United Nations attack."

Trapp raised an eyebrow. "That conclusion seems...thin."

"Thin is why we pay you the medium bucks. It's why you're on your way to Nigeria."

Madison's focus narrowed. "So the objective isn't direct action against Boko Haram. It's network mapping?"

"I don't care about their local insurgency," Mitchell said. "I care about the trail. Your job is to find out how they got those people into the country and more importantly, if anyone else is in the pipeline."

"Cover?" Trapp said.

"Robert Harding, a ruthless minerals investor with a reputation for dealing with... less-than-reputable groups. Madison, you're Elizabeth Wilbur, Bob's partner and assistant."

"Very twentieth century," she murmured.

Mitchell laughed. "Boko Haram didn't get the Me Too memo. Your legends are that you're looking to exploit their smuggling network for your own ends. Get inside, find the trafficking route, identify the network, and determine if more assets are being moved into the US. We cannot afford another Pittsburgh."

Trapp felt the familiar surge, the welcome clarity of a defined mission. This was his world. Interrogation, infiltration, and if necessary, elimination.

"The Nigerians have sanctioned this op," Mitchell continued, "but they insist on a liaison. You'll meet an NIA agent, Jelany Ikem, in-country. Intel says he's sharp—something of a rising star. He'll be your driver and guide, but he's also their eyes on you. I like the Nigerians. Don't make things awkward for me."

Madison stared at her own reflection in the dark monitor for a long moment before turning her chair to face him. Her expression was unreadable.

"So, are we going to talk about it?" she asked, her voice low and even.

Trapp didn't pretend to misunderstand. He kept his gaze fixed on the blackness outside the window. "I already apologized, Madison."

"You apologized for the outcome," she corrected him. "Not for the choice. You made a call and decided I was an acceptable loss. I just need to know if that's still on the table for this mission."

He finally turned to meet her eyes. The exhaustion was there, but so was a flicker of genuine regret. "The situations aren't the same."

"They never are," she shot back, her voice still quiet but sharp as glass. "Just know this, Jason. I'm not your asset. I'm not a tool you get to 'improvise' with. I'm your partner. You will treat me like one. Don't forget it again."

Trapp held her gaze, then gave a single, slow nod. "Understood."

THREE

Washington, D.C

THE COOL BREEZE would have been refreshing, even rejuvenating, on a sunny country morning, but in the middle of the night on a remote airfield, Fang Chen would have preferred to be pretty much anywhere else. Weirdly, it was her nose that bothered her the most, a tiny icicle that she could not cover without muffling her voice. Unfortunately, her new boss, Ambassador Lian, was wearing far less than Fang as they waited for the Gulfstream to taxi to a halt. Fang did not wish to appear weak in front of her or the men they were here to greet.

The airfield was too small for commercial passenger airliners, split in two to accommodate leisure flyers and executive clients alike, guaranteeing privacy for people like the Chinese Embassy's guest of honor.

Even powering down, the engines emitted an ear-piercing whine. The two women strode toward the Gulfstream as the door opened, revealing a plush interior. Lian was taller than

Fang by a head and possessed an athletic frame which, even in her late fifties, spoke volumes about a long and fine military career, followed by a decade in the intelligence services.

Fang was not privy to her superior's career records, and Lian had shared only occasional anecdotes and asides about her past, so Fang assumed she was not permitted to do so. She certainly trusted Fang, given the tasks she'd assigned her attaché to perform.

The first man to emerge from the jet was a beefy Chinese national whose tight-fitting suit concealed a firearm in a shoulder holster. His eyes skimmed over Fang and Lian, then scanned the near-empty runways and fields. He spoke into his lapel and stood to one side on the stairs.

An elderly man appeared at the door, his suit impeccable, his round glasses unable to hide his intense eyes. Fang estimated him to be in his eighties, and he used a cane to adapt his limp to a smoother gait. The bodyguard offered his arm all the same. It seemed a practiced routine as the older man placed his left hand on the other's arm and used his cane in his right, facilitating a steady descent to the tarmac. On the flat, the elder walked unaided, his head high, with only a slight camber to his walk.

Ambassador Lian bowed to him. Unlike Japanese culture, where bowing was as common as handshakes were in America, bowing was reserved in China for only the highest levels of respect.

"General Gao," Lian said, rising. "Welcome to America."

"Thank you, Ambassador," the general—or former general—replied without glancing at Fang. "Is he here?"

"He is." Lian gestured to Fang. "My colleague arranged a discreet location."

Colleague. Introducing Fang as a colleague, not as a secretary or even as her official position—attaché—presented her as someone Lian respected and trusted. In China, female empowerment at the highest levels of business and government was still a relatively new concept. Only women with a long history of service and accomplishment like Ambassador Lian were respected by old-school officer types like the highly decorated former general. Which meant any woman who'd reached Lian's level was ambitious and tough in equal measure.

Behind his thin lenses, Gao's eyes flicked to Fang but did not linger. "Very well. Show me."

Lian led the way, and Fang felt very small beside the pair. Both were tall, spoke with only minimal preamble, and were eager to act swiftly. Without an invitation from Gao, Fang stayed a stride behind, politeness requiring her to remain apart in case they wished to converse privately, as did the lone bodyguard.

There was little to say. Lian made small talk, which Gao returned—the flight was fine, he'd managed to sleep, relations with the Americans were returning to bearable following the Korean summit attack, and so on—until they reached the block where the amenities were based.

The bodyguard checked inside and gave the all-clear, then the party entered.

"Will my visit be recorded?" Gao asked as they passed through the entrance and paused beneath an obvious camera.

Lian glanced at Fang, who answered, meeting the man's eye. "Yes, General. But there are private places. There will be no suspicion."

The general regarded her for a long moment before Fang scurried ahead and the others followed. They passed the lounge doors with another camera and turned a corner to a block containing two more doors—one indicating male, the other female.

Fang spoke directly to the bodyguard. "The locker rooms to

the showers are empty. There is a fire exit at the far end. Please take the general through there, then turn right, where you will find a blond woman. She will take you from there."

The general looked uncertain, clearly unimpressed by Fang, but after looking to Lian for approval, he acquiesced and allowed his bodyguard to escort him inside.

Fang and Lian returned the way they'd come, diverting into the lounge. The exterior CCTV would capture them entering, but privacy was a major factor for the airfield's clientele, so there was no coverage inside this section of the building.

All except the circular serving area in the center was dimly lit, like an upmarket cocktail bar, and all the tables were spaced with plenty of carpet between them. The chairs were luxuriously upholstered in a mix of leather and cloth so patrons could choose their preference, and the booths dotted around the outside were semi-circles of comfort.

The only thing differentiating this scene from a quiet hotel lounge was that there was no barman. No other staff at all. When Fang had hired this place for the hour, she'd insisted that they would provide their own servers.

The only human present was a man in his late fifties, seated at a table out in the open with a tumbler of amber liquor at his fingertips. His small white beard and moustache reminded Fang of the pictures of the founder of a certain chicken-based fast-food chain, but his fashion sense was closer to the tech-bros of Silicon Valley—a smart suit, a polo shirt instead of a dress shirt and tie, and sneakers, accessorized with a watch that likely cost six figures. A couple of bulky rings adorned fingers not associated with his marital status.

Rafe Ashenhurst rose as the women approached, a hand extended to Lian. "Ambassador, it's great to meet in person at last."

Lian shook the hand while Ashenhurst appraised her, his

eyes roving up and down. "Likewise," she replied in perfect English. "Thank you for waiting."

"No probs," the man said, turning to Fang. "You must be the secretary who set all this up, eh?"

Although Fang was fluent in English, she had little ear for accents. Still, even she could pick up that Ashenhurst did not speak like most men of his status. He was British but didn't speak the King's English. His voice was deep, yes, but that wasn't it. There was a rough edge to him, a weird cadence that was at once friendly and somehow threatening, as if he were holding back from raising his voice.

"I did, sir, yes," Fang replied, extending a hand.

He took it softly and stared at her with a curious smile. As with Lian, his eyes roved over her. Even though she was still wearing her thick coat, she shivered with the sensation of being watched a little too closely.

"Mr. Ashenhurst," came a clipped female voice.

They all turned to find Isabella Knight accompanying General Gao from the camera-free door at the back of the lounge. It was Knight's reconnoiter that had supplied Fang with the idea of routing Gao through the shower block so that anyone reviewing the footage would see Ashenhurst in the same approximate location but leave no trail of the pair meeting.

Ashenhurst lifted his arms from his side, and his voice boomed as if greeting an old friend following a long absence. "Ah, here he is, the man himself! General—"

"No names," Gao said curtly. He spoke a little English but was not close to fluent. "Let us talk."

Fang offered refreshments, but Gao declined. He also declined a seat when offered, leaning on his cane and cocking his head toward Ashenhurst.

Gao said, "You wished to meet. I am here."

Ashenhurst seemed flustered for a moment, eyeing his drink before thinking better of it. "Thank you. Thank you. I hope it wasn't too inconvenient."

"It is highly inconvenient. But we are partners, are we not?"

Ashenhurst forced a smile, the swagger momentarily failing him. "Yes, of course. For a partnership of this magnitude, I felt it was essential we meet."

"How is business?" Gao asked, his tone cutting.

Ashenhurst visibly blanched but recovered quickly. "It is true that a handful of my other... ventures... have become unstable." He leaned forward, his voice dropping slightly, ever the salesman. "But that is good for you, General. This deal is now my primary focus. It *has* to succeed."

Gao looked unimpressed.

Lian said, "Perhaps you can assure us of progress regarding the information leaks you experienced recently."

"Right, right." Ashenhurst gathered himself, and although he didn't physically puff up his chest, his shift in tone carried that effect. "My head of security is taking care of that."

Isabella Knight took a half-step forward. Her voice was firm and authoritative, like the newsreaders Fang was familiar with, lacking the rough nature of her boss'. "Correct. We've utilized third parties, people who cannot be traced back to us. Any intelligence that has reached the NIA or the Americans will be out of date within the next twenty-four hours."

Gao looked to Lian—Knight's vocabulary too broad for a limited English-speaker. Fang translated, and Gao answered in Chinese.

"In twenty-four hours? This will be the main shipment for our bulk order?"

Fang translated to English for the British pair and strapped herself in for a slow back and forth. Better to speak plainly and without ambiguity, even if it meant conversing through her.

"The minerals have been secured," Ashenhurst said. "Transport is being arranged. The security you provided is welcome but likely unnecessary. The source has no connection to any governments, and they are eager to remain independent."

Once Fang relayed this, Lian added in Chinese, "He means the terrorists in the desert. They run the facility."

Gao nodded. "But it will be secured and processed in the same way as your batch from several weeks ago?"

"It will," Ashenhurst said. "It's all ready for your final approval. Some final tweaks, and—boom. We'll blow you away with what we've got. Exactly as you specified."

Fang wrestled with his exact meaning but got it across to Gao.

Gao said, "Tweaks? Either it is ready or it is not."

"Just some adjustments to the delivery system," Ashenhurst said. "Not the circuits or the juicy stuff you're most interested in."

"And this could not have been relayed in an email?"

"It could, but I'm a people person." Ashenhurst angled his head, eyes passing over Fang. Again, she shivered internally. When Knight gave a near-inaudible "hmm," Ashenhurst perked up, attention back firmly on Gao. "Actually, I wanted to invite you personally to my home during your assessment. There's a festival going on, so you could combine a little pleasure with your business."

Fang might have translated poorly, or perhaps Gao just didn't care. He adjusted his stance more stiffly, pulled back his shoulders, and made a sour shape with his mouth. "I take no pleasure in my business. The lives that will be lost are necessary. My discomfort is necessary. I thank you for your invitation, but I am interested only in accommodation, not parties or festivals. What you are doing may launch a war. I hope to avoid it, but you must bear in mind the human cost of our endeavor."

"Of course, of course." Ashenhurst gestured to Knight. "We will make all the arrangements."

"We are heading to Taiwan next," Knight said. "We will finalize the second phase's financing and logistics before removing personnel who know anything to a secure subsidiary in London."

Gao nodded again, his curt manner leaving no doubt that he was annoyed at this seemingly unnecessary meeting. Unnecessary, that was, except to convince the businessman before them that he was an equal partner, when nothing could be further from the truth.

Ashenhurst grinned. "I'm glad to go there personally, too. As you can see, I prefer to do things in person."

"Is that not what got your knighthood stripped?" Gao asked. "Too much in-person interaction?"

Fang chose not to translate that, figuring it was not intended for Ashenhurst's ears anyway. Instead, she said, "The general wishes to be assured your public troubles will not come to haunt you or us. And that the next time you meet, it will be to take delivery of what we have paid handsomely for."

"Abso-bloody-lutely," Ashenhurst said. "Just..." He gave a small chuckle. "Just tell your boys in the South China Sea not to shoot down my plane, okay?"

This time, Gao responded himself. "Do not provoke my countrymen. Just because the current leadership is weak and kowtows to Western imperialism, do not think they will not act against direct threats."

Ashenhurst's happiness froze in place, as if someone had whipped a rug from under him. He was considering how to reply when Knight did so for him.

"And when we are finished?" she said. "What guarantee do we have that they won't act against us?"

Gao bristled. Lian dipped her chin minutely but held her tongue. Fang thought about coming up with a suitable reply, but she was unsure of her place here. If she spoke out of turn, it could set her back with the general. Which would set her back with Lian.

Yet if she answered well, it might show him that she could do more than file papers and arrange meetings.

"If you do your part correctly," Fang said to Knight and Ashenhurst, "there will be no one left to act against you."

The general paused, appraised Fang in a way that did not make her in the least bit uncomfortable, then his mouth twitched with the shadow of a smile toward Lian.

"I believe I have taken long enough in the shower room." To Ashenhurst, he said, "We will see you in England for the final test." Then he held out one hand toward Fang. "Please, see my *colleague* if you need any further support from us."

FOUR

The heat hit them like a physical blow as they stepped off the propeller-driven Nigerian military transport onto the tarmac of the remote outpost. The sweat stains under Trapp's armpits plunged almost to his hips. Madison, if anything, looked worse. Trapp at least had practice falling asleep in aircraft whose ride was as smooth as a washer spin cycle.

A tall, sharply dressed man with an intelligent, watchful gaze approached them, extending a hand.

"Mr. Trapp, Ms. Grubbs. I'm Jelany Ikem, NIA. Welcome to my country." His handshake was firm, his English perfect. "My government has sanctioned this operation, but I must be clear: you are guests here. Any actions you take must be cleared through me first. We'll be driving to the objective together. The vehicle is this way."

Trapp noted the professional confidence and the subtle warning in Ikem's tone. This wasn't going to be a simple babysitting assignment for the Nigerian.

"Understood," Trapp said. "Lead the way."

Hours later, in a four-year-old SUV with four-year-old A/C

that felt like more of a suggestion than a feature, Trapp's lower back ached from the grueling overland journey. So far, Madison had insisted on method acting her Elizabeth Wilbur character, and Liz was no conversationalist. Jelany seemed content with his own thoughts, if occasionally somewhat bemused by his passengers' interactions.

Trapp turned his attention elsewhere, staring out through the dirt-streaked windows, where the road was a patchwork of hard red clay winding through a landscape of ochre and green. They sped by low scrub and fields dotted with clusters of trees that seemed to lean toward the horizon. Villages appeared occasionally, varying in their fortunes, some with branded retailers and two-story stone dwellings, others marked by mud-brick houses blending into the earth, punctuated by the glint of tin roofs.

"We're two minutes out," Ikem said, continuing what had become a regular countdown. The GPS in the SUV looked like any civilian mapping device but was backed by military precision and linked to a satellite acquired for their incursion.

The SUV bumped and rolled over the poorly-maintained road; the approach to the mine flattened through a barren stretch of land—not quite desert but certainly scrubland in every direction. Most of it had clearly been bulldozed with chemicals spread around to prevent regrowth.

Making it easier to defend.

As they neared their destination, the military metaphor only grew more apt. A few years earlier, Trapp had spent time in a Russian prison camp, an off-book mission that had cost him the most loving and long-lasting relationship he'd sustained as an adult. But given the lives it had saved and bad guys taken off the board, he'd sacrifice his happiness all over again. That memory had circled back to him now because of the degree of security he was witnessing here—the sentries, the guns, the double layer of razor-wire-topped chain-link fence that circled out of sight in both directions.

He glanced at the man driving. Jelany Ikem's hands were steady on the wheel, his gaze fixed on the road, but Trapp recognized the tension coiled in his shoulders. This wasn't just another assignment for the NIA agent. Mitchell's file had been brief but pointed. Ikem was a rising star in the agency, a man whose entire career had been a methodical crusade against the cancer of Boko Haram after they had raided his home village and killed his younger brother a decade ago. For Ikem, this mission wasn't about placating American allies or investigating a trafficking route. It was personal. It was a rare opportunity to use the full weight and resources of the CIA as a sledgehammer against the men who had shattered his family. Trapp saw it in the hard set of the man's jaw as they drove deeper into the territory his enemies called home. Ikem was a hunter, temporarily wearing a guide's clothes.

There was a guard waiting at the gate, flanked by armed personnel in green army-style fatigues who looked exhausted at first. But as the SUV neared and Ikem pulled the car softly to a halt to avoid kicking up dust clouds, Trapp noted the pair were tense as hell, their eyes hooded with the dead gazes he often feared more than hate-filled rancor. They'd shoot him in the head with as much emotion as flicking off a lamp.

Ikem rolled down his window, and the civilian-looking man approached with a wide smile. His faux-military style jacket was similar to the ones worn by his guards, except for the sergeant's stripes on the shoulders and the fact that it gaped open to reveal his potbelly constrained only by a white undershirt. His belt held up rough, worn trousers around his waist, hiked under the belly.

"Good afternoon," the man said with the manner of a used

car dealer. He looked past Ikem to Trapp in the back. "You are Mr. Harding, yes?"

"He is," Ikem replied firmly, offering three sets of documentation.

The man continued to ignore Ikem, watching the two white people carefully. Trapp kept his eyes forward, playing the role of a stuck-up Westerner who thinks he's better than the people he is gracing with his presence.

"I am Obasee," the man said. "I am the overseer of this facility. Given your proposal, I decided to greet you personally!"

"Nice to meet you, Mr. Obasee," Grubbs said. "It has been a long journey."

Obasee waited.

Ikem held the documents still.

Trapp turned his eyes toward the overseer and gave a slow nod. He had a role to play and would not break character now.

He said, "I prefer to see any investment firsthand. But I hate this fucking heat. So please, do what you need to do, then show us what we need to see so that we can get out of here."

It was enough. Obasee smiled and accepted the forged paperwork. He flicked through it briefly, lingering far longer on Ikem than Trapp and Grubbs combined, which brought his dead-eyed companions shuffling closer. Then Obasee gave another signal that prompted the pair to check the vehicle over. Ikem popped the trunk when instructed. Trapp forced himself to remain relaxed under their scrutiny.

Speaking to Trapp, Obasee tossed the documents back in Ikem's lap. "Good, we can *absolutely* proceed. The gate will open, and you will follow our vehicle. Do not deviate until we pull into the carport." A pointed look at Ikem. "Is that clear, friend?"

"It is," Ikem replied. "Sir."

"Good! I will give you a tour *personally*."

Obasee grinned and took off, signaling to his men that all was well. The gate trundled open to the side, wound on a winch by another sweaty, militarily dressed security guard.

Militar*ily*. Not in *military* garb.

Even in hot countries, genuine army uniforms had some heft to them, a hard-wearing quality that served their owner well, whereas all he'd seen so far were cheap knockoffs, almost fancy-dress despite their threadbare nature. That plus the men's lack of alertness and the little respect shown to their superiors all proved they were not real soldiers. Men given a gun, shown how to pull the trigger, and conditioned to value human life as much as a spider's.

Sociopathic, over-equipped rent-a-cops at best.

Obasee climbed into an ancient Land Rover with his men and drove onward. Ikem kept a dozen yards back to avoid the swell of dust in Obasee's wake. They passed between mounds of rubble, sturdy transport vehicles, and more rows of fencing mounted with observation posts.

Excessive. And not the best defensive layout.

Within the inner fence, several generators belched gray smoke, powering what appeared to be living quarters and a mess hall of sorts, and others beyond the dust kicked up by their vehicles must have served buildings and equipment too far out for them to see.

Traveling deeper, there were swells of land, ripped out by machines to get to the precious metals in the earth below. This part of the country was rich in gold and rare-earth metals, but according to satellite photos, the mine's expansion had slowed in recent years. As the technology in refining lithium—literally smashing it out of the earth—improved and demand for electric vehicles and cheap phones skyrocketed exponentially, the mine's output had resumed and the site expanded, tripling in size on the satellite photos. Digging deeper for lithium-rich ore was suddenly profitable again, albeit more costly in terms of machinery, infrastructure, and manpower.

They pulled into a rickety carport, little more than a wooden canopy that kept the sun off the Jeeps and other assorted vehicles that Trapp saw, mostly short-range transport, possibly for patrols or supply runs. Nearby were several shipping containers, some of them open and filled with tools and smaller machinery, along a walkway to a stack of prefab units that resembled the offices Trapp was used to seeing on construction sites.

Ikem got out, opened the rear door for his "boss," and although Trapp had cursed the shitty A/C on the way in, the wave of heat didn't so much hit him as soak him entirely. Nothing he hadn't felt before, but it was an irritant, nonetheless. Especially while wearing a suit.

Grubbs alighted as Obasee strode forward with his ebullient salesman manner, passing Ikem without a glance and extending his hand to Trapp. It looked sweaty even before it arrived within arm's reach. Trapp reciprocated in the Harding persona, keeping himself guarded.

Breaking the damp grip, Obasee looked at Grubbs, hands on his hips, the friendly smile pasted on.

Grubbs shifted uneasily beside him. "Is there a problem?"

Obasee's gaze flicked between them. "No problem. But we have procedures we must follow."

"You need to search us," Trapp stated.

Obasee gave a *what-can-I-do* shrug.

"It's to be expected." Trapp held out his arms for the guards' rough hands to pat him down.

They were gentler with Grubbs and rougher with Ikem, then they set about a second search of the SUV's interior. Trapp was not worried; there was nothing incriminating, except for the GPS, which was indistinguishable from a civilian screen, and the hidden compartment that they would not find without an x-ray-capable scanner. They had not risked weapons except for the standard handgun in the front that a driver like Ikem would be expected to carry and a rifle for animals who might wander into their path. No additional surveillance gear, no bugs, nothing that would get them executed, even if a scanner did appear.

They really were on their own out here.

"Clean," one guard finally reported. His friend remained silent.

"Of course it is clean. *Absoluuutely*. Thank you for your cooperation." Obasee turned with a hand outstretched like a tour guide, then stopped and gave his fakest grin yet. "Your assistant, Mr. Harding." He was gesturing toward Grubbs.

"Partner," Grubbs corrected.

Obasee conceded with an awkward nod. "Yes, partner. Our... security here... we select them from many different backgrounds. Some... they are not used to seeing a woman like this. With her hair, her neck exposed."

"Exposed?" Grubbs repeated.

Trapp didn't need to get into a feminist debate regarding Islamist militants. He said, "It's fine. We've dealt with facilities in ISIL territory. Lizzie can handle a few stares. But she has a scarf. Right?"

"Right," Grubbs said, pulling a lightweight, translucent veil over the back of her neck and hair.

Obasee didn't seem convinced by the compromise but accepted their decision.

As the trio followed him into the main area of the compound, Trapp noted how Obasee would return the greetings from guards and unarmed personnel, then slow when no greeting was forthcoming until the person in question said something in a respectful tone, which returned Obasee to sweetness and light.

Trapp wondered how a walking ego like him would fare without the armor his authority commanded.

Growing accustomed to the stifling heat, Trapp memorized all he could observe: the generators, the ground-clearing dozers and earthmovers in varying states of disrepair, the locked bunkers with warning signs, and the dozen armed men, patrolling in pairs rather than guarding specific areas, which made little sense until Trapp saw what they were probably supervising.

Although the original satellite photos showed a massive hole in the ground, a strip mine where earth was removed in huge quantities to reach the deposits below, there were entrances into the sides held in place by thick chunks of wood. Men and women—mostly men—in hard hats pushed wheelbarrows of earth out, dumped them on sluggish conveyor belts, and trudged back inside to fetch more. None looked up at the armed men watching their progress.

The miners seemed ill-equipped, dressed not in overalls but a range of clothes unsuitable for underground working—some in little more than rags.

Trapp realized that one of his assumptions had been wrong. The cleared land and guard towers weren't defensive; they were to deter workers from fleeing.

"Quite an operation," Trapp remarked, his gaze lingering on a reinforced door to their left.

Protecting people or equipment?

Obasee gave a half-grunt, half-laugh. "We take security *absoluuutely* seriously. Any investment... very safe."

That word he seemed so fond of—*absoluuutely*—was already grating on Trapp. Worth at least a slap, once he could shed his cover.

Trapp glanced back, where he'd counted at least two layers of fencing, each topped with razor wire. Surveillance cameras dotted every corner, unblinking lenses static.

He was sure some must be dummies, but with the generators working overtime, they might siphon some of the power from the industrial gear.

As they rounded a bend, taking them away from the miners, Trapp's breath caught. A group of four men—mercenaries, if he'd ever seen one—lounged near a guard post. He was startled by their muscled appearances, Caucasian and Chinese faces standing out among the local militants. Each man was heavily armed, properly dressed in ballistic vests and quality outfits, and their eyes exuded an air of menace that said, *Stay away... keep walking...*

"Interesting personnel," Grubbs said quietly enough that only Trapp could hear.

The presence of foreign mercenaries complicated things. Their manner suggested military backgrounds. Chinese or Korean, American or European, or even Russian. Certainly a few Slavic bone structures. Until they spoke, Trapp couldn't tell for sure. And there was no chit-chat here.

They knew of a few companies with interests in the mine, but only one that Trapp could see had the resources to fund this sort of op—the Ashenhurst Group. Trapp wondered if they were footing the bill for the mercenaries. And if so, why?

As they continued, Trapp tried picking out potential weaknesses: a section of fence obscured by overgrown vegetation, a guard post manned by a single, bored-looking sentry, power lines daisy-chaining generators rather than single-track cables. It was a low-tech fortress, manned by enthusiastic amateurs.

But a fortress, nonetheless.

Trapp locked on to a trio of Chinese guards standing near an access road that curled around one of the elevated sections of land. They watched Trapp's group with threats in their stares.

"What's down there?" Trapp asked.

Obasee offered another regretful shrug. "Other clients. Please, let us keep going."

"Diverse security team. Must be quite an investment."

Obasee's smile tightened. "If you choose additional security, or to supply your own people, your request will be granted. But I think you are looking for a less... premium option for your products?"

"Of course," Grubbs chimed in, a note of warning for Trapp's benefit. "Though I'm curious about the need for such... specialized personnel. Are you concerned about your employees overstepping, perhaps?"

Trapp watched Obasee's face carefully. A flicker of unease passed over it. This wasn't just about cost-effective security—there was fear inside him, too.

Chinese guards.

Foreign mercenaries.

Sections sealed off from the rest of the operation.

Which meant Trapp needed to know what they were hiding.

"This opportunity looks incredible," he said. "Now show me the *real* assets I came for."

FIVE

Inside one of the access tunnels, the stench assailed Trapp's nostrils as shadows squirmed over rough-hewn walls, cast by the swinging headlamps of passing workers. Their hollow eyes and slumped shoulders told a story Trapp could barely bring himself to think about.

"You see, gentlemen... lady..." Obasee went on, "this operation is a jewel in itself. The center of my father's empire. But I run it. Soon, it will be mine."

"Soon?"

Trapp had seen his share of megalomaniacs, but Obasee's complete disconnect from the suffering around him was particularly appalling. That could be an advantage, tagging Obasee as easily manipulated if they fed his ego just right.

"Impressive," Trapp said. "How many workers are down here?"

Obasee waved a hand dismissively. "Oh, at any one time? Maybe thirty. But we have hundreds that we can use. Many, many processing above ground. Some for transport. More for assessment and rejections. We rotate the stock to keep them compliant and healthy."

Stock...?

"But they are lucky to have work." Obasee grinned. "I am a benevolent master."

A worker stumbled nearby, the weight of his load unbalancing him. Every instinct in Trapp lurched toward intervening, but he held back.

The bigger picture.

The role he was playing.

So Trapp just stepped around the skinny African man, sighing in disgust at the inconvenience. He noted Grubbs lingering on the stumble a fraction longer, but she followed Trapp's lead.

"What are they extracting here?" Trapp asked. "Apart from lithium?"

"Ah, now we get to the good part! Follow me."

Obasee led them to a rickety elevator, the sliding cage door rattling like a hundred loose hinges as it closed behind them. It creaked as it descended in a stuttering, uneven drop, the temperature rising with every yard.

Trapp employed the rule of commercial airline travel: watch the stewardesses' reactions; if they buckle up during turbulence, you should definitely do the same. In this case, the stewardess—Obasee—remained upbeat and relaxed, so Trapp concluded the unsteady elevator and its continuous screeches and groans were perfectly normal.

After a few minutes that stretched way too long, the car emitted a sort-of howl as ancient brakes kicked in, then they clunked to a halt, allowing Obasee to wrestle the cage door open once again.

"Lithium, of course, is our primary output," Obasee

explained as they emerged into a cavernous chamber. "The reason you are here, yes?"

Trapp raised an eyebrow, making sure Obasee saw it in the wan lighting.

"I know it is essential for your fancy gadgets' batteries." Obasee's pompous tone was clearly intended to make him sound intelligent. "Phones, tablets, computers. The modern world runs on our sweat."

Not *ours*.

Theirs.

"You said *primary* output," Grubbs inquired. "What else is here?"

"Ah, that is something you will not need," Obasee said in a cheery way, but Trapp figured it had something to do with the other clients they'd passed. "I promise you, this is a new, rich vein that will please you plenty."

As they walked, Trapp catalogued every detail: the worn-out equipment, a sparse line of men and the occasional woman lugging a wheelbarrow of terrorism-bound profits, zero safety measures except for hard hats, and—frankly—the sheer scale of the operation. It wasn't just a local crime lord's project. This potentially had global reach.

"And you have other clients lined up?" Trapp asked.

Obasee's grin widened. "The world is hungry. *Absolutely*, it is. There will always be other clients. And I am the one who can cater for a feast. But I *like* you. *Both* of you." He deigned to address Grubbs for a second, then returned to Trapp. "I think we will do good business."

Around the next bend, dozens of apparently Chinese and African migrants huddled against the walls. More of those dead-eyed guards in faux-military attire gave them water in filthy bowls, a piece of bread, and what looked like overripe bananas. The workers' wrists were bound with heavy shackles chained to their ankles via a longer length of steel links. They looked scrawny and bruised. Most remained impassive, but a couple watched the contingent walk by, frozen in either fear or hope—Trapp could not tell.

"Here we have our most cost-effective labor force," Obasee said, his tone as casual as if he were discussing inventory in a warehouse. "Dissidents, mostly. Could not pay their way. We bought the debts, now they work for us. Ironic, isn't it?"

"Quite... efficient," Trapp managed.

"The smugglers bring them so far," Grubbs said, piecing it together. "Then when they can't pay the onward fees, the traffickers sell them to you."

Obasee nodded, his mouth wide in pleasure at her understanding. Trapp was impressed at how she kept it all businesslike, when he knew she'd be boiling about this as much as he was.

"Then let's talk numbers," Grubbs said.

They wandered for a few minutes more, talking yields-per-pound and dollars-per-ton, before continuing the chatter back up the elevator. Trapp played it aloof, which was not a stretch. This was Madison's field anyway, so keeping the dynamics in place was good tradecraft.

Back in the light, they blinked away the shock to their retinas and rejoined Ikem, who had been eager to remain up top. The Nigerian agent's solemn dip of his chin suggested there was plenty to discuss. Zoning out the business negotiation, Trapp followed Ikem's subtle eye-squint to the heavily armed guards patrolling the inner perimeter, mostly the mercenaries, around paths Obasee had not shown them.

"So what *is* the increased security about?" Trapp asked. "Seems like quite a heavy cost."

Obasee's smile faltered for a moment. "As I told you before, we take our clients' safety seriously."

Trapp leaned in, lowering his voice. "Come on, Obasee. You must have broken into something special to warrant this level of protection. As excited as I am about the prospect of a ready supply chain, I'm sure your father would be proud of how you've expanded his business."

The mention of his father made Obasee's chest rise. He glanced around before speaking. "You would not be interested. But we broke a new seam of a natural alloy of... ni... nio..." He seemed to be wracking his brain for the right word. "Niobic-something. Usually, we would leave it because purifying it is not profitable. But my biggest partner was interested. And has claimed it. All of it."

Niobic...

What the hell is that?

When Trapp remained silent, staring at Obasee the way he would during the quiet interlude of an interrogation, the overseer plainly grew worried and reverted to his ebullient salesman persona.

"But absolutely do not concern yourself! It has no value to cell phone manufacturers."

Trapp gave a dismissive shrug. "Then I don't care about it. My business is with your other... assets." He turned as if to leave the topic, but his curiosity got the better of him. "Still. Must be worth something if you've got this many guns protecting it."

Before Obasee could answer, Ikem cut in smoothly. "Mr. Harding is naturally cautious about any potential complications to his investment, of course."

Trapp realized Ikem had read suspicion growing at his questions. That was the right thing to do—steer the conversation back on track.

Grubbs cleared her throat. "Mr. Obasee, if I may... I

couldn't help but notice your... *efficient* labor force. Have you considered expanding their utility beyond mining?"

Trapp's pulse quickened. He wanted to follow suit but didn't quite dare in case he got in deeper than his knowledge allowed. Understanding when to leave things to the experts was a valuable skill.

Obasee's eyebrows arched. "What did you have in mind, Miss Wilbur?"

"When our factory opens, we could benefit from some additional hands," Grubbs replied. "Discreet, hardworking individuals."

A smile spread slowly across Obasee's face, lighting his eyes as if dark filaments had ignited within. "Yes, yes. We might be able to arrange something. Of course, transportation would be your responsibility. These assets are quite... delicate."

Trapp leaned into his neutral, all-business expression, the casual discussion of human trafficking and the buying and selling of people landing somewhat out of his wheelhouse. He glanced at Ikem, who pressed on likewise, although Trapp could not miss the vein that pulsed every few seconds at his temple.

"We'll need to discuss logistics," Grubbs continued smoothly. "Perhaps we can schedule a follow-up meeting?"

Obasee nodded, clearly pleased. "Yes, yes, abso*luuu*tely. Although a down payment... a reservation deposit... if you wish us to pick suitable candidates?"

Trapp was about to ask what the hell he meant, but Grubbs said, "That would be fine. We anticipated this. Perhaps now is a good time to continue our tour?"

Obasee licked his lips, happy but tense as the lucrative deal's finishing line edged closer. "I'm afraid many areas are still off-limits, so this is the extent of our demonstration. You have the statistics already, yes. That is why we are here."

"Absolutely," Trapp said with a slight curl of his lip, a tell he killed as soon as he detected it.

As they turned to leave, he glimpsed another coterie of heavily armed guards jogging from one of the private paths, jumping into open top vehicles equipped with heavy ordnance. As their engines fired, a short convoy of unmarked trucks thrummed forward, and the escort adopted front-and-rear positions to take the transports out of the facility. There were no plates, no means of identification, just the diluted primary colors of battered moving trucks that looked like old U-Hauls.

Trapp filed the observation away for later.

Returning to the SUV they'd arrived in, he reflected that he was tired, exhausted from the pretense of nonchalance more than the heat or physical effort. The tour had left him with a simmering rage that needed to boil over into action, into something that he could tell himself made his compliance worth it.

Ikem opened the trunk, and Grubbs removed a small flathead screwdriver from a toolkit with which she levered up the compartment that the earlier search had not uncovered. Trapp reached in and removed a smart burgundy briefcase.

"As discussed, a gesture of goodwill."

Obasee's eyes sparkled again with whatever dark light powered his psyche. "Ah, how thoughtful of you to bring this with you."

Trapp fought the urge to use the case as a weapon. How easy it would be to jab it into the overseer's throat, then slam one corner into his head over and over until he ceased moving.

Instead, he opened it, revealing neat stacks of cash—$50,000 in US currency.

"Perfect," Obasee said. "Absolutely perfect."

As they shook hands, Trapp couldn't help but picture the shackled workers. He didn't even try to block it out. He wanted to remember them.

As they climbed into the SUV, Trapp longed to call Mitchell immediately. But they weren't safe yet. No idea whether they were being monitored. Whether they might be attacked as they departed. As they put a mile or two between them and the compound, all three deflated in relief.

"You saw those trucks?" Ikem asked.

"Yeah, I saw them," Trapp replied, his mind racing to organize the flood of new data. He shook his head. "This isn't right. We came here looking for a simple smuggling trail. This... this is something else entirely."

"Foreign mercenaries, sealed-off sections, a secret alloy..." Grubbs listed, her brow furrowed. "And Obasee seemed terrified of his 'biggest partner,' not Boko Haram. Something else is at play here."

"I agree," Trapp said, his jaw tight. "We need to report this to Mitchell now."

He sensed he was clenching everything—his fists, his jaws, even his lats ached from the tension of repressing his urge to rip Obasee's head from his shoulders by hand. "Whatever it is, we need to bring this whole damn place down. And fast."

SIX

Washington, D.C

IT HAD BEEN A LONG DAY, like so many that had kept Mike Mitchell at work instead of home. Instead of socializing. Instead of enjoying life.

It was times like these, as he waited for the second of two doors deep within Langley to hiss open, that he wondered what he would do when he retired, how he would reprogram himself to set national security to one side and concentrate on himself and what remained of his family.

The anteroom's green light flashed on, and a friendly *ping* granted him access to the Special Operations Division Sandpit.

The Sandpit was a relatively new innovation, nicknamed such because it was where the most junior-level analysts were trialed and gained experience on low-level work. "Junior" was a bit of a misnomer, though; in the regular CIA sphere, they'd be the top of their field. But this was Special Operations. No one got into the really juicy stuff until they'd served time, proved their ability, their cool under pressure, and their understanding of the necessity of the department's existence.

Mitchell needed no reminding, and nor, it seemed, did his latest addition to the Sandpit team—a cheerful young woman named Polly Garside.

Young woman.

Mitchell chided himself. She was forty-two, with fifteen years' experience in the intelligence community. At least he had stopped referring to her as "the new girl." Not that he ever did so out loud. These days, HR had more power in the Agency than Guantanamo.

There were two other analysts working different cases, but Mitchell had trusted Polly with the uplink data concerning Trapp's observations made during his egress from the Nigerian mine.

The convoy was being escorted by mercenaries, some possibly from China and others Trapp had described in his remote debriefing as "Slavic-looking." That could mean Russian, Eastern European, or simply Scandinavian. There were a lot of inherited genes in that region. Still, it was worth following up. Larger security threats had emerged from lesser-seeming snippets of intel.

"Director Mitchell," Polly said, looking up from her screen.

She had bright copper-red hair that she swept up in a clip and wore a ruby-colored nose-stud. Not strictly office-appropriate, but not something he lost sleep over.

"Polly, yes," Mitchell replied. "I'm just passing through before going home. I wanted to check up on anything we should know about."

"Some potential fun things." Polly always sounded like she was smiling even when she wasn't. And she wasn't right now. "We had already run the signature checks for radioactive material, and there doesn't appear to be any special shielding on the vehicles, either, so we're satisfied it's negative."

Mitchell was thankful for that. They had dealt with nuclear threats in the past, and he hoped never to have to face them again. All it took was one slip.

He looked around for over-attentive ears, spotting Gary Blake and Harul Gophal at their own stations ten feet away with headphones on, listening to intercepts acquired through means that were *technically* legal but which nobody under the national security umbrella would want made public.

Mitchell pulled up a chair and sat at the edge of Polly's desk. Although only a few months into her time here, she had already proven her worth, distributing quality analysis and offering hypotheses that never overreached into fantasy or the-sky-is-falling panic.

"So what do we have?"

She concentrated on the screen for a longer moment, hit a couple of keys, and a series of windows expanded on her screen.

"The *least* interesting thing is the trucks themselves," Polly said. "There are no plates, but they conform to a batch that was supposed to be written off six months ago in Turkey. It's not uncommon for this to happen. You get a corrupt official or mechanic somewhere down the line and they think the trucks are repairable, just so much wear-and-tear that no commercial company would take them. The owners write them off and take a cash payment in return for selling them. The middlemen make a profit."

"Dangerous and illegal. But I don't think it requires our attention."

"Exactly what I thought. Then I realized we can run a trace on the shape and direction of these trucks from archived satellite imagery, and it looks like they came out of Chad."

"Chad. That's north of Nigeria, isn't it?"

"Northeast, yes. We can't trace them all the way back to the source, but we know it isn't the first time that route has been covered by at least two trucks—remarkably similar in shape to some of these."

"So they have already taken a couple of batches of whatever they're mining. How many trucks like that are there in Africa?"

"Not as many as I'd feared—they're more popular in Eastern Europe—but too many to make this stand up in a court of law, if you're asking me to swear they were the same."

Mitchell nodded. "Okay. So let's assume for a second that they could be the same. What are the implications?"

"Well, this is where I started to get all giddy." Polly gave a little chuckle. "We can make some educated guesses about the owners of these trucks based on who can afford to run a convoy line like that. There's Lau Mae Corporation from Taiwan and Ashenhurst Group who used to be based in the UK but now—"

"Let's leave the guesses for now." He wasn't ready to share with an analyst at her level that Ashenhurst was a significant player already. "We might have to circle back to it. For now, what do we *actually* know?"

"Our most solid theory is based on the observation that two of trucks that came out of that mine today also drove into Chad two months ago. That time, they were less secretive about their manifest. It was a lump of nickel alloy, enough to fill a six cubic foot crate. Also listed is niobium."

"Niobium?" Mitchell repeated, the word scratching a recently-opened cut in his mind. "What is it? Trapp mentioned something similar in his report."

Polly tapped a few keys. "It's primarily used in specialty steel, but our materials science database has it on a low-level watchlist. It's a key component in experimental superconductors."

Mitchell frowned. "Superconductors? That's R&D's headache, not Special Ops. Trapp is there to investigate a smuggling route for people, not exotic metals. The cargo is a distraction."

"But sir," Polly pressed gently, "the cost-benefit doesn't make sense. The ore is nearly worthless without complex refining. Why use mercenaries to guard a shipment of worthless rock?"

"Because Ashenhurst is involved, and nothing he does is straightforward," Mitchell said, his mind made up. "He's likely using the convoy as misdirection. Let's not get sidetracked. Package the convoy intel and send it to R&D and the Nigerians to handle. I want Trapp and Grubbs focused on the human element. That was the mission."

"Okay, sir. Not a problem." Her fingers fluttered over the keyboard, packaging the file for the NIA. "I'll just add a note about the superconductor flag..."

Mitchell stood, about to bid her goodnight when she suddenly stopped typing. Her whole body froze.

"What is it?" Mitchell inquired.

"The file... when I added the keyword 'superconductor,' it triggered something. An alert. Who is Karem Hines?"

"Never heard of him."

Mitchell came around to view her screen and read the flashing alert box.

Contact Karem Hines, DHS.

"Department of Homeland Security," Mitchell said. "I imagine he's some analyst interested in smuggling or potential nuclear materials. Maybe he's been looking into this mine."

The encrypted upload had paused at the seventy-two percent mark, and the pop-up box did not allow for a continue option. It gave a *cancel* button and a *proceed to DHS* option.

Mitchell weighed it up. They were all on the same side, after all.

"Proceed to DHS. See what it gives us."

Polly's finger was poised over her mouse button. "Can I try one other thing first?"

"Sure, go for it."

On an adjacent computer, Polly checked the internal employee list, but Hines was not on there. She accessed a more secure database with access to all government employees. At least, those not undercover. He did not show up there either.

Mitchell said, "Try private contractors. Look at the vetting department."

Polly did as requested and got a hit. She clicked on the profile, much of which was redacted. There were fifty-five pages of security checks, backgrounds on his family, and references from his university.

"Graduated from MIT, aged twenty," Mitchell said curiously as they reached his education records. "But his immediate employment after that is need-to-know. I'll have to put in a request to learn more."

"Twenty? That's young."

"Some sort of kid genius? Coding maybe."

"But why would he be interested in a convoy taking metal into Chad?"

"Let me make a quick request."

As soon as Mitchell took out his phone, an incoming call started ringing. He stared at it as if he might have accidentally caused it. The caller ID said only, *Government - Withheld*.

Meaning it was from within his own agency. But not an official CIA line, or caller ID would have given him more of a clue.

Mitchell answered.

After listening for less than twenty seconds, his blood was running cold. He could say nothing more out loud in front of Polly.

He hung up.

"What is it?" Polly asked, her voice running through with concern.

He must have looked as shocked as he felt. "I don't care how late it is. I need a meeting with Karem Hines ASAP."

SEVEN

It was three a.m. already, and Trapp paced the dimly lit villa's expansive living room, a ceiling fan wafting the cool night air around him. He'd been debriefed two hours earlier, which left him and Grubbs stuck in a safe house that had been sourced and equipped by the Agency's local stringers. But now they'd been summoned from their beds for another urgent briefing with Mitchell via the secure uplink. Not so much a *de*briefing as a *re*-briefing, and it was going mostly as he'd feared.

"Jason, your report from the mine has thrown this whole operation into chaos," Mitchell's voice crackled over the secure link, strained with frustration. "What started as a trafficking case now involves Ashenhurst, professional mercenaries, and a convoy shipping what our initial analysis says is worthless rock. None of this adds up."

"It adds up to a threat, Mike," Trapp countered, pacing the villa's marble floor. "I don't know what's in those trucks, but Ashenhurst Group didn't hire that level of muscle to protect dirt. They're dirty, Mike. We both know it. There isn't a rogue state they don't do business with. We need to go after that convoy now, before it disappears."

"Negative," Mitchell snapped. "You don't have authorization, and I can't get it without more than a gut feeling. The Nigerians sanctioned an intel-op on a trafficking route. I can't greenlight a hit on a convoy in a neighboring country. For now, your mission is to get closer to Obasee. He's your link. He knows what this is really about. Use your cover, lean on him, and find out what that cargo is and who the real buyer is."

Trapp sighed, loud enough to be heard by anyone in conference at Mitchell's end. Intentionally so.

Grubbs, who had remained seated on the plush chaise long, closed her eyes briefly before her pragmatism took over. "Sir, we believe our cover is intact. The money helped—"

"No," Trapp said. "Kissing that fat, sweaty ass won't do shit. He won't say more than he has already. If we go back, I want buttonhole cameras, and then I need a team of operators following my directions—"

Mitchell cut him off. "You know the situation in that region, Jason."

He did. All too well. Jelany Ikem had briefed them that this region was considered Boko Haram territory, and the army's stand-off with the terrorist group was very much unofficial; the murderous, raping fucks used the land for illegal activities like training, accumulating weaponry, and the sort of brainwashing and extreme worship that would make most Muslims blanch. Having witnessed the horrors of the mine, Trapp had half-expected living standards in the small town where they'd been sequestered to resemble Taliban-ruled Afghanistan. But the people were largely getting on with their lives. The world still turned, families ran their households and businesses, and as long as no one poked their noses into Boko Haram business, no one got anything shot off.

Ikem had also emphasized that the terrorist group was more like an organized crime gang with a militia arm, so it was only isolated villages that they fully occupied and defended fiercely and where they imposed their warped Islamist rule. Small towns and villages were the hubs from which they sent men out to kidnap children and where the worst of their brutality was lived out. When the Nigerian Army moved against them, finally, those outposts would be their key targets.

And here Trapp was, in a villa more akin to a tropical vacation property. He knew it fit his cover identity. Didn't stop it tasting bitter.

"Jason, I understand," Mitchell said. "The president also understands. But we need to keep the Nigerians friendly and let them handle their own backyard. You're still guests there."

Their own backyard.

Trapp's boots on the marble tile made a noise that was weirdly fascinating, like a muted movie sound effect. He paused at the window, taking in the lush grounds yet seeing nothing—nothing but gaunt faces streaked with grime, eyes hollowed out by despair, bodies bent and broken but still working.

They'd obtained and relayed scant intel. And what were his orders?

Watch and wait.

Report back.

Let the horrors continue while politicians postured.

"Understood, sir," Trapp finally said. "We do nothing."

"Not nothing, Jason." Mitchell was trying to sound sympathetic, understanding. "But we'll know more later. I have to go now. You, Madison, and Agent Ikem will wine and dine Obasee. Sweep him off his feet. Bribe him if you have to. Or simply look for leverage and exploit it. I'll be in touch as soon as you and the Army can act against them. *If* we're allowed to."

"He wants us to what? 'Use the cover'?" Trapp growled after the link went dead. "That convoy is getting farther away by the second. By the time we 'gently probe' Obasee for answers, that cargo will be in the hands of whoever is paying for those mercs. We don't have time for diplomacy."

"Those are the orders, Jason," Grubbs said. "We don't have the full picture."

"No. But I think we'll get what Mitchell needs faster with a gun to Obasee's head than sneaking around or seducing him. I mean, look at me, Madison."

She was already looking at him but said nothing.

"I mean, really *look* at me. Sure, I can do undercover, but what's my specialty?"

"Extraction," Grubbs said. "High-value targets, enemies and friends alike."

"Exactly."

Grubbs frowned, obviously missing his point.

"Mitchell sent *me*. He could have activated any number of experts in infiltration, undercover ops. But he sent *me*. He *expects* me to improvise. Even if it..." Trapp intentionally let the sentence hang.

Grubbs obliged by finishing it for him. "Even if it goes against the agreement we have with Nigeria."

It was her turn to pace the lounge. Her pumps clicked softly on the marble-style floor, a sharp contrast to the heavy clomp of Trapp's boots earlier.

Trapp wondered if he'd have taken this planned course of action when he first started working in special operations. Ever since he'd foiled a certain planned coup on the United States, Trapp had found his infrequent decisions to probe loopholes in orders far easier. Although he didn't hold much truck in the modern fetish of diagnosing a mental illness for every oddity in someone's personality, perhaps that experience had flipped a switch in him.

"I'm going to take Obasee," Trapp said, treading the line between being deadly serious and just blowing off steam. Maybe he was working himself up into a decision he'd already made. "Quiet and fast. Pretty sure there was a residential block. I can get to him—"

"No, don't be so—"

"—Either he talks, or we'll ship him out somewhere that less scrupulous folk can take their time with him. Then when we're done messing around with the trucks, we let Mike and the NIA take the operation apart."

"They won't," Ikem said.

Trapp snapped his attention to the door, unsure how long the man had been standing there or how he'd opened it without them hearing.

It was late. They were sluggish.

Still, Ikem was dressed for his part, a man made moderately wealthy by facilitating deals for people like Robert Harding. His warm smile was tempered by the seriousness in his eyes. He stepped into the room, closing the door behind him.

"A little off-the-books excursion?" Ikem said. "You might benefit from my services."

Trapp made a face. "Sharing a safe house with a spy has its downsides."

Ikem held up a hand. "Guilty."

Trapp wasn't sure how much he should share. Mitchell's interest in the trucks was more intense than it should have been; he could have been holding back. Ikem was plainly as conflicted as Trapp and Grubbs, but he had far more to lose than either of the Americans. This was his country. His *life*, if the terrorists they were deceiving uncovered his real identity.

Grubbs stepped in front of Trapp. "We appreciate the offer, Ikem. But are you sure you want to get involved? This could get messy."

Ikem's smile returned, and this time, it reached his eyes. "Obasee and men like him are a blight on my country. And I have watched you two. I know you want to act. My government will have higher priorities than this unless we force their hand. And for me, this is personal."

Trapp stood motionless, probing the questions and disparities that had weighed upon him since the first debriefing and only pressed down harder now.

"I'm no avenging angel," he said. "But this pussying around with undercover personas, playing dress-up and make-believe... it's fine to get a look around, but the more I think about it, the more I see it's a bullshit option. The least offensive way for people in Washington to claim they're doing something."

"What is your point?" Ikem asked.

"That we have an objective. Earlier this year, militarized Chinese dissidents came to the US through a ridiculously convoluted route to hide their approach and stop us backtracking to their real masters. If we want to find them, the best course of action is to turn Obasee. And it's the same solution if Mike wants to know about those trucks."

"Right." Grubbs perked up for the first time. No longer showing concern but curiosity. "So it's a case of malicious compliance?"

Trapp wasn't sure what that meant, but he trusted that Grubbs did. "Ikem, you said Boko Haram is like an organized crime group when it comes to funding?"

"Yes, yes," Ikem said. "They even have an accounting department."

Trapp assumed that was an exaggeration but took the

meaning. "So that means records. Which means, even if they're electronic, Obasee would have access."

"You're making excuses to go rogue," Grubbs said.

"It's not going rogue." Trapp smiled. "I'm improvising."

EIGHT

The scrubland was a sea of shadows. Oases of moonlight skimmed the dusty waves, but the pre-dawn gloom was dark enough to conceal their approach.

The SUV, the same one that had brought them to the mine, pulled over on a dirt road near a copse of corkwood trees surrounded by hardened mud, dark gray under the scudding clouds and intermittent light. The three operatives were silent, sitting there for a long moment.

Ikem cut the engine. "One mile to the mine perimeter. You have what you need?"

Although they'd had no means of importing specific weapons or gear, the safe house had come well-stocked with supplies an operative might need in the field, including for scenarios that called for a degree of oomph.

Trapp had checked his pack twice already, no need to second-guess himself now. "I'll radio when I'm in position."

He tested the throat mic, tapping the node against his skin twice so Ikem heard the non-verbal signal. Ikem said, "Received," and Trapp heard it through the in-ear receiver.

All set.

"Are you sure you need to do this?" Ikem asked. "We can try bribery first."

"Preparation is everything." Trapp winked at Grubbs. "Even when improvising."

"Be careful," Grubbs replied, the platitude a mild irritant but understandable.

Trapp climbed out and broke into a jog across the uneven terrain. Not an arduous task, but he stuck to the darkness, his midnight-black-and-blue getup and ski mask the best camouflage for this territory.

The perimeter fence soon loomed, and Trapp crouched, stilling himself at a rise in the hard land, scanning for patrols. The compound was heavily guarded, yes, but no matter how many army uniforms they dished out, the guards were amateurs. There were no permanent searchlights and only intermittent floodlights pointing outward. The beams didn't crisscross, leaving several feet where the dark dominated a column of ground.

There—two skinny guards in pseudomilitary gear, moving in a saunter. Bored. Having patrolled a hundred times or more without incident, why would they fear anything? If the government moved against them, the first sortie would be drone strikes, followed by a brute-force incursion by a sizeable unit. Not many people were crazy enough to break *into* a slave camp.

Trapp waited for the pair to drift into a strong beam of dazzling white light, then slipped out an unpolished K-Bar knife and arrowed silently into a dark funnel, knowing their natural night-vision would be compromised.

He intercepted the first guard with a swift strike to the neck, the razor-sharp blade slashing through cartilage and tendons and veins, leaving the man shocked, unable to move as blood gushed from the wound. Trapp evaded the spurt as the second tried to reach for his radio and raise his gun at the same time, meaning he could complete neither task, which allowed Trapp to close in and ram the knife into the man's chest.

The first guard was still on his feet, wide-eyed, his hand on the wound, but a shove from Trapp left him folded on the ground next to his comrade.

Trapp dragged the corpses to the blindside of a boulder outside the floodlights' range and kicked dust and sand over them. It wouldn't hold up to close inspection, but they'd be invisible to the guard towers.

He returned along the same path and unclipped the wire cutters from his belt. The chain-link fence—not industrial grade by any means—offered little resistance as he carved out an opening. He listened for any sign of alarm, but the night remained still except for far-off voices chatting.

Once inside, there was a second layer of fencing, but this was only maintained intermittently, either for budgetary reasons or lax planning. Still, any breakout by the captives that did not result in the fences coming down would channel them into a kill zone.

Planting the compact explosive blocks—their backup plan if something were to go wrong with Obasee's extraction—was intended to simulate a drone strike and raid by the army. It would, in theory, distract any serious resistance long enough to get Obasee somewhere private. And it was a slow, deliberate process. Evading the slack patrols and the resting guards, first concentrating on the entrance, then once he'd accessed the main body of the compound, Trapp prowled slower, choosing his moments. Setting the scene, prepping the ground.

He felt vaguely ridiculous pressed against an outbuilding, like he was playing ninja. But he was not some invisible superhero, possessed no supernatural ability to melt into shadows at will. This was not a training mission aimed at conditioning new recruits. If they caught him, he'd be tortured, then either killed or set to work in the mine himself.

Most lights here illuminated the access road and the barracks where he'd seen the unshackled workers coming and going. Then, over the mounds of discarded rocks and industrial run-off, a football-field-bright bowl of light rose into the sky, likely the mine itself, along with where they stored their slaves.

Those concentrated swaths of light allowed him to place the final charges.

A new sound froze him in place. Voices. An approaching patrol.

Trapp's heartrate spiked, but he didn't panic or freeze. He shrank smoothly between the two industrial machines he was planning to destroy and scanned his surroundings. Unlike the outer perimeter, this area was cluttered with equipment, vehicles, and low-level structures.

Footsteps.

Voices—a language in which he could say "hello," "thank you," and "two beers please."

Trapp could take them out as he had the perimeter patrol, but there were more people here. One shout, one gunshot squeezed off, and his entire plan would unravel.

Unwilling to risk a knife if they swarmed him, Trapp's fingers closed around the gun in his shoulder holster, already equipped with a suppressor. While it would only quieten the gunshot to a dull bark—not the whispered *spit* of movie-lore—if he fired beside one of the diesel generators, he'd be fine. Otherwise, all the suppressor would do was conceal his location for a short while.

The foot patrol neared.

Every instinct screamed at him to act.

But he held still.

The pair's voices rose, their footfalls loud as they passed by.

Trapp sucked in a deeper breath and released it as slowly as his lungs allowed, listening for a full minute before peeking out.

The eastern sky had begun to lighten. He hadn't planted all the surprises he'd hoped for, but it was time to go.

His limbs protested as he made his way back to the inner fence, sticking to shadows where he could, darting across the blades of light and exiting into the kill-zone, then slipping out through the hole he'd made. He paused to ensure that no signs of his intrusion remained obvious.

Once clear of the perimeter, Trapp broke into a steady jog back across the scrubland, tapping his throat mic.

"Last chance to back out. I'll be with you in ten."

NINE

At the mine complex's entrance, Trapp stepped out of the vehicle, the dry heat already building and clutching around him. He kept his chin high, chest out, his tie-less suit ensemble a better disguise than any mask, exuding an air of impatient authority.

"I'm Robert Harding," he announced. "I was here yesterday. I'd like to see Obasee. Immediately."

The guard eyed the well-dressed trio with their SUV, one hand resting on his holstered weapon while his partner handled an AK-47 as if he was either itching to fire it or was about to wield it like a club. Nerves, confusion, inexperience. All triggered by their unannounced arrival.

The first guard's eyes narrowed. More experienced than the other. A supervisor of some sort. "No appointment, sir."

"I know. Call him. Now."

The supervisor held on Trapp a long moment, and something unspoken passed between them. Something that told Trapp the man was not some idle jihadi equivalent of a rent-a-cop but assigned this duty for a reason. There was intelligence there, weighing the risk of treating "Mr. Harding" like an interloper with following orders to the letter. Perhaps this was someone with genuine military training, not a press-ganged hotheaded follower.

The intelligent guard dialed on an ancient brick of a phone and spoke to whoever answered. He hung up after a swift exchange and spoke politely but firmly. "Mr. Obasee says you aren't expected."

Trapp had rehearsed his pissed-off-millionaire routine with Grubbs as he changed out of his operational gear. "Listen to me very carefully. My people have done their due diligence, which means *I* have done my due diligence. And there are some issues that we missed earlier. Either Obasee sees me now or our deal is off."

The supervisor's head tilted, his sharp eyes watching Trapp. Again, he retrieved the phone and called through. Rapid-fire Igbo followed, a pause, then more talking. He listened, then hung up. "You are cleared. One moment, please."

They waited on a new pair of guards to arrive and take over gate duty, then the supervisor escorted the three of them in his battered Jeep through the compound, guiding them to park under the same awning as yesterday. All the way, Trapp noted the security positions, the blind spots, the open areas to avoid being cut down if they had to pull back.

Another fifty yards down the dusty, hard-packed road, men and women were starting the day, most of them shackled at their wrists and around their waists, the chains loose enough to work but plenty to hinder them should they attempt to flee. There was a small fleet of trucks, too, some open-topped, others closed. Nothing bigger than 7.5 tons, like the compact dump trucks or transports frequently hired for home moves in the States, so Trapp speculated the day's cargo would be bound for clients within Nigeria.

The supervisor marched the three of them past a series of shipping containers being used as equipment lockers, down the makeshift footpath constructed from railway sleepers to a weathered prefab building. Like a Portacabin, but unbranded. The guard knocked, a voice called back, and their escort ushered them inside.

Obasee was standing behind a cluttered desk where the remnants of what looked like eggs congealed on a plate. His open shirt was rumpled, his face unshaven, and a .38 Smith & Wesson was tucked haphazardly into his waistband.

"Mr. Harding," Obasee said in a huskier voice than previously. "Why the surprise intrusion?"

"Urgent business." Trapp's gaze hardened. "*Private* urgent business."

Obasee hesitated, then waved the guards away. "Leave us."

Trapp stared at Grubbs and Ikem. "You, too. This is between me and our friend here."

Putting Obasee on an even footing by dismissing his entourage was another prearranged tactic. Still, as the door closed after Grubbs and Ikem, Trapp felt a shiver of unease.

"Now," Trapp said, "why am I hearing whispers about Chinese investors piggybacking my deal?"

Obasee glanced over one shoulder, as if considering that the corner of the room might be listening. "How did you—"

"I have sources. What I don't have is patience. Who is your partner in Chad?"

"Chad?" This time, Obasee's eyes twitched wider before hardening, then his hand wafted in Trapp's direction, as if swatting away his concern. "That information is confidential. But if you have sources, why can they not tell you?"

Trapp stiffened his posture and gave a sharp snort. "Nothing about this should be confidential to me. I'm taking a big risk coming here. An even bigger risk investing my money."

Trapp's phone vibrated. He maintained petulant eye contact with Obasee as he fished it out of his pocket. A quick glance confirmed the coded message from Grubbs.

What it said:

I'm hungry. And I don't want to eat in this shit hole.

What it meant:

We're in position.

"Okay," Trapp said. "Seems like we get to play together awhile."

Trapp leaned forward, all smiles, and his hand shot out, fingers wrapping around the grip of the poorly concealed .38.

Obasee barely managed, "What are you—" as Trapp wrenched the weapon free, pivoted, then brought the gun crashing down on Obasee's nose, drawing a mewling gasp as he folded onto his desk.

Trapp stood over him. "You really should've talked."

They had a few minutes before someone came to check on them.

While Obasee squirmed, hands hovering over his bloodied nose, too painful to touch, Trapp sent a quick coded message to Grubbs:

We have donuts in the car.

What it meant:

Target secured.

He then turned his attention to Obasee's computer. He yanked one hand away from the man's face, wiped some blood on the overseer's trousers, and ignored his whimper of pain as Trapp forced a finger to touch the unlock button. He threw the hand back at Obasee's face, connecting with his injured nose and making him yelp.

He pointed the gun at Obasee and said, "Make one sound, and the next sound *I* make will be much louder. Clear?"

Obasee nodded, grunting in the affirmative while pressing on his face to either side of his streaming nose.

It gave Trapp no pleasure to hurt him this way, but neither did it bother him much. It was a means to an end, nothing more.

He inserted a thumb drive into the laptop. Grubbs had said the software built into the drive would initiate a data transfer but not to worry when nothing seemed to be happening. No countdown, no progress bar. The only subtle sign it was doing anything would be a pinprick of light on the underside changing from a dim red to a dim green. It would take about three minutes if the hard drive was in decent working order.

Trapp checked that Obasee was still in place, feeling sorry for himself, then scanned the office for physical evidence. A safe caught his eye.

"Combination."

Obasee made a different grunting noise and pointed at a keyboard wired to the laptop. Trapp turned it over and found a note with the word "PASSWORD12345" scrawled on it.

"No," Trapp said. "For the safe, asshole—"

Obasee lunged for the gun in Trapp's hand. Must have thought directing his attention elsewhere was a good idea. It might have been, had Trapp really been Robert Harding.

But Trapp simply stepped to one side and slapped Obasee

hard across the jaw, sending him stumbling backward, eyes widened in shock. Almost insulted.

Trapp advanced on his opponent.

"Suckered me with the pistol-whip," Obasee answered and threw a haymaker that probably would have hurt the average underling. Or slave.

Trapp easily sidestepped again, grabbed the man's arm, and slammed him face-first into the wall. The satisfying crunch of cartilage told Trapp he'd re-broken Obasee's nose, drawing a mewling noise which the wall smothered before it could become a scream for help.

He allowed Obasee to turn and face him, the blood streaming from his nostrils seemingly brighter than before, then thumped him in the gut, further cutting off his breath and causing him to slither to the floor, propped against the wall, gasping. Obasee's eyes darted, searching for an escape. But Trapp had positioned himself between his enemy and the door.

Memories of Trapp's abusive father came back to him. The scar on his neck—from a punishment involving barbed wire—felt warm. As a child, growing up and growing strong, he'd stopped that man from hurting anyone else, and now a part of him wanted to keep pummeling Obasee, to make him suffer on behalf of all those he had abused.

"Get up," Trapp said. "Slowly. Or I put you right back down."

Obasee complied, wincing as he rose to his feet. Blood still dripped, a spread of scarlet over his chest and open shirt.

Trapp checked the thumb drive. Still the dim red.

"Your computer," Trapp said. "Pull up your records. Now. I want to see for myself."

"Why?" Obasee asked, his broken nose deepening his voice, nasalizing certain letters. "What are you looking for?"

"Chinese stuff," Trapp said. "Anything Chinese."

"You're stealing it already. Why—"

"Because I'm bored of waiting. Show me what I'm going to find anyway."

"You cannot think you'll escape, can you?"

"If I can't, then it won't matter if you show me who is sending you money."

Obasee breathed hard through his mouth, his nose swollen and his eyes puffing up already. He pulled up spreadsheets and banking records while Trapp kept an eye on the door. He doubted anyone had heard their scuffle but would not be doing his job if he relaxed.

"There," Obasee said after a few seconds. "These are the China transactions."

Trapp ran his eyes over the screen without getting too close to Obasee. Large sums of money transferred from an account labelled only as "ZM."

"Who's ZM?" Trapp demanded.

"Zhao Ming," Obasee said resignedly. "A banking contact. Handles some sensitive transactions for us."

"What kind of sensitive transactions?"

"Just... moving money around. Nothing illegal."

Trapp's hand clamped down on the back of Obasee's neck, squeezing. "What does Zhao Ming do, exactly?"

"Resources. Ensures the money goes to the right place."

"What kind of *resources*? The sort I saw chained up yesterday?"

"Sometimes... yes. Workers who need jobs. Many are Chinese, turned away at the Turkish border on their way to Europe. They run out of money, get desperate enough. Zhao Ming... facilitates their transfer here."

Trapp fought to control the anger, but now that he'd started, he needed more information. "How many people are we talking about? And why?"

"I don't know exact numbers," Obasee said. "Maybe... a hundred? But they change their plans. They're given lives here first. When they earn enough, we can send them anywhere—north to Europe, west to South America."

Trapp studied Obasee's face, but he just looked defeated and scared. Probably telling the truth—he was too much of a coward to risk lying.

"In other words," he said, "you have the Chinese intercept their dissidents and use the covert route already in place to bring them here, with promises of freedom. Instead, you get your slaves, and the Chinese government punishes citizens who've run away for a better life."

Obasee held Trapp's gaze. No need to confirm. It was right there in his bloody, trembling face.

Trapp checked the thumb drive. The tiny red pinprick had turned green, meaning they now had everything from the computer.

"All right," Trapp said, disconnecting the drive. "I'll be leaving now."

Obasee blinked in confusion. "What? You think I'll just let you go?"

Trapp smiled. "Did I say, '*I'll* be leaving?' I mean *we* are leaving."

"You are insane, my friend. You will never make it."

Trapp manhandled him toward the door. "We'll see about that."

TEN

Madison Grubbs waited alongside Ikem, her heart racing in her ears but her fingers steady. They'd chosen to remain partially hidden from the main drag of the operation, ensuring they wouldn't appear suspicious next to the rows of equipment lockers—weather-beaten metal shipping containers—positioned between Obasee's office and the carport.

This was the most nerve-wracking part of the mission thus far.

While she was trained to operate in the field, "the field" had predominantly involved administrative offices until she met Jason Trapp, leaving her with scant combat experience. When firearms were involved, it took intense effort to regulate her breathing and prevent her legs from freezing up or bolting in the opposite direction. Working alongside Trapp had helped her manage, although she would never confess that to him for fear of inflating his ego.

Their first mission together had started with a jailbreak in the Middle East, escalated to a targeted attack on the US, nearly concluded violently with her own abduction, and culminated in their successful thwarting of an assassination attempt on President Charles Nash. More recently, Trapp had exploited their friendship on a mission of his own. Easy to forgive when she remembered that doing so had averted a horrific act of violence which could have destabilized America's intelligence networks. All of them.

But resentment returned when she thought about how easily he had betrayed her trust for the sake of the mission, willing to sacrifice her for the greater good. For Trapp, duty would always come first.

Two conflicting perspectives *can* coexist.

This nugget of wisdom appeared lost on the current world stage, rife as it was with debates, partisanship, and entrenched political divides. Yet it was a concept she clung to now, as firmly as the cold metal of the gun pressed against her palm.

She should follow orders.

She should do what was right.

The door to the Portacabin offices opened, and Trapp emerged, one hand behind Obasee in case he needed a human shield. Obasee was clearly hurt, so Plan A was toast; no way to take him out of the mine posing as a willing passenger.

Madison's job now was to make sure the way remained clear. She and Ikem staggered themselves along the route to the SUV, each waiting for the other to get in position before moving to the next stage. The walkway was a short length, but there were plenty of opportunities to expose themselves to passing security if they got unlucky.

Ikem was first to the carport, and he got in behind the wheel before Madison sauntered into the open and scanned the wide access road. The only personnel were a helpful distance away. As long as Obasee didn't make a run for it or cause a commotion, it would simply look like they were all having a chat.

Trapp brought Obasee close and made his own check up and down the lane.

Madison asked, "Are we going awake or asleep?"

"His choice," Trapp said, jerking his body and therefore the gun pressing into Obasee's ribs.

Obasee, blood from his nose staining his lips and clenched teeth, turned his head side to side as if expecting the cavalry.

"It's not an exact science," Madison told him. "Hitting you on the head might do more damage than we intend, but a sleeper hold might not knock you out for long enough."

"What will you do?" Obasee asked. "Stuff me in the trunk?"

Trapp hustled him to the back door of the SUV. "You're going to lie under a blanket on the floor. That way I can shoot you through the head if you try anything dumb."

"Clear," Madison said, having given a final check on their surroundings.

As Obasee got in, Trapp used the open door to shield the gun from anyone who happened by. He laid Obasee down and covered him with the promised blanket.

It was the sensible way to go. Obasee's cowardice was evident in his manner, even though he tried to put a brave face on it. Madison was sure he would be compliant.

She got in the front, and Ikem started the engine. They pulled out into the growing early morning activity with workers funneling from their barracks on routes out to their assignments. Guards accompanied them in groups, herding them toward the main access road that Madison knew led to the underground mining operation.

Then someone they recognized stepped away from the group of workers who were lining up—the supervisor from the gate, the one who had been more cautious than they'd expected, who was clearly in charge of some of the fake soldiers. And he wasn't out for a stroll.

He waved the SUV down, patting the air in the universal language of police or security services to stop the vehicle.

IT WAS a choice Trapp had faced on many occasions.

"Talk our way out?" Ikem asked. "Or shall I put my foot down?"

Another life-or-death scenario, another debate over which course of action would be least likely to get him killed.

Trapp said, "I'll talk to him, but keep the engine running."

He wound the window down as Ikem pulled to a halt, and the supervisor stood at an angle that would make it difficult for Trapp to shoot him through the door. He would have to raise the gun and point it out; by then the intelligent guard would have shot him dead.

"You are leaving already?" the supervisor said. "I received no instructions about this."

"Do you *need* instructions?" Trapp said. "Want to search us on the way out? You afraid we'll have stolen some of your rocks?"

"I am always advised about guests' movements within the complex, and I heard nothing about your meeting ending."

"I guess someone forgot." Trapp pressed his foot against Obasee's head, which was pressed against the floor. "If you need to search the car, I'll pop the trunk."

The supervisor looked back to the work detail and the harried guards shouting and pushing their prisoners around. They were waving their arms, clearly in some disarray and in need of leadership. He shook his head in annoyance and waved to two men. One of them was carrying a phone. The other, with buck teeth and ratty eyes, received a barked order and scurried away. Trapp did not risk watching where he went, knowing that would reveal his apprehension and draw suspicion.

The supervisor paused, his eyes set hard on Trapp, who had a gun in one hand and a detonator for the explosives in his pocket. He needed to avoid anything that could descend into mass violence. There were too many guards ready to pepper the car with bullets. Although he could use Obasee as a hostage, he didn't know how valuable the man really was. It was possible that whoever the supervisor worked for would see Obasee as easy to replace.

As the supervisor raised the phone to his ear, Grubbs' window rolled down. She was about to say something when the guard who'd scurried away had circled back around the SUV and was now pointing his AK47 into the vehicle.

The supervisor lowered the phone and leveled a stern gaze at Trapp. "There is no answer. He always answers. Get out of the car. Now."

Trapp circled back to the decision he'd made earlier and regulated his breathing. Calming himself. He was aware of the spike of adrenaline ramping up, his body acknowledging the signals from his brain, the signs as ingrained in him as fight-or-flight is in all humans. It always preceded violence but never descended into fear. He just needed to figure out how to take the gun off the nervous guard once he got within reach.

"Not him," the supervisor said sternly and indicated the passenger door. "Her."

EVEN THOUGH MADISON knew Trapp would be planning an exit strategy should they be unable to talk their way out of this, it didn't make it any easier to lift her hand out and open the door using the external handle. She couldn't help imagining a bullet penetrating her chest as a trigger-happy wannabe-soldier decided she was to be executed.

Trapp, seeming to remember his role, said, "You are risking a lot on this."

The supervisor offered a dead smile in return. "Just until we sort this out. I hope you understand, sir."

Madison opened the door and stepped outside, and the stinking jihadi type who had circled around the back let his AK47 dangle while he wrapped an arm around her neck, keeping her between himself and the car. She caught Ikem's anxious strengthening of his grip on the steering wheel. He was ready to move as soon as Trapp gave the order.

They had gathered a small audience. The workers were rubbernecking, watching with interest. One of the more attentive men had hair that looked like it had been dyed ginger but had since grown out, giving way to black roots. A second, much scrawnier man urged the ginger one to keep going. Both were in chains. The accompanying guards urged the line onward, but it was a half-hearted effort at best. They too were intrigued by their boss' actions.

"I will try again," the supervisor said, dialing a preset number.

The man holding Grubbs wasn't quite strangling her, but his grime transferred itself to the skin on her neck, and his sweat was pungent like overripe fruit. When his mouth came closer to her ear, his breath carried a sour stench.

The supervisor lowered the phone. "Still no answer. I will send someone to check what has happened."

"Let us on our way," Trapp said, his voice carrying the ring of authority, "or you can answer to your overseer when we pull the plug on this deal."

"Deals are not my job," the supervisor stated flatly. "Suspicious Westerners are my job."

"You won't have a job if—"

Trapp was cut off by a thud.

The supervisor's attention snapped to the lower part of the SUV where Obasee had struck.

The guns came up.

The supervisor ordered Ikem and Trapp out of the vehicle, but Trapp had ducked down, and now the supervisor stepped back while taking a crescent-shaped route for a better angle. His gun stayed aimed at the vehicle while other guards followed his orders to move in, and the man holding Grubbs pulled them away.

She was positive that if Trapp had not yanked Obasee upward and thrust his head and shoulders into the open window, they would have simply opened fire and perforated the car along with Trapp and Ikem. Trapp opened the door and bundled Obasee out, but he used his shield sensibly, not straying from the vehicle.

It was a classic standoff. Nobody moved. Nobody spoke.

Nobody, until Obasee gave a groaning plea. "What are you waiting for? Finish them."

The supervisor faltered, his earlier confidence sapped from him.

The arm snaking around Madison tightened.

That's when she spotted the shackled half-ginger prisoner nearby, inching forward just at the edge of her vision. She held her breath and tightened her grip on the arm around her neck.

Trapp plainly noticed the same movement. Lowering his chin, he constricted Obasee's neck to silence any warning.

In a desperate move, the prisoner lunged for the supervisor's gun. His frail body lacked the strength for an effective attack, but the sudden motion caused the guard to lose his balance and jerk the weapon away from Madison's head.

Madison bit down hard on the arm encircling her, tasting rancid sweat and blood before wrenching it away to create just enough space to drop to the floor.

Ikem seized the opportunity, shooting the guard with a gun he'd been concealing inside the SUV, giving Trapp the all-clear. Trapp fired three rounds into the supervisor's torso and two into the man beside him and, for one brief heartbeat as the pair crumpled to the ground, silence enveloped them.

Then chaos erupted.

Yelling and pounding boots filled the air. They would be surrounded in seconds.

"Quickly," Ikem urged, out of the SUV, helping Madison and the ginger prisoner who had assisted them to their feet.

"You are here to free us?" the prisoner asked hopefully.

Ikem didn't reply, the question shocking him as much as the incoming gunfire.

"Damn it." Trapp shoved Obasee forward so Ikem could take control of him while he removed the detonator from his pocket. He gave Ikem and Madison a final warning glance, then pressed the button.

ELEVEN

The chain reaction was as swift as it was thunderous, the outer compound erupting in a series of explosions that Trapp felt in his chest. Orange flames and black smoke boiled into the sky as the generators blew, the electricity sputtering before dying completely.

The prisoners fled back toward their barracks, stumbling and staggering, helping one another stay on their feet, while a squad of what looked like eight furious soldiers streamed from their posts near the internal fencing. Gunfire ripped all around, blowing through the SUV that Trapp, Grubbs, and Ikem were using for cover.

A nearby set of floodlights erupted in a shower of sparks, the generators' circuits blasting a lethal surge through the network. The distraction was enough as Trapp shot the two closest incoming guards and Ikem unleashed one of the AK-47s he'd acquired. It was enough—three of the gaggle fell before the others scattered to take a safer position.

Obasee's earlier bravado was evaporating, deflating his body before their eyes. "Please, I have money. I can pay you—"

"Shut up." Ikem cast a quick assessment over the SUV, which had sputtered and died under the barrage. "I will get another vehicle. One with room for us all."

"Us all?" Trapp said.

Grubbs gestured to the two workers—slaves—who had helped save her. "We can't leave them."

"Get Obasee out," Ikem said, jogging away. "I will join you."

"Grubbs—"

But Trapp couldn't call her back. She was already ushering the two bound men after Ikem, to the left, where they'd seen the fleet of battered trucks. He didn't want to leave the prisoners either, but they shouldn't risk the mission for two lives.

Except hadn't Trapp done the same in the past? Refused to compromise with human lives simply to comply with orders?

He hustled Obasee to the right, where the supervisor's Jeep was parked, just beyond the kill-zone. But two armed men barred the way. He'd caught them by surprise as much as they had him, and he was already primed—he shot them both in the head in quick succession.

The security response was mounting, though. The guard towers had emptied. Shouts rolled around, crisscrossing over each other, growing louder by the second as more level-headed personnel took charge.

Trapp used Obasee's bulk as a shield, facing him out toward the wide thoroughfare where dust swirled from the concussion blasts of the explosions as if whipped up by a desert wind.

Trapp said, "Let's see how much your friends out there value your life."

Gunfire punctuated the air. Not the racket of a full-on battle but small-arms fire at first. Then, from almost exactly where he'd expected it, came the distinctive sharp, metallic crack and two-part ka-*chunk* of AK47s—you'd never mistake it for anything else once you'd heard it.

Trapp guided Obasee in that direction around a corner formed by chunks of rock and through the swirling smoke from a wrecked diesel generator. As he moved, he caught glimpses of Ikem and Grubbs loading people onto the mine's own flatbed Jeeps and into SUVs.

What the hell are they thinking?

As much as he wanted to rip this place apart, he hadn't expected to be in the middle of it when it happened.

Ikem and Grubbs both started shooting at an enemy down one of the lanes formed of rubble and waste as workers ran for the vehicles. Two fell, cut down by the barrage from the group that Grubbs and Ikem were shooting at.

A commotion up ahead drew Trapp back to his own situation.

A team of six personnel in two open-backed wagons sped toward him from the direction in which he'd hoped to escape.

He was boxed in.

There was only one truck in the vicinity, which someone would need to drive—harder than the smaller vehicles. They were maybe a hundred feet from the Jeep, but the ground was too exposed for him to risk traversing, even with a valuable chip like Obasee.

Grubbs' voice came over the comm. "We're almost loaded. You good?"

Trapp ducked lower as a spray of bullets from a trio of reinforcements peppered the barrier. "Peachy. Is it too stupid a question to ask what the hell you're doing making so many new friends at once?"

"Very funny," Grubbs replied. "We saw an opportunity and took it. We've got drivers ready in the smaller vehicles, but we need to move. Now."

Trapp risked a glance over his cover. More guards were joining the trio, following orders from someone who plainly had experience and training. A dozen, plus a few stragglers bringing up the rear.

"Incoming," Trapp said. "Reinforcements on the way."

A barrage of gunfire assailed the concrete—a futile gesture, but one that rained chips and dust in every direction.

Obasee yelled something Trapp didn't catch, but it was probably along the lines of, "Stop shooting!"

Too bad no one could hear a thing.

Trapp heaved Obasee up and showed his face to the attackers, the overseer screaming in terror before the unit's gunfire cut out.

He wasn't hit.

Then the truck, a 7.5-tonner, roared to life, and the deafening chatter of AK-47 reports battered his ears.

Trapp watched as Ikem revved the vehicle and set off. Grubbs was riding shotgun, laying down fire from the window, but as the windshield spiderwebbed, she had to scrabble back.

He dragged Obasee to his feet and all but carried him out into the road, firing at the group from behind their boss's mass. Three gunmen fell; the rest ran for cover.

And there was plenty of cover. Rubble, machinery, an outbuilding. They were better drilled than Trapp had predicted, but they remained dangerous only in their numbers. With Obasee in play, Trapp was reasonably optimistic about his own life.

As he bundled Obasee to where Ikem could intercept them, Trapp noticed four of the freed slaves—one of whom had helped Grubbs back at the supply containers—had exited their transport and taken up arms from the handful of men that Ikem and Grubbs had felled. Whether they would be any use in a fight, Trapp couldn't tell, but even from almost a hundred feet away, he could see their determination and long-suppressed rage boiling over.

As the smaller vehicles drove by Trapp's position, the prisoners wielding guns fired ahead. One of them clearly had no clue what he was doing, and Trapp hoped he wouldn't try to take out Obasee. But the other three had some experience, enough to drive the last stand of security farther back.

The truck kept a slow pace until it reached Trapp, who climbed in the passenger side, dragging Obasee behind him. He still wanted the cover.

"Cutting it close?" Grubbs said.

Trapp pressed Obasee up against the windshield. "Just fucking gun it!"

Ikem yelled out the window and waited a couple of seconds before accelerating. The security personnel who had ventured into the road for a better angle leapt away, and gunfire erupted behind them. The truck, the Jeeps, the SUVs—none of them were bullet-resistant, and Trapp was certain they would not escape without casualties. He calculated coldly, logically, that a swift death for a handful was better than the long, drawn-out fate under which they'd have perished if they'd remained prisoners.

As they peeled away, Trapp felt a flicker of hope, of pride.

But as the main section of the compound receded behind them and the mini convoy barreled through the exit in a squeal of torn metal, Ikem said, "Shit. Brace yourselves."

"Brace for what?" Grubbs asked.

Trapp angled to view the side mirror and saw what Ikem had. RPG.

The supervising guard, the one who had organized the final defense, was aiming a shoulder-mounted tube at them. Then there was a flash of light followed by a white contrail as the rocket shot toward the fleeing truck.

A deafening boom rocked the world, shaking Trapp's skull and thumping his chest like a drum. He instinctively braced himself in his seat as the truck swerved violently. Up on two wheels, the sharp jerk flung Obasee against the door and Grubbs into the footwell. Ikem fought the wheel, tires screeching on loose gravel. For a slow-motion moment, Trapp expected to tip over. But Ikem wrenched the wheel into the momentum as a second RPG missed and hit the guard tower. The explosive force spun them ninety degrees, stalling the truck and making them a bigger target should the supervisor reload.

Ikem turned the engine over, but it chugged and sputtered.

Grubbs pulled herself up, pressing one hand to a cut on her forehead as she searched for a seatbelt with the other.

Obasee was bloodied afresh, his split brow joining his nose in streaming blood down his face onto his neck and chest.

Trapp reoriented himself, assessed he'd sustained no injuries, and took in the current situation.

The supervisor was, indeed, reloading. Behind him, his gunmen had started to regroup, and between them and the truck, the other escaping vehicles had made a break for it, streaming into the scrubland and up onto the road ahead.

Good.

Right move.

That left them with a truck full of people as a sitting duck.

Trapp opened the door and tossed Obasee out, dropped to the ground beside him, and aimed the handgun toward the guy lifting the RPG launcher.

"I've got your boy here!" Trapp shouted.

Obasee called the same words he'd used before in Igbo.

The supervisor hesitated only a second, then called back in English, "Your sacrifice will be celebrated!"

As the fanatic hefted the launcher to his shoulder, Trapp

fired three times, and hit the target at least once. The rocket-propelled grenade *whooshed* out of its launcher and spiraled up into the air, coming back to earth somewhere inside the compound with a *boom*.

But in that split second of chaos, Obasee pulled free. He gave Trapp a hard shove and ran back toward his men.

"Kill them!" Obasee yelled. "Kill them all!"

The truck fired to life, and Ikem joined Trapp, aiming after Obasee with an AK he must have snatched earlier. "Take him?"

The forces were regrouping ahead of Obasee.

"He's a good lead," Trapp said.

"If he escapes, he starts over," Ikem countered.

But there was something else, too. A darker impulse that Trapp sensed welling deep inside himself as he thought of Obasee's cruelty, the exploitation, the evil he would go on to commit.

"You know what you must do," Ikem said.

Trapp steadied his stance, gripped his gun with two hands, and aimed at the fleeing Obasee. It had only been seconds since he'd gotten free, but Trapp had weighed the morality and come to the only decision he could have.

One gunshot blasted across the land.

Obasee's body jerked, then flopped to the ground.

He twitched once, then lay still.

TWELVE

Even the thickest carpet couldn't cushion Ashenhurst's pacing. He was a thickset hound of nervous energy and had been since news landed about the raid on the mine. Isabella Knight leaned against the conference table as she watched him, arms and ankles crossed.

"Don't back down," Ashenhurst reminded her, as if she was the one who needed coaching. His eyes were locked on the oversized, wall-mounted television with the three pulsing dots denoting a connection being established. "This will go as planned if you—"

"Convince them?" Knight said.

"Stand your ground." Ashenhurst stopped pacing and faced her, chin tilted in that imperious angle she found both predictable and tiring. "It must be *us* leading *them*. No wavering, Isabella."

Isabella. He insisted on first names in private, Mister and Ms. when in esteemed company. Another irritant but not an overwhelming one.

She uncrossed her arms and checked the connection status,

taking in the wealth that radiated from every surface and gadget around them. It was like a sickness, this man's need to display his status. "They won't cut us off."

"Only if they believe we have it under control."

"Then let's convince them." She kept her voice steady, bored.

They still didn't know all the details from that morning's disaster, but the key now was to ensure it didn't look like a disaster. The only way to do it was with precision. That's why Rafe Ashenhurst had hired her. An ex-British intelligence officer, burned and demoted through no fault of her own, she had more than enough reasons to throw in with him—and the Chinese.

The screen chimed, and the three dots were replaced by General Gao. Even pixelated, the old soldier carried the stern dignity of a statesman. By his side, Fang Chen resembled a very polite ghost. Both sat in cream leather seats, and Knight imagined the rest of the jet in varying shades of excess.

"A failure of this magnitude can only be incompetence." Gao's syllables were slow and deliberate, his English functional more than fluent. "*Your* incompetence."

Next to her, Ashenhurst gave a thin smile. Calculated, not conciliatory. "The mine incident was unexpected, but—"

"Nothing should be unexpected." Gao's tone was pure steel. "We agreed you would remove the unexpected."

"Exactly. And it's being removed." Ashenhurst was speaking more quickly, a sign he was flustered, even if he didn't show it on the outside.

Beside Gao, Fang's features betrayed nothing, but Knight thought she saw a spark, a tiny flicker when the young woman's gaze rose to the screen—as if Fang was looking directly at her for a moment. Watching for a reaction?

Knight gave her nothing.

"I know what it looks like," Ashenhurst continued. "But I assure you, all is in hand."

"It looks," Gao said, "like a terrible failure." He leaned back, giving them the honor of seeing him recline in those luxurious seats. "And it threatens to expose us all."

In the silence that followed, with Ashenhurst's short, sharp glance at her, Knight took her cue. "I assured you that we would proceed. And we are."

Gao's mouth was a slit of pure discipline. "I should expect better than mere assurances."

"It was a minor interruption. We've been here before."

Gao and Fang watched her. Silent.

"These losses are the cost of doing business," Knight told him. "They pave the way for the outcome you're hoping for."

Gao's hand slapped an unseen table. "Our contacts tell us that the CIA could be in possession of important information. We understand they managed to penetrate the operation."

That was one of the details yet to reach Knight, although she would have received it soon enough.

Gao gave a dismissive shake of his head. "The trail should have been eliminated sooner."

"We will overcome this, General," Ashenhurst said.

"Your certainty is less valuable than you believe," Gao said. "I want details. I want to know how you plan to strike back."

Details. Now they were speaking Knight's language.

"Contingencies on top of contingencies," Knight said. "We have enough ore to produce twice what you need, and we have already manufactured and delivered the weaponry you requested. That feat alone should convince you we are not bumbling around in the dark. And with the mine gone, we are the only ones who can make more. In a way, the CIA has handed us a monopoly."

Gao turned to Fang for a translation. Knight had deliberately used a couple of complex words and English idioms that someone without fluency would struggle with. It gave her a few seconds more breathing room as she calculated what she could say next to further appease the man who held the fate of their company—and Knight's exorbitant bonus—in his hands.

"If the savage gave up the data, they may follow the shipment all the way to you," Gao said. "This is a problem for me. Especially if it leads them to your friends in Taiwan."

Fang looked fragile, as she so often did. But Knight had seen real fire inside her, recognizing that this was a role she played around those whose egos needed massaging. With Knight, Fang spoke with a kind of bravery Knight had to admire.

Now she wasn't exactly bombastic, but her voice was a blend of respect and confidence. "Apologies for interrupting..."

Gao's shoulders lifted, and his mouth turned down as he cast his attention onto the girl, who he plainly saw as inferior.

Fang said, "I believe Ms. Knight, General. With respect, you should trust her as well."

"Really?" Gao said.

"I have worked with Ms. Knight repeatedly these past months. Preparing your instructions, testing the limits of the US and their allies, managing different strands." Fang gave a tiny smile. "I'll take responsibility. It's as Ms. Knight says."

"So you wish this to be on your head?" Gao wasn't smiling, but he seemed satisfied. For now. "You're willing to take this risk?"

Fang's voice grew stronger. "Yes."

Gao thought about it for a silence that stretched into an uncomfortable void. "You have another chance, Mr. Ashenhurst." A generous conqueror. "But you should understand my patience is reaching its limits."

Ashenhurst pretended not to hear the threat. Knight heard it well enough.

"You want the world to fear your new weapons, General?" Knight said.

"Yes, of course," Gao answered.

"Then you will have exactly what you want, and we will show you. For now, I'll make sure the shipment is not traced to us. You will be insulated from any risk." Gao seemed skeptical, but his mood had softened. "Fine. Let us hear your contingency. How, exactly, will you rectify this situation?"

THIRTEEN

Trapp had learned a new acronym in the hours after arriving at the nearest Nigerian Army outpost to the mine.
SSS.
"The SSS are pissed."
"Why the fuck didn't you clear this with the SSS?"
And on and on, ad infinitum.

It stood for State Security Service and was the local equivalent of the FBI—responsible for domestic security and jealous of its turf.

The fluorescent lights of the nearest SSS hub were searing his retinas. For the past six hours, Trapp, Grubbs, and Ikem had been guests in the least friendly sense of the word. After the chaos at the mine—the firefight, the prison break, the death of Obasee—they hadn't been debriefed; they'd been detained. Hauled from the military outpost by grim-faced State Security Service agents, they were now under the thumb of a woman who was decidedly not impressed.

Director Olisa Ndulu, a woman whose stare could curdle

milk, had made her displeasure clear in a ten-minute tirade that could have stripped paint from the walls. They had interfered in a domestic matter, operated outside their mandate, and created a diplomatic firestorm. It was only a series of frantic, high-level calls from Mitchell back in Washington that had kept them out of an actual cell.

The compromise was this: they would remain at the SSS hub, under Ndulu's watchful eye, to monitor the convoy they claimed was a significant threat—using Nigerian aerial surveillance assets, not American. It was a gilded cage, but a cage nonetheless. And so, Trapp watched the blinking dot traverse the digital map of Nigeria, each pixel bringing the cargo closer to its unknown destination.

"This is bullshit," Trapp muttered.

Grubbs shot him a sidelong glance. "Mitchell's not taking any chances after all that trouble."

Trapp did not reply. No need. They all knew the situation. He could not shake the question, though: What was Mitchell hiding?

The CIA deputy director had been uncharacteristically tight-lipped. Something was happening behind the scenes, and being kept in the dark made Trapp's skin crawl.

Ikem leaned in, his voice low and thick. "Our new friend Olisa seems rather... pleased with recent events, no?"

Trapp's gaze flicked to Director Ndulu, who was engaged in animated conversation with a trio of analysts. A surprisingly relaxed demeanor had replaced the visible irritation she'd exuded when they first met.

"Too pleased," Trapp said. "The prison break should have her climbing the walls, not smiling like she just won the lottery."

Grubbs gave a pensive shake of the head. "You know, we

could be misreading her. What if she's as disgusted at the thought of that place as we were?"

"Could be," Trapp admitted. "Mitchell's probably taking heat from Ikem's command and the army. Dumping a shitload of displaced people on a base on the edge of Boko Haram territory? The CO didn't seem to appreciate it."

Director Ndulu's voice rose over the low hum of activity. "I hope you are finding our facilities adequate. Though I must admit, I did not expect to be hosting quite so many... guests in my command center."

The subtle emphasis on "guests" wasn't lost on Trapp. It had been used ad nauseum since arriving.

Remember you are guests here.

We will treat you well, but you must be good guests.

Trapp met Ndulu's gaze, mirroring her body language as a good operative should. "We appreciate your hospitality, Director. And your patience. I'm sure once we track this shipment to its destination, we'll be out of your hair."

Ndulu's smile seemed to genuinely reach her eyes, but her hands were still folded into each other. "No rush, Mr. Trapp. We are all on the same team here, after all."

As she walked away, Ikem raised an eyebrow. "What are you thinking we do next? Because I do not know if I can hold off my superiors much longer. They want me to come in and explain my part in this morning's actions. Although I think, like the director, they are secretly happy with the outcome."

Trapp let the question hang and returned to studying the drone tracking data on the large screen on the wall. The blinking dot representing the convoy had just reached the Nigerian border with Chad.

Grubbs brought up data on a laptop screen beside her, the same government file they had been briefed with an hour earlier. "I don't get it. We've confirmed the shipment is legit, and the paperwork's pristine. Why are we still watching this?"

Trapp shook his head, frustration evident in his taut posture. "Because something doesn't add up. The money, for one. You saw the intel from Obasee's computer. I can only guess Mitchell made a connection between this mine, the shipment, and the Chinese. Otherwise we'd be out of here by now."

"We've been wrong before," Grubbs reminded him.

"Not often enough to ignore this." Trapp faced her. "Think about it, Madison. Why would the CIA be so invested in a routine shipment?"

Grubbs opened her mouth to respond, but—

She was cut off by a thunderous roar that seemed to lift the building into the air, and the world exploded around them.

The blast hit like a punch, slamming Trapp against the console. Everything spun as the room went dark, but Trapp wasn't sure if it was his vision or the juice going out. He rolled over, catching his breath, which was tainted by the acrid scent of an electrical fire and the tang of coppery blood from a cut in his mouth.

Slumping against the desk, Trapp got his bearings. The room shuddered again as lights flickered and sparks showered from damaged equipment. He wasn't losing consciousness; it was the power dying combined with the shock.

Burning wires and melting plastic. The taste of blood persisted. His head rang, jangling for several seconds, until he forced himself to focus.

Then Trapp saw Grubbs pulling herself up toward the laptop as if it were a life preserver on a sinking ship.

"Secure the data," Trapp said with a groan, pushing shakily to his feet. He quickly assessed potential threats, escape routes, casualties. Ikem was conscious but groggy. "I'll check the perimeter."

Trapp staggered to the door, his vision and mind clearing the more he was upright. No gunshots, no follow-up explosion. He regulated his breathing, telling himself the immediate threat was over.

He ran down the corridor at an unsteady, lurching pace, alarms wailing, every third or fourth step sending a dizzy wave through him.

Even with the haze pressing in, Trapp couldn't shake a gnawing thought that the timing of the blast—right as they were tracking the convoy—was way too perfect.

Down a smoke-infested staircase, burnt rubber and scorched plastic mixed with brick dust.

On the street level floor, smoke billowed over the hallway ceilings, limiting his sight but not yet filling the space. A few more minutes and he'd be choking on every breath.

Around a final corner, the full devastation was laid bare. The once-slick entrance of the SSS hub was now a gaping wound, twisted metal contorted amid shattered concrete and small fires. Through the haze, he glimpsed the mangled remains of what had once been a vehicle, burst open like a terrible flower.

"Christ..."

Then Trapp's eyes locked on to a familiar figure picking his way through the debris—Ikem, his usually-immaculate appearance now marred by dust and a trickle of blood from a cut on his forehead. He must have descended the other fire stairwell.

"Hey!" Trapp called out, rushing to support his colleague. "You all right?"

Ikem managed a grim nod. "I've had better days. But I fear our mystery shipment has something to do with it."

The same thought Trapp had considered.

He fumbled his phone out, finding the screen cracked but operational, and hit Grubbs' number. She answered right away.

"Grubbs, the convoy," Trapp said, heading back toward the comms hub. "Have we still got it?"

"Negative," Grubbs replied. "We lost it. So did Washington."

FOURTEEN

The air in the hospital corridor was thick with the scent of antiseptic, but it didn't fully mask the smell of smoke still clinging to Trapp's clothes. Hours after the SSS hub was bombed, the aftermath was brutally clear: it had been a perfect diversion.

A tense call with Mitchell had confirmed their worst fears. While the car bomb was grabbing everyone's attention, the convoy carrying the niobium alloy had vanished across the border into Chad. Without anyone operating them, the surveillance drones had flown for miles on autopilot in exactly the wrong direction. The trail was cold.

With their only lead gone, Washington had nothing. But Trapp couldn't stand down, not when he knew what was at stake. That's what had brought him here. The survivors from the mine were the only link left.

His first witness had spoken little English, an Ethiopian man who'd traveled not for asylum or refuge but for work. There was no translator available at such short notice, so Trapp had had to muddle through.

The man had started working at the mine voluntarily, allowing his meager wages to be sent home, but after trying to leave in order to check on his family, he'd been punished, and from then on, he'd seen little outside the living quarters and the tunnels. He asked Trapp about his wife and four children back in Ethiopia, as if Trapp were a liaison helping repatriate the lost and broken, but Trapp had been unable to reassure him.

He left the room, feeling guilty that he could not convey exactly who he was and what he was doing here. Despite the doctor's pointed look of disapproval, he couldn't let it bother him.

He needed something, anything to set a proper investigation into motion, a direction in which he could aim. For too long, he'd allowed himself to be swept along, reacting instead of acting. The whole Nigeria assignment had become the kind of spaghetti-against-the-wall bullshit that led to either mission creep, in which too many threads led to too much work, or mission stalemate, where no leads presented themselves and they ended up snagging on the least-bad option.

He still wasn't sure which this was turning into.

Trapp made his way to the next patient's room.

His muscles ached from the morning's exertion, a gnawing reminder of the brutality they'd witnessed, yet the physical discomfort helped stem the exhaustion—it had been almost thirty-six hours since he'd last slept.

He paused outside the door, squaring his shoulders and blinking away his body's demand for rest. These survivors had been through so much; the least he could do was project an air of control and competence.

Pushing the door open, Trapp stood before a gaunt Chinese man propped up in bed, a saline drip in one arm, an empty soup bowl on the bed table. He could have been twenty-five or forty-five. Despite his emaciated frame, a spark of life flickered in the man's eyes as he recognized the person who had facilitated their freedom. The highlights of ginger in his hair identified him as the one who had sparked the miniature rebellion, who had taken up arms and fought alongside his fellow prisoners. Although how he'd handled a gun in this state, Trapp wasn't sure.

Adrenaline and hope were a powerful combination.

"Good morning," Trapp said. "I'm Jason. What's your name?"

Trapp already knew from the medical notes, but it was polite to ask.

The man replied, "Gin-lo."

"Mind if I ask you a few questions, Gin-lo?"

"You and your friends got us out." The man eyed Trapp warily. "Thank you." Accented English but clear, almost fluent.

"You were brave enough to help a stranger. Should be me thanking you."

"You are an American?"

"CIA," Trapp answered, matter of fact. "But don't let that put you off." He settled into a low chair beside the bed, similar to those in American hospitals. "I'm looking to shut down the people who held you captive. Their wider operation, not just the mine. Any information you provide about who runs that place could save more lives."

"You shot the overseer."

"He was just middle management. I mean, did you ever see people there who perhaps Obasee deferred to?"

A long moment of silence stretched out, the patient watching Trapp as if the CIA man might steal something. "Defer? How do you mean this?"

Trapp simplified it. "Like someone he tried hard to please. Maybe Obasee or others were scared of a visitor? Or someone else who was absent from the mine when we came."

Gin-lo had to ingest the question. Finally, he gave a small nod. "I sometimes worked in the compound. Cleaning, serving food to the bosses and their guests."

Trapp leaned forward. "What sort of guests?"

Guests—that word again.

The man's brow furrowed, his voice strained, tired. "Many African businessmen, always talking deals. There were Chinese too, but they never spoke around me."

Trapp was disappointed. Everything was too generic.

Then Gin-lo perked up. "There was one man who was different. British. He came with a Chinese party once. White, like you. But older. He came back alone sometimes."

"Alone?"

"I mean without the Chinese. He always had much security. Big men. Guns. Mostly white men."

Trapp kept his expression neutral. The danger of appearing enthusiastic was that Gin-lo might misremember something, subconsciously trying to please him.

"Can you describe any of them?" Trapp asked. "The Chinese men or the white man?"

"The Englishman... His hair was white. And a small beard. Like the American chicken colonel." Gin-lo mimed brushing an invisible beard into a point. "He had a cane, too, although I think he did not need it all the time."

Had to be Rafe Ashenhurst. His was one of the companies that Mitchell had mentioned.

As the survivor spoke, describing other people in the Englishman's party, Trapp was sure this could be a link to traffickers. How many distinctive-looking Englishmen were wealthy enough to mount dealings like that and ran operations in Chad and Nigeria?

He couldn't be that hard to find with a simple Google search. This was finally verging on definitive evidence, not the guesswork he'd been saddled with to date.

"Thank you," Trapp said. "You've been incredibly helpful. And brave. Rest now."

As he left the room, Trapp rolled his neck, easing the gathering tension as he spotted Grubbs down the hall. She'd adopted a mask of professional detachment that, he saw as she approached, could not hide the weariness in her eyes.

"Madison," he said. "What did you find?"

She fell into step beside him, switching direction. "Not much. Chinese and Africans mostly. One white man—other than you—but not much more."

Trapp nodded. "My guy had more. British accent. Obasee groveled around him. Sounds like Ashenhurst Group might be more than just a client. Hard to tell if it's the red flag we're looking for or if he's just another amoral asshole taking advantage of the situation there, but I'm guessing they're the buyers of the convoy we just lost." He rubbed the back of his neck. "It's not much, but it's better than nothing. Let's see if we can find him before Mitchell's hotshot kid takes over."

Rather than returning to the cramped and falling-apart SSS hub, they headed for their car in the parking lot, where Grubbs fired up a tablet. Trapp had given her the parameters, the key facets of what Gin-lo had told him. They started out with the Google search that he'd hoped would yield results quickly.

No such luck.

But the computer was an encrypted CIA-issued device, and thanks to the databases Grubbs was permitted to access, along with a handful she was not permitted to see but could navigate anyway, it didn't take long for her to sit back and give Trapp a smug grin.

"Rafe Ashenhurst."

Bingo.

"British national. Frequent border crossings to and from Chad. Subcontracted for Chinese infrastructure projects four years ago, owns an oil exploration company. Into drilling across Africa, more recently started up a fracking concern, *and* he's linked to a handful of shell companies that are suspected of using slave labor in their practices. Oh, and he's a big ol' sexist pig and probably a rapist. He was a knight of the realm until he all but admitted the charges with a big compensation payout. But never saw jail."

Grubbs leaned in, showing Trapp the known-associates list.

"Shady as they come," Trapp said. "Those legitimate business ties alone are a who's-who of gunrunners and terror supporters. And we circle back to our Chinese friends, too."

"If we're comparing who's-who lists, there's a healthy sprinkling of British elites. He went to college with Robert Sutherland, the current home secretary. How does a guy like this stay under the radar?"

"Money," Trapp said. "Lots of it."

A well-dressed Brit commanding respect at the mine.

Questionable ethics.

Oil and gas exploration... analyzing and buying from a mining operation.

"He's our guy," Trapp said. "Has to be."

The tablet emitted a sharp beep, then both their phones blared the same alert.

"Incoming from Washington," Grubbs said. "They want us all to be briefed right away. Secure satellite uplink only."

Trapp checked his watch. It was less than two hours since

he'd left the SSS hub. Mitchell's meeting had not been particularly long considering how much confidential intel there should've been to broach.

"I guess young Mr. Hines means business," Trapp said, starting the engine. "Let's not keep them waiting."

FIFTEEN

Washington, D.C

THE AIR in Situation Room B was cool, sterile, and thick with a tension that the advanced climate control systems couldn't scrub away. The immense, polished mahogany table reflected the muted glow of a dozen encrypted screens, but the largest, wall-mounted display at the head of the room remained blank, waiting.

Deputy Director Mike Mitchell sat straight-backed, his gaze fixed on the empty screen, his patience worn thin by hours of crisis management. Beside him, his sharpest new analyst, Polly Garside, reviewed data on a tablet, her usual cheerfulness suppressed by the gravity of the meeting.

Across from them sat Karem Hines. To Mitchell, he looked more like a grad student pulling an all-nighter than a senior researcher spat up from somewhere in the bowels of Homeland Security. He was fidgeting, his lean frame coiled with a nervous energy that seemed at odds with the immense importance of his findings.

The door hissed open, and the atmosphere in the room instantly shifted. President Charles Nash entered, his presence filling the space, his expression a mask of grim focus that Mitchell knew all too well. Mitchell and Polly rose to their feet out of habit, but Hines, apparently lost in his own world of data and theory, remained seated.

"As you were," Nash said, his voice calm but carrying an undeniable weight as he took his designated seat at the head of the table. He gestured toward the main screen. "I don't normally sit in on these, but the names involved demanded my attention. Let's get to it. Mr. Hines, you have the floor."

The screen flickered to life, displaying the tired faces of Jason Trapp and Madison Grubbs, broadcasting from a secure, makeshift command center in Lagos.

Hines cleared his throat, pushing his stylish glasses up the bridge of his nose. "Thank you, Mr. President. My department was automatically flagged by an intelligence report filed by Deputy Director Mitchell. It concerned a recent convoy shipment of a rare mineral sourced from a mine in Nigeria."

From the speakers, Trapp's voice, rough with fatigue and the static of a long-distance connection, cut in without ceremony. "The mineral is linked to Rafe Ashenhurst."

A flicker of irritation crossed Hines's face. He clearly wasn't accustomed to being interrupted. "As I was attempting to explain..."

"We don't have time for a slow-burn narrative, Hines," Mitchell said, his tone sharp. "Bottom line it for us."

Nash nodded in agreement, his gaze unwavering. "Karem, I'm declassifying Project Ultra for everyone in this room, physical and virtual. Give them the essential details. No preamble."

The authority in Nash's voice was absolute. Hines nodded,

chastened, and his fingers danced across his tablet. The main screen behind the president flickered, replacing the live feed with complex schematics and redacted documents, the words 'PROJECT ULTRA' stamped across the top in bold red.

"Project Ultra was the codename for our attempt to develop a next-generation directed energy weapon—a DEW," Hines began, his voice finding its rhythm. "It was a theoretical leap, but we ultimately abandoned it. The cost was astronomical, and the technology simply wasn't viable with our existing materials science.

"Ashenhurst approached the Pentagon years ago with a concept for a man-portable version," Hines continued, swiping to a new slide showing a 3D model of a bulky, futuristic rifle. "They passed. The power requirements were insane, and his refusal to cut ties with known terrorist organizations made him an unacceptable partner."

"Boko Haram," Trapp stated flatly from the screen. It wasn't a question.

Hines nodded. "Among others. We now believe a primitive version of this same technology was deployed on US soil. In Pittsburgh." He brought up a new set of images—autopsy photos. They were gruesome. "The victims suffered a complete, catastrophic cellular breakdown. It mimicked a hemorrhagic fever, but it left no biological trace. One agent described the scene as if the victims had been 'cooked from the inside out.' The official FBI report cited an undetectable poison, but that was a cover. They had no real answers."

Grubbs' voice was tight. "I thought the consensus was that Havana Syndrome was a non-threat. Debunked."

"Downplayed, not debunked," Trapp corrected her instantly. "There's a difference."

"This is orders of magnitude beyond Havana," Hines said, dismissing the comparison. "This is a lethal weapon. And the key to it, the reason it's suddenly viable, is the niobium alloy that was being extracted from that mine your team just leveled."

Polly Garside, who had been quietly absorbing the information, spoke up. "Niobium is a key component in low-temperature superconductors."

Trapp's frustration was audible. "Speak English, people. How does this superconductor help build a death ray?"

Hines took a deep, slightly condescending breath, as if explaining a simple concept to a child. "All conventional circuits have resistance. Energy is lost as heat. A lot of it. A superconductor has virtually zero resistance." He gestured to the schematics on the screen.

"The biggest challenge with DEWs has always been 'blooming'—the beam of energy disperses over distance, like a flashlight beam getting weaker the farther it shines. It requires immense power at the source to have any effect at range. But with a superconductor circuit, there's no energy loss. All the power is funneled directly into the beam."

"It allows the weapon to be smaller, more efficient," Grubbs extrapolated.

"And infinitely more focused," Hines confirmed. "It solves the blooming effect. It means you can project a concentrated, lethal stream of microwave energy with terrifying precision, leaving surrounding property and infrastructure almost completely untouched."

A heavy silence descended on the room as the full implication of Hines' words sank in.

Mike Mitchell felt a cold knot form in his stomach. "So Ashenhurst didn't just stumble upon a rare metal," he said slowly. "He found the missing piece to a puzzle we gave up on. He's built a weapon we deemed impossible."

"And he's preparing to sell it," Trapp's voice added grimly. "Our intel from the mine pointed to Chinese buyers."

President Nash, who had been listening intently, finally spoke, his voice cutting through the tension. "I need to know who the buyer is. Is this the same rogue faction you dealt with in New York, Trapp, or are we looking at direct involvement from the Chinese government? The response will be vastly different."

He leaned forward, his eyes locking on to the screen. "Trapp, Grubbs. I need you to get me that proof. I need to know precisely what Ashenhurst has built, and I need options to neutralize this threat. Permanently."

Hines shifted uncomfortably in his chair. "Sir, with respect... Ashenhurst's primary motivation seems to be the grudge he holds against us for rejecting his initial proposal. What if we approach him with a different offer? What if we simply... buy it? Outbid the Chinese. Seize the technology for ourselves."

SIXTEEN

Fang Chen paused outside Ambassador Lian Zhelan's office to straighten her blouse and smooth her hair. While Zhelan's predecessor preferred his state-of-the-art office to *look* state-of-the-art, the current Chinese ambassador to the United States had commissioned a switch of location within the embassy building and an extensive refurbishment to make the office resemble the interior of an egg. White walls, white ceiling, a white glass-topped desk, and a white leather chair. The carpet was off-white, close to beige.

Where the previous incumbent's office could frost over its many glass walls, these walls were made of brick, and the window was armed with a shutter in lieu of high-tech white noise. Zhelan favored the old-school methods, and she hated distractions. The only splash of color came from the non-flowering potted plants scattered liberally around.

With a deep breath, Fang shed her timid exterior. Her fingers wrapped around the brass doorknob and twisted. She entered with her head up and eyes forward, the fluttering in her stomach belying the conviction that she hoped radiated from her.

"Fang, thank you for coming so quickly. How was Taiwan?"

"It was as expected, Madam Ambassador," Fang said. "General Gao was satisfied with the arrangements, and the issue we had with the financing has been resolved. I also have the latest update from Africa."

Zhelan had been reading a thick brief bound in red leather, which she would no doubt hate. She closed the material and gave Fang an appraising look, as she often did. Although she rarely smiled and refused to give emotion even a momentary whiff of air, there was a loosening of her muscles when it was just the two of them. There had been since the day she arrived in post, having been briefed on Fang's part in the mission to disrupt an important summit earlier that year. Although it hadn't gone to plan, Zhelan—and those to whom both women were now loyal—felt she had excelled in such a short time.

From a shy, administrative attaché to almost bringing down the CIA.

General Gao still treated her as little more than a secretary, but taking her word as she vouched for Isabella Knight perhaps showed progress there, too. Yes, she wanted to do more, wanted to change the world, but did she really have the ability to work with individuals like Lian Zhelan and the general?

"Proceed, Miss Chen."

"The second allocation of funds has been transferred to the manufacturer," Fang said, consciously keeping her tone clipped and professional. "We have independently verified that production is on schedule and the prototypes are in place for a live test."

Zhelan leaned forward. "Good. And the timeline?"

"The proof of concept will be ready as agreed," Fang

replied. She couldn't help but admire the efficiency of their network, even as a part of her recoiled at the thorny question of whether she was siding with the right people.

The ambassador nodded, her fingers pressed together. "You seem hesitant. Haven't I schooled you to project confidence?"

She had, yes. Zhelan regularly offered advice and set Fang loose to put it into effect, the sort of mentor-mentee relationship Fang had always hoped for. Only, when she found herself a party to a horrible but necessary act, she still faltered. Still hugged herself to sleep at night, reminding herself why they were doing all this.

"Thank you, Ambassador," Fang said. "I just hope to serve our nation well. I sometimes worry I might not be."

Zhelan's gaze softened slightly, a hint of genuine approval in her eyes. "I know the demonstration in Pittsburgh was unpleasant, but they were enemies of both the current state *and* the new one we will build. If what Mr. Ashenhurst is selling works, we will confront American aggression head-on. *And* our weak leaders back home."

Fang's throat was tight. But she pushed the doubt aside, focusing on the good they sought to achieve. It was just so daunting some days. The reality of it.

"Is there anything else you require, madam?" Fang asked.

"Not at present. Unless there are any problems I need to be aware of?"

"The only possible issue is Jason Trapp's intervention. His team has left the mine unable to operate for the moment, and my experience with him gives me some pessimism about the trail going completely cold."

"To us?" Zhelan asked.

"I do not believe so. But he's a driven man, madam. He will pursue those responsible. I think a warning to Mr. Ashenhurst to be wary of him until the test is completed will be sufficient."

Lian Zhelan's eyes narrowed. Fang fought the urge to shrink away.

"And if the Ashenhurst side of things is compromised?"

"The circuit boards and compounds can be reproduced." Fang swallowed hard. This was a possible failure point. "We have people in place to acquire it in its entirety... should we need to dispense with Rafe Ashenhurst's services."

"'Dispense with,' Fang? I'm impressed. But your friend, Jason Trapp? Do we need to *dispense with* him too?"

Was this friendly banter, or was Zhelan making fun of her?

Fang opted to remain neutral. "The prototype components were secured before Trapp's arrival, but the original testing site is no longer viable. Mr. Ashenhurst has assured us of a new one."

Zhelan's fingers splayed on her desk, a sign that she was thinking. Before Fang had gotten to know her superior, she'd read that gesture as annoyance.

"We need more control," Fang asserted. "Trapp is out there. Ashenhurst is over-confident."

Zhelan leaned back. "And how do you propose we handle this?"

"Madam, Boko Haram troops have mobilized to secure the region around the mine. They are terrible men, but they know the terrain and have established partnerships across that part of the world. And in Europe, if it comes to it."

A flicker of approval crossed Zhelan's face.

"We use them as muscle," Fang continued. "Isabella can secure their services through the same financial channels that have worked so well to date. We warn Ashenhurst about Trapp's skills and make sure that if the American surfaces, Ashenhurst and Knight give Boko Haram the location of the man who wrecked their mining enterprise." She paused. "It keeps our hands clean. And Ashenhurst's... mostly clean."

"Do it," Zhelan said. "If you are confident we will not be implicated."

Fang bowed slightly before turning to leave. As she reached for the door handle, the familiar mask of meekness settled over her features. The transformation was instant—shoulders slumped, eyes down.

Stepping into the hallway, the door clicking shut behind her, Fang allowed herself one last thought of the dreadful power they had the potential to unleash. Then she became the quiet, unassuming woman the world expected her to be.

SEVENTEEN

Trapp and Grubbs arrived in the overpowering heat of Chad on a military transport, setting aside their elaborate undercover legends and backstories. Instead, they were armed with standard CIA identity packs naming them Jason Jones and Maddy Truby.

At the end of the single runway, they were greeted by a tall, bulky man who reminded Trapp of a Hollywood actor from the South Pacific Islands.

"I am Henry," the man said, his dazzling smile coupled with a handshake that engulfed Trapp's. "My men and I will take excellent care of you. We have a motel booked, but we'll get you to your meeting first. Is that okay with you?"

His accent was equally difficult to discern, but he seemed both friendly and professional. The private security firm had been exhaustively vetted by people in the Agency who were much more thorough than Trapp had time to be.

Henry and a small cadre of men whisked them away in a brown, worn-looking SUV—less conspicuous than a shiny black one—flanked by two others as they headed north. This diplomatic situation demanded caution, given that both Ashenhurst and the Chinese maintained a strong presence in the country. It was crucial to keep things simple: establish their intentions, acquire what Karem Hines and Mike Mitchell needed, then get out.

"Leaving Ikem behind doesn't sit right," Trapp remarked.

Grubbs sighed, agreeing despite the jurisdictional complications that bringing him would have created.

"One and a half hours," Henry said from the passenger seat. Their driver sat silent at the wheel, eyes focused ahead. "Plenty of time to rest if you need. We won't disturb you."

Henry's smile remained in place as a limo-style divider purred upward for privacy.

Grubbs closed her eyes and collapsed into a slumped position that she often claimed was comfortable. Trapp knew he should do likewise but instead focused on the barren landscape whizzing by, his thoughts drifting to Ryan Price for the first time in a while. The memory of his friend's death usually ignited a fire within him, but today he simply felt sad. Perhaps physical exhaustion was creeping in. Or the fact that this was a fishing expedition instead of extraction was dragging him down.

The arid vista surrounding the airport transformed gradually. First, they passed a township, a smattering of stone-built, single-story dwellings interspersed with occasional bars, cafés, and a garage that had once served as a gas station.

Then came more barren land on either side as the highway widened, getting less bumpy and gradually accumulating more cars with each onramp they passed. Nothing compared to the traffic-packed freeways back home, but the sudden transition from ramshackle poverty to quality infrastructure was jarring.

Soon they hit the poor neighborhoods on the city's outskirts —one-story homes, half-naked, skinny children either playing, working, or simply watching the passing vehicles—before a modern city akin to Lagos emerged, boasting straight lines and gleaming surfaces. Homes were adorned with smooth yellow plaster and terracotta-colored roofs. High-rise hotels towered above statues that watched over open parks. Specialty shops and fashion mingled with coffee shops, gentrifying urban areas like a Polaroid developing at high speed.

Soon, they skirted the river and entered what appeared to be an extensively regenerated area, a shopping mall acting as a focal point offering brands that Trapp didn't recognize but that looked expensive. A dealership displayed sports cars behind a wide front window, and above it all loomed a glass dome bearing the nation's flag.

There was wealth here, without a doubt, but knowing how a considerable portion of it was earned made Trapp uneasy.

He closed his eyes, planning to rest, but almost immediately, the privacy screen slid down with the same soft purr with which it had risen, and Henry's friendly grin returned—if it had ever faded. Grubbs stirred, blinking herself awake.

"We're thirty minutes out," Henry announced. "You ready to take the wheel?"

The three vehicles pulled into the upscale mall, allowing Grubbs and Trapp to swap into the front while their escorts would head to the motel programmed into their phones, deliver their hand luggage, and secure the building—discreetly, of course, to guard against unwanted eyes.

"Are you sure you don't want us to shadow you?" Henry asked as Trapp adjusted the driver's seat. "No problem on our end."

"Better we don't," Trapp replied. "It's a business meeting, not a ceasefire negotiation. We'd appreciate you being on standby, though. Just in case."

"You've got my number."

His "number" was actually a panic button concealed within Trapp's phone case, resembling a magnet for mounting the device in a car. If he held it for ten seconds, the phone sent an SOS, and a satellite pinpointed where Henry and his cavalry should ride in.

"Thank you," Trapp said. "Hopefully, we won't need it."

Henry patted the SUV's hood and stepped back.

Trapp and Grubbs followed the GPS onto the road, traveling alongside the Logone River before veering east into the countryside for another ten minutes. Finally, Ashenhurst's corporate office came into view—a glass monolith adjoining a motionless oil drilling facility. The polished exterior did little to mask the decay lurking beneath.

"Quite the setup," Grubbs commented.

Closer, as they passed through the perimeter, the inactive drilling towers loomed like skeletons in the distance, silent sentinels marking a once-formidable enterprise. There were no armed sentries, no barbed wire, just a welcoming parking lot half-full of mid- and high-end automobiles.

"Wasn't expecting that," Trapp noted. "Thought they'd search the car, at least."

"Yeah, it's strange." As they stepped out of the Jeep, the scorching heat wrapped around them, and the thin breeze deposited a gritty film on their skin. The N'Djamena region, at the intersection of two rivers, often experienced flooding, but Trapp doubted floodwaters ever made it this far.

As they approached the entrance, Trapp reminded himself that this was not a straightforward mission; they needed intel from Ashenhurst, who was already dealing with the enemy and could very well betray them. However, if they could eliminate the potential for the Chinese to acquire a weapon as threatening as Karem Hines had hypothesized, they had to take the chance.

The glass doors slid open with a soft hiss. A tall blond woman flanked by two bulky men in dark suits watched them enter. Although she stood unmoving, she radiated a commanding presence that demanded attention. Her gaze swept over Trapp and Grubbs, and a flicker of distaste—possibly suspicion—briefly crossed her face.

"Jason Jones," Trapp said. "And this is my associate, Madison Truby."

"Isabella Knight," the blonde stated, her voice clipped and professional. "I'm the head of security for the Ashenhurst Group. Please surrender any weapons."

Trapp retrieved a snub-nosed Glock in the clip-on holster from his belt; it might have been more suspicious had a CIA representative arrived unarmed. He handed it to the man on Knight's right. "Be careful with that."

The man remained impassive, his hooded eyes seemingly bored as he stowed the items in the waistband of his own pants, at the small of his back.

Grubbs followed suit, minus the snarky comment. Knight ran a handheld scanner over them, maintaining eye contact as if she could read their thoughts that way.

"Clear," she announced, though her tone suggested she would have preferred a reason to turn them away. "Follow me."

Leaving the security men behind, Knight led them through a series of pristine corridors: shining floors, art on the walls, air conditioning and humidifiers maintaining a cool and comfortable atmosphere. They arrived at a set of glass and steel double doors, which Knight pushed open without knocking, revealing a spacious conference room with two exits—the door they'd entered through and a smaller one to the left, likely leading to a private office. The room was dominated by a long table whose top appeared to be carved from a single tree trunk and encased in glass.

At the head of the table sat Rafe Ashenhurst. Although he appeared to be in his sixties, he retained the bearing of a fit but not overly athletic man in his forties. He had great skin, a full head of graying hair, and that odd pointy mustache-beard combo reminiscent of black-and-white Errol Flynn films.

"Welcome to Chad." He lacked the posh, plummy accent Trapp had expected, instead bringing a gravelly, clipped timbre, sounding more like a person who'd be working down in a mine than owning one. Definitely northern England. "How was your journey?"

Trapp forced a casual smile. "We appreciate you taking the time to meet with us."

"Yes, thank you," Grubbs added. "We know your previous engagement with the Agency was not as successful as either of us had hoped."

"Yep, that's one way of looking at it," Ashenhurst replied, leaning back in his leather chair, a self-satisfied smile on his lips. "All right, all right, enough with the politeness bollocks. You say our last engagement was unsuccessful; I call it one door closing but another one opening. A more expensive door."

He glanced at Knight. "Isabella, would you mind fetching some coffee for Mr. Trapp and Ms. Grubbs?"

EIGHTEEN

At mention of their real names, it took every bit of Trapp's training to keep the smile frozen in place. In his peripheral vision, he saw Grubbs' fingers twitch, although she hid her reaction otherwise.

Knight laughed. "Did you think you Americans were the only ones who could *do your own research,* as you like to say?"

It seemed more likely that the Chinese had fed Ashenhurst their true identities, which suggested that he'd told his business partners about this meeting already. Which meant there could be an ambush waiting for them as soon as they left this room.

But there was no point in denial, so Trapp smiled wider. "We expect no less, given the opportunity we're about to offer you."

"Please, I'm looking forward to it." Ashenhurst gestured for them to sit. "But as your other stooges learned, I'm very picky about opportunities."

Trapp opted to remain standing, while Grubbs took the chair at the unoccupied end of the table, facing Ashenhurst.

Knight mirrored Trapp, positioning herself in arm's length of Grubbs.

Perfect for hostage-taking.

Trapp started calculating possible scenarios, hoping that none of them would be necessary. "How about that cup of coffee?" he said to Knight.

"How about we get down to business?" Ashenhurst countered. "When people waste my time, I get impatient. And your employer already wasted plenty."

Grubbs, seeming oblivious to any threat Knight might be trying to imply by hovering near her, said, "We'd like start with your business interests in the region."

"I thought you were interested in my more, ehh, *esoteric* ventures."

"But you *are* sourcing materials here," Grubbs replied. "And in regions over the border."

Ashenhurst remained untroubled, but something flickered in Knight's expression, so fast that Trapp wasn't sure if it was anger or something else. Was it possible they'd thought the CIA didn't know about the mine?

Or was there more to Ashenhurst's connection to the mine, something they had yet to uncover?

"Yeah, yeah, there's always a challenge or two," Ashenhurst conceded. "Local instability, resource competition—the usual headaches of operating in a run-down part of the world."

Trapp seized the opening to establish the seriousness of the *opportunity*. "Speaking of instability, we've heard rumors about militant activity in areas you operate in."

"Specifically?"

"Specifically, around some of your more profitable mining operations."

Ashenhurst's eyes narrowed almost imperceptibly—his first tell. "Oh yeah? What kind of rumors?"

"The kind that suggest that you treat dealing with less-than-reputable groups as a cost of doing business rather than the red line that it is for the US government."

Trapp sensed Grubbs shift beside him but kept his gaze fixed on Ashenhurst.

"That's quite an unspoken inference, *Mr. Jones*," Ashenhurst said, his tone light—perhaps too light. "Some might even say it's a mealy-mouthed, cowardly accusation."

"Not an accusation," Grubbs interjected. "Just outlining our concerns. We cannot be seen to deal with terrorists."

"That's better. Plain speaking. 'Less-than-reputable groups.' Ha! What bollocks."

Ashenhurst laughed. Knight did not.

"And if we're speaking plainly," he continued, "I assume you think I'm in bed with these savages. Am I right?"

"Are you?" Trapp asked.

"Americans." Ashenhurst uttered the word with the same disdain one might feel after stepping on a cockroach—barefoot. "You're so bloody quick to label anyone who opposes your interests as terrorists."

Abruptly, he stood.

"I hate to speak in platitudes and soundbites, but sometimes a cliché is a cliché 'cause it's true. Today's terrorists might well be declared tomorrow's freedom fighters. Nelson Mandela was a terrorist according to both America *and* my country's greatest post-wartime leader, Lady Thatcher. Later, he got hailed a hero. Same with that Gandhi bloke in India. Should we mention the French resistance in the Second World War? Nah. History keeps vindicating people who resist oppression, whatever their methods."

Trapp felt a surge of disgust at Ashenhurst equating his allies with genuine revolutionaries. But before he could respond, Grubbs intervened.

"Mr. Ashenhurst, my apologies. It seems you misunderstand our concerns. That's our fault; we weren't clear enough. Let me state—plainly—that we are not here to judge your business practices or political affiliations."

Ashenhurst eyed Grubbs warily, his hands finding the arms of his chair as he leaned forward, intrigued.

"The US government understands the complexities of operating in this region," Grubbs continued. "In public, we must oppose 'less-than-reputable groups' with all our strength, but I don't see Boko Haram in this room. And I'm guessing there are no *direct* links. Nothing anyone involved would be stupid enough to commit to paper. If what we know and what we can prove are not the same, and we find no red flags during routine background checks, then it's possible we can do business."

Ashenhurst's expression shifted from annoyance to curiosity.

Grubbs pressed on. "If you can insulate our government from accusations of liaising with these groups, we can make it very lucrative for you. More lucrative than your current deals."

Understanding settled over Ashenhurst as he slowly returned to his seat. "I see. And what exactly are you offering me?"

Trapp analyzed the subtle shifts in Ashenhurst's posture and timed his moment. "We can ensure you have no more issues like the recent disruption to your key source of materials. That facility, by the way, is about to vanish for good. However, we can supply connections to alternative sources for easily refinable cobalt and niobium. More than sufficient for your needs—and for the weaponry we urge you to sell to us instead of our competitors."

Ashenhurst considered Trapp's proposal, his air of indifference palpable. "Mr. Trapp, I have a queue of interested parties stretching from the Middle East to Beijing and back to Timbuktu. It's very competitive. And the supply is limited."

"I'm well aware of that." Trapp tapped his fingertip on the desk. "But I assure you, none of them can offer what we can."

"A bidding war, then?" Ashenhurst asked, skepticism edging into his voice. "You want to gazump the Chinese and Russians?"

Russians? Nobody had heard a peep out of them to date, but it'd make sense for Ashenhurst to invoke them. It'd drive up the price, even if he were lying about their involvement.

And what the hell did *gazump* mean? Some British slang for *outbid*, probably.

"We can outbid the Chinese and definitely the Russians," Trapp said without missing a beat. "That's not the issue. We can also eliminate obstacles that might hinder production. Make sure that your various investments don't suddenly experience a run of bad luck."

Ashenhurst snorted. "Buy a man dinner before you attempt to extort him."

"As a valued business partner, *your* interests become *our* interests," Trapp said smoothly. "And the US government always protects its interests."

"How do I know you won't take what you want and cut me out?" Ashenhurst shook his head with mock sadness. "Why would I take that risk when my current business partners already promised to protect me from your interference?"

Exactly the opening Trapp had been looking for. "Why don't you check in with Obasee, then tell me if you're happy with the level of service your current business partners are providing in that department."

Ashenhurst's smug grin soured a little at that. Trapp pressed further.

"The incident at the mine was an example of how much

chaos two operatives can create with limited assistance from a handful of locals." Trapp took a step toward Ashenhurst. "Imagine how effective a team running a coordinated op with the full backing of the Agency could be."

Ashenhurst lost his grin completely.

"All of that *effectiveness* can be directed at you—or at your enemies. That's the real opportunity here."

The arms dealer seemed to think for a moment. Knight remained motionless in the silence, although Trapp had the impression that she was simply waiting for a signal.

He readied himself to lunge toward Grubbs. He wouldn't be fast enough to intercept a bullet if Knight pulled her gun, but he might be able to tackle the security head before she got off more than a shot or two.

But instead of making any kind of gesture, Ashenhurst said, "If I agree, I'll have some very dissatisfied customers."

"We can protect you."

"And I'll need to be compensated for *all* my losses at the mine."

Trapp took that to mean the loss of the slaves, and he must've let a hint of his revulsion show on his face because Grubbs jumped in.

"Twice what the Chinese are paying, plus protection for yourself and the promise of non-interference with all your business ventures. As long as you avoid any of those less-than-reputable parties."

"I'm not sure that's enough," Ashenhurst said. "And I still haven't heard anything to convince me you won't just blow my brains out once you've got hold of my product."

"Waste not, want not," Trapp answered. "Why would we get rid of a partner who's been so useful? Especially when they can help us keep tabs on unreputables operating within his territory."

"So now I'm your informant too."

"Business partners look after each other's interests, don't they?"

Ashenhurst stood and walked around the table, forcing Trapp to split his attention as the man approached, retrieving a lighter from an inside pocket of his suit jacket and holding it out toward Trapp. It was a classic brass Zippo-style, the gas-powered type with a sizeable flame that rarely went out.

"A token of our deal," he said.

As Trapp took the lighter, Ashenhurst leaned closer, lowering his voice. "If the Agency reneges on any aspect of the deal, even in the smallest way, I will personally come to take this lighter back. Then I'll burn you and your handlers to the fucking ground."

Trapp hoped he would. He couldn't think of anything that would give him more satisfaction than ridding the world of one Rafe Ashenhurst.

NO CONFLICT.

No extractions.

No assassinations.

Just a good, old-fashioned offer which Rafe Ashenhurst could not refuse.

As they walked out of the conference room, Madison wondered if Trapp was relieved or disappointed.

"We can find our own way out," he said to Knight, who had escorted them out of the conference room.

"You understand, we do have protocols," the security head replied.

Madison tried not to hear that as threatening. And failed.

But nothing happened as they walked to the end of the

hallway, down the staircase to the lower floor, or along another hallway that led to the lobby. The only other people they saw were two bulky men maneuvering a piece of scientific equipment that Madison couldn't identify through a propped-open door labeled with only a number: 108.

As they passed, she peeked inside.

It was a lab. Empty, sterile, with brushed metal surfaces—more like a morgue than a laboratory. Like everything else in this place, it appeared to be set up for significant operations to come.

She supposed it was too much to hope that they'd get a glimpse of the device itself.

By the time they entered the lobby, Madison was sweating despite the air conditioning. The security guard who had taken their guns when they'd come in now returned them, just as expressionless as he'd been before.

Trapp fell in beside her as they marched to the exit. The heat breathed hard and hot over them as they stepped outside, and she found it welcoming for the first time.

"What the actual fuck, Trapp?" she said. "They knew our real names."

He shrugged like that wasn't the important thing. "I've alerted Henry that we might need pulling out. They might not have executed us back there, but I'm not convinced we're out of it yet."

"Wait, I thought we nailed it back there."

"They're too well connected. The handshakes, the lighter, the fake friendliness... you didn't feel it?"

"Feeling it isn't the same as actionable data."

"It is for me. They weren't convinced. And you probably saw how pissed he was when I pretty much confessed to taking out the mine. The fact that we didn't have to shoot our way out is the most surprising aspect of this whole day."

At the car, Madison hesitated by the passenger side door. "If Knight and Ashenhurst wanted to eliminate us, they would have. Wouldn't they?"

"They're being cautious," Trapp said. "They know we're CIA, but they don't know how much exposure they've got." He opened the driver's door, looking back at the building, where Knight and two of her faithful attack dogs watched from just outside the entrance. "No, they'll put a tail on us, and if their partners in China approve, they'll move in. Hopefully, Henry'll pick us up on the road. Once we're safe, we need to hunker down and decide what to do next."

After Trapp had pressed the hidden button on his phone, they pulled out of the compact lot and onto the access road. He remained silent, as if watching for any sign of someone lying in wait. Madison focused on keeping her breathing even, letting the heat seep into her, letting it drive out the chill of fear that had settled in her bones.

They arrived at the main public road, and after another five minutes, Trapp pulled over to check his phone. There was no indicator light on the emergency call button nor anything that would alert onlookers that it had been activated. It was designed that way. The downside was that they couldn't determine if the call had gone through. If Ashenhurst's facility had shut down all radio, phone, and satellite signals, the message would not have transmitted until they were beyond the dampeners' range.

That might explain why Henry hadn't shown up yet.

Long after the projected fifteen minutes it should have taken.

"If Henry's team has been paid off," Trapp said, "we could be walking into another ambush."

"Should we call?" Madison asked. "See if anything sounds off?"

"Don't want to give them warning."

Trapp told Grubbs to navigate him to the motel rendezvous. It took them another twenty minutes to reach the parking lot of the two-story building, where Henry's SUV and a sedan were waiting. Situated on the outskirts of the city, they had easy access to the highway leading back to the airport as well as to the central area with its malls and parks.

As they surveyed the scene, Madison noticed a sentry in each vehicle and two of Henry's men loitering near the building's reception area. Much too obvious—even she had spotted them. Was that a sign that something had gone wrong or that everything was fine?

"Phone must've malfunctioned," Trapp said as he turned off the engine.

Grubb examined it. "Shouldn't have. We tested it before we set out."

"I want a shower before we talk to Mitchell."

"Just because they ID'd us doesn't mean we've—"

Trapp opened his door, cutting her off, then strode over toward the first vehicle—the tinted sedan—and rapped on the glass. "Hey, it's me!"

As Madison got out and approached, the sedan's window cracked open, but she couldn't see if it was Henry inside or someone else.

Then Trapp whipped out his gun and fired through the gap, blowing the man's head inside out just as the pair near the reception pulled semi-automatic machine guns from behind the door.

"Move!" he shouted, grabbing Madison and flinging both of them toward the rear of the car.

And once again, the world erupted into chaos and flames.

NINETEEN

Isabella Knight's pumps looked elegant but were molded for her feet and chosen because they were more than capable of standing up to a footrace. She was tall enough to not require heels, despite Rafe once informing her they would make her arse pop even more than it did in her pantsuit. She aspired to look corporate, but she would not risk her mobility just so Rafe Ashenhurst could bookmark her behind in his seedy wank-bank.

She was thinking about her footwear as she entered Rafe Ashenhurst's personal office down the hall from the conference suite because they always made more noise here. Not quite the click-click-click of traditional shoes, but on the finished marble tiles, even her thick soles announced her audibly. The space was an air-conditioned embodiment of extravagance adorned with gleaming mahogany, gilt-edged artwork, and a sweeping view that extended for miles. All this opulence for a mothballed corporate headquarters—it was typical of the aristocracy to which Rafe *wished* he belonged.

Here, appearances were paramount. Everything else followed.

Rafe Ashenhurst—once *Sir* Rafe Ashenhurst before he was strong-armed into returning his knighthood—sat behind his imposing desk, a massive piece fashioned from an oak tree sourced from land tracing back to William the Conqueror and imported at a cost of tens of thousands of pounds. Dressed in a pristine suit that likely cost more than most people earned in a month, he radiated entitlement, his sneer a blend of disdain and desire—both traits that had contributed to him losing his title. And almost an arm, when he once reached to pat Knight on the bum as a thank-you for some death or another.

Knight approached with a façade of detached professionalism. If Ashenhurst wanted to undress her with his eyes and squander his wealth on ostentatious decor, so be it—as long as her substantial paychecks continued to clear.

"Mr. Ashenhurst," she said, inclining her head slightly. "You requested a formal report on the recent security breach."

Ashenhurst's gaze shifted from ogling to piercing. "Proceed."

"I know they never denied their names, but facial recognition has confirmed it. They were Jason Trapp and Madison Grubbs, as our Chinese associates suspected."

Ashenhurst's pinkie finger drummed on the polished wood, a chunky silver ring glinting in the light. "Elaborate."

Another of the man's gimmicky traits was interjecting his conversations with unnecessarily long words, his way of impersonating the other upper-crust Brits in whose circles he moved.

Knight said, "He has a reputation that makes the Chinese nervous. Rumor from them *and* my old contacts in the Service is that he was the 'Hangman' whose codename came out in the news a few months ago."

"And what about the woman?"

"Less lethal but highly adept. They operate as a team."

"So it was a calculated op—like the mine raid that got Obasee Chidike killed."

"Actually, that brings me to my next point. The attack there was not a Nigerian-led operation aimed at suppressing the labor issue. If it was this pair, and I strongly believe they were present, they might have interrogated Obasee and tracked us down through him. Who knows what else they got hold of?"

Ashenhurst's expression darkened. "If they've compromised our development—"

"Unlikely," Knight interjected. "Our most sensitive data is compartmentalized. They were never alone here. There's no way they could piece together the full project. In fact, the only reason they might be close to understanding our objectives is the scale of the security operation you mandated."

Ashenhurst scrutinized her. "The trucks?"

Knight met Ashenhurst's gaze. "The trucks, sir. Even if Trapp wasn't present during the transport phase, it would not have gone unnoticed. If nosy bystanders didn't immediately connect the dots with the weapon test in Pittsburgh, they'd certainly be curious. As I mentioned earlier. But then again… you do prioritize customer service above all else."

"And self-preservation. Never forget that. It's what got me out of that fucking shithole neighborhood that my dad thought was somehow endearing. *Working class pride,* what bullshit." He scoffed. "Self-preservation… it's what got me my first business. It's what pushed my rivals into the damn sea. It earned me my damn knighthood, and it's what will get it back."

Knight remained silent. His rant wasn't unusual, nor was it an invitation to respond; Ashenhurst simply wanted to assert himself and shift any blame onto the circumstances.

Finally, he changed the subject. "About the operatives—

Trapp and Grubbs. If they're as connected as you reckon, then we made the right call. It's a low-risk strategy."

Isabella offered a brief nod. "Countermeasures are already in place, sir."

"And you're sure they didn't get anything valuable?"

"Not from their visit here, sir. The mine? Impossible to tell."

"You've been given resources to address the Trapp issue. Have you utilized them?"

"Fully. Although you know my misgivings. Our partners wanted discretion."

Ashenhurst shrugged. "This is my backyard. I know it better than them. And it's better this way. As long as you've done your part."

"My report to the N'Djamena police will state that we found two individuals who made appointments under false names. We assumed they were corporate spies, so we removed them. Any misfortune that befalls them afterward cannot be attributed to us."

She could feel the waves of resentment emanating from Ashenhurst, a result of his poorly hidden insecurity. Anxiety manifesting as strength. He was so close to achieving his aims: not just winning but ensuring that those who had wronged him lost. Here, her confidence clearly irritated him, challenging his false yet inflated sense of superiority.

Ashenhurst waved his hand dismissively, a gesture he usually reserved for incompetent contractors or lawyers who insisted he couldn't circumvent laws meant solely for common people. "Feed those spies to the savages, then. Are you sure they won't miss?"

The casual racism made Knight's skin crawl, but she kept her expression neutral. "I forwarded the details to the commander. However they choose to carry it out, I doubt it will be subtle. But as I mentioned, it also won't come back to us."

"Good," Ashenhurst replied. "The Chinese are eager for a demonstration. Something that aligns with the finished product."

"I'll coordinate with the tech team."

As she turned to leave, Ashenhurst's voice stopped her. "And Isabella?"

She noticed his eyes softening, his tongue probing between lips that seemed moister than before. His fingers stroked his pointed white beard.

In his haughty, fake-upper-class tone, he said, "Remember who signs your checks, Isabella. Your hesitation hasn't gone unnoticed. Are you still on board with this?"

"My loyalty is to the job, Mr. Ashenhurst. It always has been."

Knight strode out of the office. The door closed behind her with a soft click, and she allowed herself a moment to shed the man's unsettling gaze, like a dog would shake off rainwater.

As she made her way to the secure elevator, doubts about the Chinese clients gnawed at her—misgivings that Ashenhurst had ordered her to dismiss. Not just the secrecy or threat from the Americans, it was the hard deadline that bothered her most. Why would the Chinese government be so eager to acquire something if there was even the slightest chance it wasn't quite ready?

It felt more like one of Ashenhurst's arbitrary deadlines than a serious political move.

And Trapp's demise might well stall the other interested parties, but their next attempt wouldn't be agents with false names and papers.

The sooner the sale could be made, the better.

TWENTY

The air erupted with gunfire as Trapp and Grubbs sprinted across the parking lot. Bullets riddled the asphalt at their feet, sending geysers of gravel and dust into the air and peppering their legs. Subsonic rounds whistled past, their wake disturbing the air as the two men by the reception area huddled together rather than dispersing to maximize their spread. Then two more doors swung open, and men in loose, casual attire darted out with weapons primed.

"Car! Now!" Trapp shouted.

Good lord, how many times was he going to be shot at this week? He felt like he was averaging two gunfights a day.

They wove between parked vehicles for shelter. Trapp pivoted and fired two shots, taking down two of the men and sending the others scurrying for cover.

"That'll only buy a few seconds," Trapp said.

"Who the hell are they?"

"Hired muscle? Local jihadis? *That's* why Ashenhurst didn't have his people finish us back there. He knew this was waiting for us. No need to risk an execution when it can look like a terror strike."

"Terror?"

"Call it an educated guess. But these guys have the same shitty aim and tactics as the assholes at the mine. Numbers instead of strategy."

Without waiting for a debate, he grasped Grubbs' hand and pulled her back the way they'd come, toward the tinted sedan where he'd shot the man who'd pretended to be one of Henry's —ill-fitting suit, scruffy facial hair, stiff posture.

Firing off the remainder of his magazine to pin down the attackers—and to create the illusion he had more rounds than he did—Trapp yanked open the driver's side door, heaved the dead man out while snatching the Smith and Wesson from the corpse's hand, and dove in, ignoring the gore he'd spilled moments ago. Grubbs replicated his actions into the back seat and scrambled over to the passenger side.

"I'm in! Go!"

Trapp handed her the Smith as he turned the ignition. The engine roared to life, tires screeching as he floored it in reverse. Smoking rubber trailed them, closely followed by the regrouped men returning fire.

He fishtailed the vehicle out onto the road and lined the nose up with the freeway, but two vehicles approached from that direction— young men in faux-military gear out for a joyride in open-topped 4x4s.

He wrestled the wheel and accelerated, so the car spun and headed in the opposite direction. Toward the city.

Within a minute, it was a straight drag race down a long avenue, the traffic thickening as the evening surged with activity. Trapp scanned for threats and escape routes, winding the car through people departing work and narrowly evading a group of children pursuing a soccer ball from a residential block.

Grubbs gripped the headrest. "Jesus, Trapp!"

The town blurred into a montage of storefronts, cafés, and street vendors. Smartphones illuminated the faces of pedestrians oblivious to the danger until it was right on top of them.

"Any ideas on where we're headed?" Grubbs asked.

"Approximately."

"Approximately?"

"Best I can do. Lose the tail, then regroup and evac."

He swerved around a hearse, empty but for a few flowers still clinging to the inner window, then sped through an intersection, narrowly avoiding a tiny French car filled with plywood sticking out the sunroof. Trapp allowed a brief, grim smile, scolding himself for giving in to a minor thrill of adrenaline.

His relief evaporated with a glance in the rearview. The two battered vehicles—a Land Rover and a Jeep—were closing in, their exhausts belching smoke as the revs escalated.

"Company's caught up," Trapp said.

The rear window cracked and pocked with bullets from the terrorists' AK-47s but didn't shatter. Ballistic glass. It'd hold for a while.

Grubbs twisted in her seat, evaluating the threat. She checked the gun. "What am I holding here?"

"Smith and Wesson, 4506 model. It's a reliable weapon, if it's been maintained. Fully loaded, you got eight rounds in the mag. Forty-five caliber, so if you hit something, you'll only need the one shot."

"Fine." Grubbs readied it to fire and leaned out the window. "I've got three targets in the Land Rover." She fired twice, whistling in what sounded like surprise. "Make that two."

Another hail of bullets peppered their vehicle. Some people referred to ballistic glass as "bulletproof," but Trapp knew there was no such thing as bullet*proof*. Only bullet *resistant*. Eventually, with enough force, the rear window would yield.

He veered, sending a vendor's cart toppling. "Any chance you can take out their tires?"

"Driving like this? Even *you* would struggle to make that shot."

"Hold on," he said, cranking the wheel.

The car skidded into a narrow alley. The sudden maneuver caught their pursuers off guard, sending the Land Rover careening past, but the Jeep stopped to make the turn.

The alley opened to a shantytown of tents and makeshift shelters. Trapp's gut clenched at the sight. These people had nothing, and he was about to tear through their homes like a hurricane.

He eased off the gas, but not by much.

"They won't be as cautious as we are," Trapp said. "We need to make this count."

He honked the horn. People scattered, abandoning cooking fires and hauling children out of the way. The car clipped a tent, sending it tumbling.

Trapp forced himself to focus on the road. The alley ended at a wide boulevard that starkly contrasted with the poverty they had just driven through.

"Well, would you look at that," Grubbs said as they emerged onto the tree-lined street.

To their right stood the massive shopping mall they'd passed on the way in, its façade glimmering with logos of luxury brands.

"Looks closed for the night. Could work."

"What could work?"

Before he could reply, the roar of engines behind them signaled that Trapp had been right about their speed through the town. He matched their acceleration and surged ahead, mounting the curb to bypass a Mercedes.

"I can end this here." Trapp glanced in the rearview mirror again, calculating the distance, the relative speeds. "But it's gonna be messy."

A moment passed before Grubbs said, "Just do it. You know you're going to anyway."

Trapp bumped up and over the curb and veered toward the mall. The gleaming glass façade hurtled toward them, growing bigger with blistering speed.

"Brace yourself," he said.

The impact was less than he'd expected. More loud than jarring. A cacophony of shattering glass and snapping metal clattered around them as he fought to maintain control. They slalomed across the polished floor, leaving a trail of diamonds and debris in their wake.

But the place wasn't entirely empty.

"Shit." Trapp's stomach dropped.

A gaggle of stunned faces stared back at them, glasses of champagne frozen midway to their lips, canapés held aloft by waitstaff, and a buffet lined up. They had crashed into an after-hours party.

"So much for a swift ending," Grubbs said.

"New plan," he said, steering around a cluster of partygoers.

Screams filled the air as the patrons scattered en masse, champagne flutes and plates shattering on the floor. Trapp's knuckles whitened on the wheel as he swerved to avoid frantic men in tuxes steering their dates out of harm's way.

Then the pursuing vehicles crashed through the broken entrance, and gunfire erupted in deafening bursts.

"Trapp!" Grubbs shouted, ducking and covering her head as the rear window finally gave way and exploded inward. She recovered, then aimed behind them, and the Smith boomed in the tight space—one, two, three. Then three more in quick succession, as she'd have practiced at the range, before the slide racked empty. "Whatever you're planning, do it now. I'm out."

Trapp scanned ahead: the luxury car showroom he'd clocked when they entered the city.

Perfect.

He aimed the car like a torpedo.

"Hold on."

They crashed through the window into the showroom where sleek sports cars collectively worth millions of dollars lined up like glossy dominoes. Trapp felt a pang of regret as he sideswiped three of them, weaving too swiftly to identify the exact makes, but his younger self would have berated him for the damage inflicted on such exquisite machines. Paint jobs worth more than some houses were annihilated in seconds.

"What are you doing?" Grubbs yelled. "We're cornered."

"Not completely," Trapp replied, gunning it for the showroom's open front door.

The barrier to the gas pump loomed larger. He had noted it earlier when surveying the area—an unexpected alteration to the aesthetic.

With a final sweep of the wheel, Trapp bounced their battered sedan off a sleek Humvee and aimed directly at the pump. The impact jarred his teeth, but the tearing metal assured him he'd hit the mark.

As they pulled to a stop, Trapp saw that the slender pipe to the pump had ruptured, unleashing a thin but steady stream of gasoline.

"Out. Now."

As the stench of gas bloomed, mingling with burnt rubber

and exposed metal, they sprinted back into the showroom, ducking behind a gleaming red Ferrari just as the Land Rover and Jeep crashed through. The path Trapp had forged through the high-end playthings was unmistakable, and the powerful 4x4s followed it, the two men in each sweeping side to side, their AKs ready to fire as soon as they spotted Trapp and Grubbs.

But they weren't trapped. Not quite.

"We need new wheels," he said. "Think you can hotwire one of these?"

Grubbs offered a hint of a smirk. "I have a better idea." She darted toward a sleek black Maserati near the shattered window.

Trapp's hand went to his pocket, closing around the cool metal of the Zippo lighter Ashenhurst had gifted him.

The engines halted but did not shut off, and voices rose from the forecourt. They were being cautious, searching, ready to kill. No doubt they would smell the gas and be reluctant to fire indiscriminately.

Trapp glanced at Grubbs, who was focused not on the Maserati but on a key safe on the wall near an office door that read "MANAGER" in English. She had picked that lock instead of attempting to steal a $200,000 sports car directly. These days, you needed a computer for grand theft auto, not a screwdriver.

She was in, removing the key fobs one at a time, searching for the three-pronged symbol before trying the unlock button.

A Maserati convertible with the top down beeped and flashed.

The attackers' voices stopped, alerted by the new activity.

Shit.

Now they would know Trapp and Grubbs weren't outside.

No matter.

Grubbs ran to the Maserati that had beeped, slipping into the driver's seat moments before two men returned to the showroom, guns slung over their shoulders. They shouted something Trapp didn't comprehend, but it sounded like a warning.

The Maserati's engine roared to life, a deep, throbbing growl that vibrated through Trapp's ribcage. Then the passenger door popped open.

Trapp flicked open the lighter and spun the flint. The flame ignited, holding steady for several moments before he hurled it toward the leaking fuel as he dove into the Maserati's passenger seat.

"Floor it!"

Grubbs slammed her foot down.

The convertible's tires screeched against the polished floor, leaving black streaks as they tore out of the showroom and into the mall corridor. The absurdity of their situation—speeding a luxury sports car through a high-end shopping center—might have made Trapp grin if he wasn't anticipating what was about to unfold.

A deafening explosion shook the building. The shockwave hit them hard, rattling their heads and sending glass and debris cascading around them. Behind them, a massive fireball engulfed the showroom, spreading out in mushroom-shaped flames. The heat seared the back of Trapp's neck, even from this distance.

"Christ," Grubbs breathed, her eyes wide as she navigated through the chaos. "Did you know it would be that big?"

"No way of knowing how big the underground tank was. But it did the job. And the party had ended."

As they sped toward the mall's exit, the orange glow cast shadows of them on the shops they passed.

"Are you okay?" Trapp asked Grubbs, noticing a tremor in her hands.

She nodded. "Yeah. Just... processing. Remember how this was supposed to be a surveillance and intel-gathering operation?"

"You're doing great, Madison. We're almost through it."

The Maserati crashed through the already-shattered glass doors, then Grubbs steered onto the boulevard. The cool night air slapped against their sweat-slicked skin. Sirens wailed in the distance, growing louder with every second they put between the mall and themselves.

"Enjoying your ride?" Trapp asked.

Grubbs shot him a sidelong glance. She downshifted and navigated a corner smoothly. Frowned as she glanced at the dashboard. "Bad news, though. It's a showroom car—there's barely enough gas for a couple of miles."

"Then head east. We'll ditch it before we run dry and find another ride to the airport."

He leaned back in the leather seat. The adrenaline began to wane, leaving him acutely aware of every bruise and scrape.

Who exactly were these men? And if they were sent by the same people who'd run the mine, was this simple revenge, or was Ashenhurst more than just a client of theirs?

Those were questions that would have to wait.

He extracted his phone, discovered it functioning, and initiated a call to get them the hell out of the country.

TWENTY-ONE

Amid a sparse gathering of onlookers, a headscarf concealing her blond hair and Caucasian skin, Isabella Knight surveyed the wreckage, her mind calm as she controlled her breathing in a steady pattern that she'd evolved over many years. If pushed, she'd reluctantly admit it was similar to meditation. But it was not a spiritual reflection, nor even an act to clear her head to form a counter-strategy—although that was certainly a byproduct. No, concentrating on her breath, on feeling the air fill her lungs and pass up her airway and tickle the back of her mouth, was essential to prevent her from raging against the nearest person whom she could hold responsible for failure.

Or, in this case, disaster.

Rafe Ashenhurst would most certainly take it out on her. Verbally, anyway. She could handle that without ego, without striking back. Accepting blame for her boss's shortcomings was part of the job. It had been his insistence on using this rabble, who were cheaper and faster than hiring a professional team sourced from Knight's intelligence days. Twice as many hitters, half the price.

For fuck's sake...

In a UK or American city, the sidewalk would be packed with observers filming every second, taking selfies and delivering commentary. More than a sprinkling of conspiracy nuts, too. But this city was small, and although the citizens present had spent a significant portion of time recording on cellphones, the late hour and the wide police cordon had deterred the earlier throngs.

One wing of the upscale mall lay in ruins, debris strewn across the parking lot. Smoke still plumed from within, wafts of gasoline filling her nostrils as emergency services contained the aftermath. Their efforts had stemmed the spreading flames but could do little to dampen the original explosion site; containing it was their mission now.

A familiar accented voice interrupted Knight during an out-breath. But at least this one spoke passable English.

"Miss, we've searched the perimeter. No one seems to have survived."

Knight turned to the foot soldier, Halim, a man in his twenties with a nervous disposition—which was why he'd been assigned backup duty today. Knight knew he was essentially the group secretary, keeping money matters flowing, buying in kit, acquiring transport. He was a clever kid with a wealth of knowledge about a region for which borders meant nothing to Boko Haram. Now, though, with most of his team either dead or on the run, he held very still before her.

"You obtained the resources I asked for?" Knight said. "Reached out to your partners?"

Halim nodded, but uncertainty remained. "I did. But you must understand, they are recruiters. Not warriors."

Another point which Knight had communicated to Ashenhurst. But still, he'd insisted on speed over finesse, brute force over precision.

"I know you have other partners," Knight said. "Your network reaches farther than Chad and Nigeria, even if you don't. Would they be willing to travel? If we arrange it and pay them well?"

"Which partners?"

"All of them. Anyone with combat experience. They'll need to move quickly."

"Yes, Miss."

As Halim hurried away, Knight returned her attention to the mall. Her breaths deepened and slowed, but her head thickened. Ashenhurst's blind anger would only serve to hinder his objective, so Knight needed a contingency in place.

Patience.

Strategy.

These tools had elevated her to the wealthy private sector and secured her the means to retire in her late thirties, should this venture reach an amicable conclusion. Strategy would be especially crucial in the coming days. She just hoped she could convince Ashenhurst that his bull-like approach might work when demanding results from underlings in the business world, but taking out a threat like Jason Trapp was another matter entirely.

Halim returned, passing through the smattering of remaining onlookers with his head high and smile wide. He passed a phone to Knight and said, "It is unlocked. I took off the password for you and switched it to English. All the contacts you need are in there. I have sent warnings that a woman calling from this number should be trusted to make them rich."

Knight pocketed the handset. "Thank you. Is there anything else you need to tell me? Anything at all you can do that will help take out the CIA pair?"

"I do not believe so, Miss."

"Fine."

Knight slowly dropped her head, as a woman is meant to when she is concealed beneath such religious head gear, then drifted past Halim, jabbing a needle into his thigh as she moved. It was not a hypodermic, so no need for a plunger, just a single length of narrow, sharp metal, coated with a poison that attacked the body in a similar way to a rattlesnake bite. Only this concoction was around ten times more potent.

Within five seconds of emitting a tiny whimper, Halim made a choking sound. Without turning, Knight heard him stumble, and a handful of people around him gasped. She glanced back only briefly, to see him convulsing on the ground, his blood thickening, blocking arteries and backing up into his heart, killing his lungs and removing the final loose end in this awful country.

She would be glad to be free of it soon, and she would never return.

TWENTY-TWO

Mike Mitchell felt as if he had spent more time in Situation Room B than he had in his own bedroom lately. And he was growing weary of it. But if their worst-case scenario became a reality...

Karem Hines stood at the head of the room, which contained the same people as the previous day, only the screen was blank, and the sound through the speakers was a constant white noise, reminiscent of wind sweeping through a tunnel. However, the emergency transport that had whisked Trapp and Grubbs from Chad's capital city was not equipped with video satellite communications.

"I dug out the files on Ashenhurst's original proposal," Hines began. "I told you before that he had proposed a breakthrough for directed energy weapons but was low on detail, and the cost was ludicrous. It barely passed over my desk before the accountants nixed it."

"We're not here to assign blame," Mitchell said. "No need to cover your ass. Just give me your analysis now you that have more detail."

Hines seemed to be assessing Mitchell's intent, as if weighing up his need to keep his job over national security. Mitchell did not give a single shit about the mistake, if indeed it was his; he just needed intel.

Hines said, "His original proposal was never viable. But I've re-modeled the estimates based on blends of titanium, niobium, and other theoretical combinations, along with factoring in the ultra-low temperatures that we didn't think were feasible—"

"Less waffle, please," Mitchell said. "We don't know how long the connection will hold."

Hines sighed. "The formula would allow for unprecedented focusing of electromagnetic radiation, which could—and I emphasize *could*—lead to improved DEW efficiency and miniaturization potential. And I'm talking orders of magnitude beyond the kit we think was used in Pittsburgh."

"How?" Trapp's voice had an echo behind it, as if Grubbs' mic was picking up his voice, too, as he shouted over the military transport's engine noise. "And what could they do with it?"

"The process is not straightforward," Hines continued. "In conventional weapons, brute force is a significant factor, with R&D focused on generating power, maintaining thermal regulation, and maximizing range. What Ashenhurst Group initially proposed was a laser enhancement. So it would not simply be a microwave burst, either in low wavelength to trigger illness—"

"Illness like Havana Syndrome," Trapp said.

"Right. Either in low wavelengths to induce illness or higher wavelengths with more powerful beams that are hot and kinetic."

"Kinetic?" Mitchell inquired.

"Physical force behind the heated blast. Normally to scale up the power and range, the origin point—the 'gun,' if you want to simplify it—must increase in size. But if the superconductor removes all resistance from the power output, a far more condensed and focused microwave blast becomes possible."

"For which the ore taken from the mine would be invaluable?" Mitchell pressed.

"Correct. We don't know how they arrived at the formula, but theoretically, they must have resolved the challenge of both the microwave blooming and the low temperature requirements. They could even add a lightweight laser to keep the target in focus."

"Like a laser-guided missile?" Trapp asked. "But leaves no trace...?"

"A bit more complicated, but like that, yes."

"So in effect," Polly Garside said, "shifting power that would usually be lost to enhance the directed energy. Make it more focused."

"Again, it's more complicated than that, but you've got the gist."

"But the computational power would be vast too, surely? Cycling all that energy, running the coolant at the right temperature and the right quantities, and keeping the laser focus regulated to counter that 'blooming' effect you keep mentioning. It couldn't be on the device itself."

"You're right. It would require a massive bank of interlinked servers."

"You'd need somewhere to base that," Trapp said. "Meaning we can take it out."

"Correct."

Madison Grubbs spoke down the same noisy, echoing line as Trapp. "Sir, Ashenhurst holds a real grudge that we wouldn't fund his project. Even if we double what the Chinese are offering, he won't sell to us. I think he wants us to know that he's beaten us—and he holds power over us."

Hines dragged one hand over his face, fatigue wearing him down. "All because our bean counters told him 'no.' Like a toddler throwing a tantrum."

"A toddler with Chinese backers," Polly said. "And terrorists on tap."

"Let's not dwell on past decisions," Mitchell said. "We need to discuss next steps."

"Take them out?" Trapp proposed. "Remove Ashenhurst from the board, dismantle his operation. Use the information seized to develop the weapon ourselves."

"Are we looking at much smaller weapons?" Mitchell asked. "As easily smuggled as regular guns?"

Karem nodded. "Exactly. Or even drones, if you can also find a way to deploy the payload."

Trapp said, "Christ. Everything's going remote these days, even murder."

Although Trapp's words carried a hint of dark humor, Mitchell had seen the FBI report on Pittsburgh. "We still aren't sure if this is the Beijing government or the faction we dismantled in New York. If it's the latter, we have better options. If it's a legitimate pact with the Chinese, we'll have to be more cautious. Eliminate Ashenhurst's ability to sell. Dismantle the means of production."

"What are we looking at?" Hines asked. "A strike on the headquarters in Chad?"

"I don't think that will be effective," Madison answered. "The HQ is nothing but a façade. It might be operational in time, but at the moment, there's no refinery, no operations on-site."

"So where could the real operation be?" Mitchell asked. "Based on what Karem said, there must be practically an entire factory."

"That's the concern, sir," Grubbs continued. "The final

product must be assembled already. Somewhere the Chinese can test it."

She paused, and Mitchell could almost hear the gears cranking over the radio.

"The Chinese are the key, not Ashenhurst. Something in Trapp's earlier debrief about the mine..."

Her voice trailed off, and Mitchell leaned closer to the speaker. "Grubbs?"

"Sir, I need to go offline for a sec. There's something in the intel that slipped by. I won't take long."

Mitchell didn't hesitate. "Do what you need to do."

The line went dead.

Hines removed his glasses, rubbing the bridge of his nose. "If our adversaries acquire viable, field-ready units in significant numbers, we'll fall way behind before we can formulate a response."

"How long?" Mitchell asked. "Before we're outmatched?"

"Months. Worst-case scenario, weeks."

Polly looked like she wanted to speak, but an analyst seconded to Mitchell's key operation might be hesitant to speak up. Mitchell nodded to her.

"I realize we've strayed from the original mission," Polly said steadily. "But if we simply eliminate the current players, the threat remains. Someone else will seize control of the superconductor and the formula for maximizing the power. We need to dismantle the *entire* operation." She held on Mitchell a long moment before adding, "Sir."

Which meant taking down the Chinese faction involved, risking diplomatic disaster if things went wrong.

Hines asked, "Is Jason Trapp the right man for this? Him and Grubbs?"

"Absolutely," Mitchell replied without hesitation. "He may

have caused some difficulties for us, but his instincts have been correct so far."

As if on cue, Trapp's voice came through the speakers. "Grubbs has something."

Grubbs joined him. "It was in the transcript, sir. Obasee mentioned a finance guy. We don't have an exact location, but..." She paused. "Twenty-four hours. We'll track down whoever is facilitating the transactions, and from there, we can present a robust plan of action."

Mitchell nodded, while Polly maintained a neutral expression. Only Hines appeared uneasy, his fingers drumming on his thigh.

"Deputy Director," Hines said. "I caution you that this pair failed in their previous mission, then went completely off-script." He adjusted his glasses, a nervous tic that Mitchell had come to recognize in their short time together. "The risks are—"

"Necessary," Mitchell said. "Making undercover deals isn't Trapp's forte. But this is where he excels."

Hines furrowed his brow. "And what exactly is it that Trapp excels at?"

A smile tugged at the corners of Mitchell's mouth.

"You'll see," he replied.

TWENTY-THREE

Trapp's hand hovered inches from the concealed Glock at his hip. He wore another suit and another pair of fake-leather shoes to create the impression he belonged, but this time, his outfit was not to camouflage him to fool their target but to drift through an Abuja apartment block unnoticed long enough to locate their only lead to the money—and therefore, the weapon's manufacture.

"Still clear," he reported to Grubbs and Ikem, the subvocalized mic and earpiece functioning well. "Approaching the northeast stairwell."

Having returned to Nigeria to share their intel, Jelany Ikem was back on their detail, quarterbacking them as they—very unofficially—followed up. They needed to proceed in a way that Ikem's NIA was not allowed to and which the domestic SSS would not—officially—sanction.

Trapp scanned the corridor constantly, every door a potential ambush, every corner harboring an unseen bodyguard. After all, why would a man like this not protect himself? Just because their stakeout had revealed no security didn't mean he had none.

But there was no one here that Trapp could see. No sounds, except those he'd expect from a residential building in a wealthy suburb. He passed a stowed cleaning cart without incident and slipped into the stairwell, pulling the heavy fire door shut behind him with a clunk. The echo reverberated through the concrete chamber, and he cringed, listening for any hint that someone was coming to investigate.

Nothing.

He ascended swiftly and quietly, and at the top landing, he paused where a keycard reader glowed red beside the exit. Pulling a thin metal tool from his jacket pocket, he whispered, "I'm here. Going silent. Sixty seconds."

"Understood," Grubbs answered.

Trapp wedged the tool into the narrow gap between the doors, probing for the release bar. Metal scraped against metal, a barely audible scratch which in a situation like this might as well have been a gunshot.

Still, no one appeared.

The latch yielded with a soft *thunk*.

"I'm in," he said, easing the door open. "Moving to the target."

He stepped onto the penthouse level, eyes left, then right, his suit jacket open for a quick draw of the sidearm should he need it.

"Status on the alarms?" he asked.

"Disabled, but I couldn't breach the locks. You're on your own for access."

Trapp acknowledged and approached the target door—a mahogany surface polished to a gleam under recessed lighting. He retrieved a small, putty-like explosive from the pouch resting flush against his skin under his shirt and pulled it into two pieces, positioning the charges and pea-sized detonators near the door's hinges.

As he retreated to one of the sconces, he took out his phone and called up the correct app, recalling how he had tutted and grumbled like an old man as he asked Grubbs why everything had to be accessed via smartphone these days.

These days.

You're getting old, Trapp. Move with the times.

Two muffled whumps like firecrackers going off. The deadbolts' housing splintered. Trapp hurried from cover, and his foot connected solidly with the door, sending it crashing inward. He surged inside, weapon drawn as he entered the apartment. Anyone inside would be disoriented already, giving him an edge, even if there were superior numbers.

No one in the bathroom—bigger than his first apartment.

Bedroom empty—messy, sheets strewn, clothes for men and women on the floor and furniture.

Main living area—occupied. Sunken sofa, open French doors, a hot tub bubbling on the balcony outside. Three figures frozen in shock—two on the sofa, one leaping to his feet.

The leaping man, bulky and dressed in a cheap-looking tracksuit, lunged at Trapp with surprising speed. Trapp sidestepped, then his free hand shot out, striking the attacker's throat. The man gasped and stumbled. Trapp's knee connected with his head, dropping him unconscious, leaving two.

"Anyone else feeling heroic?" Trapp asked.

The young Black woman—cropped hair, pink bikini, trembling—shook her head vigorously. The other man, also Black but middle-aged and dressed in swim shorts and an open, loud shirt revealing a belly and impressive moobs, raised his hands in a placating gesture.

"Report," Grubbs said.

The fallen man was not exactly professional security, more of a brawler. This pair was surrendering with the sort of terror he'd seen only in civilians experiencing violence for the first time or in the eyes of hostages being rescued who had scarcely dared hope they might live after all.

"You," he said to the man. "Are you Dembe Lowe?"

A deeper fear flashed across the man's face.

"I asked you a question," Trapp said. "How you answer will dictate the rest of your afternoon. Are. You. Dembe. Lowe?"

The man swallowed, then nodded.

Trapp said, "Target acquired."

"Target?" Dembe said in a high-pitched voice. "I—I am a—a..."

"Relax." Trapp allowed the gun's barrel to dip but not waver. "I could've shot you ten times by now. Give me what I need, and you can go back to... whatever this is you're doing."

Dembe nodded again. Jerky. Panicked. Trapp could practically smell his fear.

Good—that made him pliable.

"Come on up," Trapp said. "All clear."

"Understood," Grubbs replied.

Trapp's mind shifted into a higher gear, cataloguing tasks. "You two, against the wall. Hands where I can see them."

As they complied, Trapp restrained the unconscious man using zip ties from his pouch.

The woman whimpered as he approached her next. "Please, I'm just—"

"You won't be hurt," Trapp interrupted. "Just cooperate."

He tied her hands before her with more zip ties and secured Dembe Lowe's behind his back, then guided the pair back to the bathroom he'd passed. He kept Dembe in sight while he threaded another couple of ties through the woman's wrist binding and attached this to a sturdy-looking pipe behind the wash basin. She was sobbing as he finished.

Trapp hated to frighten civilians this way, but sympathy was a luxury none of them could afford.

By the time he emerged to usher Dembe toward what turned out to be a home office, Grubbs had arrived. She eyed the array of screens on a glass desk with a variety of neon strips—it looked like something a teenage gamer would design.

"Impressive setup." Her gaze shifted to Dembe, who sat rigid in the ergonomic chair Trapp had placed him in. "Let's not waste time. You're the intermediary between the Chinese arms trade and the Ashenhurst Group?"

Dembe shook his head, unable to look at Trapp and the gun he held at his side. "Arms... no, no, I swear, I do nothing wrong. Nothing illegal." Sweat trickled down his forehead. "I am legitimate. One hundred percent. I just... I facilitate payments for people who want to remain anonymous."

Trapp scoffed. "Ignorance, especially willful ignorance, is no excuse for what you're doing."

"You don't understand," Dembe insisted. "I help people. Refugees. People who need to transfer money without governments tracking them. I use crypto, stable stocks. My cut is small—just five percent to cover costs. I make most of my money other ways. Mainstream trading."

As he studied Dembe's reaction, a glimmer of something gave Trapp pause. An exchanged glance with Grubbs suggested they were thinking the same way.

"Let's say we believe you," Grubbs said. "If it's true that you're such a charity-driven soul, why are you involved with the Chinese?"

Dembe's eyes widened. "I'm not! I assist people fleeing China. I do not work with their government, and certainly not arms dealers. I fund campaigns, I help find jobs and ways to bank in modern times without cash, but I stay out of the heavy stuff."

Grubbs stepped forward, standing over the man, half-naked in his swim shorts, his flabby belly spilling from his shirt. She said, "You might think you're not in deep, but your name is connected to some serious shit."

Trapp watched Dembe's face, searching for any hint of deceit, but all he saw was confusion. If he was lying, the finance man was one of the best operatives he'd encountered in years.

Grubbs continued, "What can you tell us about Zhao Ming?"

At the mention of Zhao Ming, the name that had come up during Trapp's brief interrogation of Obasee in his office, Dembe's expression shifted.

"Zhao Ming?" he said, a shiver of nerves in his voice. "She is a... she is not an arms dealer. She is a hero. Based in Taiwan, a refugee herself. She aids others and performs remarkable work. Like me, yes, she makes good money in the markets, but... we do not aid arms dealers. And China—they are who we hide people from."

Trapp leaned in closer. "Ming's name came up in connection with a mine run by Boko Haram—one employing slave labor. Your name has been linked to Zhao Ming. Since we couldn't locate her, we had to come to you. We need everything. All your dealings, all your transactions, all your clients. Easy way or hard, it's your choice."

Dembe froze. Trapp could almost see the man's mind turning behind his eyes.

When Dembe finally spoke, his voice started shaky but gained strength with each word. "No, you're wrong. Zhao Ming would never be involved in something like that. Never."

Trapp and Grubbs remained silent.

"Zhao Ming isn't a slaver. She's a hero who has saved countless lives." Dembe took a deep breath. "I won't let you tarnish her name. I will give you nothing."

Trapp sighed. "Okay, the hard way it is."

TWENTY-FOUR

"It's done," Madison declared, stretching her neck and spine to little effect.

Her eyes rested on the screen as she released an involuntary breath. While she was familiar with basic code and the nuances of digital tracking, investigating financial criminality was mentally draining. She'd been at this for two hours, utilizing passwords provided with virtually no resistance as Dembe Lowe ardently tried to prove his innocence, even as he refused to entertain the prospect that Zhao Ming was anything but a saint.

Trapp had been lingering, pacing and drinking Dembe's coffee. He'd even freed the woman from the washbasin, providing her with a robe and a place on the couch beside what had turned out to be a friend of Dembe's, who had since regained consciousness. He didn't appear to have a concussion, but his headache would linger for a while. All three were made comfortable—well, as comfortable as one can be with wrists bound in zip-ties—while Trapp monitored them. He wasn't taking any chances.

When Trapp peeked into the study, Madison added, "Dembe's legitimate. So far as I can tell, anyway. His clients are funneled through an offshore server with robust VPN cover."

She pulled up a series of documents that corroborated some of what Dembe had disclosed to them.

"He's entwined with Zhao Ming and her non-profit work, some of it straddling a very thin line of legality in most countries, especially the EU, which is where most of the refugees are headed. Backtracing the transactions reveals links to a few of the Ashenhurst Group's philanthropic offshoots."

Trapp kept half an eye on the trio, visible from the open door. "Okay, clarify 'philanthropic offshoots.'"

"Donating to charity and good causes as a tax write-off, then selling goods and services to those charities."

"So giving with one hand, taking with the other."

"Exactly. But here's the meat." She navigated through a couple of other screens and pointed to a graph. "There's been a rapid sell-off of shares in European power firms and Taiwanese tech companies—mostly shell corps with no parent companies listed but ties to banks in Hong Kong. Dembe and Zhao Ming were looking into it and considering piggybacking the trades."

"Why would Dembe do that?"

"A common tactic for small-time, aspiring-to-be-big-time traders. Follow what the super-rich are doing in the markets and imitate them as swiftly as possible. Got money to invest? The only people better to follow than the likes of Warren Buffet and Rafe Ashenhurst are the politicians in Congress and the Senate. They're immune from insider trading."

Trapp frowned. "Really? That's, like, ten years in prison for most people."

"The higher up the chain you are, the more insulated you become." She snapped her fingers and pointed again at the trades. "If you're on the inside and you learn that Microsoft is poised to supply the Pentagon's new cloud computing contract, you better adjust your portfolio to include Microsoft; if you're aware that something substantial is going to disrupt a country's tech industry, you sell ASAP."

"So someone out there, probably Chinese someones, have something major on the horizon."

"A significant win for rivals, or an event that significantly affected the Taiwanese markets."

Trapp pondered for a lengthy moment. "Like what?"

"I don't know. After 9/11, the CIA learned that numerous Saudi nationals and individuals from Al-Qaeda-associated countries had shorted airlines across the board. They made millions from it."

"Shorting—that's like gambling the stock will go down, right?"

"Right. But it's a great way to get caught, if you're too good at it. So selling is better than risking a—"

From the other room, Dembe coughed.

Trapp spun around, gun at the ready. Madison realized he hadn't checked on them in at least thirty seconds.

Trapp asked, "What?"

"I could make some suggestions," Dembe said. When no one instructed him to stop, he continued. "I believe the Ashenhurst Group has a major contract in the pipeline along with some Chinese businesses that we have not identified. Zhao Ming trusts them to fulfill their promises to our clients, and I can find nothing to indicate she is mistaken. On the other hand, of course, if a significant disaster were to occur that halted production of... er, to take one example, fracking... it could spell trouble for the industry."

"Why fracking?" Madison inquired.

"I do not know. Only that Mr. Ashenhurst bid for a new fracking contract in England, then withdrew from the running. Rumors that the government made their decision on the winning company before the bids were submitted. Not uncommon."

Trapp stopped short of thanking him, returning to Madison.

"Shrewd move," she said. "And I don't see anything in Dembe's work that indicates he's a part of it."

"Just benefiting from it."

"I know nothing," Dembe called in a pleading tone. "Please, it sounds like you are trying to rectify a great injustice. But I showed you that I knew nothing of them. Let me return to my work."

Trapp faced him again, stepping through the doorframe and holding position, gun by his side. "But now you do know. Are you going to reverse these investments? Are you going to stop working with the Ashenhurst Group?"

"I..." Dembe stared at Trapp, glancing at Grubbs as if she might support him. Then his head bowed. "I will conduct my own investigation. I will reverse anything that profits from slavery."

"Why Taiwan?" Trapp asked Grubbs. "Why not Silicon Valley firms? London?"

"Maybe something to do with the manufacturing side," Grubbs said. "The chips? They rely on precious metals, and if this superconductor can be mass-produced by one company, there's no reason to stop at DEWs."

"China wouldn't attack Taiwan directly, surely? Not to blow away a few computer chips. It's an unofficial American protectorate."

Grubbs gave a sad smile and a shrug. "They are a democracy a hundred miles off the coast of a budding authoritarian empire. But that's not why we protect them."

"It's not?"

"Nope. The industrious little bastards figured out how to turn sand into solid gold."

"You're talking about computer chips?"

"That's right. The US has spent the last eighty years blundering into Saudi Arabia's wars, and you know why?"

"Because we need their oil more than they need us."

"Exactly. Now we've got our own oil. Produce more of it than the Saudis do. But the Taiwanese make the chips, and they do it better than anyone else in the world. And unfortunately for America, no one's prospecting for silicon in the Permian Basin."

"And if niobium is the new silicon..." Trapp didn't need to finish. He faced Dembe, whose head had dropped. "And all this, you could have alerted someone about it."

When Dembe lifted his head, his eyes glistened. "I still do not believe that Zhao Ming is malevolent. Just because she allies with men like Rafe Ashenhurst does not render her a bad person."

Trapp glanced at Grubbs, moving to her other side so he could observe the three people in the lounge more clearly. "Is Zhao Ming malevolent?"

She checked her phone. "Let's see." She dialed Washington, a pre-arranged line where the right people were waiting.

"Mitchell." The gruff voice through the speaker was accompanied by the background noise of someone working a keyboard.

Madison said, "We've done everything we can at our end. How's your deep dive?"

"Hines and Garside are here. I'll let Polly explain."

"Grubbs, you're invaluable." Polly Garside's cheerful voice unexpectedly brightened the room. "That backdoor into Dembe's system is pure gold."

"Or silicon," Trapp commented with a wry smile. Then he asked Polly, "What have you got?"

"Right, so Zhao Ming? Turns out she *was* officially residing in Taiwan as a refugee. I see she was facilitating payments to assist dissidents. But here's the kicker—she's been communicating directly with Ashenhurst Group for a year. Well, with his top money people. It's not like she has Isabella Knight's personal cellphone number in her cloud account."

Trapp threw a pointed glance at Dembe, who responded with a frown.

"And now?" Trapp asked. "You emphasized she *was* in Taiwan."

"She relocated to one of her bank's other international locations," Garside said. "Along with several colleagues."

Madison felt a quiver in her stomach, the thrill of progress. "So is she a villain or a victim?"

Mitchell's voice interjected. "The last time I saw an exodus like this was right before a major attack in Islamabad. Polly, how many of Ming's colleagues departed?"

"At least a dozen," Polly replied.

"Jesus," Trapp said. "So it might not be the mining operations we need to be concerned about. We really are looking at a potential attack on Taiwan."

"Disputed territory," Hines said.

"Only if you're Chinese," Mitchell said. "The world recognizes Taiwan's independence. Beijing wants to repatriate it, like they did Hong Kong."

"What else do we have on Ming?" Madison asked. "Current location?"

After a brief pause, Hines said, "The Chinese military have

maneuvers planned in the South China Sea this week. They've strengthened their presence around Taiwan for years, but the timing feels too coincidental."

Trapp shook his head, his expression hardening. "But all this so far points to the same faction who infiltrated the peace talks in New York. Not the Chinese government."

"Trapp's right," Madison said. "Even if they wanted to execute an attack on Taiwan, what would China actually gain? The international backlash would be immense."

She stood, pacing as she articulated her thoughts. "Plus, these are high-energy weapons. That kind of technology... with their navy and air force so close... it would be like signing their name to the attack."

Trapp looked at her, still glancing back into the lounge. "What's your theory, then?"

She paused, carefully selecting her words. "It's not impossible, but maybe Zhao Ming and company aren't fleeing an attack. Perhaps Ashenhurst or his backers are moving her to protect their money. If they're funneling it to the traffickers via Zhao Ming's charities, they'll protect her."

"Or, instead of escaping, they could be moving *toward* something."

"True," Mitchell conceded. "But equally, we don't know how deeply the rebel factions have infiltrated their own institutions. Their ambassador was complicit. Who's to say military leaders aren't also involved?"

"You're suggesting a bloodless coup has already occurred?" Grubbs said.

"Even a minor incident," Hines added. "It all accumulates. An 'accidental' discharge affecting Taiwanese territory could sow doubt in the population. Psychological warfare. Escalating the threat level without committing to a full-scale invasion. Just something that brings them inches closer to what they perceive as *their* sovereign territory. Maybe it would be a test for *us*—would we really declare war on China if there was no proof they were behind the attack?"

"I'm open to any possibilities right now," Mitchell said. "We all need to be."

Nobody spoke for the longest time.

Trapp broke the silence. "Let's get to the heart of this, then. I see three options." He raised his fingers as he enumerated them. "Do nothing and hope for the best. Execute coordinated assaults to eliminate all the players we know about. Or continue on the money trail."

Madison had already plotted her preferred course. "We follow the money. It's our best chance at apprehending them all. Whatever motive these companies have for the big sell-off, it could be huge."

"Where is Zhao Ming now?" Trapp said.

Polly Garside's usual perkiness was tinged with a serious undertone. "London. She and her associates just established themselves in a subsidiary of their Taiwanese bank. Anyone want to guess who their sole client in the UK is?"

"Ashenhurst Group," Trapp stated, not even a question.

"Bingo," Polly replied.

"Then we need fresh IDs and clearance with MI5. Give me an hour with Zhao Ming, and we'll be on our way."

"It won't be that simple," Mitchell said. "The Brits don't appreciate foreigners operating like that, especially in the heart of their financial institutions. It can rub party donors the wrong way."

Trapp gave a humorless laugh and formed a grim smile, placing a hand on Madison's shoulder. "In that case, my new bride and I are going on our honeymoon. Sightseeing."

When he felt her tense, Trapp withdrew his hand from her shoulder and hit the button that severed the line.

"Rude," she said.

"He'll come through."

"No, I meant the bride thing." She smiled. "You didn't even ask my dad for permission."

"Pack your bags," he instructed her, heading back to free the prisoners. "We've got a plane to catch."

TWENTY-FIVE

As Jason Trapp and Madison Grubbs disembarked from their flight at Heathrow Airport, they exited the cabin into a tunnel insulating them against the drizzle that had speckled the windows as they'd landed. There was no sign of a welcome party in the gangway, but Trapp had half-expected someone to meet them. He'd had no contact with Mike Mitchell or the team back in Washington during the flight from Lagos International, so he was relying on updates filtering through once his cell phone connected to a local provider.

"Ever been to the UK?" Grubbs asked him.

"Once. A training exercise," Trapp replied, not elaborating on the nature of what he'd experienced alongside counterparts from the SAS and the German special forces unit from the *Kommando Spezialkräfte*.

"Have much experience with MI5?"

Trapp wished she didn't feel the need to chit-chat. They'd reached the concourse, and he had already picked up on four men and one woman following them. The surveillance team was good, blending in enough that they would not draw attention or undue questions from the public, but they clearly wanted Trapp to know they were there as he and Grubbs joined the arduous, winding line at passport control.

"MI6, sure," Trapp answered, "Royal Marines, SAS, and regular army. Don't remember crossing paths with MI5. But then if they were doing their jobs properly, I wouldn't know it was them, would I?"

Grubbs replied with an eye roll and said, "Let me save you the trouble. MI5 is domestic intelligence, unlike MI6, which operates abroad."

"Yeah, I know *that* much."

"They're watching us."

"I know that too."

After taking the civilian route through passport control, they made their way to baggage claim. The place was swarming with people from two flights, and everyone seemed to believe their rightful place was at the head of the line. Although "line" was probably a rather kind way of labeling the rabble that surrounded the conveyor belts, which were currently empty.

Then a shorter but incredibly stocky man appeared in Trapp's peripheral vision. He stared at them, his hands clasped before him. No effort to blend in the way the rest of the surveillance team had. It was as if this man was saying, "What if the two intelligence operatives didn't spot the watchers that we placed in very obvious positions and failed to be intimidated by our presence?" The man was older, at least mid-fifties, but was built like a linebacker. His bald head and worn, ruddy face gave him the appearance of a fighting dog.

Grubbs said, "They call them bulls, you know."

Trapp glanced between the man and Grubbs. "Who?"

"MI5 tactical units, plain-clothed guys—usually guys—who do the hands-on work for the intelligence officers."

"Like SWAT?"

"Not quite. They're usually more covert than that, snatching targets or taking down a threat where a uniformed response would tip them off. Usually ex-military with a bad attitude."

The "bull" turned his head, and Trapp decided to smile and give a little wave. The bull did not wave back.

They hurried through baggage claim, weaving between family members awaiting returning loved ones, some holding homemade welcome signs. There were at least three "daddies," with hearts and stars and glitter adorning the paper, and more than a few "mummies," along with some monikers that were clearly embarrassing nicknames. It wasn't quite the hubbub of a rock star or sports team returning home, yet it was busier than Trapp had expected.

But not so busy that he missed the man who walked parallel to them.

Unlike the bull and the not-so-covert surveillance team, this man had not stood out until he chose to in this moment: hipster-style beard, a soccer team's baseball cap, denim jacket over a white T-shirt, beige cargo pants, white sneakers, and a slight slump to his posture—a slump that healed itself as soon as he fell into step with Trapp and Grubbs. Until that point, Trapp might not have looked at him twice. A flicker in his eyes and the smallest stretch of his lips told Trapp he knew he'd been made.

Could've been that the change in posture wasn't intentional, that he was now on high alert and light on his feet in case he needed to move quickly. Or he wanted to be spotted, a power play to prove he could've remained hidden if he chose to. He even allowed the denim jacket to flap open a little wider, like a declaration to either Trapp or the bulls in the area.

No weapon within quick-draw range.

"Any idea who our shadow is?" Trapp asked.

Grubbs had plainly spotted him too. "No, but we haven't been briefed yet."

As if of one mind, they both pulled out their phones to see if there were any messages, which there were not.

"The House must be empty," Grubbs remarked.

"The House?" Trapp said.

"Thames House. MI5's HQ here in London."

"Thank you, Ms. Wikipedia." Trapp hefted his carry-on bag tighter to his body and patted it. "If nobody is going to say hi, that's fine by me."

"What now?"

All Trapp wanted to know was who was who, whether the expert was part of the MI5 team or if he was a threat. "Play the part for now. If you don't mind."

She allowed Trapp to put his hand around her waist, and like a couple arriving in a new country for the first time, diverted to a small store selling cheap souvenir items. There was an age gap, but not an obscene one, so they could sell it should any local law enforcement come into play. Trapp knew that MI5 could not intervene in anything but limited circumstances, such as terrorism and espionage. Watching the crowd, scanning for the aging hipster guy and not finding him, he watched the stocky bundle of muscle that intentionally stood out as he and Grubbs browsed.

They were no threat. They just wanted him to know they were watching, that they knew he was in the country.

Satisfied, Trapp bought a Union Flag pin made of metal, attached it to his T-shirt, and threw the bull a thumbs-up. Then, once Grubbs had paid for a "Mind the Gap" apron, they resumed their path out of Heathrow and into a light drizzle. Grubbs shook off Trapp's hand as soon as they reached the taxi rank.

THE LONDON Underground train doors opened, disgorging a tributary of people into the river of a hot, tightly packed station. Swimming against the incoming tide, Trapp and Grubbs were jostled this way and that as they maneuvered through the crowd until they finally managed to negotiate their way to the escalator, ascend up into the light, and scan their digital tickets at the barrier, which permitted them egress into one of London's wealthiest areas.

Canary Wharf was a financial fortress of glass and steel. Its towers crowded the skyline, and the air smelled faintly of the Thames—brackish yet industrial. As Trapp and Grubbs approached the central plaza, men and women in business suits moved with purpose through the grid of sharp lines and polished surfaces. Trapp felt scruffy in his jeans, T-shirt, and dark blue flannel jacket.

After they'd settled into separate hotel rooms—making an instant lie of their ruse as a couple—Trapp and Grubbs made their way toward the river where pockets of tourists were taking selfies and pictures of each other posing with the financial district in the background. He'd chosen a café called River View as their destination because it had a view of not only the River Thames but a 180-degree sweep of the nearby shops.

Although the fine mist of rain had since ceased, the threat of more had not diminished, so Trapp led Grubbs inside through the sliding glass doors, past an outer deck patronized by a few hardy Londoners in coats amid potted plants and aluminum chairs. There was also a separate bar, shuttered for now.

As soon as the door closed behind them, a tall, well-built man stood from his table, and Grubbs trotted toward him. Trapp joined the pair and shook the man's hand.

"Ikem, great that you could make it."

Grubbs gave him a friendly peck on the cheek as if greeting a friend. "Jelany, lovely spot we've found here."

"Yes, very lovely," Ikem replied, matching the elevated volume from both Americans. "So glad you suggested it."

"How was your flight?" Trapp asked.

"Fine, fine," Ikem replied. "Even the baby in the row behind me slept all the way through."

If there were ears nearby, they would hear only small talk. Although it might not fool the people from Thames House, it would starve listeners of facts until Trapp could identify who, if anyone, was eavesdropping nearby. There were middle-aged women enjoying a chat, a scruffy man with an open laptop who seemed uninterested in anything but his screen, and a young couple making goo-goo eyes over frothy glasses of something.

Trapp had been pleasantly surprised when the NIA had allowed Ikem to follow them to the UK. The original plan had been for the Nigerian agent to keep them under surveillance and warn of incoming trouble. But since they had been denied cooperation from MI5, who had made the point of saying "we're watching every move you make," it seemed pointless to continue with the charade of not knowing each other.

They continued banal pleasantries while ordering coffees and pastries, then took to a table where they could observe comings and goings while remaining far enough away from the windows to negate the effects of a radar mic on the glass.

"If I may speak plainly now," Ikem said, "what is our plan?"

"We got more metadata and intel mined from apps we know Zhao Ming uses," Trapp replied. "She has a routine but isn't obsessive about it."

"I thought she moved here recently," Ikem said.

"Recent is a relative term," Grubbs said. "She's been commuting between Taiwan and London for six months now.

When she's in London, she has a few favorite spots. One of them is just down there."

She was referring to the small plaza one story down from the café, in a C-shaped expanse of boutiques, a couple of bars and eateries, a donut stall, and Libby Elizabeth's Fitness Studio. Zhao Ming had a membership to the fitness studio in her phone's wallet and used it every Wednesday to attend a spin class at six p.m. whenever she was in London for more than two weeks.

"We've arranged for a rental car to be dropped in the underground parking lot," Grubbs answered. "It should be clean, but we'll sweep it anyway."

"CCTV?" Ikem asked.

"Minimal," Trapp said.

London was one of the most observed cities in the world, but there were still parts where the authorities were blind. For now.

"Her usual route from her office building to the studio is well covered. But the stairs are exposed—there's a twelve-foot gap where no one can be seen until they're already on the main plaza."

"No need to liberate the financial capital of Europe then," Ikem said.

Trapp smiled. "I'm hoping it goes a little more smoothly than the last extraction."

Ikem laughed gently, and his eyes flicked to the door, his half-open mouth frozen briefly before resuming his casual nature.

Trapp had spotted them too.

Three men with broad shoulders and close-cropped hair in smart suits had entered and were standing just inside, looking around. One of them made a beeline for the counter while the others settled around a table too small for their elbows to rest upon comfortably.

"Could just be gym bros," Grubbs said.

"Could be," Trapp agreed. "If they're supposed to be undercover surveillance, they're probably the worst I've ever seen."

Ikem stretched his fingers, then curled them into a fist before stretching them out again. "They could also be an extraction team sent to extract *our* extraction team."

"Anyone ever tell you that you have a great way with words?" Trapp glanced at the men, who were chatting among themselves. The third man was perusing the cakes. Trapp heard him ask if the brownie was vegan.

Gym muscles, big presence, no interest...

"I think we're good," Trapp said.

Grubbs fished her phone out and pretended to use the front camera to assess her hair while snapping photographs of the trio, then sent the pictures to Washington.

"So," Trapp said, "are we set?"

A chair scraped. The scruffy man who'd been working on a laptop nearby rose from his place, shut the laptop, and swept it up. After returning his cup to the counter, which was acknowledged by the barista with thanks, the man strode toward the exit. It was only as he neared that Trapp got a good look at him and noted the athletic build beneath the man's open jacket and the confident gait with which he carried himself. His wrists bore the unmistakable rope of a cable-like forearm, even though Trapp couldn't see the rest of him.

"Keep cool," Trapp told Grubbs and Ikem. "We're about to have company."

Trapp made no disguise of watching him. And the man made no effort to pretend he wasn't headed their way. He kept his hands in plain sight, holding the laptop in one as he pulled up a chair with the other. "Mind if I join you?"

"I'm guessing you'll join us anyway," Trapp replied. "Feeling shy at the airport?"

"You got it." The man had changed clothes and shed what must have been a false beard, but the way he walked, the ice-cool expression, and now his candor, told Trapp it was the same guy—and yes, he was very good at surveillance.

The guy took a seat, then placed the laptop on the table, keeping his hands on top of it. Trapp would treat the item as a recording device and not say anything incriminating. They might already have been bugged.

The newcomer offered his hand to Trapp. "Cameron Kane."

So as not to make a scene, Trapp shook it and was impressed by the grip. In return, he strengthened his own, to which the man calling himself Cameron Kane smiled and gripped harder still.

Trapp decided to be the bigger man and withdraw first.

Kane said, "It's not a pseudonym. You can have me vetted to your heart's content as soon as I've gone."

"You and your friends here to warn us off again?" Grubbs asked.

Kane chuckled and glanced derisively at the three men now sitting together, hunched over with their shoulders tensed as if wanting to impress someone. "Oh, they're not with me. They're not with anyone, as I'm sure you can tell." He looked pointedly at Trapp with that comment.

"If you're not Five, then who are you?" Trapp asked.

"Oh, I'm something much worse."

TWENTY-SIX

"I doubt any private interest has the ability to track and follow American citizens quite like us," Grubbs said. "So who are you?"

Kane carried with him a constantly amused expression, as if whatever was said to him was naïve or downright stupid. His accent sounded northern but not quite as far north as Scotland. Trapp didn't know enough to guess more specifically than that.

"I'm a peacekeeper," Kane said.

Ikem was practically mirroring Kane's body language, hands on the top of the table just like Trapp's. Grubbs kept hers in her lap. Trapp wasn't sure if she was recording the exchange with her phone or holding on to an improvised weapon. Maybe both.

"What sort of a peacekeeper?" Ikem asked.

"The sort that ensures international incidents are kept to a minimum. Zero, ideally."

"Sounds like a worthwhile career," Trapp said. "But just because you're not on MI5's payroll doesn't mean you're not on their ticket."

Kane inhaled with an unsure smile and a shake of his hand. "Let's just say I have experience in handling delicate situations."

"Using indelicate methods?"

"If my methods are indelicate, they are at least quiet."

Trapp narrowed his eyes. Kane wasn't as bulky as Trapp nor as rangy as Ikem, but he had the bearing of a seasoned veteran. He didn't threaten or try to intimidate physically. He was simply stating facts. Men with that sort of confidence were far more challenging to deal with than macho assholes.

"You're deniable," Trapp stated.

Kane shifted his posture so that he appeared more relaxed. His hands stayed where they were. "I really am here as a courtesy. You've been informed by now that the Home Secretary has decided to deny official cooperation."

"Official cooperation with what?"

Kane sighed.

Grubbs sighed.

Ikem remained impassive.

Kane dipped his chin and stared at Grubbs. "Is he usually like this?"

"No," Grubbs said. "He's *always* like this."

"Fine, we'll play it that way." Kane straightened and drummed his fingers twice on the computer before taking a theatrical breath and giving a clearly pre-rehearsed, carefully worded instruction. "As has been conveyed to President Charles Nash via your ambassador, His Majesty's government will not condone any action on British soil without the express permission of the security services. The government gives no permission for you to operate in anything other than an observational capacity and within the bounds of UK law."

Grubbs asked, "Even if we need to act to nullify a national security risk?"

"By national security risk, you mean the folk from Taiwan?" Kane resumed his usual tone, decisive and pointed. "Who have arrived *legally*, with full documentation and a business case that'll create a fuck-ton of jobs and bring a much-needed injection to a struggling financial sector?"

Trapp scoffed. "And you don't see anything off in the timing?" With only a shrug in reply, Trapp shook off the pretense. "Okay, fine, screw it. I don't care if you're recording this. If you can track us like this, I assume you know all about our investigations in Nigeria and Chad."

"You Yanks didn't invent paranoia. You just perfected it. We're treating the Chinese links with the suspicion they deserve. But you..." Kane pointed directly at Trapp. "You will do nothing to cause trouble, and you'll behave according to the laws of this land. No diplomatic immunity. No support from your station chief here. If you want to be left alone to finish your buns, all I need to hear is that you understand and will abide by UK law."

Trapp snaked an arm around Grubbs' shoulders and pulled her close. "My girlfriend and I are just here for a spot of sightseeing."

Grubbs rolled her eyes and shrugged him off.

Kane said, "No need to be cute."

"Cute?" Trapp settled his rejected hand into his lap. "Fine. If I get too... *cute*... and if you need to commit the sort of crime that'll deter an incident but isn't necessarily sanctioned in UK law..." Trapp lingered on the phrase *UK law* for emphasis. "... then it could be said you were acting independently and there would be no blowback on... Who would that be here? The director general of MI5? Or the Home secretary? Who's got you intervening in my vacation time?"

Only a sharp nasal sigh suggested Kane might be annoyed.

Trapp decided not to speak again unless prompted. Ikem

and Grubbs seemed to pick up the hint. This was Kane's gig, and it would be up to him to lead.

"Okay, listen up." Kane shifted his weight onto his elbows to either side of his computer. He wasn't quite hunched as if sharing a secret, but his voice was quieter. "I know for a fact you've been tracing a mineral that you believe will make its way to either Taiwan or the UK in the coming days."

Trapp did his best to look bored.

"There is a really muddy money trail," Kane continued, "that leads through the Middle East and around northern and central Africa, over into the western states. And that same trail leads back to one Zhao Ming, who hopes to snag British citizenship as her business moves its headquarters to the very location where we're sitting."

Kane threaded his fingers together to form a bridge on which he rested his chin and gave a smile. The man's teeth were, if not yellow, then certainly a deep shade of ivory that seemed sinister in his craggy, freshly shaven face.

But it was what he said next that chilled Trapp's blood.

"I also heard a whisper that a certain Karem Hines is seconded to the CIA's Special Operations Division. And since we know this chap's specialty is in high-tech weapons—specifically directed energy weapons like microwave emitters—it doesn't take a genius to suggest you reckon there's a troublesome item either about to be deployed or sold to people the US would rather not obtain it."

"Interesting stuff," Trapp said. "Why would you share any of this with three random strangers in a coffee shop?"

"Fine." Kane's face turned to stone. He dropped his hands to the laptop and opened it. He turned it around, and Trapp was looking at a photo of Zhao Ming, an incidental shot captured through a telephoto lens. "You want *her*."

"Very pretty," Ikem said. "But I am a married man, and this pair may be on honeymoon soon."

Kane shook his head and tapped a key, which flicked to a second photograph. Zhao Ming in a business suit striding across the same green space that Trapp and Grubbs had passed through on their way here. Another tab pulled up Zhao Ming meeting with an immaculately dressed Chinese man in a seedy-looking bar or pub filled with white working-class men—the sort of place cockney geezers would hang out in a Guy Ritchie movie.

Another photograph scrolled by in which the man sat back, apparently enjoying a joke as both he and Zhao Ming were laughing. When the third person at the table was revealed, Trapp made his first mistake.

He'd been trained to compartmentalize his feelings when something went wrong in the field, to continue to act as if everything was going perfectly to buy himself time to make a new plan. But as soon as Trapp recognized Fang Chen, his eyes narrowed, and he leaned toward the screen an inch before catching himself. Not a massive giveaway but enough.

"Thought you'd recognize that one," Kane said. "Works for the embassy, doesn't she?"

Trapp snapped his eyes up to meet Kane's. "Get to the point."

"You believe Rafe Ashenhurst is bankrolling forced labor and migrant routes in Africa. They've unearthed something they can use in a directed energy weapon, and they're selling it to the Chinese. You want to prevent that, either by acquiring the weapon for your country or to make sure it never sees the light of day. How am I doing so far?"

"I'm still listening, aren't I?"

"One of the oldest and most reliable tricks in the international terrorism book is to follow the money. Zhao Ming *is* the money. Even if she doesn't know it herself. Now as much as I'd love to believe what you're doing is a neat case of bog-standard international espionage, I still have friends around who know that's not really your main job."

"Old friends?"

"Doesn't matter. What matters is that if you are planning to extract a Taiwanese national who is currently attempting British citizenship, I may have to employ some extreme measures to avert one of those international incidents we talked about."

Trapp looked to Grubbs, who had not moved, then to Ikem, who said nothing but sat up straighter.

"I don't want the Chinese to get that weapon either," Kane said, "but any illegal activities on your part cannot draw an iota of attention from the establishment or from me. Do we have an understanding?"

"I think we do," Trapp said.

Kane rose to his feet and tucked his laptop under his arm before departing with no further pleasantries.

TWENTY-SEVEN

An hour later, Trapp was scanning the bustling plaza, observing the evening exodus from the financial centers. Beside him, Ikem remained vigilant, while Grubbs had opted to retrieve the car and meet them at the pickup.

If he was reading Kane right, the former SAS man—his former employment featuring heavily in the file Grubbs had obtained five minutes after he departed—had expressly forbidden any action that drew attention but hinted that MI5 would not intervene if Trapp kept things quiet. Meaning they were, once again, doing someone else's dirty work.

In Trapp's ear, Grubbs reported, "Sweep complete. The underground lot is a digital minefield, but I've mapped a route with minimal exposure."

He acknowledged and asked, "Status on the vehicle?"

"Clean. No surveillance devices. I'm repositioning now."

IN THE UNDERGROUND PARKING LOT, Grubbs slid behind the wheel of a nondescript Ford Focus. Her fingers flew over a tablet, displaying a 3D rendering of the plaza's camera coverage. Then she exhaled slowly, centering herself.

No matter how many times she ended up in the field with Trapp, the anxiety was always present. They could fail to secure the target, get arrested, or even die.

"Okay, Trapp," she said into her comm. "I've got a clear path from the plaza exit to our exfil. You'll have about twelve seconds of relative blindness once you've picked her up."

"Copy," Trapp replied.

Grubbs started the engine and maneuvered the car closer to the plaza-side exit, positioning it in one of the few blind spots she'd identified. As she waited, her fingers drummed on the steering wheel.

"Heads up," Trapp said. "She's on the move."

DOWN IN THE PLAZA, Jelany Ikem leaned against a storefront—just another shopper taking a moment to rest. Trapp watched from the upper-ground level by the café, leaning to enjoy a view of the river.

"Trapp," Ikem said, shifting away from the wall. "I need to check something."

"Make it quick," Trapp said, keeping the approaching Zhao Ming in his peripheral vision. "Thirty seconds."

"I only need fifteen."

Ikem wove through the crowd, no sign of stress in his pace. His height provided an advantage, and as he neared the south entrance used by river taxis and tourist boats, he identified the source of his concern.

"Potential hostile but he looks okay," Ikem said. "Alone. Minding his business."

"Copy," Trapp replied. "Get back in position."

Ikem pivoted, and Trapp timed both his direction and Zhao Ming's as she hurried from her building in garish workout attire, gym bag over one shoulder.

As she passed him, Trapp fell into step behind her, maintaining his distance to keep from alarming her. They passed the café where he and Grubbs had met Ikem—had it really only been an hour ago?

Zhao Ming approached the stairs that had once led dock workers to labor in frighteningly poor conditions but which now ferried the wealthy to overpriced indulgences.

"Approaching extraction point," he said. "She's thirty seconds from the stairs. Ikem, you in position?"

"I am," came the calm reply.

Trapp tightened his grip on the stair railing at the top, watching Zhao Ming descend.

Then Ikem, no longer calm and assured, said urgently, "I have three rough types. They spotted Ming the moment she hit the stairs."

Grubbs chimed in. "MI5 again?"

"Negative," Ikem replied, his usual jovial tone replaced by deadly seriousness. "I am certain one of them is Boko Haram. One of Obasee's foot soldiers. He was at the mine."

Trapp saw the three men. "What are they doing here?"

Grubbs' voice returned, calm and analytical. "Zhao's an obvious target. If they're worried about her, it makes sense they'd stake her out. Expect us to come looking."

"If they are worried about her," Ikem said, "it means we are in the right place."

"So much for keeping things quiet," Trapp said, reassessing. "Ikem, stay on those hostiles. Grubbs, prepare to move."

He narrowed his gaze at the men Ikem had spotted. Their twitchy behavior suggested they weren't professionals in the way he was. But they could still cause a problem.

"We need a diversion," he said. "Something not too alarming. Draw their attention away."

"What kind of diversion?" Grubbs asked.

"Do whatever I would do," he replied. "Improvise. Ikem will back you up."

There was a brief silence on the other end of the comm. Trapp could almost hear Grubbs' exasperation, then the comm went silent.

GRUBBS SAT IN THE CAR, gripping the steering wheel. "Do whatever Jason would do…"

She started the engine.

What *would* he do?

Probably something that would yield results but be ridiculously high risk.

"Damn it, Jason. Fine. Have it your way."

TRAPP WATCHED the base of the stairs—a small bubble of opportunity in the sea of surveillance cameras.

Zhao Ming, oblivious, began to descend the steps.

The three men Ikem had spotted closed in. Amateurs but still dangerous.

"Grubbs, we need you now," Trapp said.

As if she'd been waiting for his cue, a screech of tires echoed across the plaza below, and Grubbs' car careened around the corner of a delivery lane.

Trapp said, "What the hell are you doing?"

Grubbs slammed on the brakes, the car skidding to a stop a few feet from the group of suspicious men. She leapt and shouted, "Help! A man collapsed in the parking garage! I think he's having a heart attack!"

The commotion had the desired effect. The three men hesitated, their attention split between Zhao Ming and the interruption.

"Now," Trapp said.

A siren pierced the air.

Two police cars barreled into the plaza from a service road near the Thames, lights flashing blue. The vehicles screeched to a halt, blocking the most obvious escape routes. But before Trapp could respond, the suspicious men sprang into action, racing toward Zhao Ming.

TWENTY-EIGHT

Trapp quelled the surge of adrenaline through sheer force of will and experience alone. At first, he thought he had triggered a trap laid by MI5, possibly hoping to avoid embarrassment by tipping off the Met Police instead of confronting Trapp directly. But then he realized that it would be Kane who dealt with them, not the local PD.

As the two cars slowed so as not to threaten the members of the public dotting the plaza, their maneuvering was directed toward the small vehicle Grubbs had rented.

"Stick to the plan," he ordered, giving Ikem a nod and striding dynamically toward Zhao Ming.

The Taiwanese finance expert was, like many of the crowd in the outskirts, frozen, watching as Grubbs set the car in motion and sped in a circle, not so much outmaneuvering the cops but driving more dangerously than anyone would like. Including Trapp.

"For the record," he said, "that is *not* what I would have done."

Grubbs' voice was frantic as she replied, "Sue me, just get moving. Shall I pull up?"

"Negative. Keep the cops with you as long as you can hold them. I don't know if you saw the traffic earlier, but there's not much point in a high-speed pursuit through London at this time of day."

"You mean I'm screwed?"

Trapp gathered his thoughts, swallowing back the same bile and guilt that had swirled inside him months earlier when he'd implicated her in an act of treason. "I can't see a way out for you. I'm sorry."

Grubbs left it a couple of seconds before replying, "What the hell, Jason? I know it was my choice, but…" Her voice hitched, reading the same play, the same risks, as Trapp had. "I'll find a way."

"I won't leave you," Trapp said. "I'll get you out one way or another. As soon as I can."

"Don't make promises you can't keep."

"I'm ready," Ikem interrupted.

Although Trapp heard it in his earpiece, he saw the Nigerian agent closing in sideways on their target without directly looking at her, acting like a confused witness, just like her.

Trapp reached the bottom of the stairs, five feet from Zhao Ming.

Ikem was closer. He said, "This is crazy, yes?"

Zhao nodded and looked up at Ikem, then frowned. If she had been briefed on people to look out for, she would have recognized the distinctive agent, but she never got the chance to cry out.

Trapp came up behind her and poked a salt shaker that he'd lifted from the café into her back. He made it look like a friendly greeting as he said, "This is a 50-caliber Desert Eagle.

It will blow you clean in two. Don't make a noise, just come with us. You will not be harmed."

If Zhao Ming was acting, she had clearly missed her calling, as her teeth chattered audibly. "You have no idea what you're interfering with."

"Just walk," Ikem said in a kind voice. "We already know who you work for."

She stiffened for such a brief instant Trapp thought he imagined it, then obeyed, allowing the two men to flank her as they entered the underground lot through which Grubbs had made her spectacular display of improvisation.

CAMERON KANE WATCHED events unfold from a vantage point too far away for him to intervene. He was up on the ground level at one of the hooray-Henry cocktail bars that he hated so much. The advantage of this location was that he could get a fancy-Nancy glass of fruit juice without imbibing alcohol or drawing attention to the fact that he wasn't putting some nasty alcohol-free beer in his gut.

He no longer looked like a tramp, having switched his ratty fleece jacket for a cream woolen overshirt, which paired neatly with his blue jeans and red tennis shoes. With a little gel in his hair, his three o'clock shadow looked fashionably rustic rather than unclean.

But now, less than thirty minutes after he'd given them his friendliest but sternest warning, Jason Trapp, Jelany Ikem, and Madison Grubbs were proving problematic.

He was going to have to do something about this.

INSIDE THE UNDERGROUND PARKING STRUCTURE, there were two booths that could accommodate security guards, but both were empty, the guards having run out onto the plaza in pursuit of Grubbs. Being on foot, they had no means to stop her if she chose to mow them down like some psycho terrorist.

With Grubbs out of action, they needed a different egress. Most high-end vehicles and even mid-range ones would be too advanced to hotwire quickly.

"Phone," Trapp said.

Zhao gave him her cellphone, and Trapp slipped it into a pouch that shielded its RFID chip as well as all signals in and out so that it couldn't be tracked.

"There." Ikem pointed at signs to the elevators and stairs. "If we get out while the police are occupied, we can pick up a cab or something."

"Or something?" Trapp said. "Not the best plan."

"But the only one we have."

They scuttled along a painted blue strip with a white stick man denoting a pedestrian walkway, following the sign to the elevators. Trapp held the salt shaker under his shirt in case their prisoner glanced too closely. He linked his arm into hers while Ikem pushed on ten feet ahead. At the doors to the lobby, Ikem opened one to reveal a parking payment machine and the steel doors of two elevators.

What Ikem had not been expecting were two burly African men barging out and knocking him flying, his arms pinwheeling almost comically.

Trapp could not spare a second to help. He charged forward, meeting the plainly aggressive incoming pair head-on. Both had bad teeth and ill-fitting clothes, and the one in front brandished a twelve-inch blade. Knives were much easier to come by in London than guns.

Trapp parried the reaching arm, forcing the weapon to the incoming assassin's blind side, then unleashed a fierce uppercut into the man's ribs, followed by an elbow into his face. Keeping the knife away from him, he kicked his heel into the man's thigh and shoved him hard toward his compatriot, who stumbled to a halt. Trapp then launched himself with a straight boot that sent both men tumbling into a heap.

Their collapse would've been funny—reminding him of Tweedledum and Tweedledee—if they hadn't been so intent on murder.

But in the few seconds since he'd been forced to let go of her, Zhao Ming had turned and fled the way they'd come, with Ikem already in pursuit. Trapp followed in his wake, building to a sprint as he heard the two killers scramble to their feet and give chase.

Instead of heading back out into the plaza, Zhao Ming turned left and slammed through a fire door, which set off a screaming alarm and a flashing light. Trapp caught up to the exit she'd made, had a fraction of a second to take in the "Absolutely no entry to the public" sign on the door, and fell into step with Ikem, who had now grabbed their principal once again.

Zhao Ming screamed at him, and he clamped his hand over her mouth.

"Shh." He was not unduly violent with her, but bringing his face close and widening his eyes carried a threat that earned him her silence.

"We won't hurt you," Trapp said.

"But they will." Ikem indicated the doors they had just come through, where Tweedledum and Tweedledee were racing toward them again. Tweedledee still had his knife, while his friend Tweedledum carried a machete.

Trapp said, "Get her to safety. I'll catch up."

"I can help," Ikem said.

"I'll be right behind you."

Ikem obeyed and took off with Zhao Ming, who had clocked the weapons and must have concluded the lesser risk was the person who had not tried to kill her yet.

Neither of the two assassins slowed.

Trapp sidestepped to keep one of them behind the other, then threw a kick into Tweedledee's balls, doubling him immediately. Tweedledum bundled his partner out of the way and drew back the machete for an overhead slice. Trapp closed the distance, caught the man's wrist as it arched toward him, and used his momentum to spin the man over his hip.

Tweedledum slammed on his back onto the floor, and Trapp stamped on his elbow while over-rotating the wrist. A double snap of bone preceded the man's cry of pain.

Although Tweedledee was still obviously hurting, he rounded on Trapp. But Trapp had liberated his partner's machete and took Tweedledee by surprise, swinging it straight into his neck. The blade buried itself four inches into the meat, stunning him into motionless panic.

Trapp ripped it free, and the carotid sprayed a fan of blood across the smooth gray wall.

He didn't wait for Tweedledee to die; he just sprinted to catch up with Ikem.

He kept the machete with him, which was dripping red as he exited the end of the corridor, finding himself in a basic lounge intended for the parking lot workers. There was a vending machine, a couple of chairs, a coffee maker—and a woman of about sixty with tight, curly hair staring frog-eyed as Ikem asked her for what was obviously not the first time, "How do I get out? Which way?"

The woman, seeing Trapp and his bloodied blade, was about to let out a scream.

Trapp raised his finger to his lips. "My friend asked you a question. Which way?"

The woman pointed at one of the three available doors.

"Thank you, ma'am," Trapp said as Ikem slammed through the door with Zhao Ming in tow. Trapp followed them, racing into a steel staircase that took them down farther, closer to the water, where a sign pointed toward the plaza.

Ikem led them in the opposite direction, following a less-used concrete walkway with weeds and tufts of grass growing through.

Down here along the perimeter of the parking lot, there didn't seem to be any bars or eateries looking down on them, except for those on the opposite side of the Thames—too far to get any sort of read. The Millennium Dome was nearby, as were several construction projects, but again, on the wrong side of the river.

They just needed to get Zhao Ming onto public transport and away. Trapp believed she would be more cooperative now that she'd seen men attack them with blades; he could dress this up as a rescue mission rather than an interrogation.

Around the next corner, they were underground again, a long, wide corridor with sections that had been caged off for storage, leaving only a single narrow alley through which to pass.

No choice.

With Ikem ahead of Zhao Ming and Trapp behind, it was a fifty-yard dash to the next open area, where the fencing with the spear-like points would be too difficult to climb over.

Zhao Ming slowed, looking fearful.

Ikem said, "Keep going, it's fine. We will get you to safety."

Trapp pulled up short as the third man from the plaza appeared up ahead, his buck teeth visible even from this distance. He carried a six-shooter with a large-caliber barrel, the exact make impossible to tell at this distance, but its hollow black eye was leveled straight at Trapp.

A gunshot shattered the air. Not for the first time in his life, Trapp expected to die. But it was the gunman who flopped forward like a felled tree with half his head missing.

Then Cameron Kane stepped into view with a nine-millimeter Glock raised toward them.

Zhao Ming squeaked again, stifling a scream. Then said, "Please tell me he's with you."

Trapp slowed, his hands raised, the machete no threat to a man with a gun. "I'm not sure if he is or not."

"I'm not," Kane said. "But my brief is to keep the peace. So if you're going to start tearing massive parts of London up trying to get this one off the street, I can either shoot you both dead and take her myself, or you can follow me."

"Yeah, sure. What do *you* think?" Trapp said.

"Drop the blade."

Trapp did as he was told, then bent to take the gun off the terrorist, but Kane stopped him.

"No, that stays right where it is. Now move your arse or I shoot you right up it."

Trapp, annoyed at losing his chance to arm himself properly, chose the path of least resistance and did as ordered, moving toward Kane while Zhao Ming and Ikem brought up the rear.

Kane led them away from the fences at a jog, back toward the bend in the Thames.

"Where are we going?" Trapp asked.

"I've got a vehicle for you. Do not engage with any police, do not cause any more problems. Am I understood?"

"Crystal clear. Why are you helping?"

"Like I said, my job is to prevent international incidents

that could embarrass the government. I'm assuming you're not going to kill this woman."

"Of course not," Ikem said, somewhat offended.

"Good. Keep her safe, bring her back in one piece."

They pushed on through a damaged chain-link fence that Trapp held open for Ikem and Zhao. Then they ran down another overgrown lane before arriving at their final destination.

Trapp halted. He saw the same surprise in Ikem's face that he felt.

"You have got to be kidding me."

TWENTY-NINE

The wind lashed against Trapp's face, stinging his eyes as he gripped the chugging motorboat's wheel. Grease and gasoline filled the air, intertwined with the brackish aroma of the Thames. Behind him, Ikem braced against turbulent waves while Zhao Ming clung to the side, her knuckles pale and fear etched on her face.

Trapp pushed the engine to its limit, propelling the maintenance boat to thirty knots—a limit he was surprised the old vessel was able to reach. It wasn't record-breaking speed but fast enough to spray dirty water over the bow with every slap of the hull. He scanned the shoreline between rough patches, sure he'd glimpsed someone, and now he confirmed it.

Isabella Knight stood in the dock of the retail plaza, two African men flanking her, their postures tense. More Boko Haram killers.

"Shit," Trapp said. "It's her. Isabella Knight."

Ikem squinted against the glare. "Knight? Here?"

Zhao Ming was barely audible over the engine. "What does this mean?"

Trapp ignored her as more important questions surfaced. How had Knight found them so quickly? Had they been tailed from the start, or was this something more sinister?

Had Kane known she'd be waiting and diverted them in Knight's direction?

Knight and her men dashed toward the jetty where a water taxi was offloading passengers at the Canary Wharf stop.

"Hold on," Trapp warned, cranking the wheel starboard. "This might get rough."

As they sped past gleaming office buildings and luxury apartments, Trapp reckoned that if Knight and her crew had caught up with him, it meant either that the NIA or CIA had a leak or Kane had pushed them into the open on MI5's orders. But if Knight and her cohorts had already been here, lying in wait, might that spell an even bigger problem for British intelligence?

Trapp gunned the engine, eking out another couple of knots by pushing the heat into the red. The violent jolting against the tidal river threatened to tear the steering wheel from his grip, but he held on.

A quick glance behind confirmed that Knight had commandeered the water taxi. She'd donned a desert-style scarf that concealed her face and hair, as had her two buddies, the garments whipping in the wind as Knight piloted the vessel, closing the distance.

"Damn it," Trapp said. "This piece of shit won't go any faster."

Zhao Ming's terrified voice carried over boat's growl. "Why are they trying to kill us?"

"They know we're a threat," Trapp replied through clenched teeth. "You were the bait, and now they want to finish you off, too."

"But why?"

"Loose ends," Ikem answered for him.

Trapp swerved to avoid a tour boat, the passengers' shouts of surprise audible as the maintenance boat's wash rocked the glass-roofed vessel.

He called over the din, "Your Chinese friends aren't your friends. The ones backing your work with migrants? The Ashenhurst Group? They're also siphoning people away for cheap or free labor. People the Chinese government thinks are a problem."

"No," Zhao replied forcefully. "They would not!"

Trapp blazed them past Wapping; the historic docklands barely registered as Trapp focused on getting beyond Tower Bridge before Knight, so that he could at least beach the damned boat and run. The bridge's iconic shape grew bigger as they approached.

Knight was close behind, a short distance to their right. Her men aimed but refrained from shooting, the turbulence too much for a decent shot.

Trapp tightened his grip, aiming directly for one of the massive river-level bases of Tower Bridge. "Hold on!"

Ikem and Ming clung to the sides of the boat as Trapp zigzagged. The boat tasted air as it buffeted at its top speed but kept his main trajectory.

"What are you doing?" Ming cried.

Trapp was too dialed-in to respond. He eased off the throttle a fraction, allowing Knight's boat to close in. Soon they were less than ten yards away, close enough to get soaked by the maintenance boat's spray—or for a half-blind newbie to hit them if Knight stabilized her craft.

"Trapp..." Ikem's voice held a warning.

"Trust me."

The two boats pulled level, just a few lengths from plowing into the bridge stanchion, and Trapp killed the engine with one thrust of the power lever. Knight's vessel shot on ahead, her sudden correction forcing the gunmen to catch their balance. As quickly as he'd cut it, Trapp revved up his engine, slamming the throttle forward so the boat leaped ahead, veering sharply to port.

Caught off-guard, Knight fishtailed around. The collision he'd hoped for never materialized, but Knight's boat clipped the base of Tower Bridge, sending it careening to starboard, directly into the path of an unsuspecting tour boat.

Trapp lost sight of them as he maneuvered behind a massive bridge pillar, using it as a shield.

He heard no impact, so it seemed Knight would not be sinking just yet. He whipped his craft around, the engine roaring as they accelerated. Rounding the pillar, Trapp spotted Knight's damaged boat limping away from the tour barge she'd narrowly missed. He gunned the engine.

Rapidly closing the distance, Trapp tightened his grip on the wheel, the choppy waters of the Thames spraying his face.

"Brace!" he shouted.

Trapp rammed the stern of Knight's boat, crunching into their engine housing, spilling the occupants into one another and pitching them onto the deck.

Trapp allowed himself a moment of self-congratulation before reversing and throttling on ahead.

Emerging from the shadow of the bridge, a high-pitched whine cut through the air, and Trapp spotted a sleek police boat racing toward them.

"Shit."

Trapp veered away and aimed for the nearby riverbank. It was a mud-flat with stone stairs cut into the brick of the embankment, leading to a green space of trees filled with onlookers.

No choice—Grubbs was probably already under arrest, so

he and Ikem needed to stay free to use whatever Zhao Ming could give them. Plus, she'd done nothing wrong. She might be left unprotected if Trapp and Ikem were locked up.

He pressed on, angling toward a small tugboat, using them as cover, painfully conscious that the river patrol would be far faster, well-armed, and more skilled at piloting their craft.

He slowed. The boat thumped home onto the mudbank faster than he'd planned, jarring the three of them.

"Out! Now!" he shouted.

They scrambled to disembark, and Trapp's boots sank into the soggy riverbank as he hoisted Zhao out of the boat.

"We should surrender," Zhao said. "I've done nothing wrong. The police will help."

Trapp gripped her arm firmly. "Not an option."

As they lurched toward the stairs, the roar of an approaching boat gave him pause. He risked a glance and saw Knight's vessel bearing down on them, the police boat neck and neck.

Trapp reached the base of the stairs with Zhao. Ikem halted, his expression resolute.

"I'll stay behind," Ikem said. "Buy you some time."

Trapp shook his head. "Those cops are armed and trained to take out terrorist threats."

"It is our best shot. Get her out of here. I'll be in a cell with Madison, we can share a lawyer."

Trapp knew he was right, but there was another risk, one he hated to admit but had to voice. "I don't want to be indelicate, Ikem, but if they've been given a description of the men in the plaza, you—a Black man in the middle of a violent incident..."

Ikem considered a moment longer, but his mind was made up. "I know the risk. It is mine to take."

Trapp's common sense clashed with the thought of leaving his friend. But both had a more urgent duty.

With a reluctant nod, Trapp commenced with Zhao Ming up the stairs.

The second boat slammed into the shore, and before the cops could catch up, a hail of bullets tore through the air.

Zhao let out a cry as Trapp yanked her down behind the stone balustrade. The assassins' gunfire was wild yet relentless.

Trapp pushed Zhao on, both crawling. He risked a look behind them.

Where was Knight?

She'd cut and run, leaving her dogs to do the dirty work. Knew they'd be picked up as soon as she saw the cops.

And now the cops had caught up. They hadn't beached but stopped in the shallows, the armed officers wading to the riverbank with SIG MCX Carbines at their shoulders.

At their shouted warnings, the two gunmen in the beached craft reared back and aimed at the cops.

But the cops shot first, a crackle of firearms cutting down the attackers. Then they turned their attention to the other potential threat.

Trapp followed their lines of sight to see Ikem, hands raised, half-lying on his side, calling out, "I'm unarmed, don't shoot! I'm hurt. But I am cooperating fully!"

Trapp grinned. The delay while they secured Ikem would buy them time to escape. The Nigerian would end up in a cell, but they wouldn't shoot a surrendering man. Ordinary British cops didn't carry weapons—the ones who did were trained when, and when not, to use them.

He urged Zhao Ming on. "Go, but keep low."

They ascended on all fours, then scrambled to their feet at the top, Trapp half-dragging the panting woman into the park bordering the river. He could only hope Ikem's ruse would give them the head start they needed.

THIRTY

Trapp assessed them both as he slowed his pace to a fast walk: bedraggled and wet from the river spray in her workout gear, Zhao had a deer-in-the-headlights demeanor. He didn't look much better in muddy jeans, tee, and flannel jacket.

He followed the smell of greasy kebabs to a dozen vendors in small huts lining the winding path—attached to some sort of event that was petering to an end. He led Zhao to a clothing stall. The storekeeper eyed them suspiciously but gave no objection as Trapp paid for two oversized hoodies in cash. Zhao Ming's declared that she hearted London, while Trapp's was emblazoned with a bulldog in a Union Jack waistcoat driving a red double-decker bus.

Warmer and better hidden in their hoods, Trapp guided Zhao through the park, the trees offering a modicum of cover from the unflinching cameras blanketing the streets.

"You're awfully quiet," Zhao Ming observed, her earlier fear giving way.

"I'm trying to keep us alive."

Ming's steps faltered. "We can't keep running. Maybe if we turn ourselves in..."

Trapp couldn't allow that. And they were one scream away from her getting away—if she chose to run, there would be little he could do about it. All he had was her phone and the half-lie he'd spun her.

"Listen to me, Zhao," he said. "You were *bait*. For me. But now? You're a liability to them. We know, and you know, that you're part of a financial trail. They kill you, it goes cold."

"They'll—"

"Yes," Trapp said.

The park was ending, leaving them exposed.

"There," he said. "Cannon Street station. We're going underground."

Without waiting for her response, their hoods still up, Trapp guided Zhao Ming through the crowd as they descended into the station, paying at the barrier using Trapp's burner phone—which he assumed was still untraceable. At least the crowd would provide some cover.

Down two escalators and winding through tiled passages, they approached the platform. A blast of air funneled through the Tube, tousling the waiting passengers as the train trundled to a halt.

Trapp and Zhao boarded, and the doors hissed shut, sealing them in. The taste of stale underground air was a welcome change of scenery.

As the carriage lurched forward with the clatter of wheels on the track, Trapp's muscles unclenched. Finally, a chance to sit and catch their breath.

Zhao Ming slumped in the chair and leaned her head against a pole. "What happens when we surface?"

"I'm working on it, Zhao. I'm working on it."

They sat quietly for a moment, and Trapp noticed the

woman's hands clasped together. Her arms trembled, and he recognized the pure fear brought on by several near-death experiences in quick succession.

He said, "Zhao, I—"

"That's *Ms.* Zhao, by the way."

"I'm sorry, what?"

She spoke in a ramble, eyes on the floor, the terror still real, but the rapid words seemed to offer a reprieve. "Some Chinese in the West switch their surname around to match your way. I haven't. Zhao is my surname. Call me Ms. Zhao or Ming."

"Okay." Trapp had little comfort to offer. "Ming it is."

As the train rattled through the darkness, Trapp pulled out his phone, shielding the screen with his body as he composed a message.

"What are you doing now?" Ming asked.

"The only thing I can."

He hit send, knowing the message would remain dormant until they emerged from the depths of the city.

IT WASN'T clear at first whether the figure on the screen was Jason Trapp or not. Although the size matched, the wardrobe was somewhat jarring: a garish souvenir hoodie and damp jeans. But he hadn't taken the time to disguise the way he walked. A quick tap of the analysis button revealed his gait to be consistent with what they had recorded at the plaza near Canary Wharf and at Heathrow. Accompanying him must have been Zhao Ming, since both Jelany Ikem and Madison Grubbs were now in custody.

There weren't many blind spots in London, even in the tube stations, but the technology wasn't some magical Eye of Sauron. The facial recognition and gait algorithms needed time to function, and even at full capacity, they were not flawless, especially when scrutinizing dense crowds. And the London Underground always seemed to contain dense crowds.

Kane despised these meeting spots. They always reeked of urine and the base nature of human frailties. This one, behind a row of inexpensive electronic shops and secondhand phones, flanked by Georgian-era buildings now transformed into hotels, was just a short walk away. He found the contrasts of London too jarring, too overwhelming. He couldn't genuinely call it his home.

Kane handed the tablet back to the nameless bull with the buzz-cut. "It took the House an hour to find this?"

"Not my department, mate," the thuggish man in the suit replied, the muscular operative Kane had seen trying to intimidate Trapp and Grubbs at Heathrow—a literal show of strength. "But I'm guessing they wouldn't have had to if you'd done your job properly."

"The House knows I can't arrest people like Trapp and his friends, *mate*. The only way I could've stopped him from causing more trouble would be to shoot him dead."

"Yep. That's how they see it, too."

Kane ran his hand through his thick hair, fingertips kneading his scalp. "I note my reasoning in my report. If they don't like it, they can sack me."

The bull rolled his eyes upward and to the left.

"Or *can* they?" Kane pressed. "Because I'm not entirely sure this is something the DG would sanction."

The bull remained neutral, packing the tablet into a case. "The director general has final say over all operations. My understanding is they're looking to see if they have anyone more capable to do this."

"You know you don't. And since it isn't MI5 giving me my

orders, maybe you should shove that computer screen up your shaved arse."

The bull didn't rise to the provocation. In fact, he seemed to enjoy the barb. Maybe his arse was shaved, and he wanted people to know.

"Since we're discussing memory," the bull told him, "commit this to yours. It's direct from the operational chief. Jason Trapp needs to be either dead or in custody within twenty-four hours."

Kane pulled out his phone. "I assume you've got some geek squad working on alerts if he shows up." He didn't wait for confirmation. He knew it would be managed. "Get it to my phone as soon as possible. If he won't cooperate, well... offering him the carrot didn't work. Time to bring out the stick."

THIRTY-ONE

The CIA maintained a total of twenty-two safe houses in London, not counting the unofficial properties that operatives had established for themselves over the years. Trapp had never operated in this area, though, and by the time he reached the weary, run-down street, he was fatigued, cold, and in dire need of a shower. He wished he had at least a week to recuperate.

Unfortunately, such a respite was not in the cards for him or for Zhao Ming.

After changing trains three times and navigating the Tube network, Trapp finally emerged from Dagenham East underground station under a night sky and into the impoverished suburb of Barking and Dagenham. He chose this location because its profile suited his requirements: predominantly working-class, it was the kind of place where people tended to mind their own damn business.

The apartment he was headed for was situated above an empty shop owned by a company based in Slovenia and had been on the market for almost four years. The asking price was exorbitant, especially for this neighborhood. On the ground floor was what seemed to be a small, abandoned convenience store, which the faded, graffiti-adorned sign described as a 'newsagents.'

Using the RFID reader on his CIA-issue phone to disarm the electronic lock—which was disguised as a rusty Chubb mechanism—he opened the steel sheet covering the door on the side of the building. This permitted access to the regular-looking door beneath it, and once inside, they quickly closed both behind them.

Ascending the damp-smelling staircase, they encountered cheap carpeting and a rickety balustrade on the landing, along with a kitchen, bathroom, and two bedrooms. The main part of the apartment, or 'flat,' had a vague damp, musty odor from prolonged disuse. The windows could only open a crack due to metal grills designed to deter burglars and copper thieves, a common issue in areas with abandoned buildings. Trapp opted to open only those windows not visible from the street and closed the internal shutters to keep any light from escaping.

The place resembled a budget motel room, and Zhao Ming, seated on the first bed with her legs crossed, looked up at him expectantly. "Is this where you explain why this is happening?"

"You know why," Trapp said. "You're working with human traffickers and a corporate asshole who funds terrorists."

"I am not. The Ashenhurst Foundation has helped hundreds of my oppressed countrymen."

"The Ashenhurst Foundation is owned by Ashenhurst Group. Ashenhurst Group is funding terrorists, and you're hanging out with Chinese nationals who've done a lot of bad stuff to a lot of good people. You were having a drink with them recently."

Ming gave a sharp, annoyed "Ha" and shook her head. "There is no freedom without strength. My partners understand that true change requires sacrifice—a concept some Westerners can never grasp. I make sure contributions reach the right places, and—okay, I make a little with my own portfolio. But I do not consort with terrorists."

She seemed passionate, genuine. But then a lot of people Trapp had encountered seemed passionate and genuine.

He said, "If you really believe all that, you won't mind cooperating fully. If we're wrong, we walk away. If we're right, we gather the evidence we need and avert a huge attack."

Ming thought for a long, silent spell. Her voice took on a smaller note. "Do I get immunity?"

"No," Trapp replied, pulling out his phone and scrolling to a secure messaging app. "I would remind you that the people I'm looking for tried to kill you. I'm about to disclose state secrets to you. But if you're on the level, you deserve the truth."

She remained silent, but her curiosity was clearly piqued.

Trapp displayed his phone screen, revealing the messages he had requested Garside to manufacture. "Do you recognize these documents?"

Ming took the phone, examined the screen, and zoomed in to scrutinize the Chinese text.

"Where did you get this?" she asked.

"There's more."

She scrolled through additional screens sent by Polly, all of which would withstand inspection from pretty much anyone outside the Chinese government.

Trapp said, "These are messages between individuals working for us, the Chinese embassy in Washington, and the government in Beijing. You'll also find some English messages that the Ashenhurst Group incorrectly believed to be untraceable. Those people you think are assisting migrants? Who you consider your friends? They're using you as a cover: Your charity work is their shield and keeps the money flowing. Even if you're not playing both sides, you're also complicit in an illegal weapons deal involving rogue state actors."

Ming's frown deepened, her eyes vigilant as she absorbed the information. After processing everything, she let the phone slip into her lap, her resolve evidently waning.

Trapp snatched back the phone, hating the dilemma he had to force on her. "You have two options: come with me alive or die on your own." He pulled up the prearranged contact number and handed Ming the phone. "If you choose to help us dismantle Ashenhurst and remove this weapon from the market, we can grant you immunity—from US prosecution, anyway. And we'll go to bat for you with the Brits. But no promises. Press the dial button, and we can get started."

Zhao Ming hesitated for three seconds before straightening and grabbing the phone. She pressed the dial button and activated the speaker.

"Richmond Stationery Supplies. How may I direct your call?" asked the voice on the other end.

"Trapp. 9235. Alpha. Jones."

"Hold, please."

Cheerful hold music played for a few moments before a click signaled Mitchell on the line. "Trapp, do you have her? Is she safe?"

"We're both secure," Trapp replied. "And we're cooperating."

"Hi," Polly said cheerfully. "My name's Polly, and I'll be your assistant. Let's get started, shall we?"

Over the next hour, Zhao Ming outlined the connections between a network of offshore banks spanning from Hong Kong to Beijing to Taiwan. These banks appeared to handle legitimate funds intended to support refugees and protesters targeted by the Chinese government and global authorities. The Taiwanese authorities turned a blind eye to Ming's activities; while they could not officially endorse her actions, they were not obligated to intervene.

Meanwhile, a small team in Washington—Polly Garside, Karem Hines, and Mike Mitchell—monitored the intelligence being shared. They recognized many of the players involved, including known traffickers—some identified only by code names. It wouldn't take long before their true identities emerged.

Mitchell would face a choice: either dismantle these organizations or observe them to target more significant opportunities later.

Shortly before the hour concluded, Polly had analyzed several institutions and asked to speak with their witness.

"Hiya, Ming. Can I ask for a couple of clarifications?"

Ming closed her eyes, fatigue washing over her. "Of course. Anything I can do to help."

Polly either didn't catch the sarcasm or chose to disregard it. "Looking at the Goodwill Fisk Bank in Hong Kong, I've traced some shareholders back to shell corporations. These shell corporations share board members with the bank and partners who are tied to the Chinese Communist Party. This suggests that Beijing could spy on dissidents' financial arrangements."

Ming blanched. "No... that cannot be. Our bankers launder profits from illegal border crossings, yes, but the backers in China, Taiwan, and America... all are benevolent. They would not... Would they?"

Hines finally spoke up after a long silence. Until now, he had only contributed grunts and confirmed that some clients were indeed suppliers of diamonds, platinum, and gold—all raw materials for DEWs. "More to the point, these banks can facilitate military purchases without interference from places like the US. They're perfect for circumventing sanctions in dealings with rogue nations."

"Arms?" Ming interjected.

"Yes," Trapp said. "You know some of these people are arms dealers. Seemingly legal ones, mostly."

"Yes, but that doesn't automatically make them bad. All countries buy and sell weapons. Like the drone mesh that everyone is so enthusiastic about."

Trapp paused, sensing a similar uncertainty among those in Washington.

"Drone mesh?" Trapp remarked. "That sounds… foreboding."

Hines added, "Actually, it sounds like the most crucial intel on this call. Why are we only hearing it now?"

"Wait, wait," Ming said. "You don't even know what you are chasing?"

"We know what it can do," Trapp replied. "We just didn't know it had a designation."

"A drone *mesh*," Hines groaned. "That would require far more manufacturing output than we gave Ashenhurst credit for. And if it's a mesh, if he has enough computational capacity—it's still only theoretical. Honestly, we would struggle to produce it ourselves."

Mitchell asked, "What exactly are we dealing with here?"

"Constructive interference," Hines said. He *sounded* pale.

"Constructive what?"

"Individually, these DEWs are weak. Anything drone mounted would have to be. Even with a niobium semiconductor fueling it, it would be difficult to build a powerful enough emitter."

"How weak are we talking?" Trapp asked.

"Still strong enough to fry a whole platoon without breaking a sweat. On their own."

"But together...?"

"Together they could exploit a physics principle called constructive interference. Imagine dropping a pebble in a pond. Tiny ripple. Drop sixty of them in a perfectly synchronized pattern, you'd get a flood. If you align microwaves—any kind of wave—perfectly, that's what happens. They amplify each other and create one single, much more powerful wave—a needle of intense energy and power. You'd have to have a hell of a supercomputer to figure it all out, but..."

"Is that what this is?" Trapp inquired, stepping closer to the banker.

Ming looked up at him defiantly but swallowed. "I don't know the specifics, just that there's a considerable amount of money changing hands between Ashenhurst Group and Goodwill Fisk. It was nothing to do with my work, so I did not interfere."

Polly chimed in. "I've uncovered another issue. Thanks to the passwords Ming provided, I conducted an in-depth analysis to identify any anomalies."

"What anomaly?" Mitchell demanded.

"A one-time purchase made a week ago: fifty million dollars."

"Small potatoes in the arms industry," Hines said.

"Not if it's just a deposit," Ming countered.

Everyone took a moment to digest that.

Ming said, "I'm just a middleman. I help those in need, and I get to undermine China more than they undermine us. It's not perfect, and I can't pretend to be a virtuous person. But I do know where you can find a lot more of the evidence you need."

"Where?" Mitchell asked.

"Taiwan. So many of their business transactions occur there. If the Chinese want to procure arms stealthily, concealing their secrets in the midst of disputed territory is a great way to do it—especially a territory that they claim is controlled by foes who would be unlikely to look there."

"Trapp," Mitchell said, "take me off speaker."

Trapp complied and stepped out of the room.

Before he got all the way out, Ming stood and asked, "May I get some air?"

"Turn the lights off first, crack the window, and stay out of sight." Trapp exited the room with the phone, turned off the speaker function, and pressed it to his ear as he closed himself into the next bedroom. "I'm alone."

"Polly just passed me a note while you were speaking. I'd like you to hear it."

"It's all accurate," Polly said. "All verifiable."

"But?" Trapp asked.

"But it's also not very useful. It only confirms what we already thought and doesn't provide a clear course of action. To gain that clarity, she's taking us all the way to Taiwan. It's a twelve-hour journey, even on a direct flight."

Mitchell said, "She's stalling?"

"Or she doesn't know anything," Hines said. "And this has all been a waste of time."

"They wouldn't be trying to eliminate her if it was a waste of time," Trapp said.

"How do you know they aren't just trying to eliminate *you* by using her?"

"Yeah, they definitely want me dead. But she was the priority earlier today. Trust me."

"We'll go with your assessment, Jason," Mitchell said. "But you need to work on her. Gain her trust and determine exactly where we need to look in Taiwan. I can get a team over there tonight."

"Understood."

They all signed off, and Trapp returned to the room with

Zhao Ming, who had lit a cigarette and was smoking by the window.

Right in front of the window.

The lights were off, but—

The cigarette.

Suddenly, two loud pops shattered the silence, and two corresponding holes appeared in Ming's torso. Blood gushed out as she collapsed to the ground, motionless.

Trapp dove to the floor, rolled out of view, and crawled toward the dying woman.

Fucking moron.

He aimed that thought at both Ming for being careless and at himself for not giving her stricter protocols.

"Did you give them our location?"

She looked pale and terrified, her eyes wide and streaming with tears, blood pooling at her lips. "They shot *me*."

"You're going to be fine," Trapp hissed. He grabbed her shoulders and squeezed. "Did you tell anybody where we were?"

Her head shook, but Trapp realized she might not be able to hear him.

He grabbed a throw from the nearby armchair and pressed it against her wounds, both front and back, wrapping it around her to buy her more time. One bullet hole was just below the clavicle, the second near her ribs. Based on the position of the wounds and the rate she was losing blood, he doubted that she would survive long enough for help to arrive.

He crossed her arms over her chest and instructed her to apply pressure.

"I'll be back as soon as I can."

He crawled out of the room, redialing Washington as he went, and once out of sight, he rushed down the stairs into the empty shop below. He pulled open the safe and retrieved an MP5 submachine gun, a Sig Sauer B55, and several magazines.

As the line reconnected with Mitchell, Trapp said, "We're under fire. I'm going to take cover. Get me some backup."

"On its way," Mitchell replied.

"And Mike?"

"Yeah."

"I need you to find out how they keep tracking us down. And end it."

Trapp checked the guns one last time, then raced back up the stairs and prepared to defend his position.

THIRTY-TWO

Trapp kept low to the floor as he checked Zhao Ming's pulse again. Not dead yet.

He had stowed her phone in a shielded pouch, so that wasn't the source of the breach. He searched her and extracted a pair of AirPods, some keys, and her cigarettes and a lighter.

The lighter.

Of course.

It was identical to the one that Ashenhurst had gifted Trapp. This was how the Boko Haram assassins had tracked them down in Chad. And it was how they'd found Ming here.

Trapp placed the lighter on the floor and smashed it with the butt of the SIG. It shattered, revealing a transponder, which he crushed as well.

"Guess there's no point in worrying about the phone then."

Trapp pulled the phone pouch from his inside pocket and retrieved the handset, unlocking it by showing it to Ming's face.

With his back against the wall, he first fired off a message on his own handset to Mitchell to inform him that he'd located the bug. Then he turned his attention to Ming's phone.

After completing his task, he checked on the woman again. She was barely breathing.

There was nothing he could do about it. Even if he could call for help, it would arrive too late.

The safe house wasn't equipped for a siege; it was merely a weapons drop and a place to recuperate. Although he'd never managed to get the shower he desperately needed, he had swiped a change of clothes from one of the go-bags under the second bed, which were marked in his sizes.

He had to get out of here.

Many properties in Britain, especially in former industrial areas, were closely situated. The gardens often backed onto one another, sometimes separated by a narrow alley, but frequently they abutted their neighbor. The rear of the former newsagents was no different, with only a decrepit fence between property lines. He dropped out of the window, rolled over the fence, kept low, and continued over the neighbor's fence. The gardens varied in size; some were even landscaped and well-cared for, while others were overgrown, featuring rusted, inoperable trampolines and moldy plastic wading pools.

At the end of the row, Trapp scanned the streets as he would in any war zone. This close to midnight, midweek, they were very quiet, seeming eerily abandoned.

He stuffed the MP5 submachine gun he'd grabbed from the safehouse cache into the go-bag with the clothes, slipped over the final wall, and moved in the opposite direction from where the sniper must have been. There were now two blocks between him and the presumed nest.

After four blocks, he took a random street, then ducked down a gap between two houses partially blocked by wheeled garbage cans. He climbed over a low wall into a garden with a shed.

Keeping a close watch on the house for motion-sensor lights

or cameras and finding none, he advanced to the shed, jimmied the cheap lock with the gun, and slipped inside. It was crammed with junk and reeked of soil and gasoline—but he was out of sight.

Once he'd used the wet wipes for both hygiene and to remove Ming's blood, then dressed in fresh combat pants, a long-sleeved T-shirt, and a warm sweater, he wrapped his flannel jacket around himself, lay on the floor, and attempted to sleep.

He managed about two hours of rest before deciding his mind had sufficiently recharged.

Remaining in the shadows, he left his temporary shelter, returned to the street, and pulled up a walking map—he had a meeting to attend.

TRAPP'S FEET ached after three hours of walking. He couldn't return to his hotel; the authorities were searching for him, and he certainly didn't expect President Nash to advocate for his departure. His phone was dead, leaving him unable to contact Mitchell for an update. The only communication device he possessed was Zhao Ming's phone, now updated with a new passcode. He used it sparingly, glancing at it before returning it to the pouch. If it sent a signal, it would only be for a fleeting moment, allowing for a delayed response from whoever might be tracking it.

With the hoodie now part of his disguise and a feigned limp to confuse gait analysis, he eventually arrived at a location he didn't expect them to scrutinize: Canary Wharf.

Returning to the scene of the crime was not good tradecraft. But he was out of good options.

He made his way to a low-rise building that advertised

office rentals, which Zhao Ming's phone and email had instructed her business contacts to visit first thing that morning.

At 7:24 a.m., having ensured he was on the guest list, Trapp positioned himself in the lobby, in what he estimated was one of three blind spots. Although not dressed for a day of trading on the FTSE 100, he projected enough confidence that the receptionist in the hexagonal reception area confirmed he was expected and directed him to the correct room.

Walking with determination, he pushed aside the aches plaguing him. As the clock struck 7:30, he opened the door and strode into a room filled with eight Taiwanese financial analysts.

"Nobody move." Trapp casually slid the gun from his waistband, holding it at his side as the room recoiled. "This is just insurance. Do not attempt to leave."

An elderly man stood shakily, his hands raised in front of him. "Where is Zhao Ming? She said to meet here—"

"She didn't say that. I did."

"*You* sent the message?"

"Yes." Trapp pulled out the phone and accessed the saved photos and videos. He presented it to the older man, whom he assumed was in charge. "I'm sorry. This is not easy to watch."

With his free hand, Trapp pressed play, and the older man, along with the younger man and woman beside him, watched the video he had recorded before leaving. The other two remained stoic, but the older man's face paled as it revealed Zhao Ming lying motionless and bloodied.

"The people you're involved with," Trapp said, "are not who you thought they were. They are working directly with the Chinese mainland. They're looking to clean house, and they won't allow anyone who can point a finger at them to survive." He gestured toward the older man. "I'm guessing you're Larry Shian, the senior financial officer. Am I right?"

Part of Ming's declaration to Washington had named her partners and colleagues, but Trapp didn't remember all of them. Larry had anglicized his name years earlier to make introductions to Westerners smoother.

Larry said, "We guessed Zhao Ming was in danger, but we didn't realize how dire it was. That's why we agreed to meet here on short notice."

Trapp scanned the room. "Ming told us everything she knew. Which means *you* know the Ashenhurst Foundation is owned by Ashenhurst Group. Which also means you must know they're making weapons deals."

Trapp watched the man's face drain of color to a gray tint.

"I don't care about your ethics. I just need to locate the weapon Ming referred to as a 'drone mesh.'"

An athletic-looking man at the far end of the table raised a trembling hand.

"We were tracking market activity yesterday. There was a flurry of companies—shells, we think—that were shorting stocks. Zhao was suspicious and instructed us to wait for her go-ahead before we followed suit."

"Why was that significant?" Trapp asked.

"It is likely to be insider trading," Larry Shian replied. "Shorting stocks is gambling on them to fall. We would not want to be caught if those doing so were investigated. If Ashenhurst Group has a plan to take down rival companies, these trades might be connected."

The athletic guy added, "But they would only trace back to ghost corps, crypto traders... it's one way we keep the finances safe. Converting crypto into regular cash, into shares, into cash, back into crypto. But if we short the same stocks, or Ashenhurst did, it'd come back on us quickly. Especially if they all paid out."

"Paid out?" Trapp said. "Like a bookie?"

"Yes. Usually, it's someone from the City meddling with gas and oil prices, but the trades we saw were on another level."

"I need specifics," Trapp pressed him. "Which stocks are they expecting to lose the most money?"

He considered how much Ashenhurst despised being disregarded and how eager he'd been willing to sell to the Chinese to spite the US, regardless of the price.

"Think of it in terms of revenge," Trapp added. "Who can he target to bolster his own standing?"

Larry opened his mouth to speak, then closed it again and looked away. "If there is risk to us... Maybe... maybe we should take legal advice before answering any more questions."

Trapp pulled out his phone, unlocked it, and displayed a photo of Zhao Ming lying in a pool of her own blood. He thrust the image into Larry Shian's face while pointing a gun at him.

"Look closely. This isn't just a warning. This is what they did to her. What they'll do to you." His voice dripped with contempt. "I might as well shoot you right now. At least that would stop you from helping out those who want you dead."

"Okay, okay," Larry said, raising his hands in surrender.

When Trapp stepped back, he noticed the others had cowered in their seats, as if trying to hide from the man demanding they betray some weird principle of their industry.

"There's one name, one company we see repeatedly," Larry said. "He invests in both our ventures and Ashenhurst's portfolio of companies, and although he is not shorting like the other companies, he has sold many shares in companies he once championed. But he is a British *government minister*."

"Who?" Trapp inquired, urgency in his voice.

"You have to understand the consequences if he finds out that we named him." Larry seemed to consider before continuing. "He used to be the Business Secretary. He played a pivotal role in reopening the UK to fracking. He faced political pressure over the MeToo events that lost Rafe Ashenhurst his knighthood, which prevented this minister from approving Ashenhurst Group's bid for those same fracking contracts. Ashenhurst Group lost millions, had to cut up and sell branches of his company specifically set up for the fracking business that he'd assumed he would win. Now that Ashenhurst has restructured and the issue of sexism is out of the news, this minister is facilitating the Group's resurgence from his new position, using new allies."

Did they have to turn this into a riddle? "What position?"

"That's the problem. He's untouchable."

THIRTY-THREE

Mike Mitchell had confronted terrorists, hostage-takers, even irate politicians on Capitol Hill, so the situation before him should have been child's play. But he had to breathe through his nose to prevent himself from delivering a much-deserved slap to Karem Hines as the youngster paced back and forth in the operations room, his narrow frame taut with anxious energy as he vented.

He'd been building up to this since they picked up on the violence across the Thames. Nash had insisted the Washington-bound contingent observe without interference, per the UK ambassador's message. Relayed directly from the Prime Minister, the Brits were aware of Trapp's presence, had refused their usual courtesy—which was suspicious in itself—and permitted comms only to dissuade their operatives from further action.

They were supposed to persuade Trapp to turn himself in. But instead, they'd given him the fake documents designed to convince Zhao Ming that she had been a direct target since day one, instead of a loose end that it'd be nice for Ashenhurst Group to tie up along with Trapp.

Hines had threatened to go to the president to report their insubordination.

Mitchell had explained in no uncertain terms that official word was not the same as them doing their fucking duty and securing both the welfare of their operative and the safety of the United fucking States of America. Mitchell had told Hines to grow a set, which had triggered the tantrum Mitchell now endured.

"I'm a *tech* guy. I lead research teams. I'm not a spy, and I'm not an assassin's little helper. You can't expect me to—"

"Karem," Mitchell said. "Take a damn breath."

But Karem's skin was flushed with panic. "You don't understand. I've done my part. Now it's on you to find it and bring it back or wreck it so the Chinese can't have it. If you choose to disobey orders, fine. I don't care what you do, I'm out."

Mitchell's jaw tightened involuntarily. Maybe it was a generational thing, letting their feelings pour out whenever they surfaced instead of jamming them down hard and getting on with their duty. *Feelings* could be dealt with later. Duty was immediate.

Out of the corner of Mitchell's eye, he saw Polly shift uncomfortably.

"Listen to me," Mitchell growled, stepping closer to Karem. "You're worried about guilt? About messing up, not being good enough? Tough. This meltdown is squandering time we don't have."

Karem's eyes widened behind his glasses. "But—"

"No buts," Mitchell snapped. "Part of operational readiness is *waiting*. We can't just snap our fingers and get results because your short attention span demands it."

Mitchell took a deep breath himself. He needed Karem's expertise, but the kid's impatience threatened the entire operation.

He exhaled slowly. "All right, let's take a step back. Karem, give us a few more hours. When Trapp locates the weapon—and he will—we'll need you to advise on disabling it."

Hines slumped in his chair, arms folded over his chest. "Fine."

"There's a couch in my office. Get some sleep. Reboot, meditate. Whatever you need to do to clear your head."

Hines shook his head sullenly. "Like I could *sleep*. I'm wired."

"Then if you need to keep busy, let's review what we know. Garside, bring up the financials."

Polly did something on her laptop, and the large screen at the front of the room flickered to life.

"Rafe Ashenhurst's endgame still isn't clear," Mitchell said. "Knowing what we know about him, and his actions against us, we can make an educated guess. Deeply hurt when he gets rejected, he doesn't just want to win. He wants to stomp on people he sees as having wronged him. So he'll want to make his company a behemoth, and he'll do it by dominating the developing advanced weapons industry."

"Which he'll achieve," Polly added, "through controlling the materials that make them."

"But only by selling to people who he knows will stick it to the US."

Hines had seemed to regain some composure. "But like I said before—I know numbers as well as chemistry and physics. The numbers don't add up. Trapp is right—dominating DEW tech wouldn't generate the billions he'd need to make it worth all this trouble. It wouldn't replace guns, ammo, bunker-busters."

"Agreed," Polly said. "Even a big ol' success for Ashenhurst wouldn't send his rivals into a freefall deep enough for him to scoop up their businesses."

Mitchell waited for more, but suggestions seemed sparse. "What could generate that kind of windfall? What would Ashenhurst be willing to do?"

Hines shrugged, the petulant child resurfacing. When he caught Mitchell's sharp look, he sat up, seeming to be about to speak, but thought better of it.

"We're not looking for definites here," Mitchell said in his warmest tone, which wasn't exactly toasty. "No wrong answers, but we won't act on blue-sky theories. Just give me your thoughts."

"Okay." Hines sat upright like a grownup, hands in his lap. He retained an air of trepidation but spoke freely. "Something on the scale of 9/11 *might* give him what he needs financially, *if* it results in the financial downturn that we witnessed with the aviation industry.

"With billions of Chinese dollars invested in his manufacturing arm, he'll be free to buy up any crashed stocks at firesale prices. If that's fracking and mining companies, he could all but monopolize the sector."

Mitchell, pissed that he'd had to dangle a federal employee by his ankles and shake loose a theory they could work back from, absorbed what he'd said and saw that Polly understood and agreed.

"It's doubly important we support Trapp and Grubbs," Mitchell said. "Are we agreed?"

Polly nodded without hesitation. Hines stared at a spot on the floor for a long moment before leaning over as if he had a stomachache.

He righted himself and said, "Fine. I'm still on board. But you better be sure about this Trapp guy. If not, we're all screwed."

THIRTY-FOUR

It was a crisp morning, and Cameron Kane was sleep deprived. The park by Tower Bridge still bore the scars of police action from the previous day—the tape, lingering patrols to reassure the public even as Festival of Great Britain banners and bunting were strung up for the long weekend's party. The news had reported yet another gang attack, and it wouldn't be long before it dropped from the headlines.

Across the way, low-level politicians from the three main parties took turns being interviewed, showing unity in the hope of boosting their patriotic credentials. No one was more patriotic than Kane, but there was something empty, something false, about the upcoming festival. Unlike VE Day and specific celebrations like that, the concept behind this was so vague that he found it difficult to summon any enthusiasm.

The public, too, was only lukewarm—in London, anyway. The only people giddy with excitement, it seemed, were the peasants and gentry out in the sticks, the older generation of die-hard monarchists, and a subset of people Kane had never thought of as true patriots: the thuggish class who seemed to engage in competitive mourning when the Queen died, breaking out in maximum solemnity on Remembrance Day. It was fake, all for show.

Kane knew what it meant to give for his country. And no matter what hardship he endured today, no matter what shit he had to eat from his current employer, he never regretted it.

Having been summoned after a mere three hours of downtime, the only thing he had to show for a long night of work were the heavy bags under his eyes and a gnawing dread that Jason Trapp had left the city to follow a lead that Kane and MI5 had overlooked. This frustrated him even more than his aching back.

As a middle-aged man with less than ten percent body fat, he felt the cold more acutely than he had in his younger days, when he'd led his SAS squadron on endless training marches through the harsh Yorkshire Downs winters. Sitting too long on a hard bench while waiting for some insufferable paymaster was not helping, especially as he knew he was in for a roasting over the fallout from the events that had occurred on this very spot.

They'd arrested Trapp's accomplices, sure, but the real danger to peace and security was the guy Kane had helped get away. It had seemed the right thing to do at the time. Crystal balls were not standard equipment for this line of work.

The minister arrived quietly, accompanied by two undercover SO19 close-protection officers, the pair nearby in casual jogger attire—very low profile. Robert Sutherland had conducted his interviews in the media's favorite spot, and although there were plenty of other officers around, Kane hadn't bothered to pinpoint them.

The Home Secretary—responsible for the nation's security, especially through a weekend of forced patriotism—sat on the other end of the bench. He was sixty-two, on the meaty side but carried it well, a former rugby player who still partook in veterans' games occasionally, which made him a surefire vote winner. His dark hair was still full and retained boyish curls with no hint of gray. His baggy eyes stared ahead, not glancing at Kane as he approached.

"This all feels very George Smiley," Kane remarked.

"Le Carré is a classic for a reason." Sutherland, dressed in a long wool coat and a pinstripe suit with shoes that gleamed, crossed his legs and stared out at the bridge.

"You're using me."

"Not at all." Sutherland smiled to himself and lowered his chin, as if to suppress amusement. "I *would* be using you if you were actually *doing* something."

"The intel your MI5 goons sent me said he was spotted briefly in Dagenham, which is hardly precise."

"But you went there?"

"Yeah, of course. I followed the most obvious routes until I ran out of surveillance cameras. The House provided me with a contact who set me up me with local informants but nothing useful. No American bloke or Chinese girl looking for medical help or weapons—which a CIA asset usually needs."

"The Yanks and their security blankets, eh? How many informants did your contact provide?"

"Three. A drug dealer involved with the local knife and gun market, a guy who knows where to get patched-up off the books, and a loan shark with exorbitant interest rates."

"Low-level organized crime."

"The best leads I could find, but they all came up empty. So there must be a safe house in the area. But I'm just one guy, and there's a fuckload of empty properties. I can't search even half of 'em. Unless you want to authorize the Met to send a small army to sweep the area?"

Sutherland contemplated this. "I'll have someone look into

it. If they're lying low, they could still be nearby, which limits their options."

"There's another possibility."

"And that is?"

It was Kane's turn to consider his reply. "I need some guarantees."

"Guarantees?"

Sutherland must have tensed, as the two CP officers nearby ceased their stretching and glanced toward him. With his hands still in his lap, Sutherland waved the pair off with a curt chop.

"There's a good chance this is going to escalate in a way you *really* don't want it to. I need to know I'll be protected for whatever I have to do to ensure the security of the UK and its interests. I want it in writing."

This time, Sutherland did not hold back his patronizing chuckle. "Oh, Cameron." His tone turned both musing and wistful, as though he were chiding a naïve nephew. "You mentioned feeling used. Of *course*, you're being used. That's what we do with assets we have over a barrel. It's either this job or a life of scrimping and scraping in a bedsit, combining your meager military pension with whatever state benefits you can squeeze out of our fine taxpayers. Because you won't get any other sort of work. It takes an awful lot for the SAS to dishonorably discharge one of their own. Especially when word gets around."

He shifted his body fully toward Kane.

"So yes, I'm using you. And I will continue to do so until you quit." He turned back to the view. "Now you mentioned there was another option—that they might not just be lying low. Why don't you enlighten me?"

Kane could have killed Robert Sutherland three times over before the bodyguard coppers could even register that they were about to lose their jobs. They would shoot him dead or arrest him, of course, disappear him into a dark hole for the rest of his life. Kane just had to decide whether it was worth it. But as with the decision that led to his discharge from the only life that had ever mattered to him, he chose to live.

"They're Yanks," Kane said. "They feel naked without their guns. So the safe house probably armed them to the teeth, maybe even a few explosives for good measure. He could stash the girl there, get what he needs from her, then surface just long enough to take what he wants."

"And what *does* he want?" Sutherland asked, both frustrated and reasonable.

"Well, he's after this weapon that I assume you want for Great Blighty."

Sutherland's smile was thin, humorless. "What Rafe builds is his business, Cameron. That he builds it *here*, with our resources, makes it a matter of national interest. The technology is... transformative. A game-changer. We can't have your American friends trampling all over that progress because of their paranoia. Now are you going to stop him or are you telling me you haven't got the bottle?"

"That's not what I said. But it'll be well-guarded."

"My, you *are* perceptive."

"And if someone high up in the government facilitated its acquisition through favors, especially favors from enemies like your new Chinese best friends, I imagine that's an embarrassment you'd prefer to avoid."

"I hope you're not attempting to blackmail me. Or the PM. Our trade deal with China is some way off, but inviting them to our national festival is a good way to start building bridges. Wouldn't you agree?"

Kane knew he needed evidence, and he was currently without any. "What I mean is that it doesn't take much for a conspiracy to spread these days. You need to give me everything you have without worrying about who might end up embarrassed. My loyalty lies with the mission, which means cutting Trapp off and keeping whatever secrets you're worried will come out. If he's half as good as MI5 seems to think he is, he will make it to the next link." Kane inclined his head toward the Home Secretary to drive home the point. "You protect me, I'll take him out before he can scratch your name off the next honors list."

"Understood. However, it will have to be a gentleman's promise," Sutherland replied, turning his head slightly.

Kane nodded. "He's fiercely loyal to his friends and colleagues. He apparently screwed over Grubbs recently, which is unlike him, so he'll be keen to make amends. He won't want her stuck in prison for long. If the CIA disavows their actions here, he'll attempt to get her out before going after your Chinese friends or your old school chum."

"I suppose that's a possibility," Sutherland contemplated. "But wouldn't he first need a clear direction?"

"Right. His government can't provide logistical support. And he can't just break them out and hide them wherever. He'll go after that next step in the money chain."

"And you want to know who that is," Sutherland said.

"Yes."

"To summarize," Sutherland said as he retrieved an envelope from his coat, "based on your operational expertise and your understanding of Jason Trapp's movements so far, we agree that he spent the night in a safe house, acquired supplies and weapons, and intends to retrieve the Nigerian and the woman. However, this leaves three people with little to do. It's more likely he will prioritize someone who would prefer not to be... *embarrassed*, as you put it... which we do not want to happen either, since this individual..." Sutherland dipped his chin and put on his most earnest, press-friendly tone. "Whatever his shortcomings, this person of influence wishes only to improve the lives of this country's people. And you."

Sutherland slid the envelope across the bench to Kane. "This contains what you need to know about the *logistics*. Rafe's guests, his schedule, the location. Nothing more. The *what* of his project is not your concern. Your job is to stop the American from making a scene and scaring off the investors. Do we have our gentleman's agreement?"

THIRTY-FIVE

The stationary Audi was snug and warm, and now that the streetlights were starting to pop on, the tinted windows gave Trapp another layer of security. They weren't opaque by any means, but he was hidden enough from casual observers and cameras to use a pair of pocket binoculars to watch the back of the BBC studios at Millbank. He was near the river again, although ten miles west of the spot where the Met police had killed two terrorists and where Isabella Knight had gone for her impromptu swim. He had not paid for parking, but a ticket was the least of Trapp's concerns.

This was the best chance he was going to get, considering the scant information he was working on. Having learned all he could from Zhao Ming's CFO, he'd borrowed the man's high-end executive vehicle and set about formulating a plan on how best to stalk Robert Sutherland—the Home Secretary of Great Britain, equivalent to the Secretary of State in the US.

Larry had confirmed that Sutherland had very close business links to Rafe Ashenhurst. When combined with deeper background from Washington, Trapp had confirmation that Sutherland was an old university friend of Ashenhurst's and had been in the cabinet when Ashenhurst received his knighthood.

More importantly, Zhao Ming's associates were sure that Ashenhurst would have a ton of dirt on Sutherland, who had facilitated many of Ashenhurst's ventures back when Sutherland was the UK's business secretary.

When the fracking industry had haltingly reopened, Ashenhurst was at the forefront of the cavalry charge toward the UK's fuel independence, green targets be damned. He'd invested heavily in fracking equipment, going so far as to set up his own shipping arm to offset the cost of bringing it in and established a company that would sit proudly under the Ashenhurst Group's umbrella.

He'd tried shrugging off accusations of inappropriate sexual behavior toward a dozen employees over the years as "women jumping on the MeToo bandwagon," but when the accusations escalated to high-profile female business leaders who had fended off his advances, his knighthood was revoked, and he was publicly humiliated. Nor, lest the government be seen to be condoning his behavior, could Ashenhurst receive any sort of tax-payer-funded contract, such as the fracking licenses that his Cambridge buddy, Robert Sutherland, had promised.

He was out in the cold, forced to sell his fracking businesses —including a site on his doorstep—at a significant loss, which almost bankrupted him. From what Trapp had gleaned from his interactions with Ashenhurst, he still bore a mighty grudge.

Yet if he was cozy with Robert Sutherland again, it was possible Sutherland had facilitated the meeting on British soil in exchange for Chinese investment in the UK. It certainly seemed that he was willing to break rules to attract Zhao Ming's financial heft—including arranging a visit from ranking members of the Communist Party of China in the coming weeks, a couple of whom had already arrived. But was there more to it?

The photograph of Fang Chen in a London pub suggested that her boss would probably attend, even though the Chinese ambassador to the United States had no official business in the United Kingdom. Trapp had no doubt that Ambassador Zhelan had been appointed by the same faction seeking to undermine Beijing.

It was little wonder that MI5 had refused to cooperate with a CIA operation—their home secretary, currently departing the BBC's Millbank studio after a scheduled interview, had opened the door to their adversaries.

Trapp had only seconds to act. Security around the home secretary was not as tight as he would have faced reaching his own government's secretary of state, but it was still robust—four plain-clothes in his immediate vicinity and a small team from SO19 Counter-Terrorism Command nearby. Roadworks out front had pushed the small motorcade onto Lord North Street —a narrow one-way road behind the BBC building. It was quiet. Not too many passersby. Few cameras. The key was swift and surprising action that the security team could not resist. Were he seeking to kidnap or murder Sutherland, Trapp would be cut down in a heartbeat, so he'd had to come up with a better idea.

He took a leaf out of the book of many an enemy.

Having kept the car in standby mode, Trapp pulled out and accelerated hard. The electric engine hummed loudly, but even now, taking this ridiculous course of action, Trapp missed the throb of a real power train reverberating through his body.

He screeched to a halt. Late. Purposefully late, clipping the back of the armored car limo that Sutherland was being escorted into. The collision shunted the vehicle enough to make the bodyguards start. They were already drawing their weapons by the time Trapp was out of his door.

Trapp held up both his hands, letting his jacket fall open to reveal the vest to which he had strapped six packs of plastic and a dozen bags of ball bearings.

He could not have obtained these himself, so he had sent the terrified finance team out on errands for him. It had been a risk—any of them could have alerted the police, but he'd believed they were all on the same page in terms of surviving after he showed them Zhao Ming's fate.

In addition to the suicide vest, he held aloft in one hand a trigger that he depressed loosely in his fist.

He shouted, "It's a dead man's switch. You see these?" He gestured to the ball bearings around his vest. "You shoot me, these rip through you, that armored glass, and your home secretary. Not to mention whoever's in that building."

There were two Glocks on him, and he sensed the SO19 uniformed officers closing in behind. He was less than six feet away from Sutherland.

"Time to go, Mr. Secretary," Trapp said.

"Not a chance," one of the suited bodyguards replied. "Turn around and let us defuse that."

"Like you said, *not a chance.*" Trapp spoke directly to Sutherland. "I hate to coin a cliché, sir, but if I wanted to kill you, you'd be dead right now. This is my way of showing it." He emphasized the dead man's switch. "I don't *want* to die. And I don't want to kill you or the cops. I just want to know about the deal with Ashenhurst."

Sutherland held still, as Trapp was sure he'd been briefed to do in such a situation. He didn't seem overly concerned—yet.

As Trapp pulled Sutherland toward him, the guards lifted their weapons higher toward Trapp's head, as if that would stop him from releasing the switch and blowing everyone to pieces.

With the minister facing away from him, Trapp whispered urgently in his ear, "I'm not here to screw you out of your job. All politicians are corrupt, I know that. If you go, someone will just replace you. It doesn't matter to me. What matters is that you have been benefiting from Ashenhurst's dirty dealings. Don't try to deny it."

Sutherland shook his head frantically. "I don't know anything. I didn't *want* to know."

"I think you do. I think you know where the China-Ashenhurst deal is going down. I think you know where the demonstration will happen. And I think you don't care, because you think you can ride the coattails into a much-needed economic boost for Great Britain—and your own finances, to boot."

"I haven't the faintest idea what you're talking about." More than a hint of apprehension in Sutherland's voice, now.

"Your old college buddy is going to kill a ton of people to prove his weapon works. Then he's going to make a deal to sell it to the Chinese."

Sutherland's breath hitched. "Kill people? Don't be absurd. A private showcase for investors, yes, he mentioned that. To prove the technology is viable. It's just a light show, for God's sake. He would never be so insane as to conduct a lethal test on British soil."

Trapp narrowed his gaze. Sutherland seemed to believe what he was saying. "That's the problem with smart people."

"What is?"

They were speaking quietly enough for the police and security to not hear them. But it was only a matter of time until Sutherland's protectors found an opening.

"You can convince yourself of anything." Trapp gestured at the bodyguards. "Tell them to back off. Tell them it's okay."

"Why are you doing this? They're not going to let you

leave. And if you were going to blow me up... like you said, you would have done so already."

"I told you what I want. Tell me."

The lead SO19 officer shouted, "Put him down! We will use lethal force if you do not surrender!"

Trapp ignored the officer. "Come on, Bobby, tell me."

Sutherland was trembling now, eyeing his security with less faith than before. "I don't know anything about any deal. Any weapon. I wouldn't allow that on British soil."

"Think harder."

"What good will it do you?"

"I'll try to get away. Obviously. But in all likelihood, I will be arrested. So all I'm going to do is hope my people get my messages. They'll send someone else in if I don't make it."

"You're crazy."

"And you're corrupt. But I don't care. What I care about is where Rafe Ashenhurst is entertaining his Chinese guests. And when his demonstration will happen."

"*What* demonstration? I told you, I—"

"Last fucking chance, Bobby. Don't push me."

"Maybe." Sutherland was breathing fast, his words breathless. "Maybe I have a small inkling."

"Small is fine."

"They are attending one of the big parties. The Festival of Great Britain, the one down in Surrey."

"Surrey. Didn't I read something about a site down there?"

"A fracking site. It's in the vicinity of one of Rafe's properties. His personal house. He used to own the company before his business troubles forced him to sell up."

As the uniformed officers neared and another warning was shouted, Trapp backed himself against the car, keeping Sutherland snug against him.

"We're looking there too," Sutherland said. "But we've seen nothing. No indication of anything untoward. Rafe is just trying to rebuild his life after those women ruined it." Sutherland pulled up short as if he were speaking on television and realized he'd made a faux pas. "I swear, I only want what is right for Britain. Please go."

"I'm taking you with me. I need to get this intel to the right people before you lock me up."

The officers continued to shout at Trapp, "Put it down. Put. It. *Down.* You can't go anywhere."

They were closing in. And Trapp had no choice here. He could not get away. He couldn't blow them up even if he wanted to. But that was fine. He had a location, and when he surrendered, as he knew he'd probably have to, he'd get a lawyer with access to the embassy.

Suddenly, the security personnel froze. One of them touched his ear and said, "Say again."

A pause.

Then, "Please confirm."

Listening.

Then, "Acknowledged. Backing off."

The man announced loudly, "Negotiator incoming. Thirty seconds. Back off."

Negotiator?

That was quick. A bit too quick.

The police officers and bodyguards retreated. Their guns remained out but lowered. Trapp was about to drag Sutherland toward the limo and order the driver to depart when someone stepped out of the BBC building.

Cameron Kane.

"Hey there, Jase. You and I both know that's not a real vest. You're not holding a real dead man's switch. And you're definitely not a real suicide bomber. Just give yourself the fuck up, and maybe we'll get you deported home." Cameron shrugged. "In about ten years."

Trapp still held Sutherland in front of him, but now that the security personnel and police had retreated, he had a single, wafer-thin window of opportunity.

Trapp shoved Sutherland forward into Kane and sprinted behind the line of parked cars on the other side of the street.

THIRTY-SIX

"Establish a perimeter, but do not engage! I repeat, do not engage the suspect!"

As Trapp sprinted hard, his mind turned faster. Kane wanted him isolated. There would be no Met Police interrogation room. They would drop him in some hole where he would fester until the two countries needed a mutual exchange.

Only seconds ahead, Trapp evaluated angles and choke points. A narrow alley was coming up on his left, a faded "PRIVATE" sign barely discernible in the dim streetlights.

He ducked into the passageway, which opened into a miniature concealed world—a cobbled courtyard encircled by polished-brick apartments. Flowers erupted from every conceivable surface: window boxes overflowed, terracotta pots sprouted on worn stone steps, flowers even cascaded from the roofline.

The scent of lavender and roses mingled with his sweat as he stripped off the fake explosives vest and pressed himself against the wall with the passageway behind him, lowering himself behind a waist-high planter. Within seconds, he heard Kane's muted footsteps on the stone passage.

"You've run out of city, Trapp," Kane called, his voice echoing off the walls of the quaint apartment block. "Let's not make this any messier."

Trapp had been in tighter spots, but not many. This flower-filled oasis could not be his final stop. He'd been prepared to be caught and captured during his stint with the government minister, even if it meant ending up in a British prison. But now that he'd gotten away, albeit briefly, he wasn't willing to surrender.

"You don't know what they're planning, Kane," Trapp said loudly, his voice echoing as Kane's had. No way to pinpoint him.

Kane's footsteps paused. "And you do?"

Trapp allowed himself a moment to reflect. He didn't know exactly, but admitting that wouldn't hold water. "A major incident involving an accelerated directed energy weapon."

"Where and when?"

"Can't say unless you let me go."

"Oh sure," Kane said. "Let me give you my Snap handle and we can gab all night about it later."

Trapp didn't reply. Kane had sounded too close on that last word.

And, sure enough, Trapp could see the man's boots treading carefully forward.

He couldn't simply wait this out. There were only a few hiding places here. It came down to another simple, binary choice: fight or attempt to flee.

Trapp vaulted over the planter, launching at Kane. The ex-SAS officer's eyes widened, but he sidestepped, narrowly avoiding Trapp's full bodyweight. Trapp managed to reposition and land a glancing blow, but all he did was disarm his opponent.

Kane threw himself into a tackle and lifted Trapp off the ground, slamming him into a wall. Trapp jabbed an elbow into the man's neck, easing the pressure but not gaining release. Pushing away from the wall, the two men grappled like well-matched wrestlers until Trapp drove his knee toward Kane's midsection. Kane deflected it and retaliated with a vicious elbow that Trapp barely managed to slip before stepping back, putting distance between them.

"Impressive," Kane said.

Trapp didn't waste breath on a response. The close quarters of the courtyard restricted both their options, and Kane now blocked the exit.

A door swung open to reveal two young men in pajamas. One of them yelled, "What the bloody hell is going on out here? Piss off or I'm calling the police."

Trapp broke away from Kane and sprinted at the open building. The young couple tried to swing the heavy door shut, but the safety hinge was designed to move slowly. Trapp barreled past, sending them reeling.

"Sorry!" he called out before he realized he'd said it.

Maybe Britain was rubbing off on him.

Inside the lushly carpeted interior with its high ceiling and fresh-paint smell, Trapp searched for an escape route. There was no back door evident. He looked upward.

The roof.

He raced up the wide staircase. The first switchback landing had a huge window overlooking a lit vegetable garden in a shared green space.

Behind him, Kane's boots thumped on the soft flooring.

Reaching the top, the fourth floor, Trapp expected to find a roof access, but there was nothing. No door with a crash bar or heavy bolt. Just a window far above the flowery, cobbled courtyard and another door to an apartment.

"No, no!" He hammered on the door to his right. "Open up, come on! I need to get to the roof!"

A muffled voice shouted back, "Are you fuckin' mad? This building's older than your country, you Yank prick! There's no bloody roof access!"

"Please. It's an emergency!"

"Call the police then!"

A bitter laugh escaped Trapp's lips. "Ahh, shit..."

Heavy footsteps no longer approached. They had arrived.

"Nowhere left to run, Trapp," Kane said as he ascended the stairwell at a walk, eerily calm.

Trapp's gaze fell on a large potted plant by the window.

"Time to be sensible," Kane added. "We can discuss this. Work the intel."

Trapp lifted the heavy pot. "Sorry, can't do that."

Then he hurled the plant through the window. Glass shattered with a deafening crash, and the old wooden frame splintered as the pane ripped free.

Kane said, "You're insane, you know that?"

Trapp flashed a smile. "Probably." He looked out the broken window, eyeing the drainpipe to the right and the dizzying drop. "But I'm also out of options."

Trapp stepped toward the window and gripped the window frame in the gaps where the glass shards wouldn't bite into his palms. The drainpipe beckoned.

A lifeline or death.

Kane drew nearer, plainly unwilling to tackle him in case they both ended up pancaked on the cobblestones.

"Consider this, Jase." Kane was using his first name now, or rather an annoying contraction of it. Hoping to talk him down. "Even if that drainpipe holds your weight, which it probably won't, where will you go? I came after you alone out of respect for the fact I know you think you're doing the right thing. But we've locked down the entire area."

"I can't give up," Trapp replied, still facing away. "Not when you have so many people who need this to go away. Your fucking home secretary is forcing MI5 to hold back—that's why you're on me instead of them. They're more concerned about embarrassing the establishment than stopping Ashenhurst and the Chinese."

He heard Kane's frustrated exhale. "Fucking Yanks. That sodding policeman complex you won't let go of. No one else is allowed to patrol international security. Just you, right? Like we can't handle some sex-pest business knobhead."

Trapp tightened his grip on the frame, his foot probing for a purchase where he might pivot his weight to grab the pipe securely.

Surrender could mean prison.

Or it could mean a black site, endless interrogations, and the truth buried.

"Last chance, Trapp," Kane warned, tension palpable in his voice. "Don't make me—"

"Fuck it," Trapp said.

First, he took a deep breath. Then he took the biggest gamble of his life.

THIRTY-SEVEN

Madison Grubbs woke with a start to a metallic banging on the door. She pressed her elbows into the plastic mat and rose halfway, thinking how rude it was for someone to interrupt her sleep so violently. Then she remembered where she was.

She had never been in a jail cell before, and it was much different than she'd expected. Sure, she'd been arrested some months ago thanks to Trapp being a dick to her, but that was CIA holding, followed by an FBI interrogation room. Mike Mitchell had intervened before they got too heavy with her.

When she'd surrendered after her stunt at the plaza—another middle finger from Trapp, using her as a distraction—she'd pictured a large holding area: a cage full of drunks drying out and drug addicts coming down. Instead, she had been deposited in this plain, tiled box. There was a bench, a toilet with no lid or seat, and a door with one hatch for observation and a second one for passing items through. The toilet was probably the worst because she could not shake the feeling she was being watched. The next worst was the itchy gray flannel sweats she had to wear after they took her clothes.

But she endured.

As soon as the police made their presence known, she'd accepted that she would never have made it out of that plaza. She had improvised, thinking it was what Trapp might have done—big and bold—but she guessed this was how it felt to make the big sacrifice. Something Trapp had done plenty of times. Even throwing her under the treason bus, he claimed, had left him feeling worse than almost any other difficult play he'd made.

Improvising.

Fuck improvising.

Although she had known with around ninety percent clarity that Trapp would have to prioritize Zhao Ming over her, it still stung less than the other abandonment.

She had assumed her embassy would have gotten her out by now. Or at least tried.

The door opened fully, and the uniformed sergeant who had been interviewing her on and off and had attained permission to keep her locked up longer than the customary twenty-four hours entered. He was holding a sealed plastic bag containing her clothes and some oh-so-dangerous items like her belt, which she could have used to harm herself.

"I hope those are freshly laundered," Madison said.

He tossed her the package and said, "Get dressed. You're being transferred."

"Where?" she asked, ripping open the plastic.

"The security services want a word. But they don't want to step out of their cushy office building. So get dressed. You've got five minutes."

As he closed the door, Madison shouted, "I ordered the breakfast muffin. Make sure it's ready before I leave."

Silence replied.

Grubbs sighed, reflecting that perhaps Trapp's belligerence

was rubbing off on her. Or maybe she was just going stir-crazy in this Metropolitan Police cell.

True to his word, Radovanovich opened the door five minutes later.

They didn't bother handcuffing her. The sergeant and a female constable escorted her without words. She was told to sign some papers, and the duty officer explained she was not being bailed or released, but her custody was being handed over to MI5. However, she would remain the responsibility of the Metropolitan Police until Thames House took possession of her.

She was then taken to a loading bay, where a police van with a black internal cage waited. A burly young constable opened the cage door, and the woman who'd brought her from holding ushered her inside. It smelled musty, with a layer of disinfectant overriding any other unpleasantness. She guessed this vehicle more than likely doubled as a drunk tank during the night.

She sat on the hard bench and waited.

The door did not close.

Madison called to the burly constable, "Hey, let's get a move on. I've got an important appointment."

Again with the wisecracks.

After she had counted slowly to 130 in her head, a second prisoner was delivered and loaded into the van.

"Hey, Maddy," Ikem said. "It seems we're getting the band back together again."

So it wasn't just Madison who had succumbed to inappropriate humor to get through this.

"Sounds like a party," she said. Then, more sincerely, "Good to see you. They treat you okay?"

"Like a gangster at first. Then a terrorist. By now, they must have received information about me."

"Me too. Minus the gangster stuff."

The cage door slammed shut, followed by the soft thud of the outer doors.

Ikem sat back, leaning against the padded headrest. "So the Met softened us up, and MI5 will take the credit for breaking us."

"Except they already know why we're here. And the fact we're here alone in this van means Jason is still out."

The engine rumbled to life, then they were moving. Without warning, there was a sharp turn, and the traffic noise outside told Madison they were heading through the city. Whenever they slowed, what few gaps there were in the internal cage allowed the blue flashing lights to creep in, then their progress resumed quickly.

The van sped along uninterrupted for several minutes, long enough for her to guess they'd reached a freeway. The steady rhythm shattered as the van decelerated sharply, the brakes pumping hard without a skid. Through the partition, the driver's and his partner's voices suddenly erupted—no longer a low murmur, but loud, strained, and sharp with panic.

Then came the unmistakable sound of gunshots.

"Get ready," Grubbs said.

There was nothing they could use as a weapon. It wasn't like they could take their assailants by surprise, either. The internal cage left no place to hide any prep they made, and Isabella Knight's assassins would pick them off at will.

If they didn't simply blow the van to smithereens.

A loud pop burst from the rear, projecting smoke into the cabin, and the door flew open.

Madison braced.

Ikem held his chin high, his chest out, ready to meet his fate as the masked man who set another charge on the cage lock moved with haste, keeping his submachine gun in hand.

Grubbs put her fingers in her ears, and the second bang was louder, the stench of cordite wafting harshly toward her.

"Get out," the man said. His voice was pleasingly familiar.

"Trapp," she said.

"Oh my God, what is he doing now?" Ikem said as he held out a hand like a gentleman while Madison exited before him.

The daylight stung her eyes, but she blinked it away quickly. She got her bearings and found she was at the base of an elevated freeway. Traffic flowing up the ramp had come to a standstill, but a backup unit was coming toward them.

She noted that the two cops who'd been driving were now restrained in zip ties and appeared unharmed. The gunshots had been for show. There was a car in flames in the middle of the road, which she suspected had been shoved out from the alleyway to their left.

"Come on, move it," Trapp said, unlocking her cuffs and throwing the key to Ikem.

He led them out to the alleyway.

The backup unit was within small-arms fire range as it came to a halt, disgorging two armed officers with sidearms and what was clearly a positive mental attitude toward preventing their escape. They probably would succeed, as none of them were going to shoot back.

But the reason for Trapp's lack of concern soon became apparent as a trash can exploded ten feet from the cops.

As the officers retreated, a high-end BMW with tinted windows peeled out of the alleyway.

Trapp opened the back door and pinwheeled his arm. "Come on, come on. You've never been in a jailbreak before? You gotta move *fast*."

Madison dove into the back seat, followed by Ikem, and Trapp jumped into the passenger seat.

It was Cameron Kane at the wheel. "Not the best getaway

vehicle in the world, but the fucking clean air zone charges are murder for anything else. Hold on."

Kane floored it, and the high-pitched whine of the powerful electric engine resonated through the car as it accelerated hard away from the scene.

THIRTY-EIGHT

As part of the prep for the jailbreak, Trapp and Kane had manually disabled a half-dozen street cameras, hedging their bets in case their primary escape route got cut off. But for a change, everything went according to plan, so they had some privacy to switch vehicles.

This was an MG, another electric vehicle, smaller than the Audi and the BMW and far less conspicuous. A fake Uber sticker on the door made it blend in even more. It lacked tinted windows, but they had enough of a head start that they wouldn't need to drive for very long. Their destination was nearby.

"Somebody want to fill us in?" Grubbs said. "You two are best buds now?"

"I needed you out," Trapp replied. "And for that I needed guns, explosives, and someone with a place to go."

"In other words," Kane said. "I beat him and caught him, and he didn't have a choice but to cooperate."

"Cooperate," Ikem said. "That seems to be the word of the week."

"This is voluntary," Trapp said. "Just ask and we'll drop you on the street. You can surrender back to the authorities, take your chances. Both of you."

"Not happening," Grubbs said. "We see this through, they'll have no choice but to send us home, maybe even with a pat on the back."

"Don't fucking count on *that*," Kane said.

"Where are we going?" Ikem asked. "They will shut every road out of London."

"We're not going out of London," Trapp said.

"In fact," Kane said, "we're here."

They drove into what looked like a dingy alleyway, which descended into the earth and became a delivery zone with multiple signs warning that trespassers would be prosecuted or bitten by dogs, that it was the property of the Ministry of Defence, and that perpetrators were being watched.

"It's an old DCHQ listening post," Kane said. "I worked here for a bit. It's being renovated into a Cold War espionage museum. For now, it's mothballed, and no, there aren't any cameras left. Or dogs."

Kane parked, and they got out. There were eight spaces, two filled by other cars sourced from the same finance geeks as the barbecued Audi and the MG. It was cold and damp here, and Trapp was glad to ascend the stairwell to the first floor where they had set up camp.

"You never explained what the hell happened between you two," Grubbs said.

"Yes, I did," Kane replied. "I caught the bastard. Then we came to an arrangement."

"I gambled," Trapp said. "I guessed Kane here would see the bigger picture. That's why he helped us get away on the river."

"That's not why I helped you back there. My order was to

keep the chaos to a minimum. If that meant taking you out, I'd have taken you out. Giving you a boat seemed like the easier thing to do."

"Wise choice," Ikem said.

Trapp looked at Kane with annoyance, then smiled, unable to maintain the pretense. "I had the uncensored footage from the Pittsburgh massacre. I shared what I knew about the tech, along with a few state secrets about what really happened in New York."

"Jason, that's—" Grubbs cut herself off, blinking as she thought it through.

"I had no choice. If Nash or Mitchell want to jail me for it, fine. But I needed someone on my side and took a risk."

"The weapon looks horrendous," Kane said, sincerity taking over. "Scale it up, I can only imagine what a 'drone mesh' is. But that fucker Sutherland, I never liked him. He served in my unit long before my time, which is how I do occasional work for him. But he's blown all that. He might not know the full implications, but he sure as shit knows there's something dodgy going on. I've made mistakes in my life. But if what he's using me for opens the door for some hardline pricks to take over China... I'm complicit. And I can't have that."

Grubbs and Ikem took that in, gave him simultaneous nods of respect, and looked to Trapp.

"What now?" Grubbs asked. "This doesn't exactly scream 'safehouse.'"

Kane smiled as he opened the door to a floor which used to be full of digital surveillance gear, where DCHQ employees once spent their days disseminating information harvested from around the world but mainly, Kane explained, directly in London. Operators here would listen for keywords, then analyze the data, and if it was deemed necessary, they would dispatch Kane or somebody like him.

Grubbs asked, "So you were like one of the MI5 bulls, right?"

"No," Kane said seriously. "I had some finesse."

Pulling aside a floor-to-ceiling plastic tarp, Kane bade them enter his boudoir. Grubbs seemed annoyed at herself for laughing.

There were five cots laid out, a dozen more folded and stacked against one wall beside boxes of military supplies. Piles of sealed plastic boxes held packets—likely MREs—beside a refrigerator, and there were a couple of tables on which lay laptops and gun cleaning paraphernalia.

And one of the cots was occupied.

"Is that... Zhao Ming?" Ikem asked.

"Yeah," Trapp said. "She nearly died, but the bullets were through-and-through. I got the bleeding stopped, and she somehow lived through the night. Kane found her and got her medical attention before bringing her here."

"How did Knight's people find you?" Ikem asked.

"They were tracking us using a gift from Ashenhurst. The lighter."

Trapp joined her. "You awake?"

Zhao Ming's eyes fluttered and opened.

Meanwhile, Kane got on the phone and made the call he'd promised he would, having bribed some street thugs to drive a car similar to the one they'd escaped in erratically toward the M25 motorway—a good distraction, if not a perfect one.

"What help is she giving us?" Grubbs asked.

"Everything," Zhao said weakly, her voice fading in and out from visible pain. Kane had a supply of morphine, but it needed to be rationed.

"I've set up a flight from a private airfield," Trapp said. "It's a US Air Force plane heading directly to Taiwan. It'll refuel mid-flight."

"Who's flying out there?" Grubbs asked.

"I must go," Zhao murmured weakly. "I am the only one who can grant access to the servers. It is my responsibility... my burden to bear."

"I'll go with her," Trapp said. "We've traced a hell of a lot of stuff going down, but if we're going to nail the people responsible, we need more than a money trail."

Grubbs looked like she had something to say about that, but instead she pressed her lips together into a tight line.

Ikem had been hovering close by, listening. "Why don't you fill us in on what you know?"

"We think we know roughly what's happening," Trapp emphasized. "We've looked at the movement of Chinese officials, Ashenhurst's properties, and the travel itinerary for the main players. We think the testing site is a fracking operation in Surrey. Near one of the big Festival of Great Britain parties. He's going to demonstrate what the weapon can do there."

Kane returned after setting his car thieves loose. "All right, that's a go. We should be clear to head out through Brentford in thirty minutes. Once you're wheels-up, I'm sending everything I've got to the Met, to the National Crime Agency, and some gobshite journo I know at Reuters."

"Why?"

"Because MI5'll bury it," Grubbs said. "You've traced it to someone important."

"Inadvertently," Trapp said. "I'll explain more soon, but we need to get Zhao safely to the airfield and on that flight. Washington can't officially interfere here, but this will be, as far as anyone else is concerned, a US military vehicle taking a sick master sergeant for specialist treatment."

"Explain it to me again," Ikem said. "The real fight is here in Surrey. Why are you flying to Taiwan?"

"Because Kane is the hammer," Trapp replied, his voice low.

"He handles the assault here. I'm going to their financial hub to get the proof that dismantles their entire global network. If we can't stop this weapon, we need the intel to burn down everything they've ever built."

"Oh, there'll be no failing," Kane cut in, a grim smile touching his lips. "Not on my end. Those pricks at the House have finally dropped my leash. I'm going to enjoy taking Rafe Ashenhurst and his buyers apart, piece by bloody piece."

He slapped Trapp hard on the back, a gesture of aggressive camaraderie that made Trapp tense. "Isn't that right, mate?"

"So what's the play?" Kane asked, all business now. "We stop the fireworks?"

"We stop the massacre," Trapp corrected him. "But even if we do, this weapon leaves no evidence. No residue, no crater. To the world, it will just look like a catastrophic equipment failure."

Kane let out a low whistle. "And the public panics. The fracking industry's stock craters. Then a 'concerned' Rafe Ashenhurst swoops in to buy up his rivals for pennies." A dark grin spread across his face. "You have to admit, for a posh prick, it's a ballsy plan. Getting revenge on the system by owning it."

"Let's make sure it's his last," Trapp said.

Grubbs looked at Zhao Ming, reaching to touch the stricken woman's hand. Zhao lifted her head and forced a smile. Grubbs then perused the medical equipment, which extended to a saline drip and a second drip that had transfused blood into her.

"She isn't fit to travel," Grubbs stated.

"There's no other way," Trapp said. "She's a brave woman. Naïve in her choice of partners but brave. She's agreed to it, and I'll take good care of her."

"No you won't."

Trapp, having accepted his guilt, the gnawing in his gut

over what he'd had to do to Grubbs—both months ago and leaving her to be arrested in London—now felt nothing except exasperated. "Madison, I have apologized more times than I can count. I've done my best to protect you from the consequences of my actions. Even when I've screwed up, it's been because it's what I thought was the right course of action. I promise you, Madison, with Ming in my care, I will not let her—"

Grubbs was smiling.

Trapp said, "What? What is it?"

"I didn't mean you wouldn't take good care of her, Jason. I just meant that you're not going to Taiwan."

"I'm not?"

"No. I am. I'll go. You're needed here."

"Oi," Kane said. "Are you suggesting I can't handle some old public schoolboys and a handful of Chinese business types?"

"Not at all." Grubbs flashed him a grin. "I just know Jason will be a great backup for you. And he can take the heat if the cops come to arrest someone."

Trapp ran the setup through his head, reformulating the plan to send Grubbs away and keep him on point. "Impulsive decision," he said.

"Sometimes, it's necessary to improvise," Grubbs replied. "What do I need to do over there?"

"Ming needs to be there physically to access the servers and confidential files. They're locked down on air-gapped servers. No Internet access, so no possibility of hacking."

Zhao Ming spoke, her voice sounding tiny. "Biometric encryption. And this is all my fault. It's not fair to make Larry go and put himself in danger."

"Kane has her colleagues stashed at a place like this until we give them the all-clear," Trapp said.

Grubbs stood and faced the three men. "Even taking out a fracking site, it's still not big enough. One disaster, even if the body count is in the hundreds, won't cripple the industry. It certainly won't give him the apocalyptic event he needs to take over those companies at the price we think he's aiming for."

Trapp and Kane exchanged a glance. Kane gave a sarcastic shrug, and Trapp nodded slowly.

He said, "That's why, I suppose, you're going to Taiwan, and I'm heading for a British country fair. We have to figure out the missing piece. And finish it off."

THIRTY-NINE

Trapp had been prepared for his stereotypical impressions of a "traditional English village" to be shattered, but their arrival in Queensacre could not have been more quaint if Beatrix Potter herself had greeted Kane, Ikem, and Trapp and invited them to her cottage for tea and crumpets. Although still classed as a village and surrounded on all sides by the green splendor of rolling hills and farmland, it was as large as a small town with local industry and retail keeping the big brands at bay.

They rolled through the streets in the cool early morning, posing as what Kane had called "white van men" without irony, despite the fact that they were literally riding in a white panel van—a Ford Transit that was about as ubiquitous a sight in UK towns as it was in the States. Trapp got the impression Kane didn't like the vehicle or the fact that he was now operating in the dark and very much against orders, but he had been more enthusiastic about the cargo.

"I might need asylum in your fucking country when this is over," he'd said. "If you're wrong about this toff, I'll be the new Julian Assange, living in your embassy."

"Grubbs will get what we need to prove it," Trapp had assured their grouchy guide, repeating some variation of it whenever Kane expressed doubts.

It was annoying, but he needed to keep the guy on-side. Not that he believed Kane would back out now. He'd supplied weapons and transport, and when they'd researched the terrain they might need to traverse, he'd even sourced additional vehicles, which were now strapped into the back of the van.

Banners for the Festival of Britain hung across narrow streets, cabled to antique stores and cafés and flower shops, and Union flags fluttered everywhere. There was a bit of cynicism in Kane's explanation that it was all part of the current government's attempt to inject a bit of positivity into the populace, but he was probably right.

And apparently, Rafe Ashenhurst saw it as a chance to throw his hand into the balance of power in global politics, tipping the scales in favor of China—all because someone had told him "no" one time too many.

More importantly, though, this festival opened the door to inviting all manner of dignitaries from far and wide. As the village of Queensacre stirred to life for the first official day of celebration, Trapp was satisfied that he had the lay of the land memorized, as well as certain that there would be bad people waiting at Ashenhurst's estate to intercept him.

Hopefully, they wouldn't anticipate the wildcard pretending to sleep in the middle passenger seat.

"Kane, wake up," Trapp said, playing along with the ruse.

Kane came alert as fast as Trapp expected and cracked his neck as he righted himself. "We're here, then. Why not go straight to the estate? We know that's the only place 'round here with the capacity to do what we know they're doing."

"We talked this through already," Ikem said.

"I was in the land of Nod. Tell me."

"While you were resting, Washington confirmed several things for us," Trapp said. "First, the Boko Haram assholes aren't the only hired guns in play. An alert went out on the dark web that professional muscle was needed for a 'special,' which I'm guessing is us. Analysts haven't cracked the responses yet, but we know several flagged names from legit agencies also flew in on half a dozen of Ashenhurst Group's private jets."

"Private contractors," Ikem clarified.

"Eastern Europe, the old Soviet Bloc, and Turkey."

"Huh," Kane said. "What'd you do to deserve such a massive cock as an enemy?"

"I was just being my charming self. Oh, and I blew up his mine and freed a bunch of slaves."

Kane shrugged. "That'll do it."

"In addition to the muscle," Trapp said, "we've got the Chinese dignitaries bringing their own security."

"Official visitors?"

"Some, yes. Others are leading industrialists, pals of Ashenhurst and other billionaires. One in particular is of interest: Gao Shuren, a former general. Close links with the current ambassador based in Washington, who we think is dirty. Gao's itinerary has crossed with Ashenhurst's a few times, but no evidence they met. The dignitaries are one stated reason that Ashenhurst has beefed up the personnel at his estate. Claims he doesn't want the public trespassing, which apparently happens whenever there's a festival nearby. They think it's a tourist attraction, I guess."

"So a bunch of fighting arseholes tooled up to the eyeballs," Kane said.

"Indeed," Ikem agreed. "But if we know all this, they'll know we know, so countermeasures will be deployed."

"That's why we're here," Trapp said, "instead of heading straight to the manor house. We've got people working out the best way in, based on current satellite images." He pulled into a gravelly stretch of land surrounded by a low ring of steel fencing with a row of charging stations along one side. "In the meantime, we are going to keep a low profile."

The parking lot was on the edge of town near a pub, within view of a signpost pointing in three different directions at what looked like hiking trails. Trapp expected the pub did a brisk trade in the muddy boots crowd.

"Then what?" Kane asked. "After we've kept our low profile?"

"We're as sure as we can be that it'll be a drone-mounted demo," Trapp said. "This 'drone mesh' that Ming told us about. To be effective, it'll have to be satellite-fed with a ground-based processor as its origin. The computer system will be big, so shouldn't be too hard to locate. Karem Hines thinks there'll be a human override option, so all we need to do is disable their ability to fly."

"Blocking the signal is the best option," Ikem added. "Unless they have a mobile command center, the most likely position is the house."

"And they've just finished a six-month renovation." Trapp watched as cars rolled by. Pedestrians were now dotting the town, and down the main road, several white vans like theirs were parked, doors open, stalls half-erected. "He had to be preparing for this."

"And the target is some quarry?" Kane said.

Trapp pointed at one of the hills. "Can't see it from here, but just on the other side, Black Gold Investments owns what *used* to be Ashenhurst's quarry, which later became a strip mine. Tin, I'm told. Ashenhurst made it into a fracking site before he was forced to sell up. Small deposits of oil going real deep."

Kane snorted. "Bet old Rafe loved seeing that in his backyard after they shut him out for the contract. No wonder he moved to fucking Chad."

"We're only making assumptions, but it all fits together." Trapp watched a pair of larger men trying to mingle and failing. Although he was too far away to describe their faces, he directed his companions to check them out. "What do you think?"

"I think they're watching for us," Ikem said as one of the men examined his cellphone and zeroed in on some innocent member of the public before signaling to his buddy that it was nothing. "Will they have infiltrated the police?"

He was referring to two uniformed constables strolling the early crowd, their manner friendly, nods and smiles visible from their position.

"They might've spun a yarn," Kane said. "Want to neutralize 'em? Because I'd advise against it."

"Might draw attention to us," Ikem said.

Trapp had considered it, but he was on the same wavelength as the others. "I'd rather give the manor house another look."

They waited until there were more cars around, then pulled the white van onto the road leading out of town. There were actual thatched houses in Queensacre, and passing between them made Trapp wonder if he would enjoy a few days in a place like this or hate it to his very core.

The town ended in a straight cut-off. One minute surrounded by houses and flags, the next, hedgerows bordered roads too narrow for cars to pass one another. The roads weren't one-way, either. Giving way to oncoming vehicles meant utilizing gouges cut into the fields.

"Better hope we do not run into anyone we know," Ikem said at the fourth such impasse, as Trapp reversed ten feet to pull in.

"Hope," Trapp said. "The cornerstone of all great operations."

"Our targets are up at the house," Kane pointed out. "And the day they drive their own cars, I'm skating into hell."

The lane soon widened into a proper road with markings and signposts, like a civilized country should have. This led them higher into the hills and around the lip of a farm with sheep roaming free on the tarmac and fields. Then down again.

They'd come the long way around, but there, spread before them, was the sort of property Trapp had only seen in dull movies and TV shows about heiresses and princes from a hundred or more years ago. A small forest to the east. Fields to the north where cows grazed. The house itself was red brick with a slate roof, and its gardens were landscaped in a manner that made the armed patrols jarring in a perverse way that they would not be in a desert compound.

"Sprawling" was an understatement.

They were still far enough away to avoid suspicion. Trapp kept the van rolling along so that they would look like any visitor to these parts. As he drove, Ikem observed for a few minutes through binoculars, watching for patterns in the patrols.

The only feature out of place, other than the dozen or so security personnel patrolling the grounds, was the camouflaged satellite dish on the roof. Hines had told them that blowing it up might not solve the problem, as there would be redundant systems. A UAV strike or bombing run was out of the question unless the Brits perceived an immediate threat—and even then unlikely. Air strikes in the Home Counties were a surefire vote loser. So someone had to get inside, examine the setup, and neutralize it at the source.

"Shame we can't just blast our way in," Kane said.

"We do this smart," Trapp replied. "Surgical. We ride their schedule. Get in, disable the uplink, and—if we can—get out."

"If," Ikem said. "Another word we do not like for operations."

The estate disappeared behind the land as the road dipped downward, and the dirt bikes Kane had acquired rattled against each other in the back. They were definitely going to need those. Trapp's phone pinged, and he checked it out. "Washington came through. Green light. Let's do it."

FORTY

Isabella Knight rarely felt nervous, but today as she watched the gathering of stakeholders on the grand patio deck of Rafe Ashenhurst's manor house, an ominous flutter filled her belly, and her mind ran through all the doomsday scenarios she could envisage, along with the counter-measures she hoped would not be needed. In the morning sun, four Chinese men and a small woman waited patiently with hot drinks in hand, their security personnel a courteous but safe distance away.

This gathering was a culmination of a year's brilliant planning, six months of flawless execution, and a week of fuckups that could have been avoided had her boss been less trigger happy. If only he didn't insist on treating the neutralization of highly trained CIA operatives the same way he dealt with troublesome business situations—demand results, as fast and as cheaply as possible, then throw a tantrum when it didn't go his way.

That was why she had anonymously hired two gentlemen who had earned pride of place on a number of international no-fly lists and whose fees were sizable but justified by their track record. She'd faked their papers to bring them to the UK via private plane, and she had not asked permission from Ashenhurst.

The limo she'd laid on for them pulled in through the two pillars adorned with lions on the top at the entrance to the ostentatious gravel driveway. That first glimpse of the place left visitors—and employees in particular—under no illusions: Rafe Ashenhurst was a man who expected results.

The car pulled up at a circular turning point with a small fountain in its center before the house's main entrance. Demir got out first, followed by Kaya, and they reconnoitered the immediate area briefly before proceeding up the four stone stairs to the patio where the Chinese contingent was gathered.

Kilo Demir was a tall, lean man with a gaunt face. According to the crew who'd chauffeured them to England, Demir had said very little, either staring at nothing or closing his eyes to rest. Ozan Kaya, who was broader-shouldered and more physically imposing, had close-cropped hair and a neatly trimmed beard, and his eyes retained some degree of humanity. Kaya had read books or scrolled his phone throughout the long flight.

On the terrace, the Chinese contingent of four suited men and a young woman stared at the pair without a word. They stared back.

Then it was time.

Isabella Knight removed herself from the window and fell in with a crew of six men, all experienced shooters.

She took a breath and stood at the head of the group. "Let's get started, shall we?"

KNIGHT HATED MOMENTS LIKE THIS. The theatricality, in particular. Ashenhurst seizing on the kind of nonsensical staging that he had probably seen on TV shows where the nobility greeted their guests in grand settings.

Number one, keep them waiting.

Number two, make a majestic entrance.

Three...

Well, *she* was three, even though her part came first chronologically: instilling a sense of confidence in their guests before he showed himself.

"Good morning, and thank you for your patience," she said, having been instructed to use the *thank you* not the *sorry for keeping you waiting* line.

Apparently, in management speak, it was better received by clients who had been inconvenienced.

"For those who don't know me, I'm Isabella Knight, head of security, and I want to assure you that we have every contingency covered. In addition to these gentlemen, we have experts patrolling the grounds, and we've dispatched others into the village to feel out potential issues there."

Fang Chen raised her hand and asked, "Are you concerned about the British authorities intervening?"

"We expect *attempted* interference from a specific individual, if he learns of our location. But not British police or the security services."

"Jason Trapp, you mean."

"He can't affect anything here. The house is secure. We will have far more security than is required for the demonstration."

"Our intelligence suggests that he has a larger team now."

Knight sighed with as much patience as she could muster. The intelligent young woman had been impressive with her strategy and directness in her dealings with Knight, but she had to project skepticism in front of her people. If she simply accepted Knight's word—and Fang had expressed confidence in her privately—General Gao and his dignitaries, whoever they were, might believe they were somehow conspiring together.

Knight said, "We have heard some sketchy reports that perhaps his colleagues were broken free from custody. But the Met and MI5 are not saying anything publicly. I assure you we're ready for them, and I hope you are able to trust us on that."

The bulkier of the two Turks, Ozan Kaya, stepped forward. "As soon as you sight Trapp, do not hesitate to tell us. We *will* finish him."

Do not hesitate to...

A phrase more akin to corporate memo speak, although Knight doubted Kaya or Demir would know that. Or care.

She said, "Thank you, I appreciate that. But if he brings trouble, we will intercept him before he can cause any damage. You are the final contingency. Protect the area assigned to you. Are there any more questions?"

Fang had been translating for her contingent throughout, so Knight gave them a few seconds to confer before they indicated they needed no more from her.

FANG WISHED one of the representatives had wanted to ask questions, but they did not. She wanted firmer details about the geography and about the upcoming test, but that would have to wait.

As the estate security detail deployed, Isabella Knight opened the grand door, and Rafe Ashenhurst stepped out onto the patio. He paused after a few steps, framed by the columns on either side of the door, cutting an impressive figure in an impeccably tailored charcoal suit. His graying hair was combed back, and his short beard looked well-groomed, every inch of him designed to project a sense of brilliance or wealth.

"Ah, our esteemed guests," he said, wandering forward after his pause. "Welcome to my humble home."

Fang held back a scoff. *Humble.* An obscene word when spoken by a man surrounded by fountains shaped like gods and acres of gardens manicured beyond a royal standard.

"Thank you for your hospitality," Fang said.

The arrogance radiating off this man was suffocating.

As he reached the bottom step, Ashenhurst swept his arms around, gesturing at his grounds. "This... is where innovation meets inevitability. You are all here today because we share a common vision. A desire to shape the world, rather than be shaped by it."

Fang translated and saw General Gao stiffen. He did not suffer fools and believed strongly in the communist ideals, so a personification of capitalism like Rafe Ashenhurst was a bitter pill that he was barely willing to endure.

Endure. But not *indulge* for long.

Fang shared his view. Ashenhurst hadn't earned any of this. Yes, he'd started life as a poor, neglected child, but to ascend to his current station, he'd exploited, manipulated, and taken from those weaker than him. He didn't deserve what he had.

But, she had to keep reminding herself, he was useful to their objectives.

"Now," Ashenhurst continued, pacing slowly. "What you're about to witness is... transformative. Revolutionary, even."

One of the men behind Fang muttered something impatient under his breath, but she chose not to translate for Ashenhurst.

"Effectiveness is what matters," the Englishman went on. "And if *this* demonstration fails to meet your expectations, we will arrange... a larger display."

Nobody spoke. Fang's associates clasped their hands before them, not hiding their desire to get on with it.

"Rest assured," Ashenhurst said, gesturing again, this time at the fleet of cars and 4x4s waiting to take them to the test site, "we are going to do great things together."

FORTY-ONE

Madison Grubbs hit the sidewalk along with the CIA SOG—Special Operations Group—squad, hustling out of the armored SUV and into the early evening Taiwan sun, still hot despite the late hour. If she was hot in her pantsuit and ballistic vest, she could only imagine what it was like for Hawkins and his team in full tactical gear.

Their short moments on the bustling Xinyi street had passersby gawking at the procession—six men, one woman—striding toward the towering glass building.

Inside the lobby, business professionals milled around, conversations fading as they caught sight of the new arrivals. Detective Inspector Chen Wei-Ting, a woman who looked young but carried the air of a seasoned veteran, marched over to intercept them.

"Welcome to Taiwan." Flawless English, mildly accented. "I understand the need to move quickly. A threat you can neutralize?"

"That's right, ma'am," Hawkins said as politely as if he were meeting a girlfriend's mom for the first time; he'd been that way since meeting Madison, too, a genuine Southern gentleman. "I'm sorry we don't have time to brief you properly, but if you'd be so kind as to help us to the thirtieth floor, we'll keep disruption to a minimum."

"This way."

As they crossed the lobby, snippets of anxious Mandarin and Cantonese floated by from the watching civilians. Madison knew how it must look, US troops barging around on foreign soil, but Hawkins was not exaggerating about the urgency. Mitchell had paved the way, a last-minute briefing for his Taiwan counterpart to gain permission while allowing no time for leaks. When Mitchell insisted there was a major threat to Taiwan, the nature of which would remain hidden until they accessed Ming's former office, trust trumped protocol. President Nash had shelved his other business and gotten straight to work on facilitating access for Madison and Ming. Taiwan, ever aware of their neighbors' desire to bring them back into the Beijing fold, especially during maneuvers where they practiced blockading the island nation, was more than willing to grant whatever Madison needed. The cop escorting the team, Chen Wei-Ting, was the only condition that the Taiwanese government had leveled at them.

The elevator doors slid open, and the team filed in. Struggling to turn around in the tight space, Madison and Wei-Ting were dwarfed at the front as the doors slid shut. Grubbs punched the button for the thirtieth floor.

The elevator smelled of manliness and gun oil. The troops had carbines strapped to them, held at port arms, fingers over the guards, ready to defend themselves should the worst happen.

When the doors opened, she felt assaulted by the mundane —the hum of printers and the clacking of keyboards. She stepped out with the team behind her, like a gaggle of big brothers protective of their little sister. A dozen heads turned as they glided into the array of desks with the detective inspector wielding her ID and shouting in Mandarin.

Many dialects were spoken here, but Mandarin was most common, and everyone seemed to understand that they must stay where they were. A few hands raised in the surrender gesture, but most simply stood in place.

Against the wall on their left, a long, sturdy desk dominated the space, its surface crowded with a bank of computers linked to a machine that resembled a 3D printer but sleeker with a series of glowing panels and a lattice of tubes and wires that pulsed faintly with light. Madison wondered if it had anything to do with the reason they were here or if it was just some snazzy bit of tech that she'd never seen before.

From the far end where the freight elevator was located came a gurney piloted by two US Army medics who had been caring for the occupant—Ming—since they had taken off from Britain. Ming was propped up at 45 degrees, face drawn, but she'd been well enough to come off the drip and accompany them here. She'd insisted, in fact.

Madison rushed over, Chen Wei-Ting alongside her. A petty officer called Rodriguez or "Doc" maintained his distance a few feet away.

"Ming," Madison said urgently. "Where do we need to go?"

Among the workers, a bald man whose shirt stretched taut over his muscled frame watched Zhao Ming, his eyes like small dark marbles.

"She's sedated," the female medic said. "But conscious."

Another man watched just as intently as the rest of Ming's employees, but there was a tension to him that bothered Madison. Maybe it was the tattoos crawling up his thick neck from beneath his loose collar.

Ming's eyes fluttered open, fighting through the painkiller fog.

Leaning closer, Madison said, "This is the place. If we clear it out, can you point us to—"

Ming pulled her lips wide into a grimace. "Not... my... people..."

"Not your...?" Grubbs pieced together the fragments. The workers—

Straightening as slowly and calmly as she could muster, she scanned the room.

The anxious glances, the subtle shifts in posture.

The SOG team members were mirroring the civilians, picking up on some primeval instinct to warn of danger.

"Hawkins," Madison said. "May I have a word? Detective, you too."

They convened in a huddle beside an empty desk, Doc shifting back so the team maintained their 360-degree view of their surroundings.

"Ming says these aren't her people," Madison said so that only Wei-Ting and Hawkins could hear. "It's a setup. We need to clear the floor calmly and quietly, so they don't have a chance to alert anyone else. If they haven't already."

"Could be a silent alarm," Hawkins said. He touched his chest to activate his throat mic, no need to shout the order. "The civilians could be hostiles, treat as enemy combatants. Secure, and be prepared for reinforcements."

The other five soldiers remained stony-faced, minute nods the only sign they'd received an order.

The detective inspector called out instructions so the whole room of eleven could hear, hand gestures directing them toward the stairwell and elevators. A few moved reluctantly, sluggishly even. Some did not move at all.

It was Mav who made the first move, stepping toward the

bald man with the small eyes, opening one arm toward the exit. Mav's other hand gripped the carbine's handle, finger resting on the trigger guard.

The bald worker's face hardened. Then his beady eyes widened, a blend of fear and excitement etched across his face.

One of the soldiers yelled, "Gun!" although Madison wasn't clear which of the fake workers drew first. Bigger guns appeared in hands, whipped from their hiding spots under desks and in trash cans, and the US team returned fire, spreading out, weapons up, single shots returned.

The medics tipped Ming's gurney over, keeping her low to protect her. The straps kept her from tumbling to the floor, but she let out a strained whimper of pain.

Madison had her Sig Sauer in hand, and Wei-Ting pulled out her service weapon as Hawkins ushered them behind a photocopier and said, "Let us handle this."

That was the protocol, the agreement she'd made under orders from Mitchell; if things went to shit, they didn't want her getting herself shot.

As the gunfire intensified, deafening in the confined space, the SOG team fanned out, chasing down the attackers. Madison wondered, why the ruse of the workers? Why not simply have a team waiting to ambush them as soon as they arrived?

It was a lot of muscle to protect evidence of financial malfeasance.

She hoped Trapp was having more luck.

FORTY-TWO

Trapp crouched behind a gnarled oak, wishing it were nighttime and that he had a bigger team. He'd have to make do with the camo fatigues, body armor, firearms, and other gear that Kane had liberated from his former employers—especially the dirt bikes they had stashed half a click away. Trapp focused on the grounds ahead, the hundred-yard dash of open lawn between the forest's tree line and the tradesman's entrance of the grand old house.

"Movement at the main gate," Ikem reported from his nest across from where Trapp and Kane were positioned.

Trapp had a partially obscured view of the front of the house, looking down the driveway where a convoy of sleek vehicles trickled out.

"All players?" Trapp asked.

Ikem didn't reply at first, probably counting. "The four Chinese suits and the ambassador's assistant have four of their own security. Ashenhurst and Knight have six mercenaries—three front and rear."

"They think we'll hit 'em en route," Kane said.

The last vehicle disappeared, and Trapp allowed himself a slow, controlled exhale. He switched channels on the remote comms, patching into his sat phone. "Targets have vacated the premises. Give me eyes."

The voice was Mitchell's, but the encryption gave it an odd, robotic cadence. "Satellite overheads show your best approach is from the northwest corner. Two tangos to neutralize."

Trapp acknowledged, then signaled to Kane and Ikem. The trio began their approach.

Although the house was equipped with fiber optic cables, Mitchell's hackers had discovered only entertainment feeds, the usual rich-dude security, and standard computing paraphernalia. So while they had set all accessible cameras onto a loop that would obscure Trapp's approach, they hadn't located the servers, although scans confirmed a strong electromagnetic emission emanating from somewhere inside.

The local utility company had been easier to penetrate, confirming a huge increase in electricity use over the previous month, peaking in the last couple of days.

At the edge of the tree line, Trapp raised a closed fist, halting Kane, who was close by, and Ikem, who had remained at a distance. He surveyed the open ground, and the bearded hulks in body armor carrying shotguns—one of few legal weapon types in the UK, ostensibly for protecting livestock from predators but deadly all the same. Any cops happening by would just need to check their license and all would be well. The armed mercenaries were twenty yards away, their constant sweeping vigil encompassing the dense woodland along with the lawns.

Trapp was thankful for the camo gear and the evergreens. And he was thankful for the small drone that now buzzed out of the forest from Ikem's position. It was equipped with a camera, but it was a model available to anyone with a spare £150 so had a limited range.

They weren't using it as a surveillance asset, though—it was a distraction.

As the mercs' attention switched to the sky, Trapp and Kane slipped from the forest's cover and across the manicured lawn. Their sprint was swift, and the two mercs snapped around toward them too late.

Trapp had insisted they equip themselves with non-lethal weapons in case Ashenhurst's security was little more than rent-a-cops earning a living, but from what he had seen so far, these were hardened operators, battle-worn and ready to kill. So when he drove a knife into his man's neck, he felt little guilt about snuffing out the man's life.

Kane's target also fell, and they raced onward, reaching the side of the house. Trapp pressed himself against the cool stone, his breath short but controlled.

Fifty yards to the left, Ikem had made it as well. He took an iPad from his pack, a civilian device modified to scan for different types of signals. It might not do anything, depending on how they were transmitting the remote commands.

"Can you jam their signal to the drones?" Trapp asked.

Ikem shook his head. "Not a hope. But I can see many digital emissions. When I rule out the expected frequencies, I see a pulsing signal. But it looks like interference."

Trapp was already making for the tradesman's door in an alcove set away from where the nobility would once have entered at the front. It was down a flight of stairs leading to a basement level. "Too well encrypted?"

"As we suspected," Ikem said. "We will need to get closer."

Kane said, "Yep, it's inside the building."

Trapp glanced up toward Ikem, about to beckon him when

another figure rounded the corner—another patrol. Trapp and Kane were slap-bang in his eyeline, although Ikem was closer.

"Shit." Trapp reached for his sidearm, regretting that gunshots would attract attention.

But before he or Kane could act, Ikem emerged from behind a tall, dense shrub where he'd retreated without Trapp seeing him. The merc probably never knew he'd been there at all. Ikem's hand clamped over his mouth, and the blade sliced into the back of the man's neck.

Ikem dragged the body into the foliage before jogging to meet Trapp.

Kane used a miniature crowbar to jimmy the wooden door, and the disabled alarm failed to sound. Unless there was a second, air-gapped backup. Which they had to assume there could be.

Ikem peered around the jamb and shook his head. "Clear."

They advanced down the short passage into a storage area with walk-in freezers and a larder bigger than most apartments. The hotel-like kitchen was empty, the surfaces clean, but the cooking equipment was mothballed under sheets.

"Closed for the off-season," Kane commented, making the same hotel comparison Trapp had.

"No civilian staff, no witnesses," Trapp said.

Out into a corridor wide enough for two waiters and their trays, they ascended a hard staircase up to the ground floor, British SA80 rifles at their shoulders, covering every corner, every doorway. Until they came to an obviously new, heavily reinforced metal door. *Bingo.*

While Ikem checked the signal's strength and Kane watched the far end of the passage which ended in a carpeted staircase, Trapp oriented himself, confirming they were in the south section of the building, around fifty feet from the external wall. He switched the comms to sat phone and checked in.

"We're right on top of it," Trapp said.

"Fatalities?" Mitchell's robotic voice asked.

"Just the three you probably saw outside. This place is empty. They're all heading for the test site."

"Empty? No one on the source signal?"

"I know. Too easy, right? Stand by."

"Here," Kane said, running his hand over the heavy metal door. "It's flush. Can't jimmy it."

Trapp did the same, his hand passing along the door's edge, searching for vulnerabilities. "No way we're picking the lock or getting through this silently."

"Then we don't even try." Kane dug in his pack and returned with the plastic explosive he'd told Trapp was in short supply—*one try, no do-overs.*

As they pressed the puttylike material against the line where the wall met the thick, metal frame, Trapp mentally inventoried their supplies, seeing that they might come up short if the three hand grenades they'd brought failed to end the transmission.

With the charge and detonator set, they took cover at the stairs, then Kane hit the button. The explosion cracked through the hallway; it would resonate through the house and probably spread across the grounds.

"We'll have company very soon," Trapp said as they ran toward the smoking door that was now hanging half-off the wall.

"That's fine," Kane said. "We only need a few seconds to rip it to pieces." Trapp yanked at the twisted metal door. It crashed to the floor. But instead of banks of servers, a solid wall of concrete stood before them.

Kane said, "What the fucking hell is that?"

Ikem stepped into the porch, his fingers tracing over the

smooth surface. "It is seamless. Poured concrete. No access points."

The signal was definitely coming from here, and the hefty power cables proved something energy-hungry was working from this very location.

But how?

Why seal it like this?

"We can't get in," he said. "This is their failsafe. I bet it goes all the way down to the basement."

Kane confirmed it. "Even if we had more plastic, we couldn't blow it. Not without leveling half the bloody building."

Ikem frowned. "But if it's sealed like this, and the dishes on the roof are dummies, how are they transmitting?"

A chill ran throughout Trapp's body, his spine tingling as he saw the only answer. Before he could voice it, a metallic clatter echoed from the passageway.

A small, cylindrical object rolled along the floor.

"Flashbang! Down!" Trapp hit the ground flat, shielding his eyes.

The ordnance detonated in a blinding burst and deafening blast.

Trapp had no clue how many were coming to kill him.

FORTY-THREE

Madison Grubbs pressed deeper into the carpet as plaster and glass exploded around her, every breath she took reeking of gun propellant. Shouts punctuated the bursts of automatic weapons, panicked and desperate from the gang protecting the workplace, firm and commanding on the American side. Amateurs versus men whose whole life revolved around surviving such scenarios.

Shaking off the dirt, she was under no illusion that her training set her on a par with a battle-hardened military unit, but she still had eyes. And a different angle. She didn't need to cower like a damsel in distress.

One man, a guy in his twenties, scrambled frantically out of the fray, as if he was a real civilian caught up in the melee. He pressed himself up against a nearby wall; his hands were active, his face tight with concentration.

Then she saw it. Saw the thick, black stick, the binding, the wires.

A bomb.

He was twisting a detonator into the stick of what she assumed was dynamite or some construction-site explosive.

Madison launched herself forward, crouch-running to keep below the desks and out of sight of anyone who might take a pot-shot at her.

The man with the dynamite looked up.

Saw her.

Smiled.

And stuck the bomb to the underside of the long table bearing the machine that Madison had assumed was some sort of 3D printer.

She raised her gun and fired three times, taking the bomb-guy in his center mass.

A clean kill.

A fresh volley of gunfire signaled that the gangsters were regrouping and mounting a final defense, sending her diving for cover. Bullets struck the other side of the support pillar sheltering her with sharp, hollow thuds. Grubbs pressed herself against the pillar, trying to assess the situation.

The bomb was set.

"Grubbs!" Hawkins' voice came through her earpiece. "Status?"

"Alive," she replied. "But they set a charge. Timer. No clue how long."

"Copy," Hawkins said. "We're pushing forward. Stay low."

Another rally of gunfire rattled throughout the room. She risked a glance around the edge of the pillar. A man wove between cubicles, trying to flank their position.

"On your right," she said.

A burst of three cut the guy down, and Madison took the moment to sprint from cover, sliding toward the bomb like a batter diving for home base. She'd have a carpet burn to deal with later.

The bomb was not advanced: one stick, thick enough for her fingers to not quite meet around its girth, with a pin-detonator and a dial-timer. She'd seen more advanced IEDs, but she still didn't know enough about disarming something like this. No "abort" button, no red-wire, green-wire choice. What if pulling the detonator out caused a spark that set it off?

She just didn't know.

She peeled it off the table's underside, a simple sticky pad available from any stationery store holding it in place. The timer was a generic item, something from a kitchen. A simple circuit was wired into the detonator.

Less than a minute on the dial.

She scanned the battle; the operators were exchanging fire with a couple of stragglers concentrated in one section where they'd battened down behind metal filing cabinets and a barrier of upended desks.

Madison stood in place, watching the tick-tick-tick of the timer pass the ten-second mark.

It might not have been the right thing for a CIA analyst to yell at a unit of elite operators, and they might make fun of her later for such a Hollywood line, but she knew it'd get the job done.

"Fire in the hole!"

Hawkins saw her wind up her pitch and gave the order to take cover. The others took note.

She hurled the dynamite toward the enemy's improvised foxhole, the timer an awkward counterweight sending it tumbling end-over-end. It fell short, right before the filing cabinets that the gunmen were using as cover.

Silence stretched into a few seconds where the ghostly echo of a hundred gunshots whistled through her ears. She put her fingers in them and curled low.

The blast still slammed her, the shockwave rattling her

skull. She stayed down, curling tight, waiting for the ringing in her head to clear.

When she pushed herself up, the firefight was over.

The SOG team was checking the deceased hostiles, including the pair who'd been crushed when the bomb launched the cabinet against them, crushing them against the glass window, which had cracked but not smashed. A breeze ruffled the hair of a man still pinned down.

Madison pulled herself upright.

The once-pristine office was now an expanse of broken furniture and shattered glass. Bodies lay crumpled, weapons scattered.

"Clear!" someone shouted from across the room.

The "clear" confirmations kept coming as Detective Inspector Wei-Ting rejoined Madison to help check for survivors and threats. Madison stepped over an upended chair, happening on a body, a man who'd performed some Hulk-like rage-striptease, tearing his formal shirt open to reveal his undershirt and muscular torso. Tattoos spiraled up and around the man's arms, intricate designs, instantly familiar.

She pointed, waiting for Wei-Ting to look. "Triad?"

"Yes," Wei-Ting said. "Clearly."

Hawkins came up beside her, angled curiously on the body. "What in the hell are Triads doing here?"

Madison stood, brushing dust from her knees. "Beijing uses them sometimes. Chinese intelligence doesn't like to get noticed, so gangsters are a good substitute."

Wei-Ting gestured to the wreckage all around. "This whole setup, though. Bombs, weapons. A suicide mission. Triads don't operate like this."

"If other elements were ordering them to..." Madison thought back to the investigations in the aftermath of the New York attack, Trapp's solo mission that had thrown him up against a Boston chapter. "They're used to harass and even kill dissidents in other countries, sabotage businesses, and who knows what else. With enough leverage, they could make these guys stand guard and kill whoever came asking questions."

Hawkins nodded. "We'll set a perimeter in case there's more of them. Then we'll get what we came for."

Madison crossed the room to where the medics were working to stabilize Zhao Ming on the gurney. She was paler than before, blood streaking her where none had been earlier. But she was conscious.

"Ming," Grubbs said. "We need access to the systems. Now."

Ming's eyes were unfocused, her breaths short.

One of the medics opened her mouth to object, but Madison held up a hand, cutting her off. They'd been briefed that their patient was mixed up in a serious threat to national security but little else. Their mission was to keep her alive.

"That terminal," Madison said. "They tried to blow it up. If I turn it on, what do I need?"

Ming's voice was faint but clear. "My biometrics. Username is 'PhoenixRising.' Password is 'Silver' underscore 'Mirror' underscore 'forty-two.'"

Madison made her way to the table the Triad had tried to blow up, the terminal atop it a sleek, unassuming box humming faintly. Its surface was a blend of steel and glass, spools of wires coiled neatly along its crown. She couldn't shake her first impression that it had been a high-end 3D printer, but the reinforced casing and precision-engineered panels suggested something else.

An integrated keyboard and screen lay to the right of the main body, and Madison tapped the space bar to wake it up. She had memorized the username and password, and the medics were rolling Ming closer to the terminal for her fingerprint.

But there was no prompt for a username. No biometric pad, either.

"How does it work?" she asked Ming.

The woman on the gurney gazed at the machine, turning her head, her expression somewhere between a frown and a weird, confused smile. "This is not the correct terminal."

"No," Wei-Ting said, sidling forward, examining the sleek, heavy-looking machine for the first time. "But it explains why the Triads are here instead of whoever you were expecting. That isn't some Chinese weapon. It's a bank note counterfeiting machine. These people are not who you were looking for."

FORTY-FOUR

The effects of a flashbang couldn't be ignored, but they could be mitigated. As the one in Rafe Ashenhurst's palatial home detonated, Trapp jammed his fingers in his ears and pressed his palms against his eyelids. The three of them had ducked into the alcove, which also gave a small amount of shielding.

Their only edge was the hope that their attackers believed them incapacitated.

Blinking through the lingering effects, his ears still ringing despite his prep, Trapp scrambled into an upright sitting position and met Ikem's and Kane's eyes. Like him, both were blinking hard, and their heads were held heavy.

A silent understanding passed between them, the kind that only men with vast experience with violence could agree upon without words or gestures.

Through the deadness in his ears, Trapp could make out no footfalls, so he asked himself what he would do in their shoes.

The two men he had glimpsed were faces he recognized. Turks, he seemed to recall. Individuals he'd been briefed on in the past and might have even encountered at some point—

whether as colleagues or adversaries, he couldn't remember. But they were pros, and they would not simply wait around for three targets to stagger out, disoriented and ready to die.

He and Ikem erupted from their alcove, guns at the ready, but the two assassins were closer than expected. Trapp barreled into the larger of the two, a mountain of a man with dead eyes and a scar down one side of his face. Too close for either of them to raise their firearms, the Turk swung a meaty fist.

Not quite at full fighting capacity, Trapp ducked under it and drove his shoulder into the man's solar plexus.

Out of the corner of Trapp's eye, Ikem engaged the other assassin, a blur of strikes and countermeasures. Ikem was disarmed quickly, but in return, he wrenched his opponent's wrist, sending the pistol flying from the merc's grip.

"This is no way to treat guests," Ikem quipped, then threw an open palm upper cut into the man's jaw.

Trapp exchanged blows with his own enemy, thrusting a kick toward the man's groin. The man grunted, equipped with a cup that redistributed the bulk of the force of Trapp's blow, and shot out a hand. His fingers closed around Trapp's neck and began to squeeze.

AS MUCH AS Kane wanted to join the fist fight and help take down the two big bastards, he didn't believe for a moment they were alone. They had engaged Kane and his team from the left where the staircase offered good cover, but Kane had arrived from the other side. He reasoned that two approaches meant there would be two teams.

With the SA80 at his shoulder, Kane stalked in the opposite direction, expecting that Trapp and Ikem would either prevail or hold off the threat long enough that he would not suffer a bullet in the back.

He could hear very little, but his vision had cleared enough to see the way the dust moved in the next passageway, one of the advantages of emerging from within the flashbang's blast radius.

Kane could choose between moving on or holding fast and hoping whoever was backing up the two thugs showed themselves. But if they were even half as good as Kane, they would hold back unless given an order to the contrary.

Kane took a chance.

He sped up, advancing beyond the section of passage that had undergone serious construction and into the posher area that a house of this stature deserved. He did not stop, though, didn't even slow, his rubber-soled boots making no noise—of that, he was confident, regardless of what he could or couldn't hear.

Flicking the SA80 to full auto, he swung around the corner, where he expected the two-strong backup team to be waiting.

But it wasn't two, it was six.

Kane opened fire, taking the two closest to him in the head and necks as he swept his gun in an arc. Two others went down under his barrage, arms and torsos shredded, but their chests were protected by ballistic vests, meaning they were simply thrown backwards. The remaining two returned fire as Kane threw himself to the ground, using one of the fresh corpses as cover. Bullets pocked into the body's flesh, juddering it violently before Kane blasted back. His bullets tore through his target's legs, sending howls through the corridor as his rifle racked empty.

He could not afford to remain still, so he drew his Glock 19 and sprinted forward. The two mercs with the shredded legs raised their weapons, but Kane squeezed off two shots in quick succession, snapping back their heads.

That left the pair who had been wounded and hit in the ballistic vests lying winded and bleeding on their backs.

Kane looked down at them. "You were gonna kill me, yeah?"

Only one of them nodded. The other, his eyes wide, shook his head, petrified.

"And I'm guessing if I walk away from you, there's no way you won't be trying again."

The one who had nodded closed his eyes, and the one who'd tried to deny it shook his head more fervently.

Kane shot them both in the face, lifted his pistol, and made his way back toward Trapp and Ikem to see if they needed a hand.

TRAPP BROKE the assassin's grip with a double arm strike and lifted his knee up into the man's cup-protected groin, this time viciously enough to render any protection mostly useless. He gripped the man's neck and lifted his knee again, this time into his face.

His opponent got his hands in the way, dulling the blow. Trapp swung him around to be greeted by the sound of a single gunshot.

The front of the man's neck burst open, then a second gunshot tore open the top of his head. He dropped, revealing Kane holding his still-smoking gun. Kane winked.

Ikem and his opponent were wrestling, but Ikem had gained the upper hand and positioned the killer in an arm bar. Trapp snatched up the gun that the merc had dropped, pointed it at him, and pulled the trigger twice—one in the side, one in his chest, felling the angry man.

It was over.

Kane trotted toward them, glancing admiringly at Trapp's handiwork lying dead on the floor and said, "We can't do anything else here. Backup plan."

"Unfortunately, yes," Trapp said. "How many more?"

"Well, none of my bastards got away. But let's not assume anything, eh?"

THEY RAN THROUGH THE BUILDING. No resistance. Nothing, all the way to the door through which they had entered. The tree line lay a hundred yards ahead, then another stretch through the trees would take them to where they needed to be.

"We'll chance it," Trapp said. "You all good with that?"

Kane and Ikem agreed, and the three took off single file to limit the chances of a sniper taking them all.

They made it to the edge of the forest unharmed. No one came at them, no pot-shots, nothing.

It fit with everything they'd seen so far, what Trapp had prepared for—this was as much a home as an enclosure for Ashenhurst's fortune.

Security was personnel. The security detail had focused their efforts on the one area they knew Trapp had to reach, regardless of how physically well-protected it was.

The three pushed on through the trees, up an incline that tested Trapp's lung capacity, until they arrived at the small clearing on a forest track where the three dirt bikes waited, camouflaged under branches and leaves.

Trapp pulled the cover from his bike, checking the 250cc engine over as he righted it and donned clear-vision goggles.

"We've gotta catch up with Ashenhurst," he said, straddling the bike.

Ikem mounted his own machine, slotting goggles on. "They have a big head start. These are not racing bikes."

"That, my big African bundle of delight, is where you're wrong." Kane kicked his bike to life, the engine's growl rising with a twist of the throttle. "They just race on different surfaces. Valentino Rossi wouldn't be caught dead on one, but we don't have to use roads. Do we?"

"Cross-country is our best shot," Trapp said, twisting his throttle, warming the engine. He switched his comms to the sat phone but didn't need to worry about the racket; his throat mic would cut that out, and with his hearing cleared after the flashbang, his earpiece gave him direct vocals. "Let's see if we got any progress elsewhere, too."

The bikes leapt forward, weaving between trees as they plowed through the forest. He sped up while he waited on Washington. The pine-scented wind whipped at Trapp's face, dirt and forest debris speckling his goggles.

Mitchell's digitally altered voice said, "Trapp, what's your status?"

"The main signals are coming from the house, like we thought, but the servers are in some sort of bunker. They set up the position but knew we might trace it. Buried it in concrete, no telling how thick."

Hines said, "If the signal's getting out, there must be a way in. Some other transmitter we haven't seen."

"Can you locate the secondary site?" Mitchell asked.

"If we haven't seen it yet," Trapp said, "we don't have time to go rooting through farms and forests. What we need is backup. Have you spoken to the Brits again?"

There was a heavy pause before Mitchell responded. "Backup's not possible right now. Grubbs encountered some unexpected resistance in Taiwan. She's fine, but she's also hit a wall. Without hard evidence, the Brits won't move against someone connected to their home secretary."

"Sir, we don't have time for bureaucratic—"

"I know. But our hands are tied. There isn't even a single police report about gunfire in your area. They're writing it off as a hunting party. Part of the festival."

They were out of the property now, bunched together on one of those ridiculous tiny roads.

"So we're on our own," Trapp said, both to Mitchell and loud enough for Ikem and Kane to hear. "If Grubbs doesn't get the evidence they need, Sutherland and his stooges in MI5 will let this deal happen."

He ended the call with a tap of his phone, and the comms switched back to the local band where Kane and Ikem were still tuned in.

"As the crow flies, then," Kane said.

Ikem nodded, pointing at a field where sheep were grazing. "Across there, then over that hill. Rough terrain, but these bikes will handle it."

They veered off the road, tearing across open grassland. Sheep scattered, dirt flew, and each of them skidded or almost lost control as they bumped over hidden rocks, but they kept going, aiming for the first of two hills that led to the restricted area of the Black Gold fracking sight—Ashenhurst's former pride and joy. Every thump, slide, and readjustment sent a jolt through Trapp, but he pressed on, feeling the progress, no plan to speak of, and—

They crested the first, smaller hill when he heard it—a low, rhythmic *whump-whump-whump*. The others heard it too and had slowed on either side of him, but no one stopped entirely. Then the sleek black-and-white helicopter surged over the rise, its nose pointed directly at them.

FORTY-FIVE

Fang arrived at the spot overlooking the Black Gold Investments site in a small convoy consisting of the men who would approve the contract and their security detail. She doubted that public access to the land surrounding a site as sensitive as the fracking operation run would ever be allowed back home. It was fortunate, she decided, that China's enemies were so inattentive to their soft underbelly.

The perimeter of the strip mine, which resembled a quarry with a quarter of the surrounding wall missing, lay between three public rights of way, exposed to the elements. Anyone could wander the protected woodland and fields high above and far below the operation, as long as they didn't venture beyond the fences.

They weren't a real deterrent; the wire lattice strung between wooden stakes and adorned with signs every few meters was simply a public service announcement to trespassers that danger lay beyond, probably more effective in preventing hikers from perishing over the huge, dizzying drop that awaited them beyond the trees and shrubs.

It had been a very short walk from where they had left the vehicles, the distance easily covered by the men in leather loafers and their ever-present business attire despite the foliage, and even the elderly former general only needed a walking cane intermittently. The armed mercenaries, of course, traversed it easily.

While the Chinese military contractors opened the hard black cases they had lugged from the vehicles, Fang observed the industrial activity far below. She had a bird's eye view as she translated Ashenhurst's explanation for her dignitaries.

"As you can see, the site has a mobile stress unit which is used to pump water between the layers of earth and rock, creating massive amounts of pressure. They drill down to the good oil deposit, then blast through the crevices to widen them. The pressure pushes the oil to the surface, where it's gathered in those tanks."

Ashenhurst smirked and gestured at the fifty or so men and women in hard hats below, the transport vehicles, the pipes feeding into heavy machinery. "The process causes minor tremors in the earth, which the NIMBY types in these parts really despise."

"What is a NIMBY?" Fang asked.

"Oh, NIMBY is an acronym. Someone who understands the need for something like house building or mining or whatever. They vote for a government who they know will do it, but then when it appears nearby, local to them, they proudly declare 'Not In My Backyard.' See, NIMBY?"

Fang could not translate directly, so elaborated only about the tremors. She then relayed a concern voiced by General Gao, who was not willing to speak English in front of his investors. "Where is the actual weapon itself? These boxes are too small. There are too few of them."

The Chinese security personnel had finished unpacking

the cases, turning them into small trestles. Some of them contained screens which lit up but remained blank. Others folded out into a miniature square satellite dish along with a control pad that was far larger than most gaming consoles.

Ashenhurst said, "The disguised signals coordinate the drones to make it impossible to hack or intercept. It can be scaled up. In fact, it already has been."

"Yes, we know that, Mr. Ashenhurst. What we need to prove is whether it has any practical use."

"Of course, Ms. Chen. This time, we have miniaturized the tech and mounted it on the drone mesh that you requested. Today there are just six drones. The heavy-duty sort used in the film industry. But still some leagues above the average civilian model, I can assure you."

Fang relayed this to her contingent while the military personnel continued setting up.

Ashenhurst continued: "I hear your superiors in Beijing are ready to exploit a secondary site if this demonstration isn't big enough."

Fang was surprised at this. "I thought that plan was being put on hold."

He gave a small chuckle. "You are a secretary. An ambassador's secretary, of course, but..."

Fang reined in her anger and disgust as Ashenhurst moved close to her. He lifted one hand as if about to stroke her like a puppy, then thought better of it. Then he turned sharply toward the setup, checking that his own security detail was in place. Fang could hear the crackle of gunfire and muted explosions miles away on the other side of a bluff, which Fang suspected was not the original plan.

Isabella Knight had returned to the vehicles, trying to raise the people they'd left back at the estate. If she couldn't get hold of them, her task was to secure the perimeter here so that nothing could possibly go wrong.

Except that something could always go wrong. And that something was Trapp.

"We're ready," Ashenhurst said.

"What about those workers down there?" Fang Chen asked.

"Sadly, some will be killed. Most, actually. And the microwave blasts will further destabilize fragmented rock deep in the earth. Fracking means water. Microwaves make steam."

Gao stepped forward and spoke cautiously to Fang to translate. "If a normal operation's pressure from the process creates tremors, won't the overload from the energy bursts make it far worse?"

"You are a clever man," Ashenhurst said, wagging his finger, as if Gao had been keeping his intelligence to himself. "There's a strong possibility that the pressure is already building right now—as you can see, they are pumping oil out as we speak. The added heat and kinetic energy from the drone mesh will further destabilize the rock. And yes, the quakes could liquefy much of the earth above and trigger a landslide."

Fang gazed into the distance. She couldn't quite see the village of Queensacre because of the towering mound of land. But she had known the site was only allowed to continue because the village couldn't see it. "The earth over on that side."

"Correct," Ashenhurst said.

"And the village."

"Well, the demonstration, as you can see, will be small in the terms of the perimeter. But I must tell you, I've always hated that fucking village, ever since they tried to shut down this site when I owned it." He smiled, clasped his hands behind his back, and stood upright. "You will be more than impressed."

FORTY-SIX

"SPLIT UP!" Trapp yelled, throttling into a donut, flinging mud and grass high into the air—a poor smokescreen, but the best he could do at such short notice. "One of us has to get there, doesn't matter who." He pointed Kane toward a gray ribbon snaking through the green and brown landscape. "Take it!"

Kane looked like he wanted to argue, a man used to taking the lead and being at the business end of any op. But they had no time, so he launched himself back down the hillside while Trapp and Ikem pressed on.

As the helicopter banked, its rotor blades slicing the air, Trapp saw that someone was clinging to the side, the door open —one pilot, one... one what?

That was a top-end civilian aircraft, not a gunship, so if they were out here circling, waiting on a possible incursion or maybe even following them via satellite or high-altitude drone recon, they'd need additional firepower. That's what that guy was, a bearded muscle-bound pro, hefting a serious machine gun into position, braced on the skid's footplate.

"They're gaining!" Ikem urged.

"I know. This way."

The hill's contour eased, and a sharp left saw them descending, evading the first volley of gunfire as the helicopter arrowed ahead, unable to bank quickly enough.

"There."

Trapp didn't need to point. The wheat field loomed before them, golden waves rippling. Both bikes jolted as the terrain grew steeper.

The chopper had come back around and lined up its attack run from their right.

The heavy gun commenced firing, tracer rounds visible in the overcast light as they tore up the field in a pluming curtain of brown.

Trapp leaned to the right side, narrowing the angle and making the enemy miss again. The helicopter overshot as they tracked the hillside in three tight hairpins, then punched it in a straight line into a wall of eight-foot stalks.

Trapp lost sight of Ikem, becoming a blur through the dense crop. Wheat stalks whipped against his arms, stinging like tiny whips, while behind them, the helicopter righted its course and descended.

They were not concealed, only partially obscured. The gunman had given up on bullets and leaned back out, hanging on to his harness, a grenade launcher braced against his shoulder.

A pop of smoke. Then—

BOOM.

The explosion erupted to their left, dirt and wheat flying. Trapp swerved, the bike skidding sideways. Ikem cursed, barely avoiding the debris.

The helicopter circled ahead, its nose low as the gunman reloaded.

Trapp's bike, the field, the wheat... it wasn't enough. While their evasive maneuvers had distracted the pilot, the helicopter was still faster. It would take little time for them to adapt.

Another grenade whistled through the air, detonating dangerously close. The reverberation and spray of soil rattled Trapp, and his bike fishtailed. He fought to regain control, righting it by kicking the ground.

His heart pounded as the wheat field ended abruptly, giving way to open ground. The wheat had given them a modicum of cover, but now they were exposed again.

The helicopter surged forward, the gunman taking aim once more.

KANE'S BIKE screamed down the winding road, the engine furious, straining to its limit. In the rearview mirror, a Land Rover clung to his tail like a tenacious guard dog.

Knight planted backup on the road out of the estate. Of course she did.

The road curved sharply, and he leaned into the turn, tires screeching. The Land Rover followed, its bulk struggling to match his speed, its body hitting the embankment and tearing through the hedgerow. For a moment, he thought he might lose them, but his pursuer barely slowed, as if they had intentionally slapped the Land Rover against the hedges to slingshot itself around the corner. Panel work be damned.

The village was right up ahead. Brightly colored stalls lined the streets, crowds of people oblivious to the danger bearing down on them.

"Damn it."

He couldn't lead them into the middle of civilians. But the

Land Rover was closing, and the road offered no alternative escapes.

Cutting the wheel sharply, he veered off before hitting the village's main road, onto a narrow side street. This led straight into the Old Quarter, a historic section of the town. Still populated, but the concentration of people was thinner. Non-existent at first.

But then it widened onto a quaint cobbled thoroughfare, craft stalls of handmade jewelry and soap and other shit served up to those who had ventured from the main drag. The scents of fresh bread and roasted meat made him hungry, despite everything.

The Land Rover had been forced to slow due to the cobbles, but it still followed, clipping the first stall as the shoppers ran for cover, screaming.

No collateral damage.
Not here.
Never again.
He'd have to end this fast.

Kane gunned the engine, putting distance between him and the Land Rover, spotting the one chance he might have to finish this quickly. But it would not be pretty.

THE HELICOPTER'S rotors all but drowned out the sound of Trapp's bike as he and Ikem burst from the corn into the open fields. Trapp evaded a scatter of sheep that didn't know which way to run, and Ikem almost took one out before the creature reared up and switched direction.

The unfortunate detour fooled the helicopter too, flying onward before the gunner could fire another explosive their way.

Up ahead, the ground rose into a rocky outcrop, strewn with more boulders than panicked sheep. It was more direct than the valley route Trapp had intended to take to the Black Gold site, but his mind clicked into gear, a plan forming as he mapped the terrain and assessed his ride.

"Follow me," he said, veering sharply away from the easier geography and throttling it toward the rocks.

The two bikes surged forward, kicking up more dirt and gravel as they raced over the uneven slope. The helicopter adjusted its trajectory.

The gunman again leaned out with the grenade launcher.

Taking aim.

Not firing yet.

Preserving ammo for the right kill-shot.

Trapp's heart pounded as the chopper closed in, the thrum of its rotors catching up.

He just needed to climb a little higher. One more overshoot, one more slice of luck.

They were almost out of time. And land.

KANE'S BIKE RATTLED VIOLENTLY, the narrow lane a chaotic blur. Cutting the wheel, one foot steadying the skid, he took a sharp turn into a street absent of people.

Well, thank God for that.

He accelerated, full speed. The Land Rover was gaining, its bulk scraping against the walls and closed-up stores. But it squeezed through. More horses under the hood than Kane's cross-country machine, it would catch him in a straight drag-race. He just needed one accessory, and a town like this was sure to have it.

Rounding the next corner, he saw he was right.

Just what I need. Thank you.

He braked hard, sliding the bike to a stop, and leapt off. There, watched by a gaggle of diners scarfing down foot-long sausages in bread rolls, he crouched beside a huge ceramic plant pot with what looked like a banana plant sprouting from it and heaved it onto his shoulder.

The Land Rover squeezed around the corner, its driver fighting the wheel to keep it going.

Kane hurled the pot with all his strength. The heavy plant pot shattered against the windshield in a spray of soil—green leaves and roots and broken shards. The vehicle swerved, its momentum stymied.

Kane pulled his sidearm, firing relentlessly into the Land Rover's cabin. The weakened windshield caved in as gunfire echoed down the narrow street. Inside the vehicle, the bodies jerked and spasmed under the barrage, their cries mingling with the screams of onlookers.

When the gun racked empty, Kane didn't pause to check that all were dead; no telling what they'd do if they knew they were dying. He holstered his weapon, swung back onto the bike, and gunned the engine, disappearing into the maze of streets before anyone could start filming him on their mobile phones.

Let's see them write this off as a hunting party.

TRAPP GRIPPED THE HANDLEBARS, knuckles tight, hands aching. The machine beneath him vibrated hard; the hillside behind them stretched out in a jagged slope of loose stones and patches of stubborn grass. The chopper was closing in fast again, its last pot-shot flying wide, the explosion shielded by an increasingly rocky field. Trapp estimated the bulk of the shockwave went down into the ground and upward, hurling debris high into the air.

Now the helicopter was lining up another run at them, starting low, giving the guy with the grenade launcher a better, more accurate angle. Trapp figured this was their last chance. He pulled over, braced by one of the boulders that had only gotten larger the higher they trekked up the hill.

"Are you sure about this?" Ikem shouted, halting a few feet from him.

"No," Trapp replied. "If this doesn't work and they take me out, carry on. Don't help me. Clear?"

He didn't look at Ikem. Didn't wait for a reply. His eyes were locked on the helicopter as it gained ground—close enough that he could see that bastard with the grenade launcher grinning. Or thought he could. Maybe he was imagining it.

The bike's engine growled louder as he revved it. His heart pounded harder. This was a huge risk even for him.

"Get clear!" he shouted, and without waiting for a response, he kicked the bike into gear and shot forward, downward.

Toward the incoming chopper.

The aircraft dipped lower, the gunman's launcher aimed straight at Trapp.

Timing would be everything. A moving target was hard enough to hit at the best of times, but to hit a moving target from a speeding platform... the shooter had to get very lucky.

For a split second, Trapp saw it all in vivid detail—the pilot's face through the windshield, the gunman's grin, the rotor blades slicing the air.

Then he was yanking the handlebars back, as if showing off. The front tire lifted off the ground, as if the bike were an animal rearing up to ward off a predator. For a heartbeat, he was suspended, unsure if he could go through with it.

He reached down to the grenade he'd lodged in the chassis and pulled the pin on the three-second fuse.

Then he let go of the bike.

Trapp hit the ground hard, twisting so he rolled, tumbling over the terrain, pain lancing through him with every impact, while the bike shot forward, hurtling down the slope like a missile.

The gunman tracked the bike as it careened toward them. Beneath them. His grin was now a frown.

This explosion was not muffled by the landscape. A flash of light, a thumping *boom*, and the sky filled with fire and shrapnel. Not enough to destroy the helicopter directly above it, but the craft jerked violently under the shockwave, its tail spinning.

The rear rotor—a helicopter's most vulnerable point—had been hit. It spewed black smoke as the vehicle tipped sideways, then wobbled as the pilot made a last, desperate bid to stabilize.

But it was no use.

The machine veered sharply, its nose dipping as it plummeted sideways into the hillside, crashing into the rocks as the main rotor array crumpled. Flames erupted, blowing the damn thing apart, flinging metal and plastic, glass and body parts, across the ground.

Trapp lay there for a moment, the breath slammed out of him from the land-and-roll, dirt and blood in his mouth. He just stared at the wreckage, as if he had nowhere else to be.

"That," Ikem said, helping Trapp to his feet, "was both impressive and too damn close. Shall we go now?"

FORTY-SEVEN

The quarry sprawled below Fang, a jagged, crescent wound carved into the earth. Its edges were steep and raw, and even from up here, the stench of oil and damp stone drifted over the waves of noise. From her vantage, she could see most of the surface-level fracking operation—trucks rumbling, pipes snaking across the ground, and workers in hi-vis yet grimy coveralls.

A fourteen-wheeler truck with a long trailer rolled into view, its battered surface speaking of years of travel, up and down highways and motorways to industrial sites like this one. The name *Crestline Logistics* was stenciled in a deep, wine-red font across its side, bold and unassuming—a hidden subsidiary within a shell game that Ashenhurst had played with his competitors for years.

Too high for anyone at ground level to see, the trailer's roof began to retract, sliding smoothly open. Fang's breath hitched, and a chill skittered up her spine.

Ashenhurst stood a few feet away, his hands clasped behind his back. He glanced at Fang with a satisfied smirk.

Fang met his gaze. "It's functional. Already."

"Of course," Ashenhurst replied. "My security bitch says we lost contact with our people back at the house. Guessing that means those pains in my arse know they can't stop it at source. They'll be coming here, if they've worked it out. Which isn't that hard."

"What about the authorities?" Fang asked, her own anxiety a stark contrast to Ashenhurst's manufactured calm.

Ashenhurst chuckled, a dry, false sound. "The police have been handled. They won't be a problem."

"But Trapp wasn't handled," Fang countered. "You let him get away from the house. Why?"

"Because optics are everything," Ashenhurst explained, lowering his voice conspiratorially. "I can't be seen executing a CIA agent. It's too crude. But if that same agent appears to have gone rogue and is killed trying to attack me amidst a national disaster... well. I'm a hero. A survivor. And a very rich one, once the market panics."

"And a convenient scapegoat," Isabella Knight added, stepping forward. "His presence here justifies a more aggressive security response and feeds every conspiracy theory online." She turned her gaze from Fang to Ashenhurst, her voice dropping. "Our final perimeter is set. They're on their way. We should begin."

Behind Fang, the Chinese operatives shifted, their movements rushed under the watchful eyes of the businessmen as they finished setting up.

Ashenhurst swept a hand toward the truck below. "Gentlemen, the overture."

From the trailer, six quadcopter drones emerged, each the size of a small car. They rose with an eerie silence, a fine hum that barely disturbed the air as they hovered like giant, mechanized wasps.

"Individually, each drone is impressive," Ashenhurst said, his voice resonating with pride. "But together, they are revolutionary. The supercomputer back at my house isn't just flying them; it is networking them into a single weapon. Think of it less as a swarm and more as one massive, invisible lens. At my command, they can focus all their combined energy onto a target the size of a coin."

He paused, letting the implication hang in the air. "The result is a silent, traceless attack with catastrophic power. Now... shall we see it in action?"

Fang nodded slowly, her expression still neutral. "And the transmitters?"

"Hardwired underground and hidden throughout my valley. As impenetrable as the servers at my home."

My valley.

My home.

My, my, my...

Fang's attention drifted back to the quarry, to the workers below who had paused in their tasks, pointing and shouting as the drones rose slowly. A flicker of guilt twisted inside her. But this was bigger than them. Bigger than her. More important than a few lives.

Ashenhurst turned to the pilots, all of whom spoke passable English but were not quite conversational. "Let's get on with it."

As the lead pilot hit the *confirm* command, the drones ascended faster, their mechanical hums growing louder. Their sleek, angular forms cut through the damp air.

Below, the site was a maze of machinery and carved-out roads, left over from the former strip-mining operation and repurposed to extract fuel without sending men and women under the earth. Massive extraction rigs stood tall, their steel frames sending pipes snaking across the ground to carry water and chemicals to and from the storage tanks. The workers, tiny yet distinct, craned their necks to watch the drones climb higher as they slotted into a precise hexagonal formation, their underbellies shimmering faintly.

Fang's stomach tightened. She could feel Ashenhurst's eyes on her, waiting for a reaction. It was as if he believed she was more influential than the former general and the party insider—both of whom would share the final say in judging the success or failure of this display.

Or maybe it was something else. Something she'd been warned about.

Surely, he would not be stupid enough to—

"Impressive, isn't it?" Ashenhurst said, his voice projecting to all as Fang continued to translate.

On the screen in one of the black cases nearby, the graphical representation showed the drones as glowing nodes, connected by pulsing lines that represented the microwave bursts. The beams themselves were invisible, but the screen made it clear: The drones were syncing, their energy fields intertwining.

Fang could almost feel the hum in her teeth and bones.

The workers below were still staring. Some had started backing away, but the quarry walls climbed high and steep around them—the access road that served as the only way out would become a bottleneck if they tried to flee en masse.

Ashenhurst stepped closer, leaning over so Fang could feel his breath on her ear. "This is the future I've engineered. For you and your people. And now you're part of it."

The first burst of energy was silent and invisible, but its effects were immediate. The screen's lines flared brighter, the connections between the drones solidifying. The air itself seemed to vibrate.

Below, the quarry descended into a hive of chaos, the

workers scrambling like ants caught in a flood. One of the water tankers groaned, its metal frame twisting unnaturally before it buckled, spewing a torrent of water that sent workers diving for cover.

Fang's stomach tightened as she watched, her throat constricting as she told herself this was a justifiable evil, necessary to shepherd in the good that she knew was just around the corner.

Then, a generator. Its exploding mechanism rattled the observers where they stood, the pilots giving impressed hisses—"*Whoa!*" and "*Jīngrén de!*" which roughly translated as, "*Awesome!*"

Workers running toward it—brave or foolish, she couldn't tell—were caught in the invisible energy wave. They stumbled, convulsing as they doubled over, vomiting violently. On the edge of the mesh, screams cut through the chaos, raw and desperate, before they crumpled to the ground.

Ashenhurst smiled. "Of course, there are limits. We're rewriting the laws of physics here, not breaking them entirely..."

He was cut off by General Gao, who spoke in sharp Mandarin. Fang translated, her tone flat. "The general is not interested in your poetry, Mr. Ashenhurst. He is interested in results. How long can it operate?"

Ashenhurst's smile tightened for a fraction of a second before he regained his composure. "But of course. Thanks to your contribution to the conductor formula, we took a two-minute burst capacity and pushed it past ten. An eternity on the battlefield and more than enough time to provide the...'proof'... you require."

Fang forced herself to breathe, to keep her expression neutral, for the sake of Ashenhurst's smugness, for the sake of maintaining her professionalism in front of the men who would decide her—and her country's—future. But watching the impending slaughter, her thoughts were a storm of conflicting logic, tearing her apart.

She was almost relieved when the roar of an engine and the clatter of gunfire erupted around them.

FORTY-EIGHT

The assholes at the quarry's edge were in sight. Trapp had approached low and silent, keeping to the thick undergrowth with the SA80 assault rifle propped and ready to fire. There'd been eight sentries, but now there were six. Since his rendezvous with Kane at the perimeter of the Black Gold property line, they'd been all too aware of the noise they'd have to make getting here—the mercs employed to deter them must have heard them from some distance away. But the final approach had been downhill via a logging road, allowing Kane to freewheel the bike for that stretch.

With Trapp on the back of Kane's ride, they'd mapped a route using a cycling app called Komoot, taking a mountain bike trail half a click perpendicular from their destination. But still, they hadn't been sure exactly where they needed to be. That was why they'd split up, sending Ikem with an entirely different objective. They might already be too late, but given the situation, they could not rush their approach.

From Trapp's vantage point, he saw that the fracking site below was chaos—flares of fire, groaning machinery, the distant shouts of workers. But no matter how hard his instincts urged him to act, to *do something right now*, up here, on the quarry's crest, it was all about the element of surprise.

Kane's bike roared seconds earlier than planned, but that was fine; Trapp was in position. The bike skidded sideways just feet before the clearing that would have made him an easy target, the man himself dismounting and moving fast, assault rifle slung low.

They had two sets of targets, one infinitely more dangerous than the other: mercenaries trained to kill in the harshest conditions, and what they'd started to think of as the VIP contingent.

"Two tangos, east flank," Kane said from twenty feet away —in position, ready. "Mercs or VIPs?"

Their strategy was intentional and playing out as expected. Security like this prioritized protecting their principals, meaning getting them the fuck out of any situation where bullets or bombs might fly, regardless of secondary orders they might have to take out Trapp and the team. It would force them to split their muscle into fighters protecting the test flight and bodyguards forming a front-and-rear guard, rushing their human cargo to the waiting vehicles.

Trapp had wanted to disable the Land Rovers, and if they'd had more time and more cover on their approach, they would have. But a swift assessment proved it would have eaten valuable seconds that the people down in the quarry simply didn't have.

Kane's presence drew two of the two Eastern European operators while the other mercs did their jobs with the VIPs. The Chinese downed their equipment and spread out, pulling out small arms and readying to defend their position.

Curious.

But Trapp would deal with that in a moment.

The Euro-trash mercs were advancing, their movements disciplined, their weapons trained. The cold stone of a boulder pressed into Trapp's back. He could hear the crunch of boots even as he imagined Kane stashed behind the tree trunk and praying that Trapp would time the first attack correctly.

Trapp rolled to the side, came up in a crouch, and fired twice. One merc went down, clutching his chest, but his armor did its job. A third round took the man in the neck, and he dropped, gurgling.

The other ducked behind his buddy's corpse for cover, firing in Trapp's direction.

But Trapp had already vacated that spot. His turn to be the distraction. His turn to pray that Kane was as good as he seemed. They weren't exactly in sync, didn't have the history that he had with others.

He needn't have worried.

Kane engaged the second merc, peppering the ground with round after round until he drove the operator into a crawl and finished the job with a double tap to the head.

Now they just had to figure out how to eliminate the drones.

THE AIR WAS thick with smoke, the ground slick as water and fuel flowed from damaged containers as the drones continued their synchronized dance overhead. Ikem crouched behind one of the concrete barriers marking out the wide track that HGVs and 4x4s traversed in and out of the site. The SA80 supplied by Kane pressed against his shoulder. He took aim and fired at the first drone.

Missed.

Another shot, which did nothing.

Ikem frowned in frustration, steadied the stock on his shoulder, and flexed his fingers around the fore grip as he sighted the first drone and fired.

The drone jerked, but its operation seemed unaffected.

Lightweight armor, maybe?

He set the rifle to full auto and steadied his aim again, unleashing a barrage of 5.56mm rounds at the hovering drones. Something in the navigation must have flashed danger, signaling for them to speed up. They rotated too, as if in a dance, swaying from side to side in concert as they zipped around the sky like flies seeking a way into a rotting corpse. He did no more than clip two or three of them. Whatever algorithms they'd been programmed with seemed to generate a random evasion pattern.

"Jason," he said through his comms, knowing Trapp might not respond verbally. "I cannot shoot them down. I am too far away, and they are too fast. It is up to you. I will... I will do what I can here."

Workers scrambled in every direction, confusion reigning. These were working men used to coordinating in close quarters, and when disaster threatened, they did all they could for their friends. Ikem wasn't even sure they understood that the drones were the source of the destruction. Maybe if the blasting waves were visible, like a deadly aurora, they'd be able to avoid them, predict what would blow next.

The weapons they'd been briefed on were far inferior to these. People had died horribly already, and more were to come, but they had expected minimal effects on the machinery. It was then that Ikem understood: the weapon wasn't a brute-force attack on the vehicles and tanks; it was an overload, a surge of power that boiled the contents and cracked the containers. Fuel heated past burning point explodes, water becomes steam, and people's organs cook.

Ikem could not strategize any longer. There was no plan to be had other than hope people's sense of self-preservation overrode any heroism.

"Move! Move!" he yelled, running from cover.

He knew what he must look like—a man in dark fatigues, a military rifle slung over his chest, body armor. He hoped he conveyed the authority of someone on their side, like a cop or soldier.

Gesturing at a group of workers huddled near a mangled water truck, he shouted, "Head south, please—stay low and keep moving!"

One of the men started in that direction but then halted, eyes wide with terror. "But the village—my family—"

"What about it?"

"This..." He waved his hand at the place where the most drilling and insertion infrastructure was located. "Whatever's happening... it's too much. The tremors... that's the earth shifting."

Ikem turned his head, taking in not just the immediate danger but the landscape, the setup here. The drones swept the zone the worker referred to, invisible beams carving the air. He'd expected the nausea, the frying of circuits. But now the worker's determination to stay, terrified for...

The village.

"You mean it could collapse?" Ikem called back.

"Yeah!" The man thrust a finger toward the land curving upward, over the top of the quarry-like site, the topsoil juddering as another tremor shook the world. Not violent enough to throw anyone on their ass, but deep, like a man breathing with fluid on his lungs.

"Landslide," Ikem said to himself.

He darted across the open ground, over shattered glass and twisted metal. Another group was trapped on the far side of the site, cut off by a storage tank spraying brown fluid like a wounded carotid as the workers strained to get a pipe in place—presumably to drain it into an emergency backup.

The drones switched direction, moving as one, and Ikem felt the heat of the outer mesh graze his arm. A wave of nausea followed, so he pushed on through, away from the danger, taking a wider, arcing route.

Not now. Not yet.

Up close, at the periphery, the effect wasn't quite invisible. The edge of the mesh emanated a slight shimmer, like a weak light through a prism or heat on a desert tarmac road.

"This way!" he shouted, gesturing toward the quarry's perimeter. "That is the way!"

"We can't! We have to—"

"We have people who will stop this. You must move, or you will die!"

After a moment's hesitation, the three men with the pipe and the four prepping to fix it dropped their tools and scrambled toward him, faces pale even beneath the grime, the flash of nausea Ikem had felt now rolling over them, too. He counted them as they passed—five, six, seven.

Then he turned back to scan the site. There were more. Too many more. And the village—God, the village. If the hillside collapsed under the pressure overload, lifting the rock, the soil...

He forced the thought away. That was Trapp's job now. All Ikem could do was get as many out of here as possible.

FORTY-NINE

Trapp's SA80 fired twice, and the first of the Chinese operators dropped, dead. The VIPs were gone, their security with them, but the men who'd been monitoring the drones hadn't attempted to flee. In fact, they'd stayed behind in a tactically unsound position.

As Trapp received the tap on his shoulder from Kane to let him know he was covered, he noticed what the dead man had been trying to do.

He'd been setting a charge.

That meant something Trapp couldn't think about right now.

The second operative was doing the same around a black case. The metal container provided scant cover as the man's gun poked around to take potshots at the incoming Trapp.

But Kane was already overlapping as Trapp laid down covering fire. He seemed to revel in his brutal efficiency, getting in close before shooting the target in the head. Trapp had known academically the SAS were good, but seeing it in action made him a believer.

"Two down," Kane said. "Two to go."

Their opponents were professionals, no doubt about that, their reactions unhurried but by no means slow; only experience led to that level of calm under fire. But they evidently had a more important objective than survival.

"There." Trapp chopped his hand toward a cluster of boulders where the third and fourth Chinese fighters had taken cover.

Kane moved silently one way, Trapp the other, and Kane took out one with a tight cluster to the chest, the man's lightweight vest no protection from a few feet. The other, startled, glanced once at the case, then at Trapp, and almost smiled as he lay flat to the ground.

"Shit!"

Trapp rushed forward. Too slow.

The man had piled several tablets and a laptop-like device around a charge. Trapp dove for cover, and Kane disappeared, too. The charge—and the operative—exploded, taking the equipment with him.

Trapp reunited with Kane, continually scanning for stragglers or the returning security team. As Trapp's pulse dampened back to a hard drumbeat, he processed what he'd seen.

"They pretty much sacrificed themselves."

"Yeah, it was a piece of piss. The Chinese used to be tougher than that."

"They still are," Trapp said. "They were more concerned with blowing this stuff up." His attention rocked back to the fracking site. "Watch my six."

Trapp switched comms to the sat phone. "Mitchell, Hines, you there?"

"Yes," Mitchell said. "Are you okay?"

"Yeah, but no time for that. They destroyed their gear

rather than retreat. You think that means we can control the drones with it?"

"Probably, yes," Hines said. "There must be a manual override. If the pre-programmed targets go wrong or they want to abort. You'll be looking for—"

"Lemme guess. iPads, notebooks, something like that?"

"Correct. Tell me what you've got."

"What I've got," Trapp said, "is a forest full of shrapnel."

"They succeeded in destroying all the gear?" Hines sounded crestfallen. "Then there's no way to—"

"The gadgets, yeah. There's still a small satellite dish and a getup like a DJ's disco set. I can wreck it if that'll bring down the—"

"No! This isn't *Independence Day*. Blowing up the mothership won't send them to sleep. They'll just run with their programming until they've burned their fuel." Hines perked up, speaking faster, rapid-fire. "But the dish and portable tower means there's a frequency. Let's see how lazy they were. Get close to the... what did you call it? The DJ gear?"

"I'm there now." Trapp stood over the case containing the whirring device that looked like an old PC tower but with more buttons and a rectangular array of lights that reminded him of a skyscraper at night.

"Just—hold on—okay," Hines said. "I can't get in by Bluetooth. It's shielded. Oh fuck, we're done."

Mitchell said, "Pull yourself together. If it was your op, what would your backup be?"

Hines sniffed. Trapp resisted stepping in; he doubted his type of input would go down well.

Mitchell asked again, "What would *you* do?"

Hines stuttered, *ummed*, then said with a feeble croak, "I'd... I'd have a bespoke cable to hardwire in, but—"

"Jason," Mitchell pressed. "Is there anything you can use? Something that might connect an iPad or tablet?"

Trapp rummaged in the box, pulling up wires without disconnecting them. "Kane, we clear?"

"Clear!" Kane shouted back.

Trapp came up with a handful of wires and familiar connectors. "USB-C?"

"Oh! That'd work," Hines said, his voice higher in pitch, as if coming down from a panic-stricken high. "Plug it into your sat phone."

Trapp unclipped it from his gear and slotted the lead into the USB slot.

"Garside?" Mitchell's voice crackled as keyboards clattered on his end.

Below, the drones shifted their focus from the fleeing workers toward the heart of the fracking operation. Trapp watched Ikem desperately herd the last group of stragglers toward the access road.

Then it clicked. The fracking fluid. Millions of gallons of pressurized water deep underground. Ashenhurst wasn't trying to cause a tremor; he was going to flash-boil the water in the shale. He was turning the entire quarry into a subterranean steam bomb. When it blew, the quarry walls would collapse, burying everyone and everything under a mountain of earth. It would be the perfect crime: a tragic "equipment failure" with no witnesses and no evidence.

"I'm through the firewall," Hines' voice crackled, laced with tension. "But the command kernel is heavily encrypted. Whoever wrote this code was good."

"I'm glad you're a fan," Trapp snapped. "But right now I need a fucking kill switch."

Trapp watched as the drones zoned in, cutting off the only way out. They'd be on the thirty-or-so people in seconds.

Trapp said, "If you don't deal with it, we'll have multiple casualties."

"Working on it," Hines said urgently. "I've got to override the autopilot. If I can get into the command kernel—okay, got it! Sending the kill code... *now*."

The drones, angling on the fleeing workers, hesitated. Their movements stuttered in mid-air. For a long, drawn-out moment, as the silence brought on by the cutting of their motors seemed louder than anything that had come before, it seemed like they might remain in the sky, held aloft by some as yet unseen propellant.

Then, one by one, they wavered. Perhaps some thermal updraft or the residual momentum of their rotors had kept them in place. But as soon as their rotors slowed to a full stop, they dropped harmlessly to the ground, where they shattered like toys flung from a baby's stroller.

WASHINGTON, **D.C.**

THE OPERATIONS ROOM was alive with an electric thrum, and Mitchell stood at its center. The mission was a success. Around him, the team exhaled in unison.

But then he saw Karem Hines. At first, he thought maybe it was the kid's Jell-O spine collapsing now that the tension had lifted, but there was no relief there, no change in tempo or posture. Hines simply stood apart, his lean frame facing a single monitor, one finger tapping the keyboard to scroll through a wall of data. The screen reflected in his glasses, his curly hair was a mess, and he looked locked-in.

The rest of the room was breathing easy, but Hines looked like he was at a funeral.

Mitchell stepped closer. "Hines. You did good."

Karem didn't flinch. "Not now."

Mitchell wasn't used to being brushed off, especially not by a consultant half his age. But he could feel the room's relief fraying as others picked up on the analyst's seriousness. "Spit it out, Hines. Now."

Hines finally looked around.

"The satellite signal," he said. "It's still active."

"What signal?" Polly asked. "I thought you cut it manually."

"Only the local signal from the equipment Trapp secured." Hines stepped forward, his eyes now roving the room as if searching for a way out. "The guidance system is active. It's firewalled from the portable tower we just hacked, but it's still going. It shouldn't be."

Mitchell's eyes flicked to the monitor, to the lines of raw data—all meaningless to him without context. "Explain."

"We took out the drones." He paused, his voice dropping. "But the satellite that was receiving the main signal from Ashenhurst's property is still receiving and transmitting. It's feeding data. To something else."

Mitchell sensed the edges of the room closing in. "Could be a glitch? It's experimental tech."

Hines shook his head. "No glitch. Too much data being transferred. Way too much."

"So what is it feeding?"

"Don't know yet. But it's bouncing away from its original source."

Mitchell's pulse quickened. "Another target."

Hines nodded. "This isn't over."

FIFTY

The Triads' counterfeiting production line lay dormant, but Madison concentrated on the stacks of metal crates on which it was built. She knelt on threadbare carpet squares that offered practicality more than comfort, then ducked under the platform on which the printing machine was held. The metal boxes resembled self-assembly cabinets with perforations through which cool air whirred.

"Give me a hand?" she asked Dawson. "I need to get this open."

One of the team had a screwdriver. He had to unclip his weapon and backpack to crawl under to join her. He was the oddly named "Doc," a soldier whose frequent grins never quite lit up the rest of his face. Jamming the screwdriver into a seam in the metal grills, he pried it off with a big crank of his arm.

It clattered to the floor, revealing what looked like a dead bank of slots where cables used to run in and out.

He did the same with the adjoining one, behind which was an identical stack of computational relays, similarly dead.

Madison retrieved her pack and pulled out her laptop and

her pouch of cables, then connected to the primary slot in the left bank of relays. Nothing.

She tried the other and got the same goose-egg.

A third panel clanged to the ground, where a single red light remained on, unblinking beneath a single plug slot—an ISDN line, like a modem.

"Okay, now we're talking."

Madison rummaged for the right cable and, after turning off the Wi-Fi, she connected her laptop to the only live inlet, then ran a program searching for a signal. With a few deft keystrokes, the dormant computer banks whirred to life.

The cable was just long enough to stretch up to the counter so that she could stand and watch the lines of data scroll down the screen. The encryption was complex, so she'd need to risk uplinking to Langley.

The soldier called "Mac" nudged her with a sat phone. She hadn't even noticed him place or receive a call.

"Ma'am, it's Trapp."

She accepted the phone and pressed it to her ear. "Yeah, it's me."

Trapp said, "We've got a problem. Might be a big one."

"I'm a bit busy here. Not sure I can help with a problem you have in England."

"We cut out the signal to the weaponized drones, but the satellite they used is still transmitting. Hines thinks it's relaying the signal to other Chinese satellites controlling another swarm."

"Hold on, I need to think."

She hated the sensation of icy fingers tracing down her back. It meant she was formulating a thought, a theory, and probably one she'd come to wish was untrue. She turned to Ming, angled up on her gurney at around thirty degrees.

"Why is that satellite still active?" Madison asked her.

"What... satellite?" Ming answered.

The soldiers and detective seemed to pick up on her unease, on the low urgency in her tone. They all shifted their stances, as if ready to bolt or fight some more.

"And while we're at it," Madison said, "how come I can get into this system, your old records and data, but I didn't need your biometrics after all?"

Ming averted her eyes.

"*What is it?*" She slapped her hands onto the gurney, her weight making Ming jerk and wince. She ignored the medic who held out a hand as if to say, *take it easy*.

A feeling of nausea hit her, swirling with a trembling anger that caused her teeth to clench and her fist to close so tightly that her knuckles turned white. It was the exact same sensation that had washed through her when she realized Trapp had betrayed her.

"Oh my God," Grubbs said. "This is a wild goose chase, isn't it?"

Ming's head turned back to her, impassive.

"You set this up." Grubbs searched for the words, as breathless as she'd been when Trapp's scheme was laid bare for her. "It's a... you..." She couldn't think, couldn't piece it together.

Zhao Ming broke into the biggest shit-eating grin Madison had ever seen. It was as if someone had stretched out her cheeks and inserted some extra teeth.

"You set us up," Grubbs said. "Splitting us up, sending us in completely the wrong direction."

Ming chuckled, unable to kill the smile, then winced as her laughter morphed into a pained cough. "Oh, Madison. You have no idea."

Madison leaned in, the gurney rattling. "Enlighten me."

Ming lay her head back, eyes to the ceiling, the smile verging on beatific, a woman at peace. "You think you saved me? I knew they would come if you identified me, and I accepted that. A risk I welcomed. True patriots cannot be turned so easily."

"Patriots...?"

"The Great Realignment is coming, and there's nothing America can do to stop it."

Madison's body flushed through with cold. "What the hell is that? The *Great Realignment?*"

Dawson shifted closer, and so did Doc, as if the bound and crippled Zhao Ming posed a physical threat.

"The UK test," Ming said weakly, fatigue obviously playing its part. "Jason Trapp and his merry band stopped it, didn't they?"

"Yes. It's finished. It's over."

"Good."

"Good? Hundreds of people were meant to die so your faction could start production on a bigger scale. But you failed, and Ashenhurst is dead in the water."

Ming tilted her head, a smirk returning, although her voice remained weak, tired, as if fighting sleep. "The UK test was nothing more than a dry run. A proof of concept. Some of our number wanted to be cautious, to wait. But others... like me..." She trailed off before resuming with her last reserves of energy burning in her eyes. "Now others will be *forced* to move to the next phase."

"What is the next phase?"

Ming said nothing. Her eyes were closed, and the two medics moved to help her. Although fully aware now that their patient was, and always had been, America's enemy, the Hippocratic oath extended to the military, so they were duty-bound to put her health first.

Madison stepped away and returned to the sat phone. "Did you get all that?"

"Yeah," Trapp said. "The fracking site wasn't a sales pitch. It was a warm-up. I need to go do something Mitchell is not gonna like."

She knew there was no point urging Trapp to be cautious, so she just hung up. Whatever was happening, wherever the next phase was to take place, it might be located in the intel streaming through her computer right now. She had to crack it and do it fast.

More importantly, she had to keep the faith that Trapp would succeed, or all this was for nothing.

FIFTY-ONE

Isabella Knight stepped over shattered plaster, her anger a cold, hard knot in her gut. The house was a wreck, littered with the dead, and Ashenhurst was treating it like a game.

"A bit messy, wouldn't you say?" he mused, prodding a dead mercenary's boot with the toe of his expensive shoe. "I hope the next batch is worth the price."

She ignored the provocation. They had been back for five minutes, just long enough to secure the VIPs in Ashenhurst's ridiculous "operations lounge."

"The professionals I've hired will do the job," she stated flatly, meeting his gaze. "They follow my command. Now we know what Trapp is capable of, we will be prepared."

Ashenhurst reluctantly accepted her assessment before touring the charnel pit that the approach to his monstrosity now resembled. A monstrosity that would cement the Ashenhurst group as one of the wealthiest corporations on the planet.

Cement.

She hadn't meant to amuse herself with a pun like that, but considering that the machine was buried in a structure more protected than a nuclear bunker, she allowed herself a tiny smile. Ashenhurst caught it and gave a nod that she found hard to read.

Was he eyeing her up again? Or was that just the smug satisfaction of knowing that the deal was within his grasp?

Although they didn't know the full outcome of the dry run on the mine, there had been no thunderclap or enormous rumble to signal the landslide he had been salivating over. But that was a minor inconvenience. Although she was sure he was at least mildly disappointed that he hadn't managed to murder the villagers who had petitioned against his fracking project.

As Ashenhurst departed, Knight stepped around another body. She didn't believe Trapp or his friends to be supernaturally gifted, but she had witnessed how a true believer in a cause can give themselves an incalculable boost in strength, speed, and aggression when called upon.

She stood before the dummy vestibule that had attracted Trapp to this level. She'd wondered about the wisdom of spending so many millions on what might well be considered a single-use object. To get inside, to perform maintenance or to upgrade the control center, would involve ripping away a section of the house. Even the air conditioning was pumped in from a mile away through various tubes. If the enemy located one of them and bunged it up, there were plenty more to continue ventilating what must be a boiling pit of circuitry.

But Ashenhurst had ordered it this way, and his paranoia now seemed justified— he'd been thinking several moves ahead of the CIA, NIA, MI5, and whoever else might come calling. Anything short of a five-hundred-pound bomb would have little effect against the concrete pillar in which the beating heart of a new dawn in weaponry was entombed.

Her bonus was within reach. She was one day away from a long, luxurious retirement. One in which she could choose to grow fat and lazy or perhaps find something to fight for. Something in which she actually believed.

Who knew? She might even end up on the opposite side of the people she was helping arm today. Feeling something other than a numb hopelessness at the state of the world would be nice.

"Isabella," he called from the lobby. "It's time."

Ashenhurst was ready to launch the main event.

FANG CHEN WAS IMPRESSED by the operations lounge. She had been briefed on it, but no one had been permitted inside until now. The proof of concept at the mine was sufficient to assuage any fears about the effectiveness of the drone mesh, and now that Ashenhurst had satisfied his Chinese partners, it was time to show the world.

"Your additional units were shipped two days ago," Ashenhurst announced. "Thank you for the hefty deposit. I trust the remaining money will be delivered immediately after you run your own test?"

Fang translated for the Chinese-speakers.

She replied, "The funds are in escrow and only require that you deliver on your promise."

"Just a shame I can't be there to see it," Ashenhurst said.

Fang translated another question. "You will be able to deliver additional machines if the enhanced test is successful?"

"Of course," Ashenhurst said. "We have a robust supply chain ready and willing to supply what we need."

The room was decked out with screens around the walls and a huge blank one at the head of the room that currently backlit Rafe Ashenhurst. The screen flickered to life, pixelating as the images buffered, which seemed to surprise Ashenhurst.

"You may be able to witness it after all," Fang said.

The screen resolved and denoted a fleet of naval vessels on the ocean. There were no landmarks visible.

"What is that?" Ashenhurst asked.

Isabella Knight stepped out of one of the shadows cast by the massive screen. "That's a brand-spanking-new, state-of-the-art Chinese aircraft carrier. The *Fujian*?"

"Very good, Ms. Knight," General Gao said in English. "This will be its first live action encounter."

"And I suppose that water it's floating on is the South China Sea, approaching Taiwan."

"The naval maneuvers are just the stage, Mr. Ashenhurst," Fang said calmly. "Our real test requires a live target."

Apprehension flared in Ashenhurst's eyes. "A live target? My part in this was finished. This implicates me directly—this was not our agreement."

"The agreement has evolved, as has the schedule," General Gao stated flatly in English, his gaze fixed on the screen. "A new opportunity presented itself."

Isabella Knight let out a short, sharp breath, a sound devoid of humor. She muttered, more to herself than to him, "A blockade is too slow. It gives the Americans time to mobilize."

She looked from Gao to Fang. "This is faster. You're not just testing a weapon. You're starting a war."

Ashenhurst followed her logic, his voice barely a whisper. "Xinyi... our financial hub... My God, you're going to hit Taiwan."

Fang finally turned to him, her expression unreadable. "The global situation is ripe for realignment. The decision was made by leaders far beyond this room. You are a partner in this, Mr. Ashenhurst, whether you wish to be or not."

FIFTY-TWO

Alongside Ikem and Kane, Trapp continued scanning for survivors in the wreckage of the fracking operation, ignoring the Washington-based conversation that he was patched into. They weren't speaking directly to him anyway.

He wanted to go after Ashenhurst and put a bullet in him, but eliminating the middleman wouldn't avert the potential threat on its own. Plus, Trapp was invested enough in self-preservation to resist the personal vendetta he now carried, especially since such an act would land him in a British prison for twenty years or more.

Kane had already warned them that when the police arrived after responding to the mess he'd left in Queensacre—which they would very shortly—all three of them would be arrested. It was procedure. Charges would only be forthcoming if the Crown Prosecution Service deemed it "in the public interest," which Kane was convinced it would not be. All they needed was firm evidence that Ashenhurst had orchestrated the attack, and they'd be sent home with a pat on the back.

"Over there," Kane called, directing Trapp and Ikem

toward a prone figure half-buried under a twisted panel that had come loose when a transformer blew.

Trapp was there in a matter of seconds. He and Kane lifted the heavy metal while Ikem gently extracted the victim.

Dead.

They were using tarpaulins and whatever they could find to cover those who'd died—six so far. Trapp lingered on the man's face, frozen in fear and pain, committing the burns and lacerations to memory.

"*Trapp?*" Mitchell said testily, as if he'd been calling for some time. "Jason, are you there?"

"I'm here."

"London confirms—they've got what they need."

"What they need for what?" Trapp asked.

"They're going after Ashenhurst, warrants and all. And they've got a firm commitment from Taiwan to cooperate with the banking trail."

Trapp told Ikem and Kane.

"Will it be enough?" Ikem asked, his tone edged with skepticism.

Trapp wasn't sure. "Mitchell, have you heard directly from MI5? The home secretary is—"

"I know what Robert Sutherland is," Mitchell said. "And soon everyone else will, too. That's why I circumvented him. I've brought the Met's Counter Terrorism Command into the mix."

"If he knows they're on to him, he'll find a way out."

"Then we focus on stopping the next attack," Hines interrupted.

Polly was on the line, too, filtering news and helping Hines track the signals that were still zipping around up there. She said, "The Pentagon is ready to shoot down anything that even resembles an unauthorized aircraft. We can't let anything slip through."

"The satellite link from the house is still active," Hines said, his voice tight. "It's relaying across the globe. The signal terminates over the South China Sea."

"The naval maneuvers," Grubbs stated instantly from the comm link. "It has to be the fleet."

Trapp relayed the info to Ikem and Kane, shaking his head. He stared out at the distant horizon, the pieces clicking into place with horrifying speed—the money trail, the shell companies, Zhao Ming's destination.

"No," Trapp said, his voice low and urgent. "The fleet isn't the *target*. It's the launch platform." He grabbed his comms. "Madison, you're in Xinyi. Zhao Ming's entire offshore operation is there. Ashenhurst's shadow financing runs through that district."

A heavy silence fell across the line, the implication hanging in the air. It was Mitchell who broke it, his voice grim. "My God, Jason. It's not a weapons demonstration. It's a false flag."

"'They strike Xinyi," Grubbs finished, her voice strained as she realized she was at ground zero. "This place is like Taiwan's Wall Street and Silicon Valley rolled into one. An attack here would cripple the entire country. They use the DEW to make it look like a direct act of war from Beijing. America is forced to retaliate against the Chinese government..."

"...And while the world is focused on a US-China conflict, the extremist faction seizes power back home," Trapp concluded. "It's a coup."

"'They can only do it if that satellite link stays active," Hines cut in, panicked. "It all runs through the server room at the estate."

"Which is a tomb," Trapp said, slamming a fist against the quarry rock. "It's buried in concrete. We can't get to it."

"An airstrike is not an option," Mitchell stated firmly. "And letting a war break out is not something I can allow on my watch."

"And Grubbs..." Trapp could see her now, picturing her debating whether to run or keep working, trying to extract the evidence they would need to save face for the Beijing government, to prove it was not a Chinese invasion but a terrorist act. One that they needed to stop. "Madison?"

"You getting soppy on me, Jason?" Grubbs answered. "Because don't."

Trapp's stomach roiled. Not just for the people who were sure to perish under a large-scale attack, but for Grubbs in particular. He'd never forgotten what she'd gone through when she was kidnapped, never fully forgiven himself for breaching her trust.

"I sent you there, Madison," he said. "I'm sorry. Please... get safe."

"Would you?" she asked.

"You're not me."

"No. But this time, I'm in control. I think... if I'd known what you were up to when you stole my credentials... I wouldn't have let you. Not at first. But if I'd known why, and what the stakes were... I could have been persuaded."

"Time," Trapp said. "I didn't have—"

"I know. You were on a clock, and you wouldn't have persuaded me in time. I get it. But now you need to understand something for me. I'm going to get what you need to flush out Ashenhurst and whoever else is wrapped up in this. You..."

She swallowed loudly enough for all to hear. Trapp wanted to interrupt, to override her decision, but at the same time, she was right. It *was* her choice.

She said, "If you want to help me and everyone else here, take out the servers in Ashenhurst's vault. That should disrupt the signals and give us a chance." When he said nothing, she pressed, "*Jason,* do you copy?"

Trapp crouched, thinking, thinking. "It's wrapped in so much concrete, a car full of C4 would barely graze it. We'd need to get in and—"

Then he stood, the roil in his gut diminished, his muscles firing as his brain kicked into gear, signaling him to move.

"I think I know how to breach that fucking tomb."

FIFTY-THREE

The resolution of the massive screen in the operations lounge was so sharp that Fang felt like she was hovering over the deck of the aircraft carrier in person. The satellite feed was a wonder in itself, capturing every detail: the churn of the South China Sea, the sleek *Starfire* fighter-jet-like UAVs as they launched in batches of three, and the white exhaust plume trailing behind them. When the final vehicle had taken flight, the satellite repositioned, following ten clusters of six unmanned aerial vehicles over the ocean as they stuck to their pre-programmed hexagonal formations, hugging the water to evade radar detection.

"They're falling into formation," Ashenhurst said, but she barely registered it. "Exactly as they should be."

Fang was mesmerized by the honeycomb pattern the drones had formed, a geometric marvel. The *Starfires* were China's answer to the Americans' experimental YFQ-44 'Fury' drone—dart-shaped statements of technological dominance that would shame the earlier Predator models in speed, range, and efficiency.

Fang should have felt swollen with pride. This was her country's might, its destiny, a show of strength to make the world tremble. But a gnawing unease still coiled inside her.

This wasn't just a military maneuver, not some test or demonstration.

She thought of her uncle, arrested years earlier for teaching martial arts during an order to remain indoors, how he was sent to be re-educated in a special facility and was never seen or heard from again.

Was this the strength she wanted? The strength to crush all dissent and remake the rebellious into the obedient?

Yes, she told herself. *This is necessary. War is what it takes to change the world.*

And there, as the Starfires rose into the sky to deliver their lethal message, some of the biggest dissenters of all awaited: the island of Taiwan, its citizens brainwashed into believing they were not Chinese. They were about to learn what it meant to cower in the eye of a mighty storm.

USING a secure server Polly had set up, Madison frantically downloaded the data, digging like a dog for a bone rather than working like a surgeon. Anything and everything was shooting through the ether, while the team around her worked to alert the authorities of the coming danger.

"Ma'am," Dawson said, lowering his phone that was connected to the Taiwanese defense department. "It's confirmed. They're vectoring air assets but they won't make it in time. We've got maybe five minutes before—"

"Five minutes is all I need," Madison said.

Every byte of data they transmitted was essential. No point in going through all this only for the man who'd facilitated so much pain and death to walk away, his plans delayed rather than canceled.

"Is everyone out?" she asked.

"This building, ma'am, and others in the vicinity." Dawson had phoned in the highest-level warning, that Taiwan was facing its own 9-11. After years of Chinese threats, they were well-prepared for evacuations and contingencies. "Should have everyone belowground in time."

The building shuddered again, dust raining from the ceiling.

Doc called over from the windows that had cracked and lost a pane, thanks to the dynamite Madison had set off. "Got a visual."

She tore herself from the screen, focusing on where the young man was pointing. The incoming threat was little more than a scattering of black dashes on the blue sky. A shimmering, barely discernible miasma spread beneath them, like heat on a desert road—the kinetic and microwave bursts that were no doubt frying all the electronics and delicate mechanisms they flew over.

That was just the cursory, collateral damage, though. Thanks to Zhao Ming and the contingencies she had arranged with her masters, the waves would be concentrated upon them soon. No fly-past, no vomiting.

Madison and the soldiers were going to burn along with the evidence.

"Almost there," she said. "Evac your men."

"With respect, ma'am, not a chance," Dawson answered. "We're gonna give you every chance to finish what we started."

THE ROOF WAS a slab of concrete, the breeze giving cool relief under a hot blue sky. A hot blue sky that now hummed with menace.

Parker and Hsu crouched behind the low parapet, their rifles braced against the edge, barrels poking through the safety railings. Parker wiped his brow with the back of his hand, leaving a smudge of grime.

Hsu adjusted his rifle scope, squinting into the incoming haze. Below them, the city sprawled in a mass of glass, steel, and concrete, but up here, it was just wind and the incoming bogeys. The Arabs had a name for US drones that delivered payloads from too high for anyone to see: *almawt min alsama.*

Death from the heavens.

These UAVs were low, though, low enough to see them growing bigger, more distinct, their formation programmed beforehand, delivering not explosives but what the CIA woman had called "directed energy" and "microwave beams" which sounded fucking awful to Hsu.

Parker said, "They're coming in hot. You can feel it."

Hsu glanced at him. "*Feel it?* That's your intel?"

"Yeah," Parker shot back. "You wanna argue, or you wanna live?"

Hsu's finger hovered over the trigger guard. The first drone to show its sleek definition instead of just a speck appeared no larger than a bird, but it—and the others in its hexagonal cluster—was moving so fast. Growing, always growing.

Then another group of six, and another, until the sky was alive, rotating in a fast, disciplined formation.

"Let's go to work," Hsu said, his aim steady.

Hsu fired at the lead drone, but it veered sharply upward, breaking formation for a second, then reset its path, unscathed. Parker did likewise, but the entire pattern of aircraft changed direction. They set into a random pattern, a chaotic dance of banking, swooping, climbing; another dip of the wing, another maneuver. Both men reverted to bursts of three, teaming up to focus on one UAV to catch it, to predict its evasion pattern. But the drones were too fast, turning like synchronized swimmers, engines twisting and turning in unison, like the lightest-weight Harrier jets ever made. Hsu was sure they'd hit a couple of them, but it was like firing at an oncoming Jeep with a .22, the damage brushed off or deflected.

"They're too fast," Hsu said.

"No shit." Parker fired again, full auto, and this time, the target drone dipped, sputtering before it righted itself. "Keep shooting! We gotta do one of them at least!"

Hsu joined him in battering the UAVs with all they had. But they kept coming, undeterred, twisting, turning, dancing. The whine of engines got louder, and a low, resonant humming frequency made their teeth ache.

"What the hell are these things doing?" Hsu shouted.

The drones spread out now, the clusters fanning in a wide arc, zipping back and forth, looping around like acrobatic pilots at an air show.

Hsu's stomach dropped as he realized what was happening. "They're not just targeting us. They're surrounding the building."

Each unit formed a phalanx of three hexagonal patterns, rotating between themselves as if weaving a pattern, so only one was out of place at any one time. The effect was dizzying, captivating.

There was nowhere to go. The drones were too many, too fast. Hsu accepted it, an uncharacteristic tremble of his lips giving way to stiff resolve as he hefted his carbine, ready to make a final stand.

Hsu thought of his wife and his daughter's laugh as she

brought him a small bouquet of weeds she'd carefully selected from the field at the back of their house.

"Guess we keep firing," he said.

Parker nodded, taking aim. "Until we can't anymore."

Then they unleashed everything they had, hoping it would be enough but knowing that, probably, it wouldn't be.

FIFTY-FOUR

Fang Chen watched Rafe Ashenhurst bob and weave as if he was mimicking the drones. Having at first been surprised that his benefactors were moving ahead with a plan the scale of which he plainly feared, he now reveled in the attack, adopting a swagger as he narrated unnecessarily. She viewed him with a mixture of awe and revulsion, and her contempt for the weak men in suits that her own people had sent grew. As she stared at the screen showing the drones surrounding a building, she felt as if she were an ethereal spirit, watching events unfold from above.

"See the sparks there?" Ashenhurst pointed to the lower-right section of the screen. "That's the streetlights being overloaded. The precision and range is awesome, isn't it?"

Compliments fluttered around him, his subordinates eager to bask in what little glory he perceived while Fang's associates watched impassively.

"And the patterns they're flying. They'll burn through their fuel faster than hoped, but there's still a good fifteen minutes' flying time. They'll have to deploy the energy bursts soon, though."

Gao had been visibly satisfied at the initial execution, but the scaling wasn't impressing him. "What use is this if we must only use it in short sorties?"

Ashenhurst clasped his hands. "The computers powering this attack are incredibly advanced. The best money can buy. I spent as much on that as I did on the hardware you have over Taiwan right now. It has already spit out new modeling for use in your superconductor circuits. Double deployment time, and I'm sure we can tweak the delivery system."

"Hmmm." Gao watched the screen. "Fifteen minutes to eliminate all in one building? When a rocket would do it much faster?"

"Fifteen minutes on *that* building. There are many other drones, many more targets. And besides, when you've finished using this method, General, you have a nice building still in place. Just flush out the corpses and you're ready to go. Job's a good 'un."

At the last phrase, Gao looked to Fang to translate, but Fang just assumed it was another British idiom, so shook her head and called Ashenhurst an idiot in Chinese.

One of the Westerners took a brief, impossible-to-hear phone call and reported to Ashenhurst a little too loudly, "Isabella Knight reports all is still quiet. Provisions are in place."

"Of course they are," Ashenhurst replied, annoyed at his guests hearing what was obviously meant to be a subtle confirmation. "Our preparation is impeccable."

Fang knew Jason Trapp better than any dossier, better than this man's limited exposure. She'd seen Trapp in action, seen his calculated decision-making up close, and reasoned that he represented all that China feared in the collective American psyche.

"Mr. Ashenhurst," Fang said, injecting more weight into her voice. "We cannot underestimate what he is capable of. He is no obedient lapdog. He will not stop."

"Miss Chen." Ashenhurst turned to her with an impatient smile. "Our defenses have been beefed up since this morning. No amount of determination can outmaneuver the foundations protecting us—and our project."

Fang nodded, her expression placid. She preferred not to translate for the general and his cohort. But underneath, no matter how secure Ashenhurst believed his home to be, she couldn't shake the dread that Jason Trapp was somehow inevitable. Which meant Fang herself might have to take matters into her own hands—orders hailing from above even General Gao.

Ashenhurst stood with his back to the array of screens displaying the ongoing attack, Starfire UAVs swarming into formation. Fang was certain the man's positioning was intentional, the grand framing giving him gravitas despite his slight frame.

She said, "My English has improved much since living in America. So when you imply that persistence cannot penetrate reinforced concrete, I believe that is what is known in English as *hubris*."

"Spot on," Ashenhurst replied. "But when you've been around the block as many times as me, I reckon I've earned a bit of hubris."

Throughout their exchange, General Gao watched with interest. Fang felt a twinge of irritation as he leaned over and asked what was happening. She gave him a brief summary, including her concerns.

"You think you know better than our hosts?" Gao clarified in Chinese, somewhat incredulous.

"I know I do," she answered firmly. "I am not some intern here to babysit you. I serve the Chinese people with the full backing of Lian Zhelan. Having encountered our enemy before, I am certain he will attempt another attack."

Gao sat impassively, his legs crossed at the thigh, his hands in his lap. Only his head cocked slightly to show he'd heard her.

"I mean no disrespect," Fang said but maintained her steely tone. "But Ambassador Zhelan recommended me because I understand the Americans. And I understand men like this." She meant Ashenhurst. "He does not know Trapp like I do."

At the mention of *Trapp*, Ashenhurst interjected. "Perhaps, Miss Chen, you should consider taking a moment to savor our triumph. You and your bosses are about to reshape the global arms race. With my help, of course."

Before she could formulate a suitable reply, the building trembled. A low rumble began to grow and then crescendo in a cacophony of thunder as the floor beneath them shuddered violently and the walls threatened to cave in, as if a wrecking ball had slammed into the house. Ashenhurst stumbled, the huge screens flickered to black, and Fang braced herself, her expertise and exposure to the English tongue kicking in as she found her bearings.

"What," she said, "the fuck was that?"

FIFTY-FIVE

The pump-truck acquired from the fracking site roared the loudest it had so far, its engine screaming as Trapp pushed it to its limit. With the accelerator glued to the floor, Kane and Ikem held on to their seats; seatbelts didn't feel enough.

The vehicle was an enormous, bombastic work of engineering, muscling 3000 BHP; it was more than double the length of the tanker trucks. It needed to be, stacked as it was with state-of-the-art hydraulics and high-pressure mechanisms and equipped with new hoses and digital frac controls. A powerful, ballistic missile of a truck, and all but impossible to speed down the tiny countryside roads on days when the cops hadn't cordoned off the area in preparation for an armed response. But after a briefing from one of the engineering supervisors who'd worked the site since before the recent licenses were granted, Trapp believed his idea might just work.

The truck crashed through the Ashenhurst estate's wrought-iron gates, wrenching them from their hinges with a bump and a shriek. The truck lurched violently, but Trapp was set on the mansion ahead. Ikem and Kane gave grunts of stress, hands switching to grip the dashboard as the truck plowed through a stone fountain, obliterating it while slowing only a fraction. As water and debris cascaded over the windshield, he kept on going, and even though he knew it wouldn't have the impact he craved, he revved hard, cranking another gear so the truck all but yelped in pain as he floored it.

While the lawn to the right of the ornate stairs and statues wasn't quite as steep, the softer track generated more friction, more drag, and the three men in the cab jerked with the sudden change in speed. But that was nothing compared to the impact of slamming into the French doors of some dining room, ripping out a lintel along with a pile of bricks and metalwork.

For Trapp's idea to have any hope of paying off, they'd need to acquire additional firepower along the way, but this fullfrontal assault should throw off Knight's personnel, at least temporarily.

"Okay, let's move." Trapp shoved the door open and leapt out, the others following, guns up—their lack of ammo having reduced them to sidearms—all scanning for incoming. "Kane, you sure you've got this?"

"If you're sure it'll work, yeah," Kane said.

Ikem grabbed a gear bag, slinging it over his shoulder. "They should be on us any time now."

Trapp thought back to their last incursion—the blood, the bodies, and more importantly, the layout. They were in a dining room, shuttered with sheets over paintings, a long table, and chairs stacked along the wall. Having found a quick understanding over the past twenty-four hours, they fell quickly into step. Not quite a polished team but one coming together.

"Right corridor," Trapp said as they breached the mansion's interior. "I counted four guys left over, so they'll be on their way."

"Plus Knight herself," Kane added. "And I doubt she's any mug."

As they stalked onward, dragging the hose behind them, the air was thick with dust that lessened as they moved away from the crashed truck. Rounding each corner, they overlapped as they advanced, one covering the open passageway, the next advancing, then the third tagging himself in before the cycle started over.

The vestibule was in sight, its entrance a dark maw in the wrecked corridor. The walls were scarred, the floor stained with drying blood. And slumped against the doorframe was the reason their approach had been so quiet.

Trapp saw him—one of the Turkish contractors he was sure he'd killed hours ago. The man was a ruin of blood-soaked bandages and broken limbs, but his eyes were dark, steady, and fixed on Trapp. The tangle of wires and plastic explosives strapped to his torso told the rest of the story. A dead-man's switch was clutched in his one good hand. He was a human booby trap, left behind to guard the objective.

"Ikem, Kane, fall back. Now," Trapp ordered, his voice low. He recognized this man from some long-forgotten flash bulletin. Kilo Demir.

The man offered a weak, bloody smile. "No. They stay. You all die together."

Trapp's finger was steady on the trigger of his Glock, but he knew shooting was not an option. The man was waiting for it. The alcove Trapp was in offered minimal cover from that kind of blast.

"He's here for me," Trapp said into his comm, keeping his eyes locked on Demir. "Get back to the truck. Get the fountain ready and wait for my signal."

Kane gave a curt nod and disappeared back down the corridor, Ikem right behind him.

Now it was just the two of them.

"Save the speech," Trapp said, his voice flat. "There's no audience."

"You are my audience," Demir rasped, using the wall to keep himself from collapsing completely. "You are the final act. You killed me. Now I shall return the favor."

An idea—a desperate, insane idea—began to form in Trapp's mind. He needed to buy time.

"Your family gets money," Trapp said, taking a calculated step into the open. "Ashenhurst gets an empire. You see the imbalance there?"

Demir's eyes flared with hate. "You know nothing of my cause."

"I know you're a loose end he's using to clean up his mess," Trapp countered, taking another slow step. He was closer now, almost at the entrance to the vestibule. "He's not honoring you. He's disposing of you."

"Lies!" Demir spat, trying to shift his weight. The movement sent a spasm of agony through him, and his grip on the switch trembled.

That was the moment.

"Ikem, now! Full pressure!" Trapp yelled into his comm as he dove for cover behind the thick corridor wall.

He didn't see the water, but he heard it. The hose they had left on the floor behind them roared to life. It wasn't aimed at Demir but into the vestibule itself. Thousands of gallons of high-pressure water began to flood the confined space, turning the concrete chamber into a rapidly filling tank.

Demir panicked. The water surged around his shattered legs, cold and powerful, threatening to sweep him off his feet. He lost his balance, his one good hand flailing for a hold on the slick wall. In his terror and confusion, his grip on the switch went slack.

The world erupted in a deafening, concussive *BOOM*.

But the explosion was different. Tamped by the immense pressure of the water, the blast didn't expand outward in a wave of fire and shrapnel. It was contained, focused inward like a hydraulic hammer. The force of the underwater detonation struck the bunker's interior wall with unimaginable power.

Trapp pressed himself against the floor as the water and debris washed out into the corridor. The roaring stopped as Ikem cut the feed. Slowly, Trapp pushed himself up, his ears ringing, his body aching. The vestibule was a wrecked, flooded cavern, but the once-impenetrable wall now had a jagged, fist-sized hole a full foot-deep.

They weren't in. But it was a start.

FIFTY-SIX

Demir was gone, pretty much vaporized, but blood and smaller chunks of his body were fanned over the floor, walls, and ceiling. And the stench of burned explosives against concrete now mingled with it all. Nothing Trapp hadn't experienced in one form or another too many times for comfort, but it was still disgusting.

Doing his best to ignore the gore, Trapp concentrated on the one slice of luck they'd enjoyed today. He had always planned to enact this strategy once they got here and secured the additional ordnance that he was certain would be here; he just hadn't expected his enemy to set it off.

"You got the gear?" he called.

Ikem had hauled the hose with him, leaving Kane to cover their rear.

"Ready." Ikem slipped a sack off his shoulder and dropped to his knees, heaving out an attachment that narrowed the hose's stream to a diameter suitable for attaching to the pipes drilled into the earth. Then he added the second nozzle, which the supervisor who had briefed them had said they used for freeing up smaller cave-ins encountered occasionally when boring a new channel. It was narrow, not quite needlelike, but funneled the water into an even tighter pressure than the barrage that had ended Demir.

Only, there was no pipe here. No fissure in the mantle. Just a long, jagged crack in a concrete bunker.

While the crack was not deep enough to penetrate all the way to the servers, it was enough to insert the nozzle.

They worked it in as far as it would go, and Ikem twisted the valve. Water blasted out, slamming into the crack and spraying more chunks out immediately. The pressure worked at first, but there was little to push against, so it just sheared off the looser materials.

They cut the feed and waited for the water to drain out. Then they examined the crack that had increased to a gash, and Trapp used his knife to stab into it, chipping out more material before coming to a halt.

The small hole was as deep as his elbow and narrowed like a cone.

"Might be enough," he said.

Ikem saw what he'd done, and together they worked to drive the nozzle into the burrowed aperture. It needed forcing in, a good sign, since that would create a seal of sorts.

Ikem said, "Ready?"

"Okay, let's do it."

The water shot out again, a finer spray reflected back at them, proving the pressure was building up. Acting like a drill. A mighty creak eked its way out as the water's stress forced the crack wider, deeper...

More concrete groaned, then split under the assault.

"Cut it!" Trapp shouted.

Ikem did so, leaving water gushing from the fissure.

Trapp peered into the crack. He could see lights flickering

behind a second glass or Perspex shield. "It's still too small. Too damn small."

"Grenade?" Ikem said. "We have one left."

"Won't cut it." Trapp slapped the wall. "How much water we got left?"

"Cannot say. The tank was full when we started."

"Trapp! Ikem!" Kane's voice from down the corridor sounded sharp, urgent. "Bastards incoming. Must've figured they need to mop up after the vest. They'll be here in seconds."

THE CORRIDOR WAS a mess of flickering lights as Isabella moved through it, her combat boots pounding and her earpiece a mess of overlapping voices as her team scrambled to respond. She had planned for this scenario, despite her boss's belligerent denial of reality.

Amateur hour.

She placed her hand on the scanner, and the operations lounge door hissed open, having sealed itself for safety. Inside, Ashenhurst stood at the center, and his guests—wealthy, powerful, and now totally unnerved—clustered around him.

"Ms. Knight," Ashenhurst said, his voice edged with irritation. "What the hell is going on out there?"

"The expected incursion," she replied. "But as I warned you, they're not being subtle. They're not here to negotiate."

Ashenhurst's eyes narrowed. "And you didn't see this coming?"

"I said it was possible." The question stung, but she didn't let it show. "As instructed, we were prepped for covert, not a ram-raid. Best move is an invac."

Ashenhurst hesitated. "An *in*vacuation? Really? That's your solution?"

"The only one I can recommend," Knight said.

Ashenhurst exhaled sharply, his lips a thin line. "Fine. But this better not take long." He turned to the guests. "Ladies and gentlemen, we're moving to my personal safe room. Follow Ms. Knight, please."

Isabella's jaw tightened. Escort duty.

That's just fantastic.

She glanced at the group, at their fancy suits and frightened faces.

Ashenhurst stepped closer, his voice dropping. "Make sure your security goons finish this. Before the police decide to pay a visit to the loud, crashy-bangy house in the middle of a major incident."

"Understood."

Knight adjusted the strap of her tactical vest, then motioned for the group to follow.

The Chinese contingent looked like they'd rather be anywhere else—General Gao, especially. His features twisted into a scowl aimed squarely at Ashenhurst.

"This is unacceptable," Gao said, rigidly still. "We were assured the fracking site was secure. We were assured this house is secure. Now you expect us to cower in a hole? How can we trust that anything you touch is secure?"

Knight was itching to radio her team for an update, but she kept her expression neutral, supporting her prick of a boss. "Short of being entombed in concrete, the safe room is the most secure location on the estate."

Ashenhurst's smile was slick and practiced, but the strain in his eyes betrayed a simmering panic. "General Gao, I understand your frustration. Rest assured, this will not impact our agreement. In fact, I'm prepared to offer a significant discount for the inconvenience."

Gao's gaze remained stone. "You think money can compensate for incompetence?"

Fang Chen stepped forward.

"Mr. Ashenhurst," she said, her voice soft but confident. "I have a counteroffer. With your permission, General, I will wait behind and discuss it while you move to the safe room."

Knight frowned. *What the hell is she playing at?*

Ashenhurst tilted his head, intrigued. "This isn't exactly a convenient time for negotiations, Miss Chen."

Fang smiled faintly. "It's exactly the time. I'll take the chance on skipping the safe room. I trust Ms. Knight will do her job."

Knight's instincts screamed at her to intervene, but Gao cut in. "Enough. Lead the way. If this operation fails, there will be more consequences than financial ruin."

Knight nodded curtly and gestured toward the exit. "This way. Stay close."

As they moved through the corridor, her earpiece came alive, snippets of her team's chatter. They were regrouping, preparing to strike.

Good—she'd join them soon enough. First, she had to dump these liabilities in the safe room. Then she would indulge herself in a bit of good, old-fashioned payback.

FIFTY-SEVEN

Trapp pressed his shoulder against the concrete as the hiss of water flooding into the bunker became deafening, but the torrent did nothing to extinguish the lights on the servers. Ikem was stuffing material into the gash around the nozzle, rubber sealant that he'd brought from the truck, but the thick, viscous material needed time to harden, and the water leaked back out in an impressive spray.

"Keep it flowing," Trapp said. "We need more pressure."

"We're maxed out already," Kane shouted back.

Then, abruptly, the water stopped.

Trapp froze, his hand working the start/stop lever. "What the hell?"

"The pump is dead," Ikem said.

"The truck," Trapp said urgently.

The goddamn pump-truck. Someone needed to go see if it had been compromised, and Trapp wasn't about to ask Ikem or Kane to do it.

But as he stepped out of the vestibule to ask Kane to back him up, he saw Kane had already departed, and his voice over the comms confirmed it: "I'll get that contraption back on. Might need to kill a few of those cockwombling fucks first, though. Stand by."

HALFWAY ACROSS THE WORLD, Madison worked the laptop like a college student cramming in a last-minute study session. Outside, the drones had commenced their sweep of the building, and she could feel an otherworldly pulsing. For a weapon that was supposed to leave infrastructure intact, it was making a hell of a mess. Two of the operators screamed by the window, collapsing to the ground, clutching their heads, blood streaming from their noses as they crawled away from the wave's radius.

Having established their optimal formation, as reported by the pair Dawson had sent to the roof, the drones were deploying the full force of the microwave emitters—set to overload every electrical unit while boiling her and the SOG team from the inside out.

She didn't have time to process it fully, not now. The data she needed was buried here. Proof. Tangible, irrefutable proof that Ashenhurst and his dissident partners, not Beijing, were behind this. She couldn't let it slip now. No way of telling how long she'd be able to transmit with the interference closing in.

If she died here, it wouldn't be for nothing, *couldn't* be for nothing.

Another drone pulse sent a shower of sparks in a wave of color through the back half of the office, a chain-reaction of overloaded circuits that proved their time was almost up.

She just needed one more minute.

CAMERON KANE NEGOTIATED his way through the shattered remnants of the dining room, his Glock ready, his mind in a flow-state of combat readiness—every nook and cranny held danger until he confirmed it did not, every shadow was a target lurking, and he refused to face in a single direction for more than a few seconds.

The pump-truck was still wedged into the outer wall. Leaving it unattended had been a mistake, but they'd needed every hand at the site. They had hoped to quickly rip the concrete apart, not make a tiny hole.

He scanned the room again, checking every shadow, every flicker of light.

The truck was closer, its massive tires like black monolithic eyes. He could see the water gushing from a ruptured pipe, flowing around and away from the truck's base, the pump itself silent.

Trapp and Ikem were counting on him. Grubbs, too. Grubbs more than Trapp.

He took another step. The lever was within reach. He holstered the Glock, his hand stretching—

And then it hit him. Slammed into his gut, driving the air from his lungs. Whatever it was, he didn't see it. He doubled over, retching, spilling his lunch in a sour, fragrant mess. His head swam, and the room tilted, spinning around him. Pain lanced his skull, and he stumbled, knees buckling, hitting the ground in an undignified heap.

Curled into a fetal ball, his vision blurred, dark spots dancing. He reached blindly, fingers brushing the truck's tire. The rubber was cold, yet it felt like an anchor, tethering him to consciousness.

Balling all the hurt and sickness into a single, tight point, he tried to stand, but his legs wouldn't obey. His stomach churned, bile rising with an acidic trickle. His skin was on fire, every nerve screaming, yet he forced himself to focus.

They'd hit him with one of their bloody energy weapons, like the one Trapp told him about, the attack in Pittsburgh—nausea, disorientation, incapacitation. But seeing the footage was nothing compared to feeling it tear through your body.

He couldn't stay here. He had to move. Get the water flowing.

The world tilted as Kane lifted his head, vision swimming. Then, footsteps. Heavy, deliberate.

Two figures stepped into the room from outside, silhouetted against the sky. One of them carried a massive tube-shaped item, a bazooka-sized weapon with a thick cord snaking to a bulky backpack. If he'd been able to speak, he'd have made a crack about a bargain-basement Ghostbuster along with some creative profanity, but he just groaned.

"Look at this," one of the mercs said with a sneer, his Russian accent possessing an American twang. "Big bad Cameron Kane, brought to his knees. Thought you'd be harder to kill."

Others had made that mistake. Be it the Taliban or Karadzic's genocidal goons in Bosnia or some coked-up IRA foot soldiers, they'd all been wrong about him. And so had the squaddies who thought collateral damage was fun, that killing civilians who looked like the enemy was a sport. Kane had made sure none of his comrades would do such evil on his watch again, and he'd been prepared to end his career—and every friendship he'd ever fostered—to get through the other side and ground his conscience in reality.

They had all underestimated him. And these fuckers would too.

Kane had managed to draw his Glock, but his arm felt like lead.

The other merc laughed. "Boss said he'd be trouble. He don't look like trouble."

The first merc shifted, adjusting his grip on the weapon.

With a roar that tore pain from his lungs through his throat, Kane rolled onto his side, his near dead arm flipped over by his momentum as he fired one shot after the other. The Glock kicked in his hand, his wrist somehow holding up under the recoil. Both mercs jerked, their sniggering, fuck-face amusement cut short as nine-millimeter slugs ripped through them. One collapsed instantly, head snapping back; the other stumbled, clutching his hand to his collar before crumpling to the floor.

Silence.

Kane lay there, his body gasping in protest. Every movement felt like he'd been skinned, bathed in salt, and dumped in a bath of broken glass.

But he couldn't stop. Not yet.

He forced himself to his feet. His legs trembled, but he stumbled forward, one agonizing step at a time. For a flash of a moment, he was back in the Iraqi mosque ten years ago, blood on the walls and bodies twisted all around, and the laughter—the fucking laughter—of British soldiers as they mocked the dead. The ringleader had warned him not to even think about grassing them up, that they had their story straight already, and they'd burn him. That their CO, Colonel Sutherland, would protect them.

Here, now, when he reached the truck, he readied to flip the water back on.

Like cutting down that unit as they tried to murder him, the stubborn, bastard-hard trooper that he was refusing to back down, he refused to lose.

But his heart sank.

The metal casing and seal had split open. The water

pooling wasn't just a leak or pressure valve releasing. The circuits were fried, blackened and smoking, having overloaded under a surge of power.

They'd hit it with the same DEW they'd attacked Kane with. Of course they had.

He slapped the truck, the pain barely registering. He'd failed.

Again.

His legs gave out. He dropped to his knees. Stared at the ruined truck. Weakness flooded him, his stomach a churn of sickness.

What now? What the hell am I supposed to do now?

He closed his eyes. The darkness closed in. He could hold on no longer. His last thought was a wave of regret—not for himself but for the people he'd let down.

Then, nothing.

FIFTY-EIGHT

Isabella Knight adjusted the weight of the handheld directed energy cannon, its sleek casing vibrating as the charge built from the battery on her back. The leap forward they'd made with the same tech was astounding, even to a mind like hers, focused more on the use of such weapons than their origins.

Its fatal effects may have been slower than a bullet or an RPG, but its spread was wider, and in close quarters, less likely to drop a piece of ceiling to obscure an escape. Plus, the main reason she had opted for this method of execution was that it felt good.

She wasn't a psychopath—at least she didn't think she was—but there was something of a high when she finally rid herself of a stubborn target. Trapp had evaded bullets and bombs and everything else they'd thrown at him.

Taking him out this way just felt right.

Flanked by her two remaining men—both silent, both obedient—she didn't need to issue orders as they approached the dummy vestibule which Trapp and his companions had almost breached.

The long-haired man she believed was called Oleg peeled off to the right, his semi-automatic shotgun—an expensive Benelli Raffaello, the barrel of which he'd sawn off to be shorter and more mobile—loaded and held against his shoulder. He had an MP5 submachine gun strapped to his back too, but the stopping power of the Benelli made more sense.

They had followed the hose after disabling the truck so that the water was no longer a danger to the servers. All that was left was the human element.

The passageway where she expected to end this beckoned. She could hear the men inside urging their friend to hurry. They'd get no reply, she was certain.

"Knight," the second of her men hissed. Vincent, a Pole who'd served in the French Foreign Legion.

Knight raised a hand, silencing him. She didn't need his input.

The DEW didn't have a trigger but a pressure-sensitive thumb switch. It functioned less like a firearm and more like a high-pressure valve, holding back the focused microwave energy that hummed within its core. Knight applied slight pressure to the switch, feeling the weapon thrum with contained power as she rounded the final corner. If Trapp was trapped, she had more than enough charge to cook him where he stood.

She sent Vincent out to fire on them, drawing the inevitable pot shots in reply. Her thumb pressed hard and with virtually no recoil; the invisible energy burst from the barrel and scorched the air. The cries that followed were like orchestral music. She grinned and held firm as they ducked back inside.

It didn't matter. A weaker effect would reach them, but they were in an enclosed space. The two men were finished.

TRAPP'S STOMACH CHURNED, nausea clawing at his throat as sweat streamed into his eyes. The air was hot and steamy as the directed microwave energy heated the sopping carpet. His Glock gripped tightly in one hand, Trapp pressed against the wall for balance, but the wave was strong, even if he had avoided the full force.

Beside him, Ikem was hunched low, his own weapon raised, evidently feeling the same resistance as Trapp. "So we are crabs in a pot, eh? Lovely."

Trapp didn't respond. They'd heard nothing from Kane so could only fear the worst. And now they were down to their last few rounds, so firing blind was not an option, but sighting on their attackers meant stepping into the full power of the energy weapon.

"If they keep this up, they'll be out of juice soon," Trapp said.

"True. But we will already be dead."

Ikem was right. Trapp's vision wasn't quite swimming, but it was buzzing, shimmering as if he was fighting sleep as well as heat and sickness. Like malaria but steadily getting worse.

"Then we get ready to suck it up," Trapp said.

Ikem shifted onto on all fours, gun placed where he could easily snatch it up, then positioned himself like a sprinter in the blocks. "It is the only choice."

The two men shared a nod of mutual respect. No time for more than that.

"Now!" Trapp said, shoving off the wall, torpedoing into the passageway and firing two quick shots toward the first human-shaped target.

A goon with an assault rifle went down, and the other two —Knight and some big lug with a shotgun—wavered a second, ducking aside, and the scorching of Trapp's skin eased momentarily.

But only momentarily.

As they bolted the short run toward the back staircase, the water underfoot spat and boiled right away, and heat seared through Trapp's boots, up his legs, and over his back as Knight found her bearings. Trapp gritted his teeth, forcing himself to ignore the pain, staggering with the swirl in his head.

He had to dive for the stairs, Ikem two steps behind, and both of them slipped, dizzy and without a plan, no chance to finish the job. All they could do was try to survive, then find a new solution.

"Split up," Trapp said, pulling himself upright. "And fast."

HALF A WORLD AWAY, Madison's screen flashed red, a warning she didn't have time to decipher. She slammed her hand against the table, then held it, drumming a beat as another shout of defiance, of pain, rang out.

Almost there. Almost.

"Grubbs, we're out of time!"

Dawson's voice, she thought. But now her stomach turned over, her head felt hot. The radiation from above was closing in.

They were going to die. But she'd die knowing she'd done this right. Knowing they'd stopped a war.

"Got it," she said, her hand shaking while the temperature rose as if in a sauna.

She hit the final key. The screen went blank. For a moment, there was silence. Then, a massive cracking noise filled her entire world as the windows shattered, and the building shook, and glass rained down.

The building itself was dying, and Madison had mere seconds to live.

FIFTY-NINE

Ikem darted down a side hallway, eating up the distance as heavy footsteps followed. Since escaping the DEW's range, he was moving more fluidly but nothing like his old self. His head was thick, as if a migraine were threatening, but it was dissipating, not worsening.

Still, no time to think, only to act. And these long corridors were no friend to someone being chased down by a shotgun-toting killer.

Ikem took the next corner and burst into the first room he came to: a grand piano covered in a white sheet; chairs, stacked; other, more luxurious chairs upholstered in green leather, lined up against one wall; low tables, sheets covering some but not all; more ghostly objects he couldn't identify obscured by white cloth. The small corner bar was not covered, but the steplike shelves holding bottles were protected.

Ikem raced for the bar, his sudden spike in speed causing his stomach to roil, and a little vomit spurted up his throat. He swallowed it as he ducked behind the bar, ejected the pistol's magazine, and checked the bullets.

Five.

No spare mags. The rest were back in the vestibule with his pack.

"Hello-ooo," came a foreign-accented voice. Deep, taunting, threatening. "I saw your handprint. Is an obvious place to come. But only two hidey holes in here. Let's see..."

The boom of the shotgun filled the room, then the tinkling of a shredded piano told Ikem the merc was going to home in on the bar next.

Ikem popped up and fired twice, but the gunman was already covered behind the piano. Must have guessed he'd given his position away.

The shotgun boomed back, two shells blasting in quick succession, shattering bottles of booze behind Ikem, splintering wood.

Ikem fired twice more, leaving him one round as he dropped back down.

Almost out of options.

But not ideas.

"Come out, come out," the merc sang. "I am nice, really."

Ikem yanked the white sheet down and tore a strip of fabric with his teeth, hands moving quickly, mopping up the spilled spirits with one hand as he swiped what he needed with the other.

"No more games," the merc shouted, and his gun fired again, blowing out a mango-sized chunk of wood too close to Ikem for comfort.

Ikem held the vodka bottle with the white rag in the neck and struck a match from one of the boxes kindly supplied. The cloth caught fire, the flame spreading quickly. But he was soaked with booze too, and his hand briefly burned.

He hissed with the sudden pain but patted it out against his trousers.

Then Ikem rose to a crouch and called, "Got a gift for you."

He hurled the Molotov cocktail, and the bottle held steady in flight before crashing against the wall behind the piano. The spread of alcohol and fire reached its target, the alcohol igniting in a burst of flame. The man's scream accompanied a blast of the shotgun that came nowhere near Ikem, ripping apart a chair and triggering another of the piano's strangled musical notes.

Ikem calmly raised the Glock, aimed at the thrashing, burning man, and fired his final bullet into his enemy's head.

When the flaming man lay motionless on the floor, Ikem let out a shaky breath, his hands trembling slightly. One more to go. But he had no idea where Trapp had led her.

THIGHS ACHING like the morning after leg day, Trapp moved low along the wall. He'd taken as many left turns as he could and looped back toward the vestibule. He'd glimpsed Knight before rounding each bend, but the energy device was heavy, slowing her down.

Now that his head had cleared a fraction, he fashioned a new plan.

Regroup with Ikem.

Find out what happened to Kane.

Try something, anything, to cut the drones' feed.

Hell, he had no idea if it was too late already.

If Grubbs was already dead.

At the servers' entrance, the antechamber was still empty, the remnants of the steam from the assault minutes earlier lingering. The hose lay dormant.

Sending Kane alone hadn't sat well with Trapp, but there was no point second-guessing now. Knight was his priority.

Once he killed her, maybe he could get to Ashenhurst, force him to cut the line, or—

A sudden crack split the air, and Trapp ducked instinctively.

Not fast enough.

The bullet grazed his shoulder, searing like a branding iron.

Knight had resorted to a conventional firearm after all.

He hit the ground and rolled, blood spreading and dripping already. His left arm was dead, but he forced himself up onto his elbows, scanning the chamber.

Knight was close, coming closer.

She stalked into view, partly covered by the doorframe, the handgun aimed, the DEW slung over one shoulder.

"About time you slowed down," she said. "I was getting so bored of chasing you."

MADISON CROUCHED in the center of the control room. The final data packet had been sent moments ago, the last shred of intel they had. The room around her was alive with chaos. Her head was thick with migraine, her throat choked with vomit. All around her, monitors had imploded in bursts of sparks, and the sprinklers had begun spraying, drenching them in a mercifully cool rain that had begun to slowly warm. The SOG team huddled in the middle, their faces grim, weapons raised but useless.

She closed her eyes and waited for oblivion.

TRAPP'S SHOULDER flared hot where Knight's bullet tore through and radiated a dull, throbbing pain that stopped the signals from his brain reaching his muscles. The arm was dead. Oddly, the carpet beneath him was warm and damp, and he was incredibly annoyed by it.

He'd been shot before, but each time was different. No telling if he was going into shock.

He crawled backward, as if those extra split seconds of life mattered, but Knight's bullet inevitably traveled an additional few feet to reach him.

The cracked concrete wall still oozed water from the jagged gash, the leak steady, like a tire with a slow puncture. Beyond it, servers continued their calculations and their transmissions, safe behind a watertight Perspex shield.

Knight's expression remained cold.

Trapp propped himself up on one elbow, his good hand pressing against the wound.

"If you're going to do it," he said, affecting a pleading, whining tone, "shoot me in the head. Quick. Clean. No need to drag it out. Call it a professional courtesy."

Knight tilted her head. "I guess it's true. Mortality really is a great leveler." Her voice carried a cruel note. Less the calculating professional, and more an egotistical woman bent on vengeance. "You made me look incompetent. Is that a professional courtesy?"

"Please..." Trapp croaked, one hand held before him.

Knight holstered her gun and retrieved the bulky weapon from her shoulder. "I'm going to watch you vomit blood. I don't generally go in for that kind of thing, but I'll try to enjoy it."

She flicked a switch, and the battery hummed to life. She held the cannon steady, pointed at Trapp. Then she thumbed another lever, and the energy surged through the air.

Trapp braced himself as the wave hit, his body convulsing

violently. Nausea surged. Bile rose, the sharp, awful tang in his throat. Heat radiated from his core, as though his insides were being cooked alive. He gagged, blood and vomit spilling from his lips, but he forced himself to endure.

Behind him, the leak had started bubbling. It grew louder, more frantic. A hissing noise joined it, steam building behind the cracked wall.

Yes, the weapon had a wide spread, making it easier to find a target, but that meant that more than just the human target took the hit.

Trapp's vision blurred. His body trembled, folding tightly in on itself, part searing heat, part muscle contraction as the electrical signals inside him were scrambled.

But he timed it.

Sat in the corona of agony.

Waited for the exact moment.

Then, with a surge of what he knew would be a final effort, he jerked the leg he'd folded under himself, pushed off hard, and rolled to the side.

Spearing himself away from the blast zone.

The wall exploded.

A geyser of scalding steam blasted forth. Knight barely had time to register it before the torrent enveloped her. Her scream was cut short, drowned out by the hissing spray of boiling water. More cement crumbled as the shell gave way, turning the spray into a torrent, enveloping Knight and boiling her instantly.

Trapp shielded his face as he crawled into the corridor, shielded by the door jamb, but the heat seared his skin even from there.

When the steam finally subsided, Knight lay dead, her body crumpled, one arm bent the wrong way and a knee twisted into an angle that imitated an awkward sleeping position. But there was no doubt, seeing her there, boiled and lifeless on the ground.

Trapp lay there, no strength in his body, wracked with pain.

But alive.

SIXTY

In the darkness of Madison's mind, hurting like she'd never hurt in her life, it was as if the world itself was holding its breath. When she cracked an eyelid, the sky outside seemed to warp, beating in a vibrating synchronicity with her pulse. The floor rattled. Nothing electrical left to explode.

Dawson's men exchanged grim, stoic looks. One of them muttered a prayer, teeth gritted.

Madison didn't pray. She'd seen too much to expect divine intervention.

The end was upon them.

But it wasn't fire or shrapnel that hit them. No bubbling, wrenching gore as she cooked on the inside.

It was silence.

A deafening absence of sound, almost as if that had been louder than the pounding in her ears.

Then a crash, and the building shook once again.

Minutely clearer, her head rose. She blinked hard. Willed the sheen of tears to clear.

Debris rained down outside, then a huge, shadowed mass plummeted by. Something long and gray.

With wings.

She squinted as a second dropped by, this one further out, easier to see.

The assault was over. The drones that had been meant to deliver death onto this city were falling out of the sky.

FANG CHEN WALKED toward the exit of the operations lounge. General Gao strode beside her. His posture was rigid, yet his once-disparaging gaze was now tinged with reluctant respect.

"Your handling was... impressive," Gao said. "Ambassador Lian was right about you."

Fang kept her expression neutral. She didn't need—or want—compliments right now. "I did what was necessary."

Gao nodded, eyes narrowing as if reassessing her. "You have learned a lot under her. I see some of her ruthlessness has rubbed off."

Fang didn't respond immediately. She let the words hang, her mind briefly drifting to the counteroffer she had been instructed to make. One she hadn't thought herself capable of just a few months ago. But she could not allow herself to show emotion in front of the general.

Fang stepped over the sprawled body of Rafe Ashenhurst. His throat was a gaping line of crimson, his once-pristine suit now darkening incrementally. His eyes stared up at nothing, his arrogance still draining from him.

Fang didn't look back at him as they exited to where Gao assured her a vehicle was waiting, her pulse steady despite the carnage all around. Less than a year ago, it would have sent her running to hide, but now it was just another step toward the end goal.

The Great Realignment.

Fang could feel Gao's eyes on her as they reached the exit, where the other investors waited. Once, his scrutiny would have made her shrink. Not anymore.

She thought of the girl she had been so recently—timid, unsure, desperate for approval—and found an odd sense of embarrassment descend.

"Ambassador Lian will be pleased," Gao said as they emerged into fresh air. "You've proven yourself an invaluable asset to the new China."

Fang glanced at him. She'd just murdered a man for the first time, and somewhere in the back of her mind, she knew it probably would not be the last. She had crossed a line, one she couldn't uncross. But she didn't regret it.

Regret was for the weak.

And weakness was no longer a part of who she was.

As they walked toward the convoy of four vehicles, a fresh cohort of security personnel kept watch for lingering threats. The image of Ashenhurst's corpse haunted her thoughts. She would always think of that moment. Not a reminder or guilt about what she'd done but proof of what she was becoming.

Stronger.

Harder.

The new China would rise, and soon. And if more bodies needed to fall at her hand, so be it.

SIXTY-ONE

The Ashenhurst estate was a fading war zone, a smoking, stinking killing field of flashing lights competing with one another in the dark evening. It had been several hours since the first cops showed up, but medics still moved in clusters, their fluorescent vests stark against the gray, while armed cops in tactical gear swept the perimeter. Bomb disposal teams in bulky suits shuffled from the property like astronauts, their helmets removed now that they had confirmed that no explosive threats remained.

Then there were the suits. The suits containing men with grim faces and stiff backs. Their leader ignored Trapp and Ikem, his eyes evasive, as if already calculating how to spin this so it didn't splash back on him.

Trapp kept apart, reclining in the back of an ambulance, his wounded shoulder dressed and his arm strapped and pinned to his chest to limit his movement. He'd refused painkillers stronger than a few mils of morphine, insisting the paramedics leave him conscious. He'd moved to sit upright at the back, legs slung outside, a better angle to watch proceedings.

In addition to the shoulder wound—a through-and-through that hadn't touched bone, thankfully—his face was sunburned, the skin peeling in patches, and his head still throbbed with a dull, persistent migraine rhythm. Although he'd downed several pints of water at the medics' behest, he still felt dehydrated.

And exhausted.

Couldn't forget the exhaustion.

But he didn't move around. He didn't need to. The job was over. At least, the part of it that mattered to him. Cleanup wasn't his specialty.

A cop he'd never laid eyes on before appeared beside him and passed him a tablet. "Some MI5 spook said you'd want this."

Trapp thanked him but wasn't sure what for. He tapped the screen, and Madison Grubbs appeared on it. Like him, she'd been battered and blasted, and although he'd known she was alive, he was happy to see her. Also like him, she was in a medical facility, her face red and blistered, eyes sallow. At least she had a drip to one side, which Trapp would no doubt be treated to soon.

"Hey," she said.

"You look like hell, Madison. It's good to see you."

"Cut it a bit fine, Jason."

Her voice sounded as tired as he felt.

"Sorry 'bout that," he said.

"You getting soppy on me again?"

"What do you mean?"

"Setting up a face-to-face call to check on me."

Trapp wasn't firing on all cylinders yet, and he had to be mindful that his brain was still a tad sluggish. "I thought *you* called *me*."

Just then the tablet vibrated, and a banner notified him that someone else was conferencing in. He tapped it, and there was a delay while they connected to the new member of the conversation.

The screen flickered, turned gray, then Mitchell appeared, half his face filling the screen, which wobbled a couple of times. He was adjusting a web cam. When he retreated, Trapp could see President Nash standing beside him in the situation room.

"Good work," Mitchell said. "Disaster averted. For now."

Trapp nodded once, a wordless acknowledgment. He wasn't in the mood for pats on the back.

"Where's your new friend, Kane?" Mitchell asked. "Ikem? We've only had access to the Counter-Terrorism Command. Five is staying tight-lipped."

Trapp glanced toward one of three other ambulances, medics in the one on the right clustered around Kane, who lay motionless, an oxygen mask strapped to his face. Tubes snaked from his arms, feeding him fluids and painkillers.

"We think Kane will live," Trapp answered. "Organs took a beating, and he's got a world class sunburn. But as long as there's no unexpected internal bleeding, he'll recover. In time."

"And Jelany?" Grubbs asked.

Trapp's gaze shifted to the Nigerian agent, who stood a few yards away from the Brits in suits, speaking on a satellite phone.

"He's debriefing his superiors," Trapp said. "Unauthorized mission. Death and destruction. The usual. CTC haven't arrested him, but they'll have to soon. Same with me. Once they're convinced there's no more bad guys around."

Mitchell's lips pressed into a thin line. "Standard procedure with the Brits. Take it. Cooperate. We'll get you out."

"In a jiffy?" Trapp asked, affecting a mock-British accent.

Then he remembered the president was there and cut back to his serious self.

"What can you tell us about the servers?" Nash asked.

"As far as we can tell, sir, they were destroyed. We're in the clear."

Grubbs chimed in. "Sir, the Taiwanese are salvaging what they can from the drones that fell in Xinyi. They're working with us."

"Yes," Mitchell said with a glance at the president. "I'm sending Karem Hines over to assess what's salvageable."

Trapp caught the faintest twitch from Mitchell's eye at the mention of Hines' name. He didn't blame him. A pain in the ass, but if anyone could make sense of the wreckage, it would be him.

As the debriefing continued, Trapp's attention drifted toward a man in a pristine suit and a thin, gray widow's peak— no doubt MI5. The man was deep in conversation with the senior investigating officer from the Surrey Constabulary—the police service covering this jurisdiction. The MI5 man's body language was pure politics—squared shoulders, chin up, hands forming controlled, deliberate gestures.

"Trapp." President Nash's voice pulled him back into the call. "You holding up?"

"Helluva sunburn and a headache, sir," Trapp replied. "But I'll live."

"Mike, how about we let them get some sleep, and we can pick this up in the morning? They've earned some rest."

"Thank you, sir, I appreciate that," Trapp said. "But I need to be sure we covered everything. The Chinese clients? Were they definitely the same rebel faction we handled in New York?"

"We're as sure as we can be," Mitchell answered. "The data

we pulled out of Xinyi should be enough to satisfy the Senate that the Chinese government is not starting World War Three."

"But people at the highest levels are involved," Grubbs pointed out, a note of personal anger in her tone.

"Sanctions on individuals," Nash said. "That'll be the extent of it. And we have whispers that a high-ranking admiral was arrested on their new aircraft carrier. Not that Beijing will ever confirm that, but we think that's how they managed to launch so close to Taiwan."

"What about the ones sent to make the deal?" Grubbs asked.

"Gone now," Trapp said. "Probably with help from Ashenhurst's contacts in the establishment. No proof, but it stinks. If you can find someone in Five who'll investigate their home secretary, I'm betting there'll be a resignation pretty soon."

"I'll pass on what you have," Mitchell said. "But the Brits' business is the Brits' business. For now, we're sure the attack on Taiwan wasn't just about destruction. It was the opening move of a coup. Win-win for the rebels. Beijing goes to war with the US, they get the conflict they want. If Beijing backs down, it shows weakness—gives them the green light they need to take control. Even if the war didn't go their way, our military response would weaken the Chinese regime. Leave the door wide open for them to sweep in and dismantle the government."

Nash's expression darkened. "And who are 'they'? Who's running them?"

Trapp shook his head. "We don't know. Not yet. Whoever it is, they're high-ranking. Their ambassador to the US is in the mix. A retired general. Which means there'll be more military leaders who agree. For now, most are ghosts."

"And the Chinese won't acknowledge the possibility," Mitchell said. "Not to us, anyway, even in back channels." He paused, his eyes narrowing at the screen. "When this faction does surface again, when they make their move, the war we just averted could look like a playground scuffle. It isn't over. Just delayed."

"Delayed?" Nash said. "How long do we have?"

Mitchell sucked in a deep breath. "Could be they have another attack lined up for tomorrow. Could be six months from now. Or a year. But it's coming."

Nash's gaze was distant as he processed the information. "We need to be ready. Whenever they make their next move, we have to face them head-on. Especially if they succeed in unseating their president."

Trapp's fingers tightened on the tablet, fatigue draining him now but sure of what he had to say.

"No."

Nash and Mitchell stared out at him.

"With respect," Trapp added, sensing his single word reply had come across a little too sharply. "Waiting can't be an option. Sit back and let them regroup? No, sorry. We push. We force their hand. *Make* them surface before they're ready."

Nash glanced again at Mitchell, who stood stiffly to the side. The deputy director's beard shifted, a chewing motion, a sign he was considering Trapp's words carefully. Grubbs, on the smaller square on the screen, looked equally uneasy.

"He's right," Mitchell finally said. "Waiting gives them the advantage. If Trapp can provoke them into action, we might have a shot at dismantling this before it goes too far."

Nash exhaled slowly.

The silence stretched, heavy and suffocating, as the president weighed their options. Trapp could almost see the moral calculus printed on his face, balancing the idea of actively moving against powerful Chinese agents, which could encroach on the government in Beijing. And with no acknowledgment from them of a threat from within, it could look like an act of war on the Americans' part.

The abyss of gambling and hoping they cleaned their own house.

Or the potential cost of inaction.

Finally, Nash leaned forward, his eyes locking on to Trapp through the screen. "If you do this, you'll be operating without a net. No backup. No official support. If it goes wrong, we can't acknowledge your actions. You understand that?"

"Wait, what are you saying?" Grubbs asked.

Trapp didn't blink. "Understood."

The words hung in the air, a silent acknowledgment of what the president was saying. Trapp felt heavy all of a sudden, the weight of a new mission on his shoulders, adrenaline reactivated and entering his veins.

This was what he did.

What he'd always done.

But at least if he'd be working without acknowledgement, that meant that rules, red tape, and diplomacy could take a back seat.

"No," Grubbs said, reading what they were planning. "I can help. Let me help you, Jason."

"Sorry, Madison," Trapp said. "I have to go."

He hit the red telephone button, let the tablet go black, then turned it off. He closed his eyes, lay his head back on the ambulance door, and promised himself that he would rest. Sleep a little. Heal.

Then he'd be ready. He just didn't have a plan.

Not yet.

AUTHOR'S NOTE

Hi,

It's great to be back with Trapp again. Hard to believe I wrote *Dark State* over five years ago now! He is the character who changed my life and allowed me to write books for a living. I hope to be writing him for many years to come.

Shock Wave has been a long time in the making, spanning the birth of my first child and many of the sleepless nights that followed. Thanks for waiting, and I hope you enjoyed the read!

It is also the second book in an arc tracing the rise of Chinese/US competition, a subject that has fascinated me for many years, despite the many other flashpoints and hot zones around the world competing for my attention and giving me ideas. In the next book, Trapp will come face to face with one of his hardest challenges yet. More on that soon...

As for this book, Directed Energy Weapons are real, and so is the physics principle of constructive interference. Thankfully for everyone, given the proliferation of small drones across the world's conflict zones, the superconductor in *Shock Wave* was an authorial invention. Unless DARPA is cooking something up in a secret lab from a downed alien spacecraft, we're safe for the time being.

I have to go change a nappy, so I'll cut this short here. But thanks again for reading.

Jack.

ALSO BY JACK SLATER

The first instalment in a new thrilling action series that fans of the Jason Bourne and Terminal List series will love.

He can't run. He can't hide. He can't *remember*...

Six weeks ago, Gideon Ryker awoke from a coma in the French chateau where veterans of the Foreign Legion live out their final days in peace. His body is a torturer's canvas, his mind an empty slate—except for haunting dreams of a young girl's face. He doesn't even remember his name.

But he knows that a legionnaire's life is a brutal struggle. The only reward: a new identity and passport. A fresh start. You'd only take that deal if you needed to forget your past life.

Or escape it...

Clearly Gideon didn't run fast enough. Someone caught up with him once. And when a CIA hit squad arrives at the chateau, he discovers that hunting season isn't over.

But where did he come from? Who is the girl that stalks his dreams?

And why does everybody want him dead?

Head to Amazon to read **Code of Arms**, book 1 in the *Gideon Ryker* series.

FOR ALL THE LATEST NEWS

I hope you enjoyed *Shock Wave*. If you did, and don't fancy sifting through thousands of books on Amazon and leaving your next great read to chance, then sign up to my mailing list and be the first to hear when I release a new book.

Visit - www.jack-slater.com/updates.

Thanks so much for reading!

Jack.

Printed in Dunstable, United Kingdom